Skeletons

JANE FALLON

PENGUIN BOOKS

PENGUIN BOOKS

Published by the Penguin Group
Penguin Books Ltd, 80 Strand, London WC2R 0RL, England
Penguin Group (USA) Inc., 375 Hudson Street, New York, New York 10014, USA
Penguin Group (Canada), 90 Eglinton Avenue East, Suite 700, Toronto, Ontario, Canada M4P 2Y3
(a division of Pearson Penguin Canada Inc.)
Penguin Ireland, 25 St Stephen's Green, Dublin 2, Ireland (a division of Penguin Books Ltd)
Penguin Group (Australia), 707 Collins Street, Melbourne, Victoria 3008,
Australia (a division of Pearson Australia Group Pty Ltd)
Penguin Books India Pvt Ltd, 11 Community Centre,
Panchsheel Park, New Delhi – 110 017, India
Penguin Group (NZ), 67 Apollo Drive, Rosedale, Auckland 0632, New Zealand
(a division of Pearson New Zealand Ltd)
Penguin Books (South Africa) (Pty) Ltd, Block D, Rosebank Office Park, 181 Jan Smuts Avenue,

I

All Jen Masterson had ever wanted was an ordinary life. It wasn't a very glamorous ambition, admittedly. Not one she would have mentioned to her school careers adviser. But she'd worked hard to achieve it. She had made the right choices, finessed the rough edges, manipulated her little corner of the world so that it suited her perfectly. For the most part, anyway.

Married to the same man, Jason, for twenty years. Two children, Simone and Emily. A job in a hotel with a modicum of status and responsibility – not so much that it kept her awake at night, but just enough for her to feel that she hadn't completely wasted her adult life and university education. A small house in a part of London where it was still possible to walk to the shops without fearing for your life. So long as it was daylight, that was. And you made sure not to make eye contact with anyone. Her in-laws a manageable three miles away. Her own mother, thankfully, further. She was happy. And she was prepared to fight to keep it that way, if she had to.

She often looked around at her friends' lives – her best mate and sister-in-law, Poppy, in particular – and counted her blessings. It wasn't that she thought her lot was better than anybody else's. It was just that it was right for her. There were definitely areas that could have been improved on. But no one could have it all, Jen believed. You just had to decide what really mattered.

She knew she was average-looking for a start. Five foot three, fiery red locks, a smattering of freckles. On a good hair day, she was Julianne Moore. On a bad, Little Orphan Annie. She had inherited skinny from her mother. This she had always thought was a good thing, until, one day, the magazines were full of curvy burlesque girls with breasts and hips and all sorts of things Jen simply didn't have in her repertoire, and her ironing-board-straight-up-and-down flatness had suddenly struck her as cold and uninviting.

But she just told herself that everything was cyclical. That, if she was patient, soon enough the curvy girls would be back on the Atkins Diet and trying to flatten out their oversized cleavages so they could wear shift dresses. Meanwhile, her underwear drawer concealed an array of chicken fillets of varying shapes and sizes for when a bust was absolutely essential. She lived in fear of one of them falling out of her top, or being burst by a random fork.

In actuality, Jen was far more attractive than she gave herself credit for. Not to mention smart, funny, loyal. A good mother, a loving wife, a supportive friend, a conscientious colleague. A model daughter-in-law. (Only a so-so daughter, but more of that later.) She had a lot going for her.

She had no reason to suspect that it was all about to change.

But it was.

And, if truth be told, even if she had, it was out of her

hands. There was simply nothing she could have done to prevent it.

Later, she would think how funny it was – the way people could be so deluded. By 'people' she meant herself, of course. How she could have thought she'd created the perfect life when, in fact, it was one gust of wind away from toppling over and crashing to the ground.

Pull out the wrong card, nudge the wrong Jenga block, and the whole thing could collapse around your ears, however sturdy you thought you had made the foundations.

When she saw what she saw, Jen knew that it was a chink in the armour. A scratch on the glossy finish. What she didn't understand – and why would she? – was that that first tiny fissure would allow in the drip that became a flood. That that first flap of a butterfly's wings would eventually cause the tsunami. Of course she didn't. If she had, then maybe she would have handled things differently.

She might have looked away, pretended she hadn't noticed. She might have decided that, really, it was none of her business. Better still, she might have turned on her mid-height uniform heels and run in the other direction.

2

Jen looked at her watch. There were still three and a half hours to go until her shift ended. She was only a little over halfway through the day. Despite the fact that she liked her job, she didn't like it *that* much. She would still rather be almost anywhere other than here.

She had worked her way up – over the fifteen years since her youngest, Emily, had started nursery – to become the reception manager at a smart boutique hotel in an area of London that had happily been called Fitzrovia for years, but which was now trying to rebrand itself (somewhat desperately, it seemed to Jen) as Noho.

Becoming a manager meant that she earned slightly more money, while still seeming to do exactly the same job she had always done, except for being allowed to boss a couple of people around. Truthfully, she didn't really enjoy that side of things as much as she had thought she might. She would blush when she had to reprimand a junior colleague for arriving late, stutter when she was forced to correct their desk-side manner. She wasn't entirely comfortable becoming one of 'them' after years of being one of 'us'.

The Fitzrovia Hotel cultivated a chichi image. Flock wallpaper and dark wood. Large works of modern art by exciting up-and-coming (read: cheap) artists. At least, they may have been up and coming when the hotel had

4

opened in the mid-eighties. Now they were all up and gone, as far as Jen could tell. None of them on to greater things.

A spiky iron sculpture took pride of place in reception, occasionally threatening to spear one of the guests who walked too close, the embodiment of the phrase 'a lawsuit waiting to happen'. The desk behind which Jen spent her days was fashioned from battered copper-coloured metal. Occasionally, when one of the front-of-house staff was having a bad day, they would hit it with whatever implement they could lay their hands on. No one ever seemed to notice a few new dents.

The hotel bar and restaurant attracted the beautiful and not quite so beautiful people who worked in the nearby media companies and art galleries that had gravitated to the area from Soho, drawn to its lower rents and more bohemian atmosphere. (Faux bohemian, Jen always thought – bohemian with a trust fund.) While the occasional visiting TV or movie star who hadn't been able to get a room at The Charlotte Street, but didn't want to suffer the more establishment formality of The Dorchester or Claridge's, would sometimes show up to stay the night.

Jen rarely mixed with them. She generally spent a lot of time dealing with personal assistants, managers, managers' assistants – and even assistants' assistants. One time, there had been a third assistant. The assistant to the assistant of the assistant. That was how important she was considered in the world. She got to deal with the help's help's help.

Apart from the odd celebrity, the hotel's guests were

mainly made up of well-to-do tourists and a loyal handful of regulars who made The Fitzrovia their home whenever they were in London on business. It was a friendly place. Only thirty-two rooms. Small enough that they could cater to people's individual needs. Big enough to get noticed.

'Any plans for the weekend?' Her colleague, the imaginatively named Neil McNeil, who was on the desk with her, asked his usual Friday afternoon question.

'Family,' Jen answered, as she always did.

'My wife says the family that plays together stays together . . .'

Jen liked Neil well enough, had been working next to him for years, but every other sentence he uttered began with, 'My wife says . . .' It was almost as if, all the time you were speaking, he was only listening just long enough to get a clue as to which wifely piece of wisdom he could quote back at you. Jen had sometimes worried that if she ever met Neil's wife, the first thing she might say would be, 'Will you stop being such a know-all?'

Most of the full-time staff at the hotel had been there so long they were like family. The dysfunctional kind. The kind you know you have to see, but you hope aren't going to invite themselves for Christmas. Jen, Neil and fellow receptionist Judy Sampson had been working together for nearly twelve years. The general manager, David, had been telling them all what to do for eight. It was rumoured that Margaret in housekeeping had been at The Fitzrovia since the first day it opened, in 1985. No one actually knew if the rumour was true, because Margaret was the hotel bitch and engaging her in conversation meant listening to hours on end of mean-spirited diatribe about your co-workers. Few people had the stomach for it.

Back in those days, so rumour had it, the hotel had employed twice the staff it boasted now: a guest liaison manager, an events organizer, a dedicated concierge sitting at a desk opposite reception. That had been in the days when The Fitzrovia had been hoping to compete with the big boys. The big boys had clearly won. The Fitzrovia had cut back and accepted its chic boutique status. Jen was glad. She liked the intimacy, the chance to pay attention to the details.

As jobs went, it suited Jen perfectly. She had always been able to fit her shifts around the needs of her family. Now she mentally tried to plan what to get for dinner. She often did this when Neil was talking to her. She could plot through the whole of a recipe followed by a shopping list, in her head, while he told her an anecdote. She had the art of smiling and nodding in all the right places down to a T, while all that was going through her head was: salmon or chicken? Mash or rice?

'. . . and the thing is, that it doesn't. I mean, not necessarily.'

She caught the tail end of Neil's train of thought, had no idea what he was referring to. 'Um . . . no, I suppose not.'

'That's what I said. Unbelievable, isn't it?'

'Unbelievable,' Jen agreed, clueless, surreptitiously checking her watch again.

Waking up early on Saturday morning, Jen allowed herself to indulge in the fantasy that she was going to have to drag herself out of bed and to the freezing bus stop, before rolling over and settling back down for a couple of blissful hours more. Jason was oblivious, lying on his side. She snuggled up to his warm back, draped her arm round his stomach. This was her favourite time of the week. Actually, she couldn't imagine anyone for whom that wasn't true. Was there anyone in the world who, if asked, would say 'I'm happiest at nine o'clock on a Monday morning when I have the whole week at work to look forward to'? Maybe – if your job was testing mattresses, or helping Ben and Jerry decide which flavour combinations would make the best ice cream.

Five minutes later, she realized there was no chance of her going back to sleep. It felt strange, knowing that neither of the girls was home. Of course, this had happened many times before – they had often stayed over at friends' houses at the weekends – but it was the thought that neither of them was going to be coming back in the foreseeable future that made everything different. Emily had left for Leeds University a week ago, excited but teary, two years after Simone had departed for Durham, and Jen knew it was going to take a bit of getting used to. She was trying to look at it as an opportunity, an adventure, a new chapter. Trying to suppress her fears that life was never going to be the same again. That she wasn't entirely sure if she knew who she and Jason were any more now they were back to being two halves of a couple rather than Mum and Dad. Time would tell if she was right.

It wasn't as if they had still done things together very often, the three of them, since Simone had left home.

Emily had usually had plans that didn't involve her parents. But somehow, knowing that she was just a Tube ride away, that she would sweep in at some point – even if it was just to get changed and sweep out again – had given their lives a framework. They were parents. That was what they did. They hovered about on the periphery of their growing children's lives, waiting to step in and do parenty things. Waiting to be needed.

Jen said a silent thank you that they had the rest of the family around them. Jason's parents, his two sisters, Poppy and Jessie. Poppy's daughter, Jessie's husband. They were a unit, a clan, as close-knit as a family could be without it all tipping over into movie-of-the-week creepiness. They loved to spend time together, gathered in one place as often as they could. Now her girls would come and go less often. That would be the only difference.

For this first weekend, though, distraction was the only solution. No point hanging about at home wondering what their next move should be, sitting by the house phone in case Simone or Emily called, like faithful old Greyfriars Bobby pining on his master's grave. They needed a plan, a distraction, a configuration of smoke and mirrors that would allow them to pretend that nothing had really changed. We're just having a day out without our daughters. No big deal. It's not as if they've both left home and the house feels empty and soulless. It's not as if I'm scared I don't know who we are without them.

Jen's first thought was Poppy, Jason's middle sibling and her closest friend. They could have lunch, do a bit of early Christmas shopping in Richmond (very early, even for her, a woman who liked to have purchased all her presents by the time anyone else had started), go for a walk along the river if the weather was nice. By the time Jason woke up, half an hour later, she had his whole day mapped out like an overachieving hothouse parent.

3

Poppy unwound her scarf from her neck and then proceeded to wind it back round again more tightly. The day was sunny but deceptively cold. The leaves had already started to leave the trees behind, and they kicked them up underfoot as they walked. Jason strode on ahead with Poppy's four-year-old daughter, Maisie, pointing out the ducks and the boats, occasionally grabbing her hand or the hood of her jacket when she strayed too close to the edge of the riverbank.

'Do you think I'm getting a moustache?' Poppy said, out of nowhere.

'Let me see.'

Poppy pushed her face close to Jen's, and Jen screwed up her eyes and scrutinized her sister-in-law's upper lip.

'No. I mean, no more so than anyone else. There's hair, but it's blonde. I'd never have noticed, if you hadn't pointed it out.'

'Shit. I'll have to add it to my list of things to get waxed.'

Jen laughed. 'You can't see it. I should never have said –'

'No. You're the only person I can trust to tell me how it is.'

'OK, so how about me?'

Poppy peered at her. 'I can't tell. I need my glasses.'

They walked on in silence for a few moments.

'So I'm guessing you were looking at Jason this morning and thinking, "What are we going to do with the rest of our lives now both girls have left home?"'

'Witch.'

'It's a syndrome. I read about it.'

It might not seem ideal, having your sister-in-law for your best friend. There ought to have been whole areas that were taboo, subjects off the menu because they were just too revealing, but Jen and Poppy had a 'no boundaries' rule that they had deemed essential if their friendship was going to trump their familial relationship. Luckily, Jen and Jason's marriage was largely drama free so Poppy had never been called on to take sides. Not so far.

'It's just going to take a bit of adjusting to,' Jen said now. 'For both of us.'

'I bet you end up having another baby.' Poppy smirked.

Jen pulled a face that said 'no way'. 'We're going to run around doing all the things we couldn't do with kids in tow.'

'Such as?'

'I have no idea. Going dogging. Or taking drugs. What do unencumbered people do?'

'I have a four-year-old, don't ask me.'

'Maybe we'll go travelling, something like that.'

'What? Backpacks and Birkenstocks? I can't see it, somehow.'

'I mean more like a long holiday. Nothing too intrepid. Nice hotels and scheduled flights.'

'Can you afford to do that?'

'No.'

'If I were you, I'd just enjoy the peace and quiet. Lounge

around a bit without anyone asking you to make them a sandwich or give them a lift to a party.'

Jen sighed. 'We can babysit Maisie whenever you like. Look at Jason,' she said, pointing up ahead, where Jason was now carrying his niece on his shoulders and pretending theatrically to drop her every few steps. 'He's in his element.'

Jason revelled in being a parent as much as Jen did. Adored family life. It was one of the things that had attracted her to him early on – his love of spending time with his family, his desire to be a father himself. Fatherhood, he had said to her once after Simone was born, made him feel like a man. He had said it as if it was a joke, and she had laughed along with him, but she knew he'd really meant it underneath. And he'd been good at it too. Still was, she reminded herself. Or, at least, still would be whenever he got the chance.

'Great,' Poppy smiled. 'You can have her every weekend. Recapture your golden years of parenting while I run around and have fun. That way, everyone's happy.'

'OK, well. Maybe not whenever you like. But sometimes.'

'You just need to give it a bit of time to work out who you are without the girls around. It's not like you're not parents any more. Just not full time. Or is that too many negatives? You know what I mean.'

Jen looked at her. 'Have you been reading *Psychologies* magazine in the doctor's waiting room again?'

Poppy laughed, pushed her dark (pink-streaked) hair away from her face and tucked it behind her ear. She and Jen were only a couple of years apart – forty-one and forty-three – but Poppy was steadfastly refusing to accept it gracefully. She somehow got away with it, too, managing to seem – to Jen, anyway – cool and carefree rather than deluded and tragic. Both of Jason's sisters seemed younger than their years. Poppy because she cultivated a laid-back, youthful image, Jessie because she acted up like the spoiled, indulged, youngest sibling that she was. As a counterbalance, Jason had assumed the responsible, reliable, elder brother mantle early on – another trait that Jen had found irresistible.

'No. But I do watch *Loose Women* sometimes. Same thing.'

Jason turned round, Maisie swaying like the head of a sunflower on his shoulders.

'Gaucho?' he said, pointing to the restaurant up ahead.

'Lovely!' she called back.

By the time they got home, it was nearly dark and it was all they could do to summon up the energy to eat off their laps, flipping between *Strictly* and *The X Factor*. They had walked miles, trailed round the shops half-heartedly, stopped for lunch and then coffee. By ten o'clock they were both dropping off, cuddled up on the sofa, and decided to call it a night. Jen nestled into Jason's proffered arm, and was congratulating herself on a successful waste of a day when she fell asleep.

4

In her compact but perfectly formed flat on the top floor of a white stuccoed house, in a once run-down but now regenerated square off the seafront in Brighton, Cass Richards brooded about her own life while she studied herself in the mirror and plucked at her stray eyebrow hairs. She screwed up her eyes, trying to get a good view through the detritus of necklaces and hairbands and scarves that hung over the sides of the glass. She really must declutter one of these days.

Her hair was freshly washed and wrapped in a towel. A choice of two outfits was laid out on her bed next door. It was Saturday night and, as on most Saturday nights, that meant going out. Usually to a party or a dinner. Tonight was a party. A friend of a colleague was celebrating something or other, she forgot what. They all blurred into one endless event after a while. This one was being held in the colleague's friend's house in Rottingdean. She knew the one, a characterful flint-walled pile near the pond. She had often driven past it. Admired it from a distance. It promised to be fun. If the friend owned the property, he – or it might have been a she, she couldn't remember – must be doing OK, so hopefully there would be some interesting people there. By which she meant useful people. Good contacts. She was always on the lookout for good contacts.

She treated these events like work. Dressed smartly. No more than one glass of wine. No shovelling in the canapés like it was your last meal. Network, network, network. You couldn't overestimate the importance of making new connections.

Her job was her success story. That was the one thing she had got right. So far, anyway. To be fair, it was all she had been concentrating on. She liked to see herself as a work in progress. Everything else – social life, family, relationships – was a bit of a fuck up, admittedly. She had read a book once, one of those self-help manuals that were mostly bought by people who were probably beyond it, and it had suggested making a list of all the things in your life that needed attention. She had been exhausted just by the thought of it, hadn't been able to put pen to paper. Over the page, it had encouraged a second exercise entitled 'All the things I like about me'. She had thrown the book in the bin.

The thing was, success at work was there if she wanted it. It was completely within her control. It was up to her to make something of her life. Everything else could wait.

Most of her friends were far less focused than she was. They fell into two camps: the ones who had simply taken jobs that paid the rent, that were a means to an end, and nothing else; and those who, like herself, were working at building a career. She was the only one who rarely took a day off, though. Who had tunnel vision. For Cass it had always been about setting herself up for success. She had no interest in running around like the oldest adolescent in town, drinking and smoking and pretending that going to clubs until four in the morning and waking up next to some bloke whose name you couldn't remember was what you really wanted to be doing. She wanted to make something of herself. Do well. Make her parents proud.

She wanted to stand out.

Actually, she usually found these events exhausting. Halfway through the evening, she would always think about making her excuses, ringing her friend Kara and heading to a bar for a few glasses of something fizzy. Letting her hair down a bit for once. But she knew she had to seize every opportunity that was presented to her. If work was the only area of her life where she could call the shots, then work was going to come first.

She was a realist above all else. Circumstances had forced her to be. She was in an impossible situation; there could be no happy ending – at least, not as far as she could see. So she had learned just to accept things as they were. Not always graciously, admittedly.

That was too much to ask.

5

Jen and Jason were spending Sunday afternoon as they spent five out of six Sunday afternoons – or six out of seven, if Jen could get away with it – at Jason's family's rambling childhood home in Twickenham.

Despite the fact that his parents, Charles and Amelia Masterson, now lived there alone, and that it was really far too big for them – something everyone was studiously avoiding pointing out, so afraid were they that one day Riverdale might have to be sold, and they wouldn't just lose the bricks and mortar but also the fulcrum round which the whole family rotated – the house never seemed empty. Probably because it never got the chance to be. The Mastersons liked to congregate. And Riverdale was where they liked to do it best.

Most Sundays, along with Jen and Jason, Simone and Emily, there would be Poppy and Maisie, as well as Jessie and her husband, Martin. They didn't restrict themselves to weekends either. Didn't need a birthday or an anniversary as an excuse. The sun rising in the morning was enough of a reason for a Masterson get-together.

Admittedly, most women's worst nightmare would be to marry a man whose idea of a good night out was dinner with his parents, or a drink with his sisters. For Jen it was the culmination of everything she had ever wished for.

Jen's own family was called Elaine.

She was it. The sum total of Jen's living relatives – well, with one exception, and he didn't count. It was just her and Elaine, and it had been that way since her dad had walked out and left them when Jen was eight years old. She loved her mum, of course she did, she just sometimes wished she could multiply her.

When she was seven, Jen had wanted two things: for her parents to start talking again; and for some brothers and sisters to come along to keep her company while she sat on the landing and listened to the silence. It wasn't that her mum and dad didn't speak – it hadn't got to the 'Jenny, would you ask your father to pass the salt' stage yet. They just didn't speak unless they had to. There was no conversation. Nothing beyond the absolute essentials.

Most evenings, her dad would go out straight after tea and come home, three or four hours later, smelling like beer and kebabs from the nearby takeaway. Once, a local stray had followed him home, tail wagging, clearly convinced that Rory must have been concealing some tasty meat about his person because of his habit of stuffing a doner into his pocket to keep it warm, and the resulting aroma that clung stubbornly to his clothes.

By the time she was nine, those seemed like the halcyon days. Her father had gone, and he didn't seem to be coming back. Her desire for siblings had never abated.

Without her dad there, home had felt oppressive, the

long silences even more suffocating. Never mind that, in the last year or so, her father's noise had mostly been the clatter he made when he fell down the stairs, or his party trick of burping the national anthem when he'd had a few. A skill that had always made her mother seethe. At least there had been evidence of life.

She assumed that her mum and dad must have loved each other once. In fact, she knew they had, had a vague but compelling memory of fun family days out before it all went wrong. Rory had been a joker, always kidding around, doing impressions, funny walks, pulling faces, anything to make her laugh. And she could remember Elaine joining in. With the laughing, that is, not the face pulling. She could remember a time when she didn't have a knot of anxiety in her stomach, waiting for him to get home from work, for the heavy atmosphere to descend, when he would pick her up and twirl her round until she begged him to stop. Actually, maybe he had already started drinking then because, looking back, he had had scant regard for her safety, flinging her up in the air and barely catching her, Jen gasping with laughter and, probably, fear.

He was a man of big gestures, coming home on different occasions with a go-kart, a disgruntled-looking hamster in a cage, a Kenwood food mixer, and presenting them to Jen and Elaine with a flourish. She had wondered, later, whether he had won them off his mates in a card game. Whether other wives and children had woken up bemused by one of their possessions having inexplicably disappeared. Some other little girl crying because Hammy seemed to have escaped and taken his cage with him. No one had ever seemed to ask.

She had seen the photos of her parents with their arms round each other, smiling broadly for the camera. Their wedding, with Rory's Zapata moustache and Elaine's heavy fringe and honey-blonde bouffant locks. One and a half sets of grandparents still living, none of whom Jen could really remember ever meeting, dressed in their best. Everyone looking proud and happy and hopeful.

Not only was Jen an only child, but so were her parents. The only child of only children. Grandparents long gone by the time Jen was really aware they had ever existed. And once Rory had disappeared so completely from her life, Jen became the only child of an only parent. It should have been the two of them against the world. Instead, Jen had decided to blame all Rory's faults and shortcomings on her mum, Elaine. It was irrational, she had realized once she grew up a bit, but since when did rationality ever get in the way of family resentments?

She had accepted every invitation that came her way, any excuse to get out of the house and away from her mother's stubborn determination that everything was going to be absolutely fine with just the pair of them. She had sought out friends who lived in noisy, crowded households, sitting quietly in the background, observing rather than taking part. Always the shy girl on the outskirts. And, as soon as she was old enough, she'd applied to go to college as far away from home as she could and still be in the same country. Actually, she had tried to go to Scotland at first but, in the end, she had had to plump for her third choice, Newcastle, where she'd lived in twenty-four-hour-party halls and then a house shared with five others. The noise never bothered her. She had revelled in the chaos and the drama. Anything was preferable to silence.

The first time Jason had taken her to meet his own family, about six months after they had started dating – having met when Jen, fresh out of university, back living in a bed-sit down south and at a loss for what to do with her English degree, had volunteered to help organize a production at the local council-run theatre where Jason was the stressed-out would-be director attempting to pull the whole show together – Jen had stared in open-mouthed amazement at the anarchy, the warmth and the bickering that had filled their kitchen. Mostly the bickering. The Masterson girls could have won competitions in arguing. Synchronized squabbling. '55 kg and under' teasing. The contrast with her own teenage home couldn't have been more extreme.

The house – a large but still somehow cosy-looking Arts and Crafts detached on a quiet residential road leading away from the centre of Twickenham – had smelled of fresh coffee and baking biscuits. Jen remembered thinking there were no hard edges; everything was drowning in soft furnishings. It had reminded her of a padded cell – only, one made by Laura Ashley and featured on the pages of *Homes & Gardens*. The family was clearly as artsy and craftsy as their house, because there were pictures tacked up all over the kitchen walls (some of which, she later discovered, dated back to when Jason was about three years old), and home-made-looking artefacts of varying degrees of ability everywhere she turned.

'Jason made that in school,' one of his sisters – Jen

hadn't worked out who was who yet – had said as she'd pointed to a misshapen pottery thing that Jen had assumed was meant to be a vase of some kind, but which now held pens in the middle of the kitchen table.

'Good, huh?' She had rolled her eyes as she said it, so luckily Jen had known she was meant to laugh. 'Mum still has everything any of us has ever produced. It's like the most pointless museum ever.'

Most of the family had been there. His mother, the two sisters, Poppy and Jessie. It had been Poppy, the middle of the three children, who had spoken to Jen she'd discovered when she was introduced. Jen had tried to hide in a corner, overwhelmed by the two confident girls, an amorphous ever-moving cloud of long hair, perfume and sarcastic remarks. She had found them terrifying. Not because they were mean, but because they were so self-assured. They had been handed the world without even trying, why wouldn't they be confident in their own fabulousness? So she had given up making an effort to talk, and she'd sat in a large armchair that had almost swallowed her up, speaking only when spoken to.

'What do you do?' Jessie, the youngest at sixteen, had barked at her. Short, dark haired and ethereal-looking, she had draped her stick-thin frame in some kind of long wispy number. If Jen hadn't known already, she would have guessed that Jessie was headed for drama school. Jason had told her his sister was a natural actress, blessed with a talent for making up stories, self-obsession and histrionics.

'Um . . .' Jen had said. 'Nothing really, at the moment. I'm looking.'

'What about your dad? What does he do?' Jessie had carried on.

Jen had imagined this was what it must have felt like to be interrogated by the Gestapo – except they might have been more interested in her responses. Jessie was painting her toenails while she talked, and only giving Jen half her attention.

Jen had absolutely no idea of the answer to that question. Drank? She hadn't seen Rory for years at that point so, for all she knew, he could have been the man who had come to fix her boiler the week before.

'I don't know, really,' she had answered, and Jessie had looked at her as if she thought Jason might have brought home the village idiot.

'Have you never asked?'

Jen had ignored the question. She'd guessed that Jason hadn't filled them in on her family history.

'Jason says he met you at the theatre.' Jessie pronounced each syllable separately, relishing them all: thee-ate-er.

'Yes,' Jen had said, looking to Jason to help her out, but he was playing with the family's cat, and seemed oblivious to her plight.

She'd tried to conjure up some interesting anecdote or other, but everything she could think of seemed to have some kind of 'R' rated element: unsuitable for public consumption. 'The first time we had sex was on the stage, actually, after everyone had gone home,' or, 'Did he tell you about when we caught the leading man giving the boy who played his brother a blow job in the props cupboard?' So she had just said nothing.

'What were you doing?'

'I was helping out.' Oh, the sparkling wit. Move over, Oscar Wilde.

'For God's sake, Jess, leave the poor girl alone.' This from Poppy, the other one, the middle sister, whose grungy get-up and unwashed hair couldn't hide the fact that she had a face that probably made grown men weep. Sloping hazel eyes had gazed at Jen sympathetically from under a spiky fringe. 'It's just that you're the first girl Jason has ever brought home, so we're naturally curious.'

Jason had looked up from his position on the carpet. 'You are such a liar.'

Poppy had given Jen a big smile. 'We were beginning to get worried . . . you know.'

Jason had thrown a cushion at his sister. It had actually missed Poppy completely and hit Jen in the eye, but she'd tried to ignore the fact she thought she might be going blind and she'd laughed along. It had seemed like the right thing to do. And, if she hadn't, she'd been afraid she might cry.

Jason's mother, Amelia, had made tea. Home-baked scones, salmon-paste sandwiches and a Victoria sponge. The stuff of Enid Blyton families, not something Jen's mum would ever have had the time – or even the inclination – to do. It had struck Jen when Jason had first introduced her that if you ever had to explain to an alien what a mother was, you could just show them a picture of Amelia. She was so soft, so warm, so maternal-looking, covered in flour from baking treats for her children. Either that, or her cocaine habit was out of control. Jen had nearly asked if she could sit on her lap.

Elaine was all angles. Elbows and knees sharp like compasses. Skin scratchy like sandpaper. On the rare occasions Jen condescended to give her a hug, she couldn't help feeling there was a danger she might snap her in half.

'Do you take sugar, Jennifer?'

'It's Jen, Mum,' Jason had cut in. He had heard Jen say the same thing many times, although she hadn't been intending to insist on her preferred name here so soon.

'My fault, Jason did tell me.' Amelia had smiled, and the room had practically lit up. Jen had actually looked round to see if someone had turned a light on.

Jen hadn't wanted to seem greedy by saying, 'Yes, three please,' so she had muttered a word that had come out a cross between 'one' and 'two', meaning Amelia had had to ask the same question again.

Jen had known that she wasn't making a great impression. She wouldn't have warmed to herself as a potential daughter-stroke-sister-in-law, in all honesty. She'd wished, and not for the first time in her life, that she was more polished, more . . . accomplished. Or, at least, more socialized. She'd felt like one of those children found living in the woods who has been brought up by a wolf pack and has never had human contact before. All she could do was grunt. They were lucky she didn't sit on the floor, lift her leg and start grooming her bits noisily.

'Come up to my room,' Poppy had said, out of nowhere. 'I'm going to a party tonight and I have literally no idea what to wear. I've been home too long; you're the first person I've seen in weeks with any sense of style, so you can help me pick something out.'

Jen had almost kissed her with gratitude, nearly falling

over the now sleeping cat in her hurry to get out and away from the questioning.

And then Jason's father, Charles, had walked in. The sun had come out, birds sang, flowers bloomed.

'You must be Jen.' He had smiled his big, expansive smile. 'Welcome to the madhouse. Are they torturing you yet?'

Jen had smiled nervously. 'No . . . of course not.'

'I bet they are. Take it as a compliment. If they didn't like the look of you, they wouldn't bother. They're all bark.'

Charles had swept Amelia up into a floury hug, seemingly oblivious to the white powdery mess that transferred itself to his suit. Jen had actually been surprised that he was dressed so formally given the bohemian get-up favoured by the others. Even Amelia was wearing a floaty scarf with her pinny. She knew, though, that he had his own business, something in property, so he probably had to make a good impression. Later, she'd learned that Charles was always well turned out. Even on days when he didn't visit the office, he was never less than impeccably attired. No lounging around in his PJs, or old gardening trousers, for him. He was up, showered, shaved and dressed to impress by breakfasttime.

Amelia had laughed and pushed him off, waving her pastry-sticky fingers at him as a threat. Jen had tried to imagine Elaine doing the same to Rory, but the only image she could come up with was her mum hitting her dad with a newspaper when he had tried to help himself to the cooking sherry once. Neither of them had been laughing.

Up in Poppy's old room – a treasure trove of her childhood things, Rothko and Pollock posters, and a heaped-up clothes mountain sitting in the centre like an altar – Poppy had sat on the bed cross-legged and indicated for Jen to sit next to her.

'Ignore Jess,' she had said, conspiratorially. 'She has a tendency to say inappropriate things. It comes from thinking you're God's gift and everyone will be fascinated by whatever you utter.'

Jen had laughed. 'Honestly, she was fine.'

'It's all to do with being the youngest. You get away with more. Myself, I'm the overlooked middle child.' She'd leaned across and dragged over a floral dress from the pile on the floor. 'How about this? Too Lady Di?'

'A bit. Maybe if you wore it with engineer boots?'

'Don't have any.' She scrabbled around under the bed. 'Converse?'

'Perfect.'

'If I can find them. So how about you? Youngest? Eldest?'

'Both. I'm the only one.'

Poppy had stopped in her rummaging and looked at her as if that was the strangest concept she had ever heard. 'God. Grim.'

Jen, who was used to people telling her she was lucky to have all of her mother's attention, or not to have to wear hand-me-down clothes or share a bedroom, had screwed up her face in response. 'It is a bit.'

'Hey, do you want to come to this party?'

'Oh, I don't –' Jen had started to say, but Poppy had continued, 'Shit, no, Jason won't go. He hates all my friends. Come without him.'

Jen had laughed. 'Better not.'

'Well, next time.'

'Great.'

'Or we could meet up in London. I mean, if you're going to be part of the family we really should get to know each other properly.'

'Bit early for that, I think. I wouldn't buy a hat yet –'

'Oh no, he's got to settle down with you. He's got no choice. I've always been terrified he'd marry some girl I didn't like. Can you imagine what that'd . . .? Well, no, I don't suppose you can. And that lot all love you too, I can tell,' she'd said, indicating the downstairs.

And, just like that, Jen had acquired a best friend.

At some point, when they were sitting around the table after lunch, Poppy had produced a tin full of old photos and proceeded to show Jen every embarrassing haircut Jason had ever had – along with pictures of him in fancy dress, or school plays, or dressed as a page boy for a cousin's wedding. To Jen he had looked adorable in every different incarnation, but what had captivated her more, what she could hardly bear to tear her eyes away from, was what was around him. The crowded messy life of a family – happy, smiling, pouting, sulking, it didn't matter. They were an entity, a team, a gang.

And all the while Amelia had beamed, as if all she had ever desired was right there in that room, and Charles had sat at the head of the table smiling, making jokes, making his children laugh, making Jen feel at home. A patriarch completely happy with his lot.

By the time she and Jason had left to go home, a few days later, she was in love with them all in different ways.

Even Jessie. She had nearly refused to leave, climbed up on the roof and claimed squatter's rights. She'd wanted to stay in that overstuffed, noisy, *alive* house for ever and be a part of their lives. They were everything she had always imagined the perfect family would be. She'd known that, more than anything, she wanted to join this clan. She had wanted to turn the clock back to her lonely childhood so they could adopt her.

About a week later, Jason had asked her to move in with him and she hadn't even hesitated before saying yes. Over the years, they had all become such important allies in her life that on the (very) rare occasions she and Jason had a fight that lasted into the evening, what kept her awake wasn't worrying about who would get the house, it was how she would be able to win custody of her in-laws.

6

Jen lived in a permanent state of feeling bad where her own mother was concerned. Lived with the guilt while steadfastly refusing to do the one thing that would ease it, which would have been to make the trip to see Elaine more often. She knew that her mum looked forward to their visits like, she imagined, Lindsay Lohan looked forward to the pub opening. She always got a cake in, even though Jen had told her a million times that she was trying to go cold turkey where sugar was concerned. And then Jen would feel she had to eat a slice, but was resentful at the same time, so she'd end up with all the calories without even any of the enjoyment.

Elaine would make a list between visits of all the things she wanted to remember to tell her daughter and, every time, Jen would catch herself sneaking a look to see if her mother was getting near to the end and she could make her excuses and leave.

She knew she had to be there. She wanted to be there, wanted to be a dutiful daughter and to pay her mum back for the fact that she had done so much for her, bringing Jen up on her own after Rory had left, working full time but never deliberately making her daughter feel as though she was hard done by. Jen had done that on her own. It was just that the second Jen arrived, she couldn't wait to leave again. She would spend hours beating herself up about it, promising herself that the next time she would stay longer, look happier, try harder, but then the day would come around, and she would be somehow incapable of behaving any differently.

She didn't know why her mother brought out the worst in her. Elaine had never done anything but try to do her best. Actually, a thought had occasionally inveigled its way into the back of Jen's mind, hovering there until she forced it out again: it was her mother's trying that did it. It was too much, too revealing, too in need of her attention.

Elaine Blaine. Even her name was laughable. Jen had asked her once, when she was a teenager, why she had given up her own, more majestic surname, Rochester, for something that sounded like the start of a limerick.

'Because that's what people do when they get married,' Elaine had said, as if that settled the matter.

Even after Rory had left, she had clung to the name like a life raft, unwilling to let the last part of him go.

Elaine liked routine. She had made it an art form once she and Jen were on their own. It could have been her specialist subject on *Mastermind*. What time will you get up every morning for the rest of your life? What time will you make yourself a pot of tea every afternoon? What day will you stock up at the Co-op?

Meals were allocated a night and never rotated, so Jen always knew that if it was Tuesday, it was fish fingers, oven chips and peas, but Thursdays meant spaghetti Bolognese. As far as she knew, Elaine still ate the same daily specials on the requisite day. Certainly Sundays, the only day she and Jason ever visited, was still roast. Jen had seen the frozen packets of individual chicken breasts lined up in the freezer like coffins, next to the already partially roasted potatoes and Yorkshire puddings.

'Can't we have something different?' she had asked once, when she was about fourteen. A Wednesday, it must have been, because Elaine had taken a packet of ham out of the fridge, and lettuce and tomatoes to make a salad.

'Ham salad today, you know that,' Elaine had said cheerfully.

'Let's save that for tomorrow. I could make baked potatoes. With beans. Or scrambled eggs.'

'Baked potatoes is Friday,' Elaine had said, as if that was stated in the Bible, and who was she to argue? Thou shalt only eat baked potatoes on a Friday. Thou shalt not covet thy neighbour's spuds. 'If you want to help, you can slice the tomatoes.'

Jen had stamped her foot. Literally stamped it like a cartoon rendition of a sulky child. 'God, Mum, what does it matter? If we feel like having something else, then let's have something else.'

'I feel like ham salad,' Elaine had said in a small but determined voice. 'It's Wednesday.'

It was only more recently that Jen had realized that Elaine probably thought that by taking control of what she had it in her power to influence, she could make her daughter feel secure in the wake of the devastating break-up. It hadn't worked. Jen had felt scornful, even ashamed, of her mother's lack of adventure and flair. Irritated by her practical ordinariness. No wonder her father had felt he couldn't stay; he would have been bored to tears by the day-to-day mundanity. She had had no doubt he would come and rescue her from it one day.

Clearly, he hadn't.

Now, every Sunday, Jen and Jason would either drive to Jen's mum's house – where they would use up all their conversation in the first five minutes, and then sit for hours in an oppressive silence punctuated every now and then by Elaine asking if they wanted more tea, or if they'd heard about the plans to build new homes on a local field that Jen had played rounders on, once, thirty years ago – or to the far more lively and joyous environs of Jason's parents' home.

Every Sunday morning, when Jen woke up, her first thought was always to work out whether she was in for a day of pleasure or pain. This week, thankfully, it had been pleasure.

7

Jen had brought with her: a bag stuffed with a large pumpkin she had picked up at the farmers' market and that she knew was the perfect size and shape to be carved by Amelia, and to adorn the front step later in the month; a copy of a free magazine that had been put through her door that contained an article on the Bloomsbury set, which she thought her mother-in-law might find interesting; and a scarf for Charles that she had found in one of the more upmarket charity shops and knew would compliment his favourite autumn overcoat.

She liked it best when the whole family was there. You never really knew who was coming until you arrived. It was an open house. No need to book. Amelia would always cook enough to feed a small country, and whoever turned up turned up. Jen had sometimes wondered if her in-laws had to eat Sunday-lunch leftovers all week, some weeks. In fact, she knew they did. Charles had often joked about it.

'Any word from Jess?' she said to Jason as they drove up through Richmond.

'Coming, I think.'

She reached over and rubbed the back of his head. With his three-day-old stubble and the new grade-two-all-over haircut he had finally resorted to (after catching sight of his recently acquired balding spot in a random combination of mirrors in a department store changing room, which meant he got a rare glimpse of the back of his own head), Jen had started to think he looked a little like a fuzzy tennis ball. It suited him. Gave him a sort of rugged Action Man look that was completely at odds with his character. Jason Statham with a soft spot for kittens. Christian Bale with a penchant for Aran jumpers.

'I still can't get used to it,' she said, referring to his shorn hair. 'You look like a squaddie.'

Jason raised an eyebrow, a habit that used to make her go weak at the knees when she had first met him. 'Oh, you like that, huh?'

'That depends. Can you do a hundred press-ups and run twenty miles in boots that are too big for you?'

'Of course.'

'Liar.'

'OK, but I could do about eight press-ups and run two miles if I had very comfy trainers. But I need the ones that are built up on one side because I over-pronate.'

'Right, you pass the test.'

'Really?' he said, taking her hand. He raised it to his lips and kissed the tips of her fingers. 'You're that easy?'

Jen laughed. 'Desperate is the word. You're basically the best I can do.'

Jen and Jason's initial attraction had been one of those eyes-across-a-crowded-room, I-have-no-idea-who-you-are-but-I-want-to-throw-you-on-the-floor-and-ravage-you kind of things. From her point of view, at least. She had always assumed he had felt the same, although – who knew? – maybe he just hadn't had the energy to fight her off. After all, trying to set up a production of a mind-numbingly pretentious new play, written by a local would-be Harold Pinter, with a bunch of amateurs light on talent but heavy on attitude was exhausting, he'd told her the first time they had stayed behind after rehearsals to share a warm can of lager that he had produced from his bag.

'Rewrite it,' Jen had said, offering him a drag on her cigarette. 'You're the director, I'm sure that's your pre-rogative. Make it so all the ones who are rubbish die by the end of Act One.'

Jason had laughed. 'I don't think that would be allowed. This is community theatre. It's meant to be inclusive.'

Jen had yawned and stretched, noticing, with satisfac-tion, that Jason couldn't resist checking her out as she did so.

'Honestly? Who cares? It's only going to be their par-ents or their husbands and wives in the audience, anyway. You could stick them up there reciting nursery rhymes and their loved ones would probably be impressed.'

'Oh God, why did I get myself into this?'

'So you could meet me,' Jen had said, and then she'd blushed at her own forwardness.

Jason had given her a look that had made her stomach flip – and every other part of her body, for that matter. And then he'd leaned over and kissed her. She could remember the moment exactly. The thrill that had gone through her. And then he had broken off and started coughing so hard his eyes had begun to water.

'Sorry, sorry,' he'd said, his voice cracking. 'That's what comes of pretending I smoke to impress you.'

They had been together ever since.

When Amelia opened the door, the familiar scent swept out after her. Still baking and coffee, but these days joined by the lilies she kept in a large vase in the hallway, and the cigars that Charles liked to enjoy after dinner some nights. Jen had always thought she should bottle it, call it 'Home' and sell it as a room spray to people who were living apart from their loved ones.

She tried to imagine what the scent of her own child-hood home might be marketed as. 'Bad Atmosphere' or 'Frigidity', maybe. 'Tension' by Lancôme.

She chided herself immediately, as she always did, for comparing her own family negatively to her adopted one. It was never going to be a fair fight. There were no level playing fields. People were dealt different hands and, how-ever hard you tried, you couldn't make a royal flush out of sixes and sevens. It simply wasn't possible.

They were the first to arrive and, as usual, they all fell into their assigned roles. Charles handed round the gin and tonics. Jen followed Amelia to the kitchen and did whatever she could see needed doing, while Jason caught up with his dad in the living room. It was a masterclass in gender stereotyping and one that, Jen knew full well, like most women of her generation, she would scorn under any other circumstances. She had tried on occasion, though, to accept Amelia's protests that she didn't need help, and to sit and chat with the rest of the family in the hour before they ate, but she hadn't been able to resist the smells and the warmth and the acceptance of Amelia's kitchen.

So, on Masterson Sundays, she allowed herself to indulge her inner unreconstructed 1970s woman. When Poppy and Jessie arrived, they would laugh at her, as they always did, happy to let Amelia do what she loved to do and only offering up the minimum of assistance.

'So how's it been?' Amelia asked as she whisked flour into the gravy.

Jen knew immediately what she was referring to.

She had thought that Simone leaving home, two years earlier, would have gone some way to preparing her for the time when she and Jason would be left on their own. But, although she had missed her desperately – could almost feel her absence as a presence, somehow, like a black hole, a vortex in the middle of their house – it was nothing compared to now. She had still had one child at home. She had still had a purpose, an identity. She'd comforted herself by transferring all her attention to her younger daughter, shoved her head down into the sand and refused to look to the future, stubbornly failing to make any long-term plans. To be fair, Jason had reacted in exactly the same way, and they had never really discussed what might come later.

Jen and Jason had always known Simone wouldn't be an only child. In fact, once she had found out she was pregnant, Jen had been adamant that their offspring would never have the lonely upbringing she herself had endured, and Jason had readily acquiesced. Emily had come along eighteen months later, before either of them could change their minds. If she hadn't, Jen often said, they would have tried IVF, adoption, kidnapping, anything. Got a dog and put a dress on it, if all else had failed.

They'd decided very swiftly, though, that while one might be bad, three would have been way too much of a good thing. Two, in this instance, was the magic number.

Amelia totally understood the void that Emily's departure would have left. They had talked about it often in the weeks that had led up to her going. Amelia had been through it herself, of course, although after drama school Jessie had moved back home without a second thought and happily fallen back into the role of dependent daughter, allowing her mother to cook for her and do her washing. Even though Jen had always thought they should throw her back out, make her understand what it was like to have to fend for herself, she was now secretly harbouring hopes that in three years' time Emily might do the same.

'Pretty awful. Although I'm not sure it's quite sunk in yet. I keep waiting for her to walk through the front door.'

'You'll get used to it. And these days they seem to keep in touch much more regularly than they used to. Mobile phones, I suppose.'

'She's called me every day,' Jen said, and made an apologetic face as if to say, 'I really don't have anything to complain about.'

'Well, there you go. Although don't expect that to last. Once she settles in, gets into the swing of it –'

'I know. Then it'll be me phoning her.'

Amelia leaned over and gave her a hug. 'Like I said, you'll get used to it.'

'Jason is pretending he's fine about it, but I know he's checking her Facebook status every thirty seconds.'

Amelia smiled. 'I remember Charles kept making excuses to visit his Highgate branch when Poppy first went to St Martins, and she was living in Hackney. And then he'd say, "Well, as I was over that side of town anyway, I thought I might as well keep going and visit her." In the end, she had to ask him to call first because he was cramping her style.'

'Are you talking about me?' Charles appeared at the door, fresh drinks in hand. Whoever hadn't volunteered for driving duty was always half-cut by the time lunchtime was over.

Charles looked, as he always looked, ready for his close-up. Jen had never seen him anything other than tanned, shaved and smelling of Molton Brown shower gel and Geo. F. Trumper cologne. (She had no idea how he kept up the tan in rainy London. Regular sprays in a St Tropez booth, maybe. She found it hard to imagine him in the regulation paper thong, lifting one leg and then the other while a barely-out-of-her-teens girl squirted brown liquid over his inner thighs). Even when she and Jason had stayed at the house, or they had all gone away for a weekend together, it had been the same. Any time of the day or night. He was like one of those women who are so afraid of their partners seeing them without make-up that they sleep in their full slap, lying motionless on their backs all night in the hope of not smudging their mascara, and then set the alarm for half an hour before their husband gets up so they can cleanse and reapply the whole lot while he's still snoring.

Jen had always admired the fact that Charles made such an effort, even if he sometimes did get it a bit wrong: his hair a touch too big, his tan a shade too orange, his heels verging a little too close to Cuban. It was sweet. Endearing. Lovable.

'Now, why would you think that?' Amelia said.

'Lucky guess,' he said, and planted a kiss on the top of each of their heads as he handed them new glasses and took the empty ones to the sink to rinse out.

'You should be so lucky,' Amelia said, twinkling at Jen as she teased him. 'Charles always thinks everyone's talking about him. Not because he's paranoid, but because he thinks he's the most interesting topic there is, isn't that right, dear?'

Charles looked mock horrified. 'See what I have to put up with, Jen? My own wife –'

'Oh, get out the violins,' Amelia said.

Charles sidled up behind her and wrapped his arms round her, squeezing tight. 'You know you love me, really.'

'Maybe,' Amelia said, coquettishly.

Charles squeezed more tightly.

'OK, yes, I do, now get off me.' She batted him away with a tea towel.

'See . . .' Charles smiled a victorious smile at Jen as he went to leave the kitchen again with the two clean glasses – Sundays were always a relay of clean and dirty glasses for Charles. It never seemed to occur to him that he could just refill the ones each of them had already used. 'I'm irresistible.'

The front door banged, announcing the arrival of

Poppy and Maisie, closely followed by a heavily first-time pregnant Jessie, and Martin. Coats were dumped on the backs of chairs, more gin and tonics appeared. Jessie and Martin joined Jason and Charles in the living room while Poppy slumped at the kitchen table. Amelia had set paints and paper out for Maisie, and she gravitated towards them like an addict to a rock of crack.

'She's definitely a Masterson,' Amelia said approvingly.

Jessie heaved herself into the room. On her still skinny frame her seven-month baby bump made her look like she was attempting to smuggle a spacehopper through customs. She held on to her lower back and moaned theatrically.

'They're all discussing cars in there. It's like an episode of bloody *Top Gear*.'

'Aaah, is no one talking about you?' Poppy smiled a sarcastic smile.

Jen stifled a laugh. Jessie-baiting was one of Poppy's favourite pastimes. It was almost too easy.

'Mum . . .' Jessie whined. Exactly, Jen imagined, as she would have when she and Poppy were ten and thirteen.

Amelia put a glass of apple juice down in front of her. 'She's only teasing.'

Jen stepped in. 'How are you feeling, Jess? She kicking much yet?'

Jessie and Martin had opted not to find out the sex of their baby, but the rest of the family was just assuming it would be a girl. The Mastersons specialized in having girls. Jason, they all agreed, had been an anomaly. The only boy of his, or the next, generation among the whole extended clan.

Jessie turned to Jen, happy that she was the main topic

again. 'Like crazy. I think she – or he, obviously – is going to be a dancer. I've been doing this pregnancy yoga and I swear the baby tries to join in –'

'She's probably just attention seeking. I wonder who she takes after?' Poppy chipped in.

'I'm not even listening to you.' Jessie held up her hand. 'It's like you don't exist.'

If she ignored the way they had all aged, Jen could have believed she was back in the early 1990s. The arguments were the same, the decor had barely changed – except for a few coats of the same colour paint, which had all then been completely recovered with the same old artwork. Even Jason's misshapen pot still held pens in the middle of the table. She wouldn't have wanted it any other way.

'What else can I do?' she said, putting her arms round her mother-in-law from behind as she stood at the stove.

'Nothing.' Amelia lifted up one of Jen's hands, and kissed it. 'Sit down and enjoy yourself.'

At lunch Charles liked to rehash old family in-jokes. When he took his first mouthful of lamb, he clutched his throat dramatically, like he always did, and pretended to keel over in a death throe.

'Charles, stop it,' Amelia said, smiling.

Charles, as always, sat up with a triumphant look on his face. 'Just kidding. It's delicious.'

He took another bite. Did it again. Maisie squealed hysterically, exactly as Simone and Emily used to when they were little. The more times he did it, the funnier she thought it was.

Then the reminiscences started. Just as in all families, the old well-worn anecdotes would be aired again and again, with everyone chipping in to add their favourite parts. Typically Amelia or Charles would run through the time Jason got his thumb stuck in a bottle of ketchup and had to go to Casualty, the time Jessie made a snowman and brought it inside and hid it under her bed, not realizing it would melt all over the floor, and the time Charles drove the car to Battersea with Poppy's favourite bear and the house keys on the roof.

'And they were still there when he arrived!' Amelia would say. Then everyone would join her in the next sentence. 'All the way from Twickenham to Battersea.'

And then they would start on stories that included Jen, so she didn't feel left out. The time they had all gone away for the weekend and Jen had cooked a chicken with the giblets still tucked up in their plastic bag inside, the time she'd offered fifty pence to what she thought was a tramp only for it to turn out to be one of Charles and Amelia's wealthy bohemian neighbours enjoying a short rest on a park bench.

There were countless running gags in the Masterson family. Not to mention rituals and traditions. Tangible evidence of a shared happy past. They were incomprehensible to the outside world and, no doubt, rather self-indulgent and annoying to those not involved. A little bit 'Aren't we great?', a touch 'Do you see how close we must be?', a smidgen 'We're very pleased with ourselves!'.

As for Jen, they made her feel warm and fuzzy. Included. Loved.

Then Charles would toast Amelia and thank her for the

meal, as he always did. They would all clink glasses, echoing his thanks and secretly congratulating themselves on how fortunate they were.

'I hope we're like them when we've been married for forty-five years,' Jen said to Jason in the car on the way home, not for the first time.

'What? Me making the same old jokes and you still laughing?'

'Exactly. It's so sweet.'

'Well,' Jason said, reaching out and putting a hand on her knee. 'I can certainly keep to my end of the bargain. It's you who'll have the hard job of pretending you still find me funny.'

'I've already got away with it for twenty-two,' Jen said, laughing. 'What's the difference?'

8

For Charles and Amelia's upcoming forty-fifth wedding anniversary Jen and Jason had organized a few days away near Oxford for the four of them. That is, Jen had done all the organizing and Jason had cheered her on from the sidelines. They had wanted to get the whole clan down there, but it had proved impossible to pin down dates they could all do, so they were having a family party the following weekend too. Simone and Emily had already booked their train tickets home for that one.

In a moment of madness Jen had come up with the idea of making a DVD as a present for her in-laws. A document of the whole extended family sharing memories and mementos. As soon as she'd suggested it, she had been overwhelmed by the practicalities of making it happen – until Jessie, surprisingly, had offered to drive across the country to the various aunts and uncles and cousins, recording their messages on her camcorder and trawling through their old family photos. That was the thing about Jessie. She could be infuriatingly selfish and thoughtless at times, but then out of nowhere she would do something so incredibly generous or kind that everything else would be forgotten.

'You and Poppy have work,' she'd said, when she'd called Jen to suggest her plan. 'And this is probably the last time I'll be of any use to anyone before the baby comes and I'm out of action for God knows how long.'

'I'm sure we can just ask them to record something on their phones and email it to us,' Jen had said.

'No way. If we're going to do it, we need to do it properly. Plus it'll give me an excuse to get away while Martin decorates the nursery.'

Meanwhile, Jen had arranged to spend an evening round at Poppy's, making a list of everyone who should be included and emailing them to let them know what was required.

'So I've got a date,' Poppy said, as soon as Maisie had been tucked up in bed and the wine opened. They had got as far as writing down the names of all Charles and Amelia's siblings before they got sidetracked. A job that had taken them approximately one and a half minutes.

Poppy's announcement, in itself, wasn't really news. Poppy often went on dates. First dates, second dates, third dates. A few times she had seen someone for a couple of weeks, or even months, before either she or he – usually she, it seemed to Jen – decided they could do better. Jen had always found her sister-in-law's tales of single life both entertaining and alarming. Her relationships always came with bucketfuls of added drama. She had a predilection for complicated men – ones with addictions and neuroses and, occasionally, although she never found out until it was too late, wives. It was a constant whirl of fights, tears and extravagant make-ups in Poppy's world. Jen couldn't see the attraction herself.

'Good for you. Who is he?'

'Well, his name's Ryan, he's forty-two, separated, soon to be divorced, two children – eleven and nine – that he has at the weekends, and he runs his own company. Importing furniture from the Far East.'

'Where did you meet him?'

Poppy paused just long enough for Jen to start to wonder what was going to come next.

'Well . . . OK, I'm just going to tell you and then you can laugh in my face.'

'Poppy! What?'

'You have to promise not to tell the others first.'

'Of course.'

'I met him online, all right? I signed up with one of those dating sites. So. Now you know.'

Jen realized she was sitting there open-mouthed. She couldn't have been more surprised if Poppy had told her she'd met this man at a Christian prayer meeting, or a stamp-collecting convention.

'You've been online dating, and you didn't tell me?'

'I'm telling you now, aren't I? He's the first one I'm meeting.'

'You know what I mean.'

'I knew you'd just say the only people on there would be saddos or rapists. Or both.'

'Well, actually, I wouldn't, because you're on there now, and you're not a saddo. Or a rapist. Honestly, I think it's a good idea.'

'Really?'

'Really. It's the only way anyone seems to meet anyone these days, according to the papers.'

Strictly speaking, this wasn't the truth. Jen actually did feel quite alarmed that Poppy would look for her future among the kind of people who, she imagined, would put themselves out there, on the internet. Drop-dead gorgeous Poppy, with her line in smart put-downs and the way she could fill a room just by smiling. She had always been the crush object of all the cool blokes – the desirable, moody ones. Did she really need to advertise for a date?

'You don't think it makes me look desperate?'

'No more than usual.'

'Gosh, you're funny.'

'I know. I can't help myself. Seriously, though, even though I don't think it's sad at all, be careful. Promise me you'll meet him in a public place and you'll tell me exactly where you're going to be and when. Just in case.'

'I'm not stupid. We're having lunch on Wednesday at the Soho Hotel. And I've already told him that, if we get on, I want to talk to either his ex-wife or his mother before we go out on a proper date, to check he's really who he says he is. I'm not taking the risk he's happily married and just wants a bit on the side.'

'And he said OK?'

'Yep. And I've already checked out his company's website, and it all seems to be above board. His name is on there and they have a warehouse in Acton. I phoned up and asked about ordering a sideboard, and it seemed like they'd have been happy to deliver one to me if I'd said I wanted it.'

'Jesus. Now it's him I'm worried for.'

'And I've told him if he doesn't look like his picture, then I'm turning round and walking straight out again. There will be no chance to try to win me over with his sparkling personality, so he may as well 'fess up now.'

'Oh my God, Pop. You're being serious, aren't you?'

'Of course. He needs to know there's no point even

trying to get one over on me about anything. Start as you mean to go on.'

Jen couldn't help laughing. 'I hope he still turns up.'

'I know. I might well have put him off for life, but then, if he's easily put off, it's good that I find that out now. God, he'd better be nice after all this.'

'Too right. He'll have me to answer to if he isn't.'

Poppy leaned over and filled Jen's glass. 'Maybe I'll bring him to the party, if he turns out to be the man of my dreams.'

'Now I feel really sorry for him. Being scrutinized by all the Mastersons at once.'

'You remember what that was like, right?'

'Terrifying. Let's hope he's thick-skinned.'

'Anyway, like I said, don't tell anyone.'

'I'm not even going to dignify that by answering. Again. How many years – '

'I know, I know,' Poppy interrupted. 'Forget I said it. Have another glass of wine.'

Jen was indulging in a bit of Neil-baiting. She and Judy currently had a bet going to see how many times they could get Neil to mention his wife during an eight-hour shift. Judy was currently in the lead with nine, although with no independent adjudicator Jen wasn't sure how much she could trust her opponent.

She had started a conversation about running, because she thought she could remember that being one of Mrs Neil's interests. (Neither of them knew her name, and it didn't occur to either of them to ask – too much time had passed. And, anyhow, they couldn't imagine any name that would be appropriate and so had decided it was better not to know.) But that attack was thwarted when the phone rang and interrupted her.

She was racking her brain for a way to bring the conversation back round. Or even for anything else to talk about, and sod the bet. Working side by side with someone for hours at a time meant that you soon ran out of things to say. They all knew far more about each other than they did some of their closest friends.

Neil seemed to have no general conversation. No opinion of his own to offer on anything, just his wife's. Sometimes hours could pass without him talking at all beyond the repetitive procedural business of the hotel. And then Jen's shift would crawl by. She would feel like she was moving in slow motion. Wading through the day as if through a vat of treacle. Hence she didn't feel too bad about trying to poke him into scoring her a point or two.

They had been locked into a resounding silence for so long that, at one point, Jen felt as if she might doze off. The hotel was quiet, caught in the lull between the summer tourists and the pre-Christmas rush of shoppers and partygoers.

'What do you think of Woody Allen?' she said, slightly desperately, remembering that Neil had once mentioned buying Mrs Neil a DVD of *Manhattan Murder Mystery*.

'My wife thinks he's a genius . . .' Neil said.

Jen congratulated herself silently, and then wondered whether Judy would try to claim her question had been a leading one.

Neil was detailing which of Woody Allen's films his

wife liked and which she didn't, the exact moment at which she thought he had lost his touch, her thoughts about his controversial love life. Jen looked at her watch surreptitiously. Two hours to go. She tried to stifle a yawn.

'I hate to interrupt your nap,' a voice said, and Jen jumped.

'I'm so sorry,' she said, looking up and trying to give the impression she was wide awake and fully engaged.

She was relieved when she saw it was one of the regulars, a Mr Hoskins, Sean, standing there with an amused smile on his face. They had many repeat guests – it was one of the things the hotel prided itself on, making sure people would feel so welcome they would want to come again. Sean was some kind of vintage dealer, with a shop in the Cotswolds somewhere, and he came down every four weeks or so to trawl through the markets and car-boot sales around the seamier parts of London, in search of treasure. Jen remembered one of the chambermaids telling her he had a life-sized mannequin in his room once, and that he'd left it lying on the bed, under the covers, as a joke.

He was one of her favourites, actually. He always took the time to chat to the staff – something a lot of the guests clearly thought was beneath them – and he had a sarcastic tone that always made her laugh. It didn't hurt that he was attractive either. Not in an obvious way. He was in his early forties, she would guess, maybe forty-five. Dark hair that he wore short on the sides and swept back on top, with a few specks of grey appearing around his hairline. Bluey-grey eyes. He was nice enough looking, nothing special. But when he said something funny – or when he laughed at something someone else said – his face really came to life. His eyes positively twinkled, the raft of little lines around them giving away that he laughed often.

Not that Jen was interested. That had never been her style. She had never in her twenty-two years with Jason gone beyond a teasing playful flirtation with any other man. It had simply never occurred to her that she might. But having Sean around definitely made the days pass more quickly.

'Mr Hoskins. Nice to see you again. And apologies. Again.'

'Shall I go away and come back later?'

Jen knew he was joking. Neil, on the other hand, completely missed the point. He was one of those people who didn't always quite get when others were being flippant. He took everything at face value. Jen had long ago learned that using sarcasm was pointless where Neil was concerned.

'I can book you in, Mr Hoskins,' he said, as if Jen might really be about to take him up on his offer to go away so she could have a snooze.

'It's fine, Neil,' she said. 'It's all under control. Well, actually, it's not. I'm afraid the internet's down, so I can't check you in officially. I'm afraid it means I have no idea which room you've been allocated either.'

She was relieved that Sean laughed. Some guests would – understandably – be furious if they'd had a long journey and then the hotel couldn't even offer them anything other than a seat at the bar. Especially when they'd had to stand at reception being ignored before finding that out.

'Just give me any old key and I'll go and make myself at

home. You might have to warn the other guests they could find a strange man asleep in their bed, though.'

'I am so sorry.'

'Do you remember the days when we used to write stuff down? What were we thinking?'

Jen smiled. 'If you'd like to wait in the bar, you can have a drink on us and then I'll come and get you as soon as we can sort this out.'

'What if it's not fixed till tomorrow? Will you bring me in a duvet?'

'Of course. I hear the floor's quite comfy in there. It's sprung, apparently.'

'Oh, I'm sure it'll be working soon,' Neil piped up. He shot Jen a look. 'If not, we'll help you find another hotel, obviously.'

'Oh God, no,' Sean said. 'This is why I love this place, there's never a dull moment.'

'Nice bloke,' Neil said when Sean had moved off towards the bar. 'My wife loves all that vintage stuff he deals in. I'm not so sure myself.'

Bingo! thought Jen. Five mentions, not a bad morning's work.

By the time lunchtime came round, she was desperate to get out and get some fresh air. She hadn't seen Charles since the weekend, and she thought it might be fun to catch up and to tell him in depth about Emily's first experiences away at uni (her current favourite topic; she could bore for England, and frequently did – it was a shame, really, that she had missed the meeting where they chose the new disciplines for the next Olympics), and so she put her coat on over her uniform (brown pencil skirt, green shirt and brown cardigan or jacket, black court shoes; it was channelling Mussolini a little too much for Jen's liking, but not bad, actually, as uniforms went) and did what she had done many times before, walked round the corner in the hopes of surprising Charles at his office.

Technically he was retired, but his name was still above the door. He was still a partner, although he'd handed over the reins to one of his protégés a couple of years ago, and he still liked to drop in a few times a week to survey his kingdom.

The flagship branch of Masterson Property, and the one where Charles liked to spend his time, was a three-minute walk from The Fitzrovia. In a district of restaurants, media companies and art galleries the facade stood out like a brash cousin at a royal wedding. The obligatory photographs of swanky properties filled the windows, although rarely with the prices attached. It was just assumed that if you crossed the threshold to enquire, then you had already resigned yourself to the fact that there were going to be an awful lot of zeros attached.

Somehow, over the years, Charles had also become British TV's go-to property expert. In fact, now they had him on to talk about anything – the recession, the disappearance of the green belt, the state of the nation. It had started about fifteen years earlier, when one of his clients, who happened to work for Sky News, had asked him to go on air to talk about the trends in house prices. He had done so well they'd asked him back and, since then, he had become a regular fixture on shows like *Daybreak* and *The One Show*. Jen didn't always agree with his views – he was increasingly booked to espouse a 'We're all going to hell in a handcart if we don't sort out the moral decline of our society' viewpoint. And he'd become a sort of pin-up boy for the Countryside Alliance and *Daily Telegraph* readers. But that was just his public persona. To his adoring family and friends he was still a pussy cat in real life – a rational, reasonable, charming, funny man.

Later, she would wish that she'd stayed in the staffroom and eaten the sandwich she'd brought in with her, as she so often did. That she'd ignored the fact the sun was shining for possibly the last time that year, and put her feet up. That she had gone out five minutes later, turned left instead of right, kept her eyes firmly on the pavement in front of her.

But it was too late. Once she'd seen what she'd seen, she couldn't un-see it. Couldn't pretend she didn't know what she knew. Couldn't rewind, erase and rewrite. However much she might want to.

9

It was something about the way they were looking at each other that made her stop and look. Ordinarily she would have run across the road to say hello, eager as a Labrador at the sound of a tin opener, but not today. Something wasn't right. It was Charles, there was no doubt about it. She could spot his tall imposing figure in any crowd. But she had no idea who the woman was. And, whoever she was, he was standing too close to her, paying her too much attention.

Thankfully she spotted them when she was still far enough away that they hadn't yet noticed her. Now she had stopped, she didn't know what to do with herself, so she rummaged through her bag, as though she was looking for something important, while actually keeping her eyes firmly on the two people on the other side of the road.

She didn't know what it was exactly that made her so sure this was no ordinary conversation. It was a combination of impressions. A collection of nuances that added up to something bigger – she just didn't know what. For a start, although she couldn't hear what they were saying, Jen was pretty sure they were arguing. Not an all-out row – she couldn't imagine Charles would ever sink to that level out here, in the street, whoever he was with – but one of those small, snipey squabbles that couples have.

You know the ones. They're usually about who left the top off the shampoo or whose shoes trod mud into the carpet. The important stuff. The stuff that you only ever get worked up about with people you know intimately.

They were talking quietly, seemingly aware enough of their surroundings to want to make sure they weren't overheard – they had tucked themselves into the entrance to a little cobbled alley, as if standing two feet away from the main street might render them invisible – but not so aware that they could wait until they were alone to say whatever they had to say. The way you just can't help yourself, sometimes. You have to get something off your chest, never mind if you're in the checkout queue at Tesco's and your next-door neighbour is behind you ear-wigging. Hoping to hear some gossip she can pass on. Suddenly it's crucial that you tell your husband that you've always hated the way he picks at the stuff between his toes while he's watching TV.

The woman was a few inches shorter than Charles, so she was having to look up to get his attention, straining to pull herself up to her full height, almost on tiptoes. She looked young. Compared to him, anyway. Despite the fact that something was clearly wrong between them, Jen thought he looked concerned for her, anxious to get his point across but without letting things get out of hand. She knew that face so well, she could read his expressions, even from a distance.

She stood there watching, transfixed. An insistent alarm was ringing in her head. Something was wrong. Something was threatening her perfect family life. She knew she should probably turn round and walk back to the hotel, but she couldn't seem to tear herself away. Poppy had once said that Jen would definitely be the person who caused a pile-up on the motorway because she was craning her neck to look at the rear-ended car on the other side. Twenty people dead instead of one case of whiplash. Nosy woman causes M1 carnage. It wasn't that she *was* nosy necessarily – actually, scratch that, she was. She was just interested, she would protest. She liked to know what was going on. She always had to find out what happened next. And in this instance, if she was being honest, it felt as if she had a right to know. Or, at least, that no one would have expected her to turn a blind eye and ignore it. Whatever *it* was.

As she watched, the woman put a manicured hand on Charles's arm and he looked down at it, as if startled by the contact. He didn't shake it off straight away, like Jen expected him to, either. He left it there for a moment longer than felt right, and then he removed it gently, holding it in his own and massaging the back of it with his fingers. Looking at the woman intently. Looking around to make sure he hadn't been seen. Looking like a man Jen had never met.

Jen, across the street, stepped back into the doorway of a restaurant. Just missed falling down a hatch in the pavement where kitchen staff were stashing boxes unloaded from the back of a van.

'Lady!' one of them shouted, waving his arm at her.

'Shit, sorry,' Jen said, as quietly as she could, without actually whispering.

She thought about calling out. Or running across the road to surprise them. Jumping out shouting 'Gotcha!', setting off streamers and blowing a party whistle. Anything that would break the moment. But first she needed to decide if what she thought she was seeing was really what she thought she was seeing. She had a history of jumping to conclusions. Something else Poppy liked to remind her about.

Really, though, there was no doubt. Jen took a deep breath, felt it catch in the back of her throat. Told herself to calm down. For a minute or so, she just watched the man she had thought was so familiar to her, and the woman she had never seen before, and then, after she was sure she'd taken in the whole scene – after she'd seen as much as she needed to see, and before she could talk herself out of it – she forced a smile on to her face and started to walk towards them.

10

'Charles.'

If you put her on the stand, made her swear on the Bible, Jen would have to say that he jumped. Certainly he took an almost imperceptible step away from the woman as he turned to see who was calling him. And there was also no denying that he looked panicked for a split second when he realized it was his daughter-in-law. Then he forced his features into a smile, but she knew him far too well. She could tell that it wasn't genuine.

'Jen, what a lovely surprise.'

For a moment, Jen didn't know what to say because, having intended to suggest lunch, she now couldn't imagine anything she wanted to do less. Or what she could talk about in its place.

'I'm on my way to meet someone.' She looked at her watch hammily, as if to emphasize the point. 'I was just going to stick my head round the door to say hello, and then rush off again. And then . . . here you are . . . in the street.' She could almost feel the wave of relief as it flooded his face. She would be gone in a moment.

'Well, it's always good to see you, even if it's only in passing,' he said, making as if to move away.

Jen took a step forward, extended her right hand to the young woman at Charles's side. She wasn't letting him get away that easily.

'Hi, I'm Jen. I'm Charles's daughter-in-law.'

As she waited for the woman's response – 'Hi, I'm X, I'm Charles's mistress' maybe? Or 'I'm a prostitute he's hired for a quick one, we were just arguing about the fee' – Jen got the chance to give her a quick appraisal. She was even younger than Jen had thought at first. Late twenties, maybe. Thirty at the most. She was taller than Jen, something that, despite all her better instincts, always made Jen feel a little inadequate. She noticed the woman's brown, thick, shiny hair, worn long and loose, her dark eyes and her slim figure. OK skin. Attractive but not a head-turner. Quite ordinary, really.

Jen always noticed when women had good hair. Her own was out-of-control curly. The hours of her life she had lost to hair straighteners would have added up to a lifetime for some animals. Not elephants, maybe, but guinea pigs, say, or hamsters. She lived in fear of drizzle or humidity. She fantasized about chemical blow-dries and months of smooth silky locks. Who cared if the formaldehyde took years off her life? At least she would be a sleekly coiffeured corpse. Luckily for the two girls, they had inherited their father's family's poker straightness. Dark brown for Simone, and Jen's all-out red for Emily.

The irony of regularly dying the roots of her hair a colour she had hated her whole childhood was not lost on Jen. For the record, she loved it now. Once she was out of an environment where people shouted 'Ginger' (to rhyme with 'wringer', not 'whinger' because that, somehow, turned a colour into an insult) at her at every available occasion, she had started to revel in her difference. Possibly at about the same time as some artsy boy she was

63

seeing had told her she reminded him of a Titian painting. She had never claimed she wasn't superficial.

She had inherited the colour from Rory's side of the family, apparently. It had bypassed him but his grandmother, he had informed her when she was little, had had a fine head of flaming locks. It had made her feel special when he'd told her that. Connected to ancestors she had never known.

These days she tended to keep it in a ponytail, in an effort to minimize potential weather-induced horrors. Now she felt herself tuck a strand that had come loose behind her ear. A reflex action that, if you knew her well, would probably have been a dead giveaway that she was feeling awkward. It was her default gesture when she didn't know what else to do with her hands. Ever since she had realized that, she would try to pre-empt it by doing something else, but she'd lose concentration for a second and there it was again.

Finally, the woman seemed to realize that she was expected to respond, and she shook Jen's offered hand.

'Cass Richards,' she said. 'Nice to meet you.'

'Cass is looking for a place in town.' Charles jumped in before Cass could say anything to the contrary. Anything incriminating. ('I'm a sex surrogate. I get paid by the hour to try to coax it back to life.')

'I've just been showing her what we've got available at the moment but, you know, the market's slow . . .' He tailed off without completing the sentence.

Jen had to resist the urge to ask questions, to put this Cass on the spot by asking her what area she was considering and how many rooms. She knew she wouldn't have the answers ready.

'Well . . .' She decided to let Charles off the hook for the moment. She needed to regroup, to assimilate what she thought she'd learned, to make sure she wasn't rushing headlong towards a ridiculous conclusion.

'Like I said, I have a friend to meet, so I should go. Bye, Charles.'

She accepted his proffered kiss on the cheek.

'Nice to meet you,' she said to Cass as she moved off. 'Good luck with the house hunting.'

Cass smiled politely. 'Thanks. Good to meet you too.'

Jen resisted the urge to look back as she rounded the bend into Rathbone Place. She knew there would be nothing she would want to see.

She had lost her appetite, and any ideas she might have had about luxuriating with a snack in the sun had withered and died. Charles, having an affair? She couldn't believe it could be true. She simply couldn't compute that he would do that to Amelia. Sweet, loving, devoted Amelia. Or to Jason and his daughters. To her, for that matter. To the entity known as the Masterson Family. He had principles, morals, standards. She knew he didn't take his role as husband and father lightly. She knew he was the opposite of the man she had called Dad.

She tried to assess the evidence rationally. A young woman with shiny hair had put her hand on Charles's arm and he had failed to shake it off immediately. Then he had held it in his own for a few seconds, no more. It was hardly a smoking gun. What had really given them away was much more indefinable. The argument, the atmosphere, something in the way they looked at each other, the way

Charles started when Jen had called his name. It all added up to something. She just couldn't be sure what exactly.

Usually, when anything interesting happened in Jen's life she would reach for her phone and hit Poppy's number. Poppy was always her first port of call in a crisis. Somehow, that didn't feel like the thing to do in this case.

'I think your dad might be having an affair . . .' might not be the best opening line of a conversation she'd ever thought of.

'So guess what? Charles has got a bit on the side . . .'

'Did you know your father can still get it up?'

No.

Plus she knew that she had a habit of making something out of nothing. There was the time when she'd told everyone at work that Judy was pregnant, when she had just put on a couple of pounds, or when she'd insisted to Poppy that the bloke painting her living room had a crush on her, and then he'd told them about his upcoming wedding. To a man. It was just that sometimes she wanted things to be true so much she convinced herself that they were. This time, obviously, was not one of those occasions.

She walked on towards Oxford Street, thinking about how much Jason adored his dad. How he had always held him up as an example – and it had never been challenged by her – of the husband and father he aspired to be himself.

She pictured Amelia in her cosy, welcoming house that she had worked lovingly for years to turn into a home that her whole family would want to return to every chance they got. Poppy who was Charles's uncrowned favourite

– he would never have admitted to it, but his pride in her success and the way she was managing to juggle her career in advertising with being a single mum to four-year-old Maisie positively burst out of him whenever they were together. And Jessie who, at thirty-seven, was still the baby of the family, and who loved her dad so much she would probably still sit on his knee and insist he read her a story, if he would let her.

She thought of how much they meant to her as a family, how, since they'd all but fostered her twenty-two years ago, she had felt like they'd filled a hole in her life that her dad had created when he'd left and that she and her mum had steadily made deeper every year, chipping away relentlessly at the foundations of their relationship like would-be prison escapees.

It couldn't be true.

By the time she got back to the hotel after forty-five minutes of aimless wandering around Soho, Neil had been replaced by Judy. Ordinarily this would have filled Jen with joy. They could spend the afternoon gossiping and chatting, and the time would pass by in a heartbeat. Today, though, she would have found Neil's long silences a relief.

She considered, for a brief second, whether she could confide in Judy about what she thought she'd witnessed, but she knew that, fond as she was of her, confident as she was that Judy would sympathize and probably give her some sound advice about what she should do next, Judy had no filter, no concept of keeping things to herself. She parroted out whatever she had heard, regardless, completely unaware that sometimes discretion might be best.

Consequently, Jen knew that Cathy from housekeeping had once had sex with a guest whose room she was meant to be cleaning, that Graham the doorman (or Graham Roper the Doorman Groper, as she and Judy had once nicknamed him, because he had hands that didn't so much wander as run ahead with purpose) had a penchant for lunchtime visits to strip clubs, and that Nick, the head waiter in the restaurant, had been blessed with a third nipple right in the centre of his chest. There was no malice in

Judy's sharing of stories, she just couldn't help herself. It was as if she leaked, and there was nothing she could do to make it stop.

If it hadn't been to do with Charles, Jen might have been tempted to tell her, anyway. She desperately wanted to say it out loud to someone. To see if it sounded ridiculous, or plausible, when it came out of her mouth. But her father-in-law's minor celebrity status meant that her suspicions would spread around the hotel like wildfire and, before she knew it, the tabloids would probably be camping out on his doorstep, rifling through his bins and taking photographs of Amelia from unflattering angles, emphasizing her wattle and comparative lack of sex appeal.

For a fleeting moment, she even wondered if she should tell Jason what she had seen. She knew she couldn't do it, though. Couldn't be the one to shatter his idealized vision of his father. Not when she wasn't sure, anyway. Not when what she had seen might have a hundred innocent explanations. If only she could think what one of them might be.

The afternoon turned out to be a write-off as far as work was concerned. Jen tried, and failed, to concentrate, and when she accidentally called the representative of a well-known macho Scottish actor, who was expected to arrive the following day, and told him that she had organized the Brazilian wax his client had requested in the hotel spa, she realized it was time to give up and go home. So she claimed a sudden-onset migraine and the need to go and lie down in a darkened room. Fortunately, she had so rarely taken a sick day in all her years on the job that no one questioned whether she was telling the truth and, in fact, their genuine concern for her almost made her come clean and admit that she was lying. She refused David's offer of a cab, insisting that she was OK to negotiate the Tube, and left as quickly as she could get away.

Sean Hoskins was unloading boxes from a taxi as she left.

'Escaping?' he said as she passed, head down. She really didn't want to talk to anyone.

'Something like that. Going home, actually. I've got a migraine.'

'Oh, I'm sorry,' he said, sounding genuinely concerned. 'Can I do anything? I could run round to Boots . . .'

She felt bad that she was including him in her lie. Touched that he would care enough to offer to help. She forced a smile. 'No. Thank you. I've got stuff at home.'

'Do you want my taxi? I won't be a minute.'

'Honestly, I'm fine. But thanks again.'

He peered into one of the boxes he had stacked up on the pavement. 'I've got a melamine tea set from the nineteen fifties in here, if that's any good.'

Jen laughed. 'I'm OK for kitsch tableware, actually.'

'Hope you feel better,' he called after her as she walked off.

The house always seemed to Jen like a completely different place when no one else was home, echoey and somehow shabbier. Not that it didn't always look a little shabby around the edges. Lived in. Knackered, actually. It sounded grand, saying they had a house in London, but in reality it was tiny. Basically a two-up, two-down with a bit of a kitchen extension. It was in the middle of a terrace of Victorian cottages that had been built for railway workers or something similar. Short, undernourished, nineteenth-century people, anyway. It sat in a well-kept road, and their neighbours were quiet and had plants in their little front gardens, rather than the old motorbikes and broken fridges that were the accessory du jour in the street they had lived in before. They had a small patio out the back that was a sun trap, with room for four chairs, if you didn't mind all sitting in a tight row, like you were at the cinema.

Jen loved it.

They had moved there when Simone was about sixteen months, and Emily was well on the way, and she had never wanted to go anywhere else, even though they had always all been tripping over each other, fighting over whose turn it was to use the one bathroom, moaning about the lack of cupboard space and soundproofing.

When the girls were home she barely noticed the clutter, but now she had to force herself to turn a blind eye to it and head straight for the kitchen. She had decided on her journey home that she would cook Jason his favourite meal – a calorie-laden and time-consuming fish pie. She wanted to do something nice for him, but not so nice that he would realize something was wrong. As if she might be able to offset some of the damage his father was doing by feeding him a tasty bit of haddock in a white sauce.

She knew that if he asked her if everything was OK, she would probably blurt out what she had seen – and that was the last thing she wanted to do. That would be on a par with announcing to your five-year-old that the tooth fairy was a kiddie fiddler, or that SpongeBob and Patrick secretly hated each other. She needed to process, to decide what she should do next, before she acted.

Spending an afternoon cooking wasn't Jen's natural inclination, but she knew that if she didn't get on with it right away, the chances of it happening once Jason got home were minimal. She would get caught up in the stories of his students – he worked, these days, teaching drama at the local sixth-form college – and opening a bottle of wine, and they would end up with grilled fish and boiled potatoes for tea. Nice, but not exactly the point. Besides, the mindless tasks of cubing the haddock, boiling and then mashing the potatoes and making the creamy sauce would give her the chance to think things through properly.

She forced herself to replay lunchtime's events one more time, frame by frame. Whatever way she looked at it – fast, slow, forwards, backwards – the impression it left was the same. She tried to take herself out of the picture, to imagine the encounter from the disinterested viewpoint of a stranger. What would she have inferred if she had caught sight of Charles and Cass, knowing neither of them? She ran the film again. There was no doubt. She would barely have noticed them, just another couple, albeit of the May and December variety – or more like March and November – but a couple without a doubt, so relaxed were they with each other, so intimate their body language. Shit.

If she was right – and the jury was still out on that one – then doing nothing in a hurry was definitely the best option. She was all too aware, though, that it wasn't

in her nature just to let it lie. If Charles was seeing someone, then he needed to be taken to task. She couldn't just
stand on the sidelines and watch him destroy his family.
Her family. She needed time to think.

She heard the front door bang, announcing that Jason was
home.

'Hello!' she called out, putting on as cheerful a voice as
she could muster, which, given the mood she was in,
wasn't very convincing. 'I'm in the kitchen.'

'What have I done to deserve this?' Jason asked as he
peered over her shoulder.

Jen turned round and planted a kiss on the end of his
nose. 'I had a migraine. Actually, that's not really true. I
skived off. I thought I'd come home and be a domestic
goddess, for once.'

'Well, I'm impressed, although you really should be
wearing an apron and kitten heels.'

'And I bought a cheesecake.'

'You bought it? You didn't spend all day slaving over it?
Shame on you,' he said, laughing. 'What kind of a wife are
you?'

She pushed him away playfully. 'One who will throw
this whole creation in the bin in a moment and open a tin
of beans.'

'I love it when you get angry.'

She pulled him back into a hug. 'Love you too.'

'OK, that's it, what have you done?'

'I miss having people to wait on,' she said. 'You're going
to have to let me spoil you for a bit, while I get used to
both girls being gone.'

'Spoil away.' Jason kissed her on the forehead. 'If you want, I could start moaning and throwing tantrums and telling you I hate you, and then it'd be as if they'd never left.'

'Perfect,' Jen said. 'And throw in some crying for good measure.'

'Do you remember when Simone threatened to leave home because we wouldn't let her paint her half of the bedroom black?'

And they were off into a happy reminiscence about when the girls were little – their favourite way of passing the time these days. Jen pushed Charles out of her mind. Tried to think about anything else.

Cass put down the newspaper she was pretending to read and pressed the button on the remote to mute the TV. She was finding it hard to concentrate. Ever since they had bumped into Charles's daughter-in-law earlier – Jen, that was her name – she had been aware of a flicker of anxiety in her stomach. At least, she thought it was anxiety. It had occurred to her that it might be anticipation. She knew that a part of her wanted everything to come out into the open. Even though that would probably be catastrophic. It was like when you leaned over a too-high railing. Who hadn't thought, 'What if I jump?' Who hadn't wanted to push things too far, just to see what would happen?

Or maybe that was just her.

In reality, though, she knew that she would never force the issue. She had no doubt that, if she did so, she would be running the risk of losing Charles from her life altogether. In fact, not even running the risk, it was a certainty. He had told her many times that he couldn't openly acknowledge her. He had too much to lose. She almost certainly wouldn't see him for dust. And, despite everything, she really did believe that he loved his family in Twickenham. All of them, even his wife, Amelia.

It had felt so strange – thrilling, almost – to meet the woman who was married to his son. Jason, she knew, was the eldest. Then there were the two girls, Poppy and Jessie. Their names were all so familiar to her. There were grandchildren too. Three, as far as she knew. She didn't often ask, and he didn't often share. Actually, she had told him a while ago, when they were having one of their fights (they often argued – in fact, they had been squabbling about something or other when Jen had come along) that she didn't want to hear any more. She didn't care about Amelia, Jason, Poppy or Jessie. They were nothing to her.

She hadn't really meant it.

Still, it had given her an undeniable buzz. Meeting Jen. Shaking hands with her. Knowing she held all the cards. It had passed through her mind that with one sentence she could blow the whole thing apart. Throw their secret out into the open and watch his family implode. She could inflict unimaginable cruelty with just a few words. Thank God she hadn't done it, hadn't been overtaken by an urge to self-destruct. It was a powerful weapon to have, but one she knew she would never use. It frightened her just how tempted she had been.

It wasn't in her nature to be mean. She was a people-pleaser, she always had been. At school she had always been the one with her hand up, whether she knew the answer or not. Please, Miss! Choose me! Like me! It was pitiful, really, her need for approbation. No wonder she had never met a man who actually wanted to plump for her as his life partner. She was too needy, too clingy, too afraid of rejection. She had always pushed her suitors away eventually, driven them to the point where they would turn round and say they'd had enough, and then she'd felt overwhelmingly let down when they left. Everything was a test to her. And few people ever passed.

Her mum had always told her she should just relax, be herself, and not over-think things too much. But since when had her mum been an expert on relationships? She hardly had an exemplary track record herself.

That reminded her. She must ring her mum. She usually tried to call her every other day, but sometimes she was so busy at work she would forget. Work had a tendency to take over her life, if she let it. She tried to remember if Barbara had said she was going out. Her mum had a hectic social life that usually eclipsed her daughter's. Partly it came with her job. Barbara worked in the offices of a finance company – doing admin, nothing too glamorous – but the staff seemed to still be stuck on the eighties' maxim of 'work hard, play hard' and Barbara was always going for drinks and cocktails after work. Not that Cass could remember the eighties. She was barely even two when they ended. But she'd seen *Wall Street*.

Barbara picked up on the second ring.

'Darling, hello.'

'Hi, Mum. I've not called you in the middle of something, have I?'

'No, of course not, how are you?' Barbara always said this, whenever Cass asked, so for all Cass knew she could have been in the middle of performing heart surgery, but set it aside to chat to her daughter.

'Fine. Having a night in.'

'Me too. I'm treating myself to a glass of wine before I start cooking.'

Cass knew that cooking meant popping a ready meal for one into the microwave. Barbara used to love to cook. She would come home from work every evening and prepare elaborate meals, sipping on a big glass of wine while she threw things flamboyantly around the kitchen. Now she rarely bothered. Cass, living on her own as she did, empathized. She could never understand why anyone would buy all the separate ingredients and spend hours putting them together when you could just opt for the finished product.

'What are you having? I've got a Waitrose lasagne. It doesn't look as good as yours, though.'

Barbara laughed. 'You should come home, then. I'll make you one. If I can remember how.'

'Maybe at the weekend.'

'Really? That would be lovely.'

'I'll drive up and we can load up at M&S.'

They talked for a couple of minutes about nothing much: Barbara's frozen shoulder and the appointment she had with the doctor for a couple of days' time; a dinner party she was going to the following night; the problems Cass was having with her washing machine. Even though neither of them would have admitted it, it was hard to find new things to talk about when they spoke so often.

Afterwards, Cass decided to have a long bath and then an early night. She needed to process what had happened, go through it moment by moment and wring every last trivial detail out of the memory. She needed to get it straight in her head before she could allow herself to think what, if anything, might happen next.

13

There was, Jen thought, only one thing she could do short of hurling unproven accusations or inviting her father-in-law and Cass Richards on to *Jeremy Kyle* to explain themselves. If Charles was doing something so out of character as seeing another woman, then she was sure she would be able to read it on his face if she got him alone. He would no doubt have spent the night worrying about whether or not she'd guessed, whether he'd given himself away. She needed to see him before he had had time to compose himself.

She dialled his mobile before she could talk herself out of it.

'Morning, sweetheart.' His voice sang out to her with his customary greeting.

She had always loved how both Charles and Amelia had, over the years, started to address her in the same way they did their two daughters. He sounded so like his normal self that she wondered, for a moment, whether she had imagined the whole thing. Maybe Charles treated all his clients like that, holding their hands, massaging their fingers, squabbling with them? It was an unusual way of conducting business, but it wasn't impossible.

She had to talk over the sounds coming from the back of the hotel kitchen. The crash of plates and the inane chatter of the two teenage pot washers. Personal calls were strictly forbidden on reception and so the staff usually chose to hover in the blind alley behind the ground floor, jostling for position with the air-con units and the bins.

'Hi. I was just wondering if you were in town today. I was going to lure you out with the promise of a coffee and a bit of carrot cake.'

'Lovely. As it happens, I am. What time's your break?'

She tried not to think too hard about why he would be in the area for a second day in a row. Perhaps it was a prestigious new property. He still liked to swoop in and pick off the best ones for himself, when he could. It was the sport of it that he enjoyed. Much more so than the money it brought in.

'I'm on an early, so lunch is eleven till twelve. Any good?'

'Perfect,' he said. 'Valentino's?'

It must be a good sign that he's so willing to meet up, Jen thought as she ended the call. Surely if he was feeling guilty, rattled by yesterday's near miss, he would have made an excuse. Claimed a prior engagement, or pretended that he was at home in Twickenham with a good book. She allowed herself to relax just a little. Told herself everything was going to be fine. Wished she found herself more believable.

Charles was already sitting in their favourite corner when she arrived. Coffee pot and two cups in front of him. Tan gleaming. Whitened teeth sparkling. He stood up when he saw her, as he always did. She had always found his old-fashioned manners charming. The last of the real gentlemen. Even Jason, who had largely modelled himself on his father, had given up on that one years ago. Probably because Jen had laughed at him whenever he did it.

'We're not in the Deep South now,' she had said the first time. 'It's not 1860.'

Charles smiled a wide, confident smile. Jen mirrored it. He looked, she noticed, like he didn't have a care in the world, like the last time he had seen her he'd been handing paper money to a beggar, rather than holding hands with a woman who wasn't his wife.

She scanned his face for hidden meanings. Obviously, he wasn't about to say, 'So you know that woman you saw me with . . .' but Jen had thought there would be something there. A nervousness, a warning, an apology. In fact, he just looked the same.

They leaned into a hug. Charles pulled out a chair for Jen to sit. So far, so routine.

'Coffee?' he asked rhetorically, the jug already hovering.

'Lovely.'

He looked exactly the same as he always did. She didn't know what she had been expecting. A black cape and a moustache to twirl, maybe?

Charles was peering into her cup. 'Dirty,' he said, picking it up and rubbing at a minuscule spot of something or other.

'It's fine –'

'No, it's the principle.' He waved his arm to attract a waiter. 'My beautiful companion's cup is a little dirty . . .' he said.

'I'm his daughter-in-law,' Jen interrupted, she didn't

know why, it just came out. She realized that she didn't want the waiter to think she was anything other than a member of Charles's family. Not his latest conquest, she thought, and felt immediately queasy.

The waiter hurried off apologetically, probably to spit on to the stain and return the same cup back to her.

Jen briefly tried to imagine how she would feel, a woman of forty-three, if this seventy-three-year-old man was her lover. It was impossible to see him as anything other than a father figure. What was this Cass Richards thinking? Maybe she had a thing for the marriage of fake tan, tooth whitener and white hair. Or maybe, more likely, she had a thing for wealthy men who had enough of a modicum of fame that they could get a table at the top restaurants at short notice.

'Sorry again, Mr Masterson,' the waiter said as he placed a fresh cup in front of Jen. She noticed that he didn't even acknowledge her. She was used to it. Once someone had remembered where they recognized Charles from, they often found it impossible to focus on anyone other than him. It didn't matter that their treatment of whoever he was with became borderline rude – they couldn't seem to help themselves. It was incredible the effect a famous face – however far down the alphabetical list (and Charles was probably a D at best) – could have. Jen couldn't imagine what this Marco (as his name badge proclaimed) would have done if someone from *TOWIE* had walked in. Imploded, probably. Literally died of excitement.

'Not your fault at all,' Charles said, doing a fine impression of a priest granting absolution. Probably imagining to himself how the waiter would go home and tell his girlfriend that Charles Masterson was absolutely charming in real life, just like you'd imagine he would be.

Stop it, Jen told herself. She never criticized Charles, even to herself in the privacy of her own head. She mustn't allow her possibly unfounded assumptions to make her start now. Not until she knew what was going on.

'So,' she said, once the waiter had left, now practically bowing and scraping, 'how's your week been so far?' It was an anodyne enough question. There was no hint of an accusation in it.

'Exhausting,' he said with a big smile on his face. 'I can't remember how long it's been since I did two days' work in the same week.'

Jen laughed, as she knew she was supposed to. 'What, is there a rush on high-end property at the moment or something?'

'Couple of prime places I want to handle myself. You know I love the big ones. We've got this one house in Mayfair. Used to be an embassy. Hasn't been on the market for fifty-odd years, but they've just got permission to turn it back into a home. It'll go for thirty-five million easily. More, probably, if we market it in China and Russia . . .'

Charles had a habit of raising his voice whenever they were out in public. He became more animated, punctuating whatever he was saying with big hand gestures and laughing a little too loudly and too long. Particularly at something he had said himself. Jen had noticed it many times, had always told herself she was imagining it, that he probably found it harder to hear in crowded places and so overcompensated or something. But he was doing it now. There was no doubt he was playing to the audience of the other customers. Hoping they would turn round and notice him. Anticipating the little frisson of excitement when someone realized whose presence they were in.

She adjusted her own voice down a notch in the hope that he would follow. She wasn't in the mood to indulge his little ego trip.

'The world's gone mad.' She had always been fascinated by the people who bought the properties Charles dealt in. It was like a parallel universe. One in which someone's family home could cost several hundred times more than Jen could ever hope to earn in her lifetime.

'It'll probably end up being a second home that they'll use twice a year,' Charles guffawed.

Jen swallowed, now was her chance.

'So . . . that woman you were talking to yesterday. What was her name? Cath?'

Did she imagine it? Did Charles's mask slip just a tiny bit?

'Oh, her. Cass, I think her name is. What about her?'

Cass Richards, Jen thought. You know her name as well as I do. A knot started to form in her stomach. She couldn't imagine Charles forgetting the name of a potential buyer who had come to him with millions of pounds she wanted to spend on a flat.

'She's not in line for the thirty-five-million-pound house?'

Charles raised his eyes wide. 'What? Goodness, no. She's just looking for an apartment. Much more modest.'

'Well, you say that, but I imagine Masterson Property doesn't really do modest. Not in the real sense.'

'No . . . true.' He stirred his spoon round in his coffee, even though he was way too conscious of his calorie intake to ever add sugar. Charles still went to the gym regularly. Something that Jen had always admired, grateful that he was so mindful of his health. More likely his concern was how he looked in his boxers, it occurred to her now.

'What does she do for a living?'

'Who . . . Cass Whatever-Her-Name-Is? I have no idea.'

'Don't you have to check out potential buyers, make sure they're not time-wasters, that they can really afford the asking price?'

Jen knew this was the case. Charles had explained to her before that Masterson Property prided itself on only presenting credible buyers to sellers.

'Of course. But yesterday was the first time she came in. She will have filled out all the credit-check forms, and someone will be processing them as we speak.'

'Maybe she has a rich husband.' Jen hated herself for sounding as if she assumed a woman would need to have attached herself to a wealthy man in order to afford a high-end property. But she couldn't worry about her feminist credentials now. She just wanted to press Charles's buttons and see how he reacted.

He seemed to have completely regained his composure. 'Probably. I have no idea. I leave all that side of things to someone else, these days.'

She knew she couldn't push it any more. It wasn't as if

he was suddenly going to confess whatever it was he was up to. There was no doubt in her mind that his pretence of ignorance when she had mentioned Cass had not been genuine. He had recovered quickly, though. Covered up the traces.

She had just one more reaction she wanted to gauge. 'Anyway, enough about work. How's Amelia?' She looked him directly in the eye as she said it, challenged him to look away.

'Making the Christmas pudding,' he said, chuckling indulgently. His smile seemed to reach his eyes. It still made him happy to think about his wife. That, or he could add Oscar-worthy actor to his CV. Now she was seriously confused. 'I swear she starts earlier every year.'

'No,' Jen said fondly, 'pudding in the second week of October, cake the third. It's always the same.'

'Well, she seemed to be enjoying herself, anyway.'

There was only one explanation she could think of. Charles was a practised liar. This wasn't a new skill he'd had to learn over the past few weeks, or months – this was a way of life.

He looked at his nails nonchalantly. All fine here. Nothing suspicious.

What kind of a seventy-three-year-old man had his nails manicured regularly? Jen thought, noticing how perfect they were – how perfect they always were – buffed and shiny, all the same length. A ridiculous one, that was who. One who cared way too much about the way he looked.

She kept the conversation on neutral ground for the rest of her break, fabricated a need to go to the chemist so she could leave ten minutes early, and tried not to recoil when he moved to hug her goodbye.

'Feeling better?'

Jen struggled to think what Sean was referring to, remembered her fake migraine just in time.

'Much. Thanks,' she said, way too brightly.

'Really? Because you look like you're ready to deck someone.'

'Are you checking out?' She couldn't be bothered to engage in their usual banter. Everything felt trivial and pointless compared with what had happened.

Sean looked a little shocked at her tone. He handed over his Visa debit card. 'Yes. Please.'

Jen knew she was being curt, didn't want to take it out on the guests. 'Sorry ... I'm just ... something's happened, that's all.'

'Oh ... OK ... Are you all right? I mean ... is it serious?'

Jen felt bad that he looked concerned for her. A worried friend, rather than a polite acquaintance. She thought for a moment. She was alone on reception until Judy came back from her break. Sean was one of the only people she knew who had no idea who her father-in-law was. She looked around, to check Graham the doorman wasn't within earshot. Why not? Say it out loud, and see what happened.

'Well, since you ask, I think I've just found out that my father-in-law is having an affair. With a woman less than half his age, not that that makes any difference. The point is that he's cheating on my mother-in-law, and it'll break her heart. Not to mention what it'll do to their children – my husband and his sisters, that is. And he's the least likely man you'd ever think . . . I just can't believe it, that's all.' She looked at him, waited for a reaction.

'God, I'm so sorry. That must be rough.'

'I'm trying to decide what to do.'

Sean looked confused. 'Do?'

'I can't just let it happen.'

Sean held up his hand. 'Oh no, no, no, no, no.'

Jen couldn't help it, she smiled. 'If you don't think I should do anything, just say so, really –'

'Rule number one, don't put yourself in the middle of other people's relationships.'

'Rule number one of what exactly?'

'No idea. But it makes sense.'

'You think I should just stand back and let it happen?'

Sean shrugged. 'I honestly don't know, but do you want to risk it all coming out into the open? Have your mother-in-law find out?'

'No. God . . .'

'Maybe he's having a midlife crisis –'

Jen interrupted. 'He's seventy-three.'

'OK, well, an old-life crisis, then. What I mean is, awful as it must be, perhaps it'll burn itself out, he'll realize he's made a big mistake.'

'It just doesn't seem right, that's all.'

Out of the corner of her eye she could see Judy on her way back from lunch. Heels click-clicking on the shabby-chic wooden floor.

'Anyway, never mind. Forget I said anything.'

She was grateful that Sean noticed Judy, took the hint.

She busied herself with the computer, printing off his receipt.

'Leaving us already?' Judy said as she got to the desk, her coat half off.

'Too much of a good thing,' Sean said.

Jen swiped his card. She didn't know what she had been thinking about, really, confiding in a near stranger.

14

Sunday lunchtime came round again all too quickly. This was always the case, obviously, but this particular weekend Jen barely even noticed Saturday whizz by, so preoccupied was she with hoping the next day would never arrive.

They were heading over to Twickenham. Only this time she wasn't looking forward to a cosy family lunch; she was dreading seeing her in-laws. It felt as if there would be a whole subtext present that hadn't been there before. She couldn't deny that she was curious to know if Charles was acting any differently around Amelia – furtively, like a man with a secret – but, at the same time, she didn't think she could bear to see it, if he was.

There had been Christmas shopping, she could remember that much. Stupidly they'd gone to Westfield – thinking it would still be reasonably quiet, as it wasn't yet November. Of course it had been packed with shoppers, the lights and tree already in situ, a red-suited Father Christmas ringing a bell and ho, ho, hoing all over the place.

They had braved M&S and bought a cashmere-mix sweater for Amelia, and a similar one for Elaine. The rest of the afternoon was spent trailing around, deciding not to go into various shops because they looked too crowded, and – for Jen, anyway – slowly losing the will to live.

'How about a pashmina?' Jason would offer up a random suggestion every now and then.

'For who?'

'For *whom*?' he'd said with a smirk, because he knew it would wind her up.

She hadn't felt like playing. 'Who for?'

'I don't know. Any of them.'

Jen had a list in her pocket with the names of all Jason's uncles, aunts and cousins they had to find something for, as well as the rest of the family. 'None of them want a pashmina/a foot spa/a bathrobe,' she would say huffily in response to whatever generic item he had suggested. Jason had never been a great present buyer in Jen's eyes. Not for want of enthusiasm. 'We need to find something more personal.'

'For all twenty-two of them?' Jason had said, dragging his feet like a sulky toddler.

Jen loved Christmas – she always had. Every year she spent December in an excited state of anticipation, planning and scheming, hiding presents at the back of cupboards, stockpiling treats. What she couldn't bear, though, was Christmas in October – even Christmas in September, in some stores. In fact, hadn't Harrods opened its festive department at the end of August last year? She was sure she could remember seeing Santa sweating in a surprise late-summer heatwave. Red-faced and angry, necking back cans of Diet Coke.

There had been no joy in wrestling through the sweaty, frantic throng. There hadn't even been a restaurant or cafe they could retreat to that didn't have queues halfway out of the door, apart from the champagne bar – and that was out of the question, obviously, although tempting. Afternoon glasses of champagne didn't fit into their tight Christmas budget. Plus, to Jen, it had felt flat without the girls. They had both tried to get excited, but it was all show and she had realized pretty swiftly that they were only doing so in an effort to make the other one happy. She'd wondered, briefly, if this was how it was going to be from now on. The two of them tiptoeing around, trying to pretend that everything was the same as it had always been. A lifelong game of make-believe. It was too depressing to contemplate.

Eventually, they'd decided to cut their losses and give up early. Jen had ended up spending the evening shopping on the internet, even though that really had no fun attached to it at all. Ordering a beautiful gift felt no different from ordering groceries.

She woke up on Sunday morning with a sinking feeling. She pulled the covers over her head and tried to go back to sleep, but it was hopeless. As soon as her mind was distracted by something, she knew she might as well get up, because no amount of lying there would make her drift off again. She looked at the clock on the bedside table. Seven fifteen. Great. So much for a lovely lazy weekend lie-in. She knew that Jason wouldn't thank her for being disturbed this early, even if she brought him a cup of tea. She crept out of bed and across the bedroom, feeling for the door handle in the dark.

She sat at the kitchen table, nursing a mug, willing the day to be over. She couldn't even think about lunchtime. Couldn't imagine sitting through the meal watching Charles acting as though this was any normal day. Although she supposed it was, for him.

'Did I tell you Dad asked us to pick up a bottle of wine on our way?'

She jumped as she realized Jason was standing right there behind her. She hadn't heard him get up, had no idea how long she had been sitting there staring off into space. She felt momentarily panicked. She hadn't told Jason she had met up with Charles earlier in the week. She hadn't felt she could mention it without giving away the fact that everything wasn't quite as it should be. Without blushing, or tripping over her words, or – God forbid – spilling out her suspicions and shattering his world. She hated secrets, and this was why. What if Charles had said something? Would Jason think it was odd that it had apparently slipped her mind? Be non-committal, she thought. Don't give yourself away.

She looked across at him. 'When did you speak to your dad?' she asked, trying not to sound too interested.

'Yesterday. He just called to check we were still coming.'

'Oh,' she said. 'Right.'

'Are you OK? You look a bit . . .'

She seized on that thought like a heroin addict finding contraband in a methadone clinic. 'Actually, I feel awful. Migraine. I've been sick a couple of times.'

Jason was all concern. 'That's what you get for feigning an illness to skive off work,' he said, putting a cool hand on her forehead. 'It's payback.'

Jen nodded in what she hoped was a pitiful way. 'I think maybe I should go back to bed for a bit.'

'I'll call Dad and tell him we can't come.'

'No, you go.' Jen already knew that neither Poppy nor Jessie could make it to Twickenham that weekend. She hated to think of Amelia up to her ears in roast beef and gravy, with only her faithless husband for company. 'They're expecting us, it's not fair to let them down.'

'If you're sure you'll be OK. I'll make it a quick one.'

She was relieved. She didn't think she could keep up the pretence for the next few hours with Jason worriedly watching over her. By the time he got back, she could claim to be on the mend. It could be the fastest migraine in history.

15

'What do you think Cass is short for?' Jen said casually to Neil, at work the next day. She was foolishly hoping he wouldn't quiz her on why she was asking. Just shootin' the breeze, wondering idly about the derivation of certain names, no reason.

'Cassie? Or Cassandra, probably. Or Casper, if it's a bloke.'

'Cassandra. That would be good. It's unusual.'

'Who are we talking about?'

'No one.'

'Oh, right. How about Cassiopeia? Cassidy?'

'Mmm, maybe.'

'Cassius? Caspian?'

'It doesn't matter, really.'

It was strange with Neil, he could sit there in silence all day but, once you gave him a topic, set him off on a path, it was sometimes hard to get him to stop. She couldn't really tell him it was only the girls' names she was interested in, because then he would ask her why. She would have to suffer him burbling on for a while. Now he seemed to be googling the answer. She inhaled deeply.

'Cascada? Cascata? Cassia? Cassta? God, there's all sorts on here.'

Jen couldn't think how to get him on to another track.

'What's your wife's name, Neil?' she said, in a fit of

inspiration. 'In all these years, I don't think you've ever told me.'

'I must have.'

'No. Pretty sure you haven't.'

'Well, that's –' he said, and then mercifully the phone rang. Neil sprang into professional mode. 'Hello. Reception. How can I help you, Mrs Richardson?'

Jen busied herself double-checking that the rooms that had been vacated that morning were clean and ready for reoccupation. She was desperate to be alone to think.

'I've agreed a late checkout for Mrs Richardson tomorrow. One o'clock,' Neil said, when he eventually got off the phone.

This was another habit of Neil's. He would invariably spell out all the details of any interaction he had with the guests – regardless of whether you were standing right there, listening to every word of his conversation, or not. For him this passed as repartee. Jen had clearly heard him say, 'So, just to confirm, you're fine to stay in the room till one tomorrow, Mrs Richardson,' about ten seconds before.

'Fine.'

'Because we have a couple checking into a standard double who aren't going to get here till the evening. I double-checked.'

Jen knew this too. She had heard him tell Mrs Richardson the exact same thing, after he had gone through the future bookings on the computer.

'Right,' she said, and tried to look as if she was absorbed in what she was doing.

It was either famine or feast with Neil.

'What were we talking about?' he asked.

Jen acted like she didn't remember. 'Oh, I don't know. Nothing important. I'm just going over the housekeeping report, actually.'

She tried googling both Cass and Cassandra – the most likely of all the names Neil had offered up in her opinion – Richards while she was at work, when Neil was on his break, but people kept coming over and it was a strict rule at the hotel that no personal business be conducted on the computers at reception. When one of the new junior staff she was meant to be training looked over her shoulder and asked her what she was doing, she knew she had to give it up.

'I'm just checking no one's been using the computer for anything other than hotel business,' she said, somewhat unconvincingly, exiting the page as quickly as she could. 'I like to go through the history every once in a while, just to be sure.'

The junior looked taken aback. 'That sounds a bit draconian.'

'Hotel policy. I don't make the rules.'

Truthfully, Jen had no idea what she was intending to do once – if – she tracked Cass Richards down. She just wanted to do something, anything, because she felt so powerless. It was out of the question that she was going to ignore what she had seen and let Charles destroy the family – she knew that much. She thought, maybe, if she could find out a bit about Cass, then that might help her decide on her next move. Maybe she could get in touch with her, and tell her Charles had a loving wife and adoring family that he was risking by being with her. Maybe, even though she was having an affair with a married man, she would have some sense of decency under there somewhere and do the right thing. She knew that wouldn't solve the bigger problem of Charles, of whether this was who he really was – a man who cheated on his oblivious loved ones – but it would at least remove the immediate threat. That was what Jen was telling herself, anyway.

There was no harm in finding out who Cass was. It would satisfy her curiosity to a certain extent. And then she could decide what to do with that information, if anything, later on.

She didn't want to use the computer at home, because it felt both wrong and foolish to leave something on the history that her unsuspecting husband might stumble across one day – like those people who secretly get off on eating a whole packet of Jaffa Cakes in one sitting, but then hate themselves for it, so they leave the wrapping right there on top of all the rubbish in the bin, subconsciously hoping their partner will find it. So, at lunchtime, she took herself off to an internet cafe on Charing Cross Road, bought a coffee and a sandwich, paid for forty-five minutes' access, and settled down.

The cafe had the air of a sixth form common room. Handwritten notices adorned every spare inch of the walls, advertising rooms to let or help with computer skills. There was a distinct aroma of unwashed clothes in the place. The funk of forty thousand rucksacks. Her coffee tasted of dishwasher soap.

There were various people called Cass or Cassandra

Richards on Facebook and Twitter but they were too old, too young or on the wrong side of the world. There were several who had no details, not even a photograph on show. There were a couple of others whose pictures may have been Cass when she was younger, but it was almost impossible to tell. Jen kept going. There were Cassandra Richardses working in Woking and Hull, but one gave horse-riding lessons and the other worked in the refuse department of the local council, and neither of those seemed right. Although what she had to base that feeling on, she didn't know. There was one who lived in Coventry. Jen racked her brain. Had there been any clues when they'd met?

She couldn't remember Cass having had a Midlands accent, but she had barely said a whole sentence and, even if she didn't, that didn't mean anything. You could be brought up in London and then move to Coventry. You could go off and become an officer in the refuse department at Hull City Council, for that matter.

She had already used up twenty-eight of her forty-five minutes. She needed a strategy. Concentric circles, she decided. She would start by checking out all the Cassandra Richardses in London and then, if none of them came through, widen out the search from there. One-sixth of the country's population lived in the capital. Good odds.

She rushed through the list, discarding as many as she could on the grounds of age, nationality, anything. She was left with three that seemed to merit further investigation. She pored over any details she could find about the first – listed as a systems analyst in Barking. She wrote down the number of her office. She would decide what to do with it later. The second had a Facebook page that Jen was denied access to. She was a member of a sailing club in Westminster, and had taken part in their annual race. On their website there was a picture of her with a trophy. A smiling, pretty, athletic-looking black woman who had come in second place. Jen scored her name off the list.

The third seemed to be very gregarious. She had a Facebook page, a Twitter account (Jen scrolled back – no mention of meeting up with her lover at his office recently – in fact, most of her tweets were pictures of her two dogs) and a blog where she wrote about baking. On the blog she mentioned her husband and three children. Jen didn't even want to think about what Cass might be doing to her own family, as well as the Mastersons. She also talked about her weight and her futile attempts to exercise and resist the call of home-made scones. 'Scales still hitting sixteen stone four!' Jen read on one recent entry.

Next.

So, after all that, she was left with the systems analyst in Barking and a phone number. It could be her, it was possible. It just hardly felt inspiring, that was all. There were probably countless more Cassandra Richardses she had missed. Or she may have disregarded the right one for the wrong reason. Or Cass might live in Wales or Cornwall. Or she might be called Cassiopeia. Or she might have absolutely no presence on the internet, although Jen wasn't sure that was possible these days. She started to pack up her things. She would call the Barking number and see what she could find out. After that, who knew? Maybe this was someone's way of trying to tell her she should leave well alone. Not that Jen believed in that stuff – fate and karma and spirit guides – that was much more Jessie's arena. At this point, though, she was prepared to accept anything.

There were a couple of minutes left on the clock, but she didn't have the heart to start a whole new search. She was about to close down the screen when she thought maybe she should hit 'images' for the hell of it. She clicked on it and, just like that, there she was. 'Cassandra Richards' brought up a picture – several times, actually – dotted among various other Cassandra Richardses, some of whom Jen recognized already from her trawl.

It was her, there was no doubt about it.

Jen clicked on one of the pictures and then gasped as she saw the text beneath it. It was a spread from a regional magazine. One of those pages of photographs from some kind of social gathering, a charity event or the opening of a new bar. Jen had never understood them. Who was looking at them? How crucial was it to anyone to see what the people from their local car dealership wore to a party? Cassandra stood next to a man, both smiling at the camera, glasses of champagne in their hands. 'Cassandra Richards, Senior Property Agent at Masterson Property in Brighton, and Andrew Burford from the London Head Office' the caption declared.

The girl who was working behind the counter came over to tell Jen that her time was up.

'Two more minutes,' she said, waving the girl away. 'I'll pay.'

She tried to take it in. Cass was a senior member of staff at Masterson Property. Charles's company. Of course, that made sense, in a way. He had to have met her somewhere. But it also made it far more complicated. Even if they ended their relationship, they were still going to see each other. There were no guarantees.

Jen scanned the page again, looking for a date. It was right there in the top left-hand corner: 9 May 2011. More than two years ago. Cass was already working for Charles two years ago.

She was going to be late back to work. She printed off the page, paid for her extra time, and left.

Jen raged the whole afternoon, swinging between anger and confusion about what it all might mean. Had Charles been seeing Cass all that time? Did that mean it was serious? More than just – she used 'just' in the loosest possible sense, meaning it only comparatively – a fling. Of course, they might have worked together for years and their relationship had only turned into something else more recently. She hated not knowing.

A wolf in sheep's clothing, that's what Charles had turned out to be. A snake in the grass. She often found herself thinking in idioms when she was stressed. Better late than never. He who laughs last laughs longest. It takes two to tango. Her mind would throw one out for every occasion. She usually had the sense to keep them there, to not let them out of her mouth.

She was crashing pots and pans around the kitchen, trying to take her frustration out on the dishwasher, when Jason appeared and unravelled himself from his scarf and jacket. He always arrived home from work a mess after his bike ride, but today, because it was raining, he looked like a rather mangy otter, freshly dragged from the river. Jen tried to ignore the lake that was forming around his feet.

'What's up with you?'

She gave him a hug to hopefully demonstrate to him that he wasn't the cause of her mood, and to give herself a moment to think. Now they were both dripping. She could have gone straight from her kitchen and won a wet T-shirt competition. If what they were judging you on was how wet you could get your T-shirt, and nothing else, that was.

'David. He's trying to change all the rotas. He thinks it's not fair that some of us always get to do the most popular shifts.'

In reality, it was Jen who had the final say on the shifts each receptionist worked. David had never been anything other than sympathetic about the fact that Jen wanted her hours to fit around her family. Even now she had no children at home, he was still happy to let her cherry-pick. She made a mental note to be extra nice to him, to make up for her slander.

'He'll never do it. He won't have the guts.'

'Well, he'd better not,' Jen said, getting into her role.

It was frightening how easy she was finding it to lie to Jason. Alarming how readily she could justify to herself that she was doing it for the right reasons. Jason would be devastated if he learned the truth about his father. He idolized him. As did the rest of the family, for that matter. If she had to tell a few white lies to protect them, was that so bad? At least until she found out for certain exactly what it was Charles was guilty of. A petty, impulsive crime of passion or a premeditated, cold-hearted, calculated felony.

'I'd resign, if he did.'

Jason laughed. 'Yeah, right.'

Even though Jen was making up her dilemma, she was a little offended at Jason's response. Implicit in it was the fact that she had settled years ago, that she had no ambition. He was right, of course, but that wasn't the point. At least, she *had* always had an ambition, and that had been to create a family. She had always told herself that once Simone and Emily had both left home, she would have time to pursue her passion. If only she had a passion to pursue.

'I might surprise you one day.'

'Oh, Dad's on *The One Show* tonight, by the way. Feature about national service.'

'Oh, right,' Jen said, unsure what else to say.

'I've set it to record, in case we forget.'

'Great.'

At eight minutes past seven, they were in front of the TV, inevitably. Plates on their laps, glasses of wine on the coffee table in front of them. Jen's father-in-law ambled through a pre-recorded feature on post-war compulsory military service. Some kind of significant anniversary had apparently occurred earlier in the year – fifty years since it had ended, something like that – and Charles had tracked down (that is to say, the show's researchers had tracked down) a few old boys who had done their stint in the 1950s.

Short film over and back to the studio where the two presenters tried to feign interest. Charles was sitting on the sofa opposite them. He looked just as he always looked: thick shock of near-white hair combed just so, his slightly too orange tan and his jaunty, brightly coloured shirt that contrasted oh so beautifully with his dark grey suit. The idea of a woman so much younger than him – so much younger than her, in fact – looking at him and thinking 'phwoar' was incomprehensible, Jen thought, as she watched. Flattering him by hanging on to his every word and telling him his liver spots made him distinguished and therefore sexy. It didn't bear thinking about. She shuddered.

'So,' the male half of the duo said, 'what's your feeling, Charles? Should we bring it back?'

Charles smiled his 'I'm on TV' smile. 'Well, it certainly didn't do me any harm.'

'Do you think it made a real difference to society, though?' the female presenter asked in a bored voice. The regular hosts were both on holiday, and the two stand-ins were struggling to act as though they cared about anything except the fact they were getting prime-time exposure.

'Oh, definitely. I think we were taught to have proper values. Young lads nowadays have no idea how to hold down a job or keep a family together, because they've never experienced real discipline.'

'He's a natural, isn't he?' Jason said proudly.

'He certainly is,' Jen said. 'You really feel like he means it.'

'You do.'

Jason thought she was paying his father a compliment. She wasn't.

They watched the rest of the show in silence. Jen wanted to fill it, but she suddenly didn't know how. It struck her that their default topic of conversation may have left home with their daughters. She had never realized before how much of their common ground revolved around the girls' movements. And whatever gossip there was from the rest of the family, of course, but that now felt like a topic she wanted to avoid. Surely they had had more in common than that? Years of a shared – and she had thought happy – life. She felt suddenly light-headed, as if she was standing on the ledge of a tall building. She closed her eyes, breathed in slowly.

She tried to think if anything funny had happened at work, but the only thing that kept coming into her head was an image of Charles and Cass Richards. It clogged up her brain like duckweed, refusing to budge, blocking out all other thoughts. So she stayed silent. She was scared of what might come out if she opened her mouth.

16

Every year, the whole Masterson family got together to celebrate Jessie's birthday at the end of October. Not that her birthday was actually *at* the end of October. Nothing with Jessie could be that straightforward. It had begun when she was nine and, incensed that she had been born on Boxing Day and so, however hard her parents had tried, the two celebrations tended to merge into one, she had announced that from now on she was going to have an official birthday two months earlier, on the twenty-sixth of October.

To all intents and purposes the rest of the family had forgotten when her actual special day had been. Except for Amelia, that was, who still liked to regale them all with the story of the time she went into labour while she was cooking Christmas lunch. Usually when she was in the middle of preparing some other family feast, leaving them all to try to block out the image of her waters breaking all over the lovely terracotta tiled floor.

Ever since she had been old enough to demand it, Jessie had had a family party on the nearest Saturday, and everyone was expected not only to be there but to stay over too. No excuses. None of them even bothered to check it was still happening, they just kept that weekend clear in their diaries. It was a fact of life.

Not that Jessie was a natural host. Far from it. She left all the planning for the celebration to her husband, Martin, and everything else – meals, washing up, bed-making – to the rest of the family.

'It's my birthday,' she would say, with all the maturity of someone who was turning eight, rather than thirty-eight, if anyone suggested she so much as switch the kettle on. For some reason, they all allowed her to get away with it. Almost certainly because they couldn't face the tears and sulks if they didn't. This year, because her first baby was due in a couple of weeks' time, she would undoubtedly be even more demanding and they would all respond in kind, by being increasingly indulgent.

Jen's birthdays, growing up, had always been quite quiet affairs. At least, after Rory had left. There had once been a party with a couple of her school friends. Well, Elaine had called it a party – it had really been a slightly more elaborate tea than usual (chicken and egg sandwiches, and on a Tuesday, positively daring). But Jen had found her mother fussing around them too humiliating, her anxiety that they all have a good time palpable. She had never wanted to repeat the experience.

Elaine would usually appear at the foot of her bed, early in the morning, wrapped gift in hand.

'Morning, birthday girl.'

Jen, sleepy-eyed and only half awake, would open her present, which was always something she wanted, something sensible and practical. She had invariably guessed exactly what it was likely to be in the weeks before.

'Thanks, Mum.' She would accept her mum's offer of a hug, and that would be it. Celebration over.

Then she would go to school, or out on her bike, and Elaine would go to work or to do the weekly shop. The first thing Jen would do when she got home would be to check if anything had arrived for her in the second post.

It never had.

She had always felt resentful that her big day would, by and large, pass without a fuss.

She felt bad whenever she remembered that now. She'd been too young to understand that her dad upping and going was just as – or maybe even more – devastating for her mother as for her. Another thing for her to feel guilty about. Add it to the list.

Jen and Jason usually drove down to Jessie and Martin's in Petworth on the Saturday morning – more room this year now neither Simone nor Emily would be with them, although she didn't want to dwell on that one too much – hopefully in time to spend a couple of hours in the pretty little town centre before the party, and then travelled back on the Sunday, after lunch, talked out and exhausted. It had always been one of Jen's favourite weekends of the year.

Until now, that is, of course. Now she would have volunteered for a stint in Afghanistan to get out of it.

'I hate the way she just assumes everyone else has as much time as she does,' she heard herself moan as they set off, fraught and in bad spirits. 'I mean, it would never occur to Jessie that, for some of us, the weekends are precious.'

'I thought you loved it,' Jason said.

And Jen had to say, 'Yes, I do, I'm just knackered.'

'It's a family tradition. What are you going to do?' He shrugged.

Jen's family didn't really go in for traditions – unless you counted the days-of-the-week meals, or the regularity with which Elaine told Jen they were much better off without her dad. Usually crying as she said it, which didn't really give the point the reinforcement it needed. Jason's, on the other hand, was dripping with them.

'That might be true, but it's a family tradition that she invented when she was little so that she would get more presents. It hardly counts.'

'What's up with you?'

'Nothing. Why does something have to be up?' She snapped at him, knew she was sounding petulant, but she couldn't seem to help herself.

'It'll be fun,' he said, as if that was that. There was no point Jen pursuing it – it wasn't as if Jason was about to say, 'Well, let's not go, then, if you're tired. We'll shoot off to Paris on the Eurostar instead.'

This had always been Jason's way of dealing with things. He refused to be drawn into an argument. Couldn't see the point. They had had fights occasionally – of course, they had – just not very often, and never very serious. She could have counted on one hand the times they had raised their voices at one another. Jason was reasonable and reasoned, level-tempered and level-headed. And Jen had always loved that about him, had worked hard to be the same. She had always counted it as one of her successes, the fact that they rarely fought.

She had no idea why she was suddenly sniping at him now, of all times.

'I know it will,' she said, reaching over and squeezing his knee. 'I'm just letting off steam.'

Safety in numbers, that was her plan. Don't be alone with anyone, and don't even think about the rot at the centre of her in-laws' marriage. She just had to get through this weekend first. This weekend was about Jessie's birthday, about the family enjoying celebrating with her, about Amelia loving having them all under one roof. Jen was going to have to stick her head firmly down into the sand, and keep it there, until it was over.

The truth was, she was dreading it. Dreading seeing Charles, knowing what she knew. Dreading seeing Amelia, knowing how big an unexploded bomb was buried under her life, ticking away, waiting to go off. Dreading giving herself away.

For the next forty minutes they drove in the strange new silence that seemed to have entered their relationship. Eventually, Jen decided to call both Simone and then Emily on the hands-free phone, on the pretext of trying to pin them down about what they might want for Christmas. Simone, as always, had no idea.

'Just give me the money,' she said, as she did every year.

'No. You know that's not allowed.'

'I can pay off my overdraft –'

'If you can't think of anything, we'll just choose something ourselves,' Jason piped up.

Jen felt the tension ease.

'You like Justin Bieber, don't you?'

'*Da-a-ad* . . .' Simone said, elongating the word so that it sounded like it had three distinct syllables.

Jen laughed. Simone was so easy to tease.

Emily had very definite ideas about what she would like, as Jen had known she would.

'I need a Kindle. Everyone else has one. I'm the only saddo still lugging real books around.'

'Wow, that must be really awful,' Jen said, and she was gratified to see that Jason smirked.

'I mean, I have to carry this great big bag. It's tragic.'

'Gosh, yes,' Jen continued. 'God forbid you should be expected to lift some textbooks. It's practically slave labour. I'd sue.'

'Ha, ha,' Emily said. 'You're so funny, Mum.'

'I know, it's a gift.'

'I wish I could be at Auntie Jessie's party,' Emily said.

Jen felt the hollow at the pit of her stomach contract. This would be the first year neither of her daughters would be there.

'Me too,' she said. 'Do you think you might be able to get home for a weekend any time soon?' She tried to keep the desperation out of her voice, could almost hear herself channelling Elaine, hated herself for it.

'I'll try. I don't know, there's so much going on . . . Christmas, though. Oh, and Granny and Grandpa's anniversary party, I should be OK for that.'

Oh God, the anniversary party.

'OK, sweetie. Love you.'

'You too,' Emily sang back.

Jason chimed in cheerfully, 'Me three.'

Emily laughed. 'You sound like Grandpa.'

Jen didn't even want to think about that one.

'It's good that she's having such a great time,' Jason said, when she had hung up.

'I know. It is.'

'And the party is only a few weeks away.'

'Five weeks.'

'It'll go by in no time. And remember, we've got Oxford before that.'

Oh God. Oxford.

Amelia was waiting at the front door when they arrived (having called when they were five minutes away, as they always did). Soft, sweet, warm and apparently secure in the unconditional love of her family. Seeing her standing in the doorway of Jessie and Martin's cottage brought a lump to Jen's throat. A cottage was how Jessie always referred to it, by the way. It had a thatched roof. That, in Jessie's eyes, gave it cottage status. To the rest of the family it was a palace. A rambling, rather ramshackle palace, but one which could accommodate both Jen's terrace and Poppy's flat and still have room to spare.

'You made good time,' Amelia said, beaming.

'M25 was deserted,' Jason said, sweeping her up in a big embrace so that her feet almost left the floor. Jen tried to imagine picking her own mum up and twirling her round. She'd probably snap in half. She'd certainly think her daughter had lost her mind. They had never been demonstrative.

Amelia laughed and pushed him away, hugging Jen

into her in one smooth movement. As ever, she smelled of something clean and citrusy. Jen squeezed her tightly.

'You look lovely, dear.'

'You too,' Jen said, because Amelia did.

Amelia always looked lovely. Not always groomed – sometimes with a bit of stray tomato puree in her hair – but lovely, nevertheless. Just a bit tired around the edges. She cared more about making her family a nice cake than having her nails done. Which, to Jen, had always seemed like a good thing. Maybe she'd been wrong.

She leaned down and buried her face in her mother-in-law's hair. Her smooth blonde-white bob smelled of lemons. Fresh, wholesome. Jen squeezed the familiar soft curves. She didn't think she had ever known Amelia do any exercise beyond the long walks the whole family used to take at the weekends, along the river or up through Richmond Park. No 'Legs, Bums and Tums' for her. That was more Charles's domain. Although it wasn't necessarily his own that he was interested in. Her brain offered up a snapshot of Cass's well-toned calves. She brushed it aside.

'I've just put the kettle on,' Amelia said.

Over her mother-in-law's shoulder Jen could see Charles appear in the doorway. She kept her eyes down, putting off the moment.

'Jessie's in the kitchen.'

Jen nearly said, 'What's she doing in there?' because she had never seen Jessie lift a finger, but then she realized that Amelia would have been in there with her, spoiling her rotten, until the rest of them arrived.

'Hello, sweetheart,' Charles said, and grabbed her in an embrace.

She felt sick. She knew she mustn't look him in the eye, because she would surely give away the fact that she'd gone from considering him the closest thing she had to a father, to thinking he was a despicable creep, who might as well be wearing a grubby mac with a pocket full of toffees. Nought to sixty in record time. She stood rigid and waited for it to be over.

'Hi, Charles.'

He was wearing some kind of a cravat affair, tucked into the open neck of his shirt, she noticed. Before, Jen would have thought how sweet, how adorable that he still made such an effort. Now she just thought he looked ridiculous. An ageing fop.

'How's my favourite daughter-in-law?' Another long-running in-joke.

'Good, thank you. I'm good.'

Jason was brandishing a box of six bottles of sparkling wine. 'Supplies,' he said, handing it over to his father. 'Where's Martin?'

'Doing something in the basement,' Amelia said. 'Fixing the washing machine, I think. Of course, it's decided to go on the blink when there's a house full. Go down and find him.'

Jason ditched their case in the hall and hurried downstairs like an eager child. The men attached to the Masterson women were so used to being outnumbered by females that they grasped every chance they got to take part in a bit of full-on male bonding.

'Play nicely,' Jen called after him.

Amelia fussed around with the kettle and the teapot while Jen settled herself at the kitchen table with Jessie. Charles had thankfully disappeared. Jen imagined he was in the living room, relishing playing barman in a different setting, lining everything up so that he could offer everyone a drink.

'So . . .' she said. 'Happy birthday.'

'Thirty-eight effing years old. Can you believe it?'

'You don't look it, Jess.' She knew just how to get on the good side of this particular sister-in-law.

'OK, for that you get a piece of the birthday cake early. Will you get it out of the fridge, Mum?'

'I'll do it.' Jen hated the way Jessie always barked orders at Amelia, as if she was a stroppy teenager. 'Amelia, sit down with us.'

Amelia obliged, happy to do whatever anybody asked of her. 'I wonder what time Poppy will get here?'

'Why didn't she come with you?' Jessie demanded. 'That would have made more sense than her getting the train, surely.'

'She took Maisie to the seaside yesterday. They stayed in Bognor.'

'Jesus. Really? Why?'

Just at that moment the doorbell rang and Poppy let herself in, holding Maisie with one hand and dragging a large suitcase with the other.

'Don't you ever lock your front door?' she asked as she gave Jessie a cursory hug.

'This is the countryside,' Jessie said smugly. 'No need.'

Amelia swept Maisie up, sitting her granddaughter on her lap.

'How long have you come for?' Jessie demanded, eyeing Poppy's suitcase.

'I have a four-year-old, Jess. You'll soon find out what that's like,' Poppy said tetchily.

'OK, OK, I only asked –'

'This is my favourite weekend of the year,' Amelia interrupted, oblivious. 'Now all we need is for Charles to make the gin and tonics, and it'll be perfect.'

17

'So,' Poppy said, when they somehow found themselves on their own for a few minutes. Actually, Jen had gone to use the bathroom and, when she came out, her sister-in-law had pounced on her like a trapdoor spider.

'What's new with you?'

Jen had been dreading this question. Obviously, she wasn't about to blurt out her suspicions, but she was terrified Poppy would know she was holding something back. Poppy had this kind of bullshit radar that could cut through anything. Jen had once tried to keep from her the fact that she was pissed off with Jessie over something she'd said to Jason. (She couldn't now remember what it had been about – Jessie had an endless back catalogue of harsh remarks and faux pas. It had been a long time ago, when Jen didn't know them all so well, and she hadn't wanted to criticize one sister to another. These days, dissecting Jessie was one of Jen and Poppy's favourite pastimes.) Anyway, Poppy had seen through it in an instant, refusing to get off the phone until Jen had told her what was wrong.

Actually, that was when they had made their 'no taboos' rule. Jen had stuck to it ever since, more or less, and as far as she knew, so had Poppy.

'Nothing much. Oh, how did the date go?'

Poppy sighed. Poppy was a great sigher. 'It didn't.'

'Ryan didn't show up?'

'No. Well, he didn't stand me up either. He emailed me the day before and said he'd been thinking about all those demands I'd made, and there was no point in us meeting. He basically said that if I was that pushy now, he couldn't imagine what I'd be like to go out with, and he didn't think it was worth finding out.'

'He said that?'

'Well, that was the subtext. He was much more circumspect. But I knew what he was getting at.'

'Or perhaps he just didn't look like his picture after all.'

Poppy laughed. 'Maybe. I did wonder if it was really all my fault or whether it was more that he had something to hide. Like acne scars. Or a wife.'

'So . . . what now?'

'I'll keep trawling. Someone else will catch my eye one of these days. It's a shame. I quite liked the look of him.'

'Like you said before, better to find out now. His loss.'

'Don't say anything, will you?'

'How many times? As if.'

'Not even Jason.'

'Not even Jason. Although I don't think he'd judge.'

'No, Jen.'

Jen started edging towards the safety of company, hoping Poppy would follow.

'Is something up?' Poppy said. The question Jen had been dreading. 'You seem a bit low.'

'No,' Jen shot back, far too quickly. 'Everything's fine.'

'Where are those girls?' she heard Amelia calling from the kitchen.

Jen breathed an almost audible sigh of relief. 'Here!' she called back, and started to head in that direction. If she was going to keep her suspicions to herself, then she was going to need to become a better actor.

Halfway through lunch Jen realized she felt exhausted. Eight people around one dinner table all shouting to be heard. Plus one soon-to-be-delivered baby – who was probably rethinking its decision to be born into this family at all, by now.

Jessie had reduced them all to tears of laughter re-enacting a recent antenatal class that had dealt with breach births and forceps and all manner of other horrors, describing how one of the other mothers-to-be had kept saying, 'I'm not giving anyone permission to do that to me. I just want that on record,' over and over again.

Amelia kept slightly misunderstanding the point of the story and saying things like, 'Were they actually trying to make her sign a consent form, then?' or, 'Had she gone into labour during the class?' which would set everyone off again.

Then, almost immediately, Jessie and Poppy started to have a fight because Jessie thought Poppy had made a disparaging comment about the size of her car – when, in fact, all Poppy had done was make a joke about it being bigger than her own flat. It might have been, actually, Jen thought. It was close. It threatened to develop into one of those 'You're always putting me down', 'You think you're better than the rest of us', 'Well, you're just jealous, you always have been' fights that happened every couple of years and could blight a whole weekend.

'You always do this. You always ruin it,' Jessie said, becoming tearful.

Martin ran a protective hand over her belly and said, 'It's OK, Jess, don't get upset.'

'Oh, for God's sake,' Poppy said fractiously. 'Grow up, Jess.'

'Girls!' Charles said, a warning note in his voice.

Jen still hadn't really been able to look at him. She was sure he had noticed, because out of the corner of her eye she could see him watching her every now and then. She'd decided that, if challenged, she would claim another migraine. A special kind of migraine that somehow rendered it possible to make eye contact with every person in the room except one.

'Have I already told you about John from next door tripping down his front steps and breaking his ankle?' Amelia suddenly asked, out of nowhere. This was always her tactic whenever a squabble broke out, pretend she hadn't noticed it, and it might just go away.

'I didn't start it,' Poppy said defensively. 'All I did was make a joke about the car being big. It wasn't a value judgement.'

'He's been in St Thomas's for a week and a half, waiting to have physio. They can't send him home, because there's no one to look after him.'

'Can't social services send someone round?' Jason chipped in, trying to help derail the train.

Jessie's eyes welled up with big fat tears. 'I've lost my appetite now. I'm going to go and lie down.'

Jessie could have won competitions in crying. A shelf full of trophies for weeping, bawling and sobbing. A certificate for first prize in the blubbering open. She was a frequent and dramatic crier. Of course, she was also an actress, so Jen never knew how seriously to take her histrionics. She always fooled Martin, though. In all honesty, Jen usually just pretended it wasn't happening, but with Jessie about to give birth any moment, she felt she perhaps ought to indulge her.

'How's the nesting been, Jess? Have you been tempted to clean out all the kitchen cupboards yet?'

Jessie turned to her, all smiles again, now she was the focus of attention. 'Oh God, yes. And I've started baking, haven't I, Martin? I mean, I've never been interested in making a cake in my life and now I can't stop.'

'And I have the expanding girth to prove it,' Martin said fondly. Martin already had three grown-up children by his first wife, and had never intended to have a second family, but – and Jen had to give him credit here – once Jessie had announced she was pregnant, he had thrown himself into the role all over again with enthusiasm. He was still a big part of his older kids' lives too and, unlike most men who end up with much younger second wives, he had actually been divorced from their mother before Jessie had come along. He was a nice man, Jen thought, if a little too fond of babying Jessie who, in turn, was all too happy to be babied and treated like an indulged child rather than a wife. She had a tendency to treat Martin like a necessary irritation, and Jen often found herself feeling sorry for him. He, on the other hand, seemed oblivious. He adored his wife and was blind to any of her faults.

Just like that, the tension dissipated and all attention

turned back to Jessie and the impending arrival of a new addition to the family. It was always that way. Privately, Jen called it the Masterson tidal system. Out of nowhere, something would come along and wash away whatever had been there before. It was totally unpredictable. At first, Jen had watched in horror as Poppy and Jessie would go at it tooth and nail. How could two people she loved so much be throwing such hurtful darts at one another? It was only after she had survived her own first fight with Jessie that she realized Jessie calling her a 'fucking annoying bitch' meant that she was totally accepted. It was almost a sign of affection. Like when a cat lifts its tail and pees up your curtains.

'Please, have a boy,' Jason was saying now, removing any last traces of tension in the air.

'I'll do my best,' Jessie said, mock serious.

'No chance,' Charles said, knocking back the last of his wine. 'Not in this family.'

'God, we're like freaks,' Poppy chipped in. 'Biologically unable to produce males.'

'Good,' Jessie said, laughing. 'Who needs them, anyway?'

Jen did her best to smile along with everyone, but really she was scrutinizing her father-in-law. He was smiling at his wife fondly, laughing like he hadn't a care in the world. She couldn't work it out. How could he be so blasé, so unconcerned, so ... oblivious? How could he be so exactly like his usual relaxed, easy-going self, if he had a whole secret life going on?

He was flanked on one side by Jessie and on the other by Maisie. Leaning back in his chair, taking it all in, smiling expansively, loving every moment. He looked up and caught her eye. She looked away.

This wasn't Charles. This wasn't her adored father-in-law. This was a man who cheated on his wife – a man who had purported to be a shining example of stable husband and fatherhood to his three children his whole life, while practising anything other than what he preached himself. Someone who, it turned out, was not the man all the people around the table, basking in his paternal glow, had always thought he was. This man felt like a stranger.

In the past few days, she had started to question whether everyone she knew mightn't be harbouring a big secret. Not Jason, obviously. She had never doubted him. But now she found herself looking at Martin, wondering whether he might be a secret philanderer. God knows, living with Jessie couldn't be easy. Or did he like to dress up in her clothes whenever she went out? Or put a nappy on and get spanked by random strangers when his wife thought he was down the pub?

Unlikely, Jen knew, but suddenly anything seemed possible. Maybe Poppy was an alcoholic or a bulimic or had an addiction to sticking a compass into her thigh? Perhaps Jessie had a fancy man in Bognor? Or maybe she went shoplifting whenever she got the chance? Actually, that last one didn't seem so incredible. She had an inflated enough sense of entitlement – it might well stretch to thinking shops ought to give her stuff for free.

How did you ever truly know that the people you were close to were really the people you thought they were? Maybe if she had been there the day Charles had first laid eyes on Cass, it would have been obvious. He would have come home looking different, smelling different, casually dropping the name of a woman he'd just met into the conversation.

Maybe there were always signs, it was just whether you chose to read them, or not.

18

'Everything all right, sweetheart?' Charles loomed large in the doorway of the slightly mouldy-smelling bedroom that had been allocated to Jen and Jason for the night. She had sneaked upstairs to unpack their things, safe in the knowledge that overindulgence in food and wine had left the rest of the family almost comatose in the living room. Apparently, she'd been wrong.

Jen jumped, tried to laugh it off, managed to drop the clothes hangers she'd been holding.

'You startled me.'

Charles turned on his megawatt smile. 'I just thought you seemed a bit quiet at lunch, that's all.'

He was fishing. He was worried that she'd seen through his charade of pretending Cass was his client, and he was trying to find out how serious the damage was.

'Nothing wrong, is there?'

'No! Of course not.'

'Ah, there you are . . .'

Jen almost cried with relief as she saw her mother-in-law appear in the hallway.

'. . . I have cake, and I can't seem to get any takers. You're my last hope.'

Jen leaned over and hugged her with relief. 'Are you trying to kill us all?' she said, with a forced laugh. 'If I eat any more, I'll explode, but I will come down with you, though.'

She began to follow Amelia down the stairs, leaving Charles hovering in the doorway of the bedroom.

'I think an afternoon nap's on the cards, don't you?' she said, not looking back.

Sometime later – she still didn't know if it was twenty minutes or two hours – Jen became aware of Martin standing white-faced in the doorway. The rest of the family were dozing in their armchairs. Only Jessie was nowhere to be seen.

'I think it's started,' he said to no one in particular.

'Shit. Are you sure?' She leapt up, feeling she should do something, although not entirely certain what.

'What?' Jason said groggily. It had gone dark outside, and it might as well have been six in the morning as six in the evening to the people inside. 'What's happening?'

'The baby.'

'I'll ring for an ambulance,' Jason said dramatically, wide awake now. 'None of us can drive her to the hospital, we're all over the limit.'

'No. Wait. How far apart are her contractions?'

'I haven't timed them,' Martin said. 'Should I?' He had clearly forgotten anything he had learned in antenatal class. Or at the births of his three older children come to that.

'Yes,' Jen said, glad of something constructive to do. 'I'll come in with you. Jason, make us some coffee, will you?'

'Has something happened?' Amelia was saying as they left the room.

'What's going on?' Poppy added. 'What time is it?'

*

Jessie was half sitting, half lying on the bed, pale and sweating, hair fanned out on the pillow as if it had been arranged by a stylist. Jen thought she looked more like Kristen Stewart's older sister playing someone who was in labour than someone who was actually in labour. She had never really seen Jessie act, by the way. Not because she hadn't made the effort, but because Jessie's career always seemed to be lodged more in her head than in reality. She had played a car crash victim in *Casualty* once, but that was about it. Jen remembered her being incensed that her head had been bandaged in such a way that her face was unrecognizable.

'Why did no one tell me contractions were this painful?' she demanded when she saw Jen now.

'I'm sure they did, Jess. Do you want me to get your mum? Or one of the others?'

Jessie grabbed Jen's wrist. 'No, you stay.' She sat up and shouted, 'Jason, get Mum!'

Jen wasn't sure he'd heard her, but then Jessie let out an almighty scream. Jen was convinced she was shouting more loudly now that she had an audience, thereby ensuring that no one in the house could remain in ignorance of what was going on for long. The performance opportunity of a lifetime.

The next few hours were a blur. Jen, Poppy and Amelia sat around the bed timing, soothing and advising, while Martin held Jessie's hand and wiped her forehead tenderly. Jason had eventually managed to track down a midwife at the nearest hospital, in Arundel, and was now barking occasional pieces of information through the door.

'She says to call back when they're about four minutes

apart. When she has three in ten minutes, that's when it all starts getting really serious,' he shouted, running back downstairs to make more coffee and check on Maisie – who was hiding out in the living room, probably traumatized by the sick cow noises coming from her aunt's bedroom.

'I told her we'd all had a few drinks, and she told me off, but then I explained it was a birthday lunch – and that the baby wasn't due for two weeks, anyway – and she was a bit nicer after that. She gave me the number of a local mini-cab firm,' he called out the next time they heard from him. 'She's trying to track down your allocated person.'

Jessie let out another almighty wail, and dug her nails into Martin's hand, almost drawing blood.

'How long?' Jason shouted through the door.

'Five and a half minutes since the last one,' someone said.

'Oh Jesus,' they heard him mutter.

'How are you feeling?' Jen squeezed her sister-in-law's free hand.

'I'm still here, aren't I?' Jessie said through gritted teeth.

'Our midwife is lovely, isn't she, Jess? I wonder where she is. Did she say if she had holiday booked?' Martin said, out of nowhere. 'It seems odd to let someone else deliver the baby.'

'I don't care if the postman delivers it, just get this fucking thing out of me,' Jessie said, causing the rest of them to stifle a laugh.

Three hours later, they were all still sitting there.

'Me and Dad have made sandwiches,' Jason said,

popping his head round the door. 'If anyone can face eating. And Dad wants to know if anyone wants a drink.'

'Is Maisie OK?'

'Fine. She's eaten. Don't worry about her. It's giving us something to do, otherwise we'd just feel helpless.'

Jen blew him a kiss just as Jessie let out another roar.

'Oh my God, I'm out of here,' Jason said, beating a hasty retreat. 'How long?' he called as he went.

'Still five and a half,' Poppy shouted. 'Tell Maisie I'll come down and say goodnight to her in a minute.'

In the end, the midwife – not Jessie and Martin's allocated one, but a friendly, competent-seeming woman nonetheless – came to the house, arriving at four in the morning and shooing all of them except Martin out of the room. They all congregated in the living room, which was spotless, Jason and Charles obviously having discovered that cleaning was a good displacement activity.

'You've even organized the books in the bookshelves, by the look of it,' Poppy said, incredulous.

'By topic,' Jason said. 'Actually, before the midwife arrived we were about to go for alphabetical.'

Even if it hadn't been for the array of noises coming from upstairs, no one would have dared to even think of going to sleep. Jen tried to persuade Amelia to lie down for a while, but she wouldn't hear of it – although they all promised to rouse her, if anything happened.

Jen snuggled up with Jason on one of the big sofas. It was the colour of undercooked liver and smelled of wet dog, despite the fact that Jessie and Martin's beloved old beagle, Sparky, had finally keeled over about six months before. Actually, their whole house was the colour of undercooked liver and smelled of dog. You couldn't accuse them of not being committed.

Although she was shattered, Jen could still feel the adrenaline rushing around her body. Everyone was a bit hyper, a bit wired, a bit on edge. Excited, like they were kids, and it was the night before Christmas. Like they were all involved in a big adventure together.

By midday, they had all slept a bit – on and off – despite the noise. They had half-heartedly made breakfast and picked at it, and a few of them had showered and changed, quickly, so as not to miss anything.

Jen was trying to think what they should do if the baby had still not arrived by the time she and Jason intended to leave for home. You heard about women who had long labours – thirty-six hours, forty-eight, even sixty – all the time, but both of them had to be at work the next day and neither had the kind of job where you could just take the day off with no notice. It felt wrong to go before it was over, though. It would be like leaving a cinema without seeing the end of the film. Walking out of the football stadium just before there was a last-minute goal. Well, on a much grander, more important scale, obviously.

She was just about to ask Jason what he thought they should do when a telltale wail suddenly announced the arrival of the newest member of the Masterson clan. They all sat bolt upright, not knowing what was expected of them. Jason got hold of Jen's hand and hung on to it. No one said anything until a couple of minutes later, when Martin ran down the stairs, stuck his head round the door, a look of sheer delight on his face, and said, 'Girl!' before turning round and running back up again.

As if on cue, Poppy, Amelia and Jen all burst into tears. Jen looked at Charles and saw that he had a smile on his face like the Cheshire Cat. Like he couldn't have been more proud. Like all that mattered to him was his family.

She no longer had any doubt. Whatever it was that was going on, it had to stop.

19

She had dialled the number before she had really thought about what it was she was doing. She had no idea what she was going to say, no plan beyond making the call, maybe setting up an appointment she could cancel, or not, later on. She had spent some time back in the internet cafe browsing the Masterson Property website, checking out the high-end houses in the Brighton area, making a note of the ones that had Cass Richards listed as the agent. She wondered what the other people in there were researching. Who, these days, didn't have a laptop or at least a phone they could get internet access on? They must all be looking up something they wanted to keep secret, something that couldn't be traced back to them.

Great, now she was choosing to spend her free time with would-be suicide bombers and people who got off on dodgy porn.

She almost hung up when the woman answered the phone. This was ridiculous. She had practised her cover story several times, but she overcompensated by rambling on to the receptionist about having to relocate for work and needing to be somewhere where there were good schools for her kids and she could ride a horse. She had never ridden a horse in her life, but it sounded like the kind of thing someone who was interested in the house she was enquiring about might like to do.

The receptionist interrupted her in the end, obviously bored to tears. 'I'll ask Cass Richards to call you back, and you can sort out a time with her. She's the agent for this property.'

'Perfect,' Jen said, thankful to have been derailed.

'What's your name?'

She had agonized about how to deal with this question when it arose. Her surname would be a dead giveaway, and ring alarm bells with Cass before they'd even met. She knew that once Cass clapped eyes on her, she would probably remember her face. And the truth was that she fully intended to tell her exactly who she was, even if she didn't. But she didn't want to give away too much in advance. In truth, she didn't want Cass to be ready for her; she wanted to take her by surprise.

'Jennifer Blaine,' she said, with as much confidence as she could muster. She could always claim that she still used her maiden name, as so many women did these days. As she would have done herself, if she didn't hate it so much. Or if her desire to officially be a Masterson hadn't superseded everything else.

She gave the woman her number, made an excuse that her landline wasn't working at the moment, hung up and waited. It was out of her hands now.

Half an hour later, her mobile rang while she was checking in a couple from Canterbury. She felt it buzz in her pocket – ringtones were strictly forbidden for hotel staff on duty – and it took all her willpower not to at least see who was calling. Once she had handed the couple over to Graham Roper the Doorman Groper, who was hovering with their luggage, she fished it out of her pocket. A number beginning with 01273 was listed as a missed call. A Brighton number.

'Back in a sec,' she said to Judy. She walked through the foyer and out on to the pavement. Cass hadn't left a message, so there was nothing to do but to call the number back. She heard it ring twice.

'Cass Richards.'

Jen heard a voice on the other end, and nearly dropped her phone. She suddenly couldn't think of anything to say.

'Hello?' Cass said, an impatient tone creeping into her voice.

'Hi!'

'Hello, who is this?'

'Hi, sorry, my name is Jennifer Blaine, I think you just called me. About the house in Roedean Crescent –'

'Jennifer, hello. So you'd like to have a look around?'

Jen noticed Cass sounded more perky, now she had the sniff of a sale. 'Yes. Please. If that's possible.'

'Of course. Today?'

'No! Maybe on Thursday? I have to come down from London.'

She had tentatively arranged to have a day's holiday on Thursday. She could get the train down, meet up with Cass and be back before anyone really noticed she was gone.

They agreed a time, and Cass gave her the full address.

'How are you fixed?' she asked, just as Jen thought she was home and dry. 'Do you have an offer on your place?'

'Second home,' Jen said confidently. That seemed like

the least complicated scenario to posit. She heard Cass's interest in her go up a notch.

'So . . . are you a cash buyer?'

Why not? It was almost fun to play the carefree rich card for a few moments.

'Yes. No chain, no complications.'

'Well, that will be very attractive to my vendor. Let's hope you like the place.'

Jen ended the call, walked back in and bypassed reception, going straight to the Ladies where she promptly threw up.

By Wednesday evening, she was seriously thinking of cancelling her appointment. What was the best that could come of it? That Cass would realize she'd been rumbled and would be furious that Jen had wasted her valuable time? That she'd tell Charles what had happened, and then Jen's relationship with him could never be the same? Not that she was sure it could be now, anyway.

She had thought through, carefully, exactly what she was hoping for. In the most perfect version of the plan, Cass would turn out to be a woman of scruples who would be shocked and horrified to discover that her lover was still happily living with his wife. She had only entered into the relationship because she had been sure he was separated, she would never intentionally steal another woman's man, devastate his family. Jen realized that Charles wasn't coming out of her wished-for scenario in a particularly flattering light. She could worry about that later. What mattered was that Cass would tell her she was going to break it off immediately. She would let Charles know in no uncertain terms that what they had been doing, for however long, was wrong.

Of course, inevitably, it didn't turn out like that.

On the way to the station, Jen remembered she hadn't called Poppy since baby Violet's birth a few days before. While she was still nervous about talking to her sister-in-law, she knew that she had to try to carry on as though everything was normal. They rarely, if ever, went more than two days without speaking.

'I found a grey pube,' she said, as soon as Poppy answered. Her plan was that if she launched into a random topic, then Poppy would be wrong-footed and wouldn't ask her how anything else in her life was going. For the record, she had not discovered a grey pubic hair. Not yet. Although she was pretty sure it wouldn't be long.

'Jesus. No hello?'

'This is an emergency, can't you tell?' she said.

Poppy laughed. 'I assume you pulled it out?'

'Of course, but now what? It's only a matter of time before they all turn, and then . . . well, God knows.'

'Hollywood wax?'

'Please! I'm not going to lie around while some poor woman gets paid seven pounds an hour to poke about down there. I feel bad enough when I just get it tidied up.'

'So what are you suggesting? Dyeing it?'

'Maybe I could use that stuff men have for touching up their beards.'

Poppy squealed. 'Or ask your hairdresser to do it when she does your roots.'

'God, I really do not want to get old. This is the kind of stuff no one warns you about.'

'What else is new, or have you just been examining yourself for signs of ageing?'

'Shit, I have to go, my stop's coming up.'

It wasn't. In actuality, she was still standing at the side of the road, waiting for a bus to take her to Victoria.

20

By the time the train pulled into Brighton station, she had almost forgotten her mission. She had done such a good job of blanking out the impending horror. Just having a nice day out at the seaside. Ice cream, donkey rides and kiss-me-quick hats. It came back to her with a sickening thud when she was in the taxi, driving down towards the coast road. Whatever this was, it wasn't a holiday.

She arrived in Roedean Crescent a few minutes early, paid the driver, and hovered about outside the house for a few moments, unsure what to do.

The street was a stunner, with majestic views over the sea at the front, and rolling countryside at the back. The boats in the marina twinkled white down below, like so many rows of pearly false teeth. Jen paced up and down, trying to get straight in her head what exactly she was going to say, why exactly she was there.

Cass was being ambushed, she almost certainly wouldn't appreciate that. For all Jen knew, she could be a psycho. A real, live Bea from *Prisoner: Cell Block H*, prone to stabbing and gouging, rather than having a nice middle-class chat about how sorry she was for anything she might inadvertently have done. Jen thought about chickening out, leaving before Cass arrived, hot-footing it back to London and pretending it had all been a dream.

Too late. A chic little red Fiat 500 pulled up, and there

she was. Jen was able to get a better look at her before Cass really looked up and registered who it was that was waiting for her. She had slightly sticky-out front teeth, something Jen hadn't notice the first time she had met her – she wasn't talking Goofy, just a hint of an overbite – and a nose that was small, and cute. The combination gave her an approachable look, a cartoon girl next door. She didn't look like a home-wrecker. The shiny brown hair was looking, well, brown and shiny. Jen patted down her blow-dried and flat-ironed locks that always smelled faintly of burning, these days. They were starting to frizz in the drizzle.

Cass was wearing a dark grey skirt and a jacket – estate agent uniform – but this one was stylishly cut, nipped in at the waist and with a hint of a pinstripe. Underneath she had a magenta T-shirt that stopped the whole look from becoming too masculine. Jen watched as she reached for a black pea coat from the back of the car and pulled it on over the top, and felt suddenly inadequate in her own jeans, Ugg rip-offs and parka-style jacket.

She could hear herself breathing in and out. She steadied herself for the moment when Cass would recognize her, would want to know what the hell she was doing there. She waited, as Cass started to walk towards her, her heels clicking on the pavement. And there it was, an almost imperceptible flicker, a brief frown.

'Hi,' Jen said nervously. She felt sick.

Cass looked at her quizzically. 'Hello. Are you Jennifer Blaine?'

'Yes. Sort of.'

'Didn't we meet before?' It took a moment for Cass to

put all the pieces together. 'In London, wasn't it? Aren't you Charles Masterson's daughter-in-law?'

Jen hesitated for a moment. Nodded. 'That's why I'm here.'

'Ah. You're not really looking for a second home by the sea?'

'Sorry.'

Cass folded her arms. 'Care to explain?'

'If you've got a couple of minutes.'

'What I've got is a homeowner expecting someone to be looking over her house at midday. I need to go and tell her the appointment's been cancelled.'

'Can I wait for you? We could get a coffee or something, I don't know.'

Cass didn't answer, just turned in the direction of the front door and marched up the path. Jen had no idea what to make of her cool demeanour. She hadn't exactly been friendly – but then, who could blame her? She had been sideswiped, jumped from behind; she was probably trying to gather her thoughts and work out exactly what was going on. Or else she had a machete stashed in her client's front garden for emergencies, and she had decided this was one.

Jen waited while Cass spoke to a woman on the doorstep for a minute or so, and then came back down.

'So,' Cass said. 'What's all this about?'

'Do you want to get a drink? Go to a cafe, or a pub, or something.'

'I don't really have time. Just tell me what's going on, Jennifer –'

'Jen,' she interrupted. She couldn't help herself. When-

142

ever anyone called her Jennifer, she felt as if she was being told off. Actually, in this case, maybe she was.

'Why would you come all the way down here, pretending you were interested in buying a house? I assume because you know who I am.'

Jen nodded. Said nothing.

'Did Dad tell you?'

Jen opened her mouth to speak. Shut it again. Tried to compute what she had just heard. Couldn't. It felt as if everything went into slow motion. Cass was looking at her expectantly, waiting for an answer, but Jen couldn't think of what to say for the white noise in her head. She wondered if she'd heard correctly.

'Dad?'

'Charles. That's why you're here, isn't it?'

'You're . . .?' She couldn't say it. She took in Cass's wide brown eyes, so like Charles's and Jason's. And Jessie's, come to that. The hair. Poppy and Jessie both had shiny dark tresses that Jen had always envied. She remembered Amelia showing her a photo of Charles from the beginning of the seventies, laughing at his long silky hair, falling past his shoulders like a girl in a Timotei advert, showing her that that was where the two girls had inherited it from. Make that three, maybe. Three girls. How had she not seen it?

The cute nose and the overbite must be courtesy of her mother. Whoever she was.

Cass interrupted her thought process. 'I'm getting really confused now, and I don't have time for this, to be honest.'

'You're his daughter?'

'Who did you think I was?'

'I . . . actually, this is pretty grim . . . I thought he was having an affair with you.'

Thankfully, Cass actually smiled. 'Jesus, that *is* grim.'

'I had no idea.' Jen was aware that she was standing there with her mouth open again. She couldn't seem to close it, as if she wanted there to be a physical manifestation of her shock. She simply couldn't take it in. This woman was Charles's daughter. A sister Jason, Poppy and Jessie knew nothing about. A million questions rushed into her head at the same time. She had no chance of saying anything even halfway intelligible.

The day had suddenly turned black and windy. Jen let out an involuntary shiver and pulled her coat more tightly around her.

Cass seemed to take pity on her. 'Do you want to sit in my car and talk? It'll be warmer.'

'Definitely.'

'So,' Cass said, as she turned the engine on and the heating up, 'I can tell this is a shock.'

'You can say that again. I thought . . . I could barely believe he might have a girlfriend, but a daughter . . .'

Cass was silent for a moment. Jen tried to work out what that signified, couldn't.

'What do you want me to tell you?'

'I don't know. Everything. How old are you?'

'Twenty-five.'

'So Jason – that's my husband, by the way – would have been eighteen. God, Jessie was only thirteen. She's the youngest.'

'I know.'

'So you knew you had a brother and two sisters?'

'I did. Not that I really think of them like that.'

'And that Charles is still with their mother. Amelia.'

Cass nodded. 'I've always wondered what she was like, actually.'

'She's lovely. Motherly. Kind. Sweet. She adores him, adores her family. I always thought they were so happy.'

'Lucky them.'

Jen didn't have to be Miss Marple to detect the hint of sarcasm in Cass's voice.

'You think otherwise?'

'Who knows? There must have been something wrong.'

It annoyed Jen that Cass was speaking as though she was an authority on Charles and Amelia's relationship. She felt as if Cass was overstepping a line. 'Well, maybe twenty-five years ago, they had a blip. To me they've always seemed like one of the happiest couples I've ever known.'

Cass smiled, but not in a good way. Not in a way that said, 'Let's be friends.' More, 'I'd like to cut you up and eat your kidneys.'

'I'll ignore the suggestion that I'm a "blip". I don't think a man being with a woman who wasn't his wife for fifteen years points to a happy marriage.'

Jen felt the blood rush from her head. Actually felt it, like when you stand up too quickly and have to hold on to the arm of the sofa to stop yourself from falling over. Outside, people were battling against the wind, leaning into it to fight their way down the street. She wondered if she had really just heard what she thought she'd heard.

'What do you mean? Fifteen years?'

Cass looked at her. Blinked. 'My mum and dad. They were together till I was fifteen. Actually, that makes it sixteen years, I guess. OK, so he could hardly ever stay over, and he never came to parents' evenings, but we had the house, the dog, the three-piece suite. He was there whenever he could be.'

Jen thought about Charles and Amelia's beautiful family home. The way they had always made it feel like the most loving, safe, welcoming place she had ever been.

'Charles doesn't even like dogs,' was her genius retort.

'Well, he definitely seemed to like Buster. He got him for me for my eighth birthday.'

'Are you saying he was around for your whole childhood? He was like your proper dad?'

'Apart from the fact we never went on holiday together, and I couldn't understand why I wasn't allowed to use his surname, yes.'

'So they split up, what . . . ten years ago?' Jason and Jen had been together for twenty-two years in total so, for the first twelve she had known Charles, he had been sneaking off to be with Cass's mum. It didn't seem possible.

'They're still in touch, actually. They've somehow managed to stay friends, which is more than I've ever been capable of with any of my exes.'

Jen tried to get it straight in her head. 'They were together for sixteen years?'

Cass nodded. 'Yep. She had the ring and everything. Not that they were ever married, obviously, but he always told her that, in his eyes, they were.'

'This is . . . I don't know what to say. It's insane.'

'Well, it doesn't make much sense, that's true.'

'And there's just you. Please tell me there aren't any others?'

'Just me. I think Mum would have loved a few more, but Dad . . . you know. So it was just me and her most of the time.'

It struck Jen that, devastated as Jason and his sisters would be if they ever discovered Charles had a secret family, Cass was pretty hard done by herself. She couldn't imagine having a brother and two sisters and never being allowed to even meet them. She would have killed for one sibling, let alone three.

'I know how that feels.'

'You're an only child?'

Jen nodded. 'And my dad basically disappeared out of our lives when I was eight.'

Cass nodded sympathetically. 'That sucks.'

'And your mum – how did she . . . I mean, was she OK with it all?'

'Of course not, although she tried to pretend it was all fine. I think she always believed he'd leave Amelia one day and they'd be together properly. It was pathetic, really.'

'How did you end up working with him? If, well, you sound like you have a lot of anger towards him. Which is understandable, obviously.'

'It was his idea. He said it would be a way for us to spend time together, and that he wanted to feel he had been able to help me get started on a career. I was just out of college, no idea what to do with my life. Of course, I hadn't really thought through that I wouldn't be able to tell anyone there who I actually was. After a while, though,

I was glad no one knew, because I didn't want it to look like I was being given any special favours. And then, after a year or so, I moved down here and I've been here ever since. Dad never really had much interaction with the regional branches – beyond popping down a few times a year to congratulate us all, or tell us to work harder. And I'm good at it. Really good. I'm going to set up on my own, eventually.'

'He never worried that it would all blow up in his face? That he'd get caught out?'

Cass shrugged. 'He made it pretty clear that if we ever said anything, he'd have to disappear from our lives altogether. It was always plain that his legitimate family came first. Or the kids did, at least. And then his new career came along . . .'

'I'm sorry. What a mess.'

'It's just how it was. We were hard done by, but so were Amelia and the others, I suppose. At least we knew where we stood. I sometimes think that's better than your whole life having been a lie.'

'And you've never been curious . . . to meet your brother and sisters?'

'My half-brother and half-sisters? Honestly, no. They're not really my siblings. They're just random people who are Dad's kids by someone I've never met. It's not the same.'

'They're related to you. That must count.'

'You know what? When I was young, I sometimes wanted a brother or a sister. It never even occurred to me that Dad's other family could fill that role. When I was ten, Jessie was . . . what? Twenty-three? We were hardly going to start having sleepovers.'

'You obviously don't know Jessie,' Jen said, attempting a joke.

Cass just looked at her.

Jen fished in her bag for her phone. 'I've brought photos, look. Jason and I have been married for twenty years, by the way . . . well, I suppose you know that.'

'That's a long time, these days. I'm a fuck up at relationships myself,' Cass said. 'It's hard to trust anyone when you really know what people are capable of.'

'I suppose you've seen pictures of them already,' Jen said, finding a recent one of Jason, anyway.

'Of course.' Cass took the phone, and studied the picture. 'Wow, he's getting old.'

Jen realized Cass couldn't have seen him lately. It seemed to her that Jason had got older in tiny, almost imperceptible, increments. It wasn't like he woke up one morning last week and suddenly looked middle-aged. Even despite the radical haircut.

'Charles hasn't shown you any recent ones, then?'

'I don't think he likes to be reminded of his double life too often.'

'That's Poppy,' Jen said, showing her a snap she had taken of herself and Poppy gurning up at the camera, in a slightly drunken embrace, Jen straining to hold the phone far enough away to include them both in the picture.

'She looks like Dad.'

'I don't think I have any pictures of Jessie . . .' Jen felt herself babbling on, couldn't stop. 'This phone is quite new, so –'

'Jennifer . . . Jen, what do you actually want?'

'I have no idea. The idea was to tell you Charles had a

loving family at home and to ask you to break it off with him.'

'Well, that went to plan.'

Jen exhaled loudly. 'Please, don't tell Charles I was here.'

'You really think Amelia has never known all these years?'

'God, no. Of course not. And she mustn't. It would devastate her.'

'It's OK. I'm used to being Dad's guilty little secret.'

A slight edge crept into her voice as she said this. Almost undetectable, but there, nonetheless.

'Do you know why I haven't seen any recent photos of Jason?' she said, and then she carried on, not waiting for an answer, 'Because I asked Dad not to show me any more. Do you have any idea what it's like knowing all your life that your dad has three other children who get all his attention? Ones who can actually be seen out in public with him?'

Jen didn't say anything. There wasn't really anything else she could say.

'I'm sorry, Jen, you seem like a nice woman, and I'm sure Jason is a good guy, if you say so. I'm sure all of them are.'

'I don't know what to think. Jesus. That is really fucked up.'

'Well, it isn't *The Brady Bunch*, that's for certain.'

'They mustn't ever find out.' Jen realized that this secret was going to have to stay just that, a secret.

No one would benefit from it being brought out into the open. Not Jason, who had spent his whole life idolizing his dad, not his sisters, who would probably never get over finding out that their whole happy upbringing had been a sham, not Amelia, who would surely crumble in the face of the truth. And, if she was being honest, not her either. Because if Charles's secret came out, then how could the family – *her* family – ever stay together?

A flicker of irritation, or even anger, passed across Cass's face. 'God, no, the chosen ones must never be disabused.'

'How would it help anyone, if four more people had their lives ruined? More, actually, because my kids . . . they love Charles.'

'Ah yes, the grandchildren. That just about sealed the deal. Once they started coming along, there was no question my mum was going to get her happy ending. Even if they did drag it out for a few more years.'

'They're just kids still. They're not to blame in any of this.'

'They're not that much younger than me, are they?' Cass snapped.

'They're eighteen and twenty,' Jen said. 'They've barely even left home.'

'Sorry, that was uncalled for. Sometimes it just makes me angry, that's all, but I have to remember it's Dad I should be angry at, not the rest of them.'

'I shouldn't have come down. I don't know what I thought I was hoping to achieve, but I've just managed to upset you. I'm sorry.'

'Stop apologizing. You weren't to know.'

They sat there, not saying anything for a moment.

'I should go,' Jen said, leaning down to pick up her bag. 'I have to get back to London.'

She could hardly think straight, her mind was so crowded with images of Charles with another woman, Charles bringing up a strange little girl who called him Dad, him arriving at their house after a day at work, slinging his coat on a hook, fixing a gin and tonic, putting on his slippers, sitting in his favourite chair, temporarily forgetting he had a wife and three children at home because he had what amounted to another wife and a daughter here. How was it possible to carry that off for sixteen-odd years, and still have your family believe you were the perfect father?

She wondered, briefly, whether Cass was a fantasist, making the whole story up to be dramatic. It was something she could imagine Jessie doing to get sympathy. But there was no doubt in her mind, really. There was no question that this whole thing had turned out to be a bigger, much more complicated mess than she had ever imagined.

21

Cass was celebrating. A house she was looking after on the Hove seafront had just set off a bidding war between two parties, and she'd managed to get one of them to agree to pay £44,000 above the asking price. The owners had been delighted, of course, because these were credible buyers too. Cass had checked out their financials. There was only a chain of one. The sellers hadn't yet exchanged on their new place but had agreed to put their things into storage and rent a flat for a while, if they had to. Not that the recession really seemed to be affecting the buying power of the kind of people who bought houses from Masterson Property, but it had made them more cautious in one way. No one was going to risk missing out on a great deal.

Of course, she knew from experience that anything could still go wrong. She had encountered every kind of road block in her years on the job. Surveys, neighbours, schools, the wrong kind of light, bad feng shui – anything could cause people to pull out, it seemed. Some just flat out changed their minds, decided to stay put or move to a different city altogether. She had a good feeling about the Stanhopes, though. And her intuition was usually pretty reliable.

Of course, she hadn't spotted that Jennifer Blaine aka Jen Masterson was a faker on the phone. Her sixth sense had been caught napping. Taking a day off.

She had been desperate to tell someone about what had

happened, but it was out of the question that she share her story with any of her colleagues. No one at work knew she was Charles's daughter, and she wanted it to stay that way. Not least because she didn't think any of them would appreciate having been lied to for three years. That left either her mum or Kara, who were the only people who had been party to every grim detail. She knew her mother would only worry. Barbara lived both in hope that Charles would rekindle their relationship one day, and fear of it being discovered, thereby ensuring there was no chance.

So she'd called Kara and persuaded her to drive down from Haywards Heath for a drink. And then the offer on the house had come, and they had decided to turn it into a celebration. They were sitting drinking tall glasses of champagne from extravagantly shaped flutes, at a table looking out over the dark seafront.

'What did she look like?' Kara asked, dropping an ice cube into her champagne. Kara always asked for ice cubes on the side with any drink, and would plop them in, one by one, swirling them around until they melted. She thought it helped limit her alcohol consumption and therefore her calorie intake.

'Pretty, I suppose. Red hair.'

Kara was a looks fascist. She believed that appearance was everything. Super skinny and groomed to perfection, she worked hard to disguise the fact that her face was a little on the plain side, too square and with a nose that was a touch too prominent to be considered conventionally beautiful. She had very specific criteria on which she judged other women's looks.

'Thin?'

Cass shrugged. 'Normal, I guess. What does it matter, anyway? She's not the one who's related to me.'

'I just want to get the full picture. Who would play her in a film?'

Cass struggled to think. It was always much easier to play along with Kara than to ignore her. 'Julianne Moore? She has red hair, doesn't she? But younger.'

'I have no idea who that is.'

'Yes, you do.'

'What about Nicole Kidman? She's on the red side of blonde.'

'She looks nothing like Nicole Kidman.'

'That girl in *The Help*?'

'For God's sake, Kara. I'm trying to tell you what happened –'

'OK. Well, I'll just picture the one from *The Help*, then.'

'Fine, if that makes you happy. Not so pale, though. And forty years old.'

She told Kara the whole story, from the phone call through to her and Jen saying an awkward goodbye. She hadn't known how to leave it, really. Once Jen had discovered that she was Charles's daughter, rather than his lover (God, that didn't even bear thinking about, although it had seemed quite funny later on, and Kara thought it was hysterical. 'I've always had a bit of a crush on your dad, actually,' she had said, and Cass had held up her hand: 'Enough') it had been clear she had no idea what to do next, what she should say. It had been obvious that her instinct was to protect her family, the real family, and who could blame her? Cass had been irritated, though. Pushed to one side and made to stand in the wings, again.

She had offered Jen a lift back to Brighton station. It had been pissing down, after all, and it would have seemed heartless not to. Jen had refused, though. Eager to get away and process the new information she had discovered, no doubt. Eager to put some distance between them. She had asked Cass to direct her to a bus stop, and the last Cass had seen of her she'd been slogging along the road leaning into the almost horizontal rain. Cass had at least managed to persuade her to accept an old umbrella she had in the boot of her car, and Jen had clutched it close to her head in an attempt to stop it blowing inside out. She had waved as Cass drove off.

It was a shame, really. She had seemed like a nice enough woman, and Cass could do with having a few more friends who knew about her situation. Kara was great – they had known each other since forever, since secondary school, and Kara didn't just know about Charles, she had met him several times at the house in Iver Heath – but she could be hard work. And sometimes Cass just felt like offloading all her frustrations and resentments without having to play twenty questions. Especially after she and her dad had had one of their fights.

They were always rowing. Usually initiated by her. Cass knew, deep down, that what she was doing was pushing him as far as she could to see if – when – he would reject her completely. It was classic insecure behaviour. Make that classic insecure adolescent behaviour; she had just never managed to outgrow that stage.

She adored her dad. Both adored and hated him. He had created a life for her and her mum that could never have had a happy ending. Of course, her mum had been as much to blame. What had she been thinking, taking up with another woman's husband? In Barbara's mind it had been some kind of all-consuming romantic impulse she had been powerless to ignore. To Cass it had always seemed a bit sad, a bit tacky. Not to mention deluded. They were always destined to be the poor relations.

When she got to the end of her story, Kara reached out across the table and took her hand.

'He's got a lot to answer for, your dad.'

Cass smiled at her. She knew that, for all her faults, Kara completely got it, completely understood her anger and sadness and confusion, without her having to spell it out. There was a lot to be said for a shared history, and Kara was the closest thing to a sister she had ever had. The others, Poppy and Jessie, didn't count.

She had been thinking about what Jen had said about her own father. Was it worse to have grown up not knowing your father at all from the age of eight, because he hadn't cared enough to keep in touch? Or to grow up knowing your dad cared about you, but not being able to claim him as your own? It was a toss-up.

'Let's not talk about him any more. I'll get another round.'

Jen could barely take it in. On the way home, she had stared out of the window at the passing countryside and tried to get things straight in her head. Was Cass being Charles's daughter better or worse than her being his mistress? On the one hand, it was a relief to know that Charles wasn't sneaking out to have sex with a woman young enough to be his daughter. On the other hand, the woman young enough to be his daughter – the woman she had thought he was sneaking off to have sex with – *was* his daughter. A mistress could be got rid of. A daughter, Jen assumed, was for life.

And a woman who was Charles's daughter was also Jason, Poppy and Jessie's sister, like it or not. Nothing could change that now.

And even if Charles wasn't cheating on Amelia now, he had spent sixteen years doing so. Cass's mother hadn't just been a passing fling that he may have regretted immediately. She had held as significant a role in his life as his wife had. Well, almost. He must have loved her, anyway. Moved beyond the sex to the companionship and comfort of a real relationship. As betrayals went, it was about as bad as it got.

But the point was that nothing could change it now. Charles had another daughter. Whatever Jen did or didn't do couldn't make that fact go away.

'Margaret from work's just found out she has a half-brother from her dad's first marriage,' Jen said to Jason, trying to sound gossipy rather than giving the information any gravitas.

She wanted to test the water, check that she was doing the right thing if she decided to keep Charles's secret to herself. OK, so the scenario she was positing wasn't quite the same but the key issues were.

She knew that if she had more family somewhere herself, however remote or unconventional, she wouldn't want to be kept from them. Jason had numbers on his side, though, enough to go around. Hopefully, that might make a difference.

'Really?' Jason said, taking his eyes off the TV for a moment to look at her.

They were settled down in front of *Autumnwatch*, glasses of wine in hand, dinner cleared away.

She nodded, trying her hardest to look as if she was just telling him an interesting snippet from work. 'She's trying to decide whether to track him down, or not.'

'Why?'

'What do you mean, why? Because he's her brother.'

'Well, he's not really, is he? I mean, they share a bit of DNA but that's about it.'

This took Jen by surprise. Jason was so big on family that she'd expected an entirely different response. 'But, you'd be curious, wouldn't you? I think I would.'

'Maybe to see what they looked like, but that would be about it. I mean, if he was her full brother who got adopted, then, yes, maybe, but a half . . . I don't know. It's not that big a deal, I don't think.'

Jen had thought about it, thought about nothing else, it seemed, since her meeting with Cass. She didn't agree – she would have been happy to grasp on to anyone who was a half, a quarter, anything. But then she didn't even have a cousin to speak of, so she would probably have laid claim to a monkey in a suit if someone had told her it had agreed to be her family. Hearing him say this definitely made her decision less burdensome, though.

'I think I'd want to,' she said.

She needed to make sure Jason was adamant. No room for maybes.

'That's because it's different for you,' he said, stretching a hand over and patting her leg.

She felt a little as if he was treating her like the family dog, or even a horse.

'Miss Only-Child-Of-Only-Children-Of-Only-Children.' He smiled at her, so she knew he was teasing.

'Probably.'

Luckily, Cass had expressed no interest in hooking up with her second family. If Jason didn't think he would have any motivation to meet a half-brother or -sister either, then she didn't feel as if she was depriving him by not telling him his father had had a child with his bit on the side. All that would achieve would be to break up both his family and his heart. OK, panic over. She knew what she had to do.

She had opened a can of worms but now she was closing it again. Quickly, before any of them escaped. Sealing the lid, nailing it down, hiding it under the bed.

22

It was amazing how once you decided to act as if something had never happened, you could almost make yourself believe it was true. Apart from still feeling deeply uneasy (not to mention queasy) in Charles's presence, Jen found she could function in a way that pretty much passed for normal. If enough time went by, she felt as if she might even forget about it altogether. It would become nothing more than a bizarre but vivid dream – or maybe more of a nightmare.

She was hoping it would be like a stain on the carpet, gradually receding as the months went on, just a residual shadow left that she would bury at the back of her mind and forget. It was worth a try. She tried to ignore the fact that there was a mark on their living-room rug from when she had spilled red wine on it about ten years ago. Still as vivid and bloody as the day it had happened.

They were slobbing around at home one Saturday afternoon a couple of weeks later, just the two of them, Jen and Jason, pyjamas still on, knowing they should go out and do something, but unable to face the ice and slush that had overtaken the streets, when Jen's mobile rang. She picked it up and looked to see who was calling, expecting to see Poppy's number, or Amelia's. Neither of them ever called on the house phone, these days. When she saw the name, she almost dropped it again.

Cass R.

She hit decline, switched the phone to silent in case it rang again.

'Who was that?' Jason looked up from his paper, only half interested.

'Jessie. I can't face another conversation about cracked nipples.'

'You should have put her on to me. I'm an expert.'

Jessie was proving to be a somewhat neurotic first-time mother, unsurprisingly, and had taken to calling Jen or Poppy at all hours of the day and night and opening the conversation with such gems as, 'My nipples are literally falling off, I mean, literally. I'm not joking,' and, 'Her poop is coming out green. It's like pond water. Should I call the doctor?'

One time, Jason had answered and, before he could even say hello, Jessie had declared, 'Martin wants to have sex with me already, but I told him it looks like roadkill down there at the moment. I don't want him anywhere near it.'

Jason had calmly replied, 'I agree. I imagine it's ghastly,' and handed the phone over to Jen, saying, 'I think she wants you.'

She tried to imagine why Cass might be phoning. She knew Cass had her number – Jen had called her back about the Roedean Crescent house, after all, and she had given Jen her own mobile number at the same time, just in case either of them was running late.

And, to Jen's shame, she had drunk texted her, the night after she got back from Brighton. She and Jason had shared a bottle of wine when they got home from work, and Jen had started to feel more and more righteously indignant on Cass's behalf, despite her promise to herself to bury the news. She had tried to imagine Jason acknowledging Simone as his daughter, but not Emily. Showing one of them off – like Charles had always loved to do with Poppy and Jessie – and refusing the other's pleas for recognition.

She remembered Jessie's wedding to Martin and the way Charles had beamed on his walk up the aisle, pride dripping off him like sweat. And that made her think about how, when she had married Jason and had had no male relative to give her away (it had been out of the question that she would tell Rory she was getting married – even if she had known where to send the invitation – let alone invite him to play a part in the ceremony), Charles had stepped in willingly, and Jen had felt so proud on his arm. In his speech he had said that the cliché about gaining a daughter had never been more true. He said it as if he was thrilled to be increasing his flock. No hint that in a field outside, somewhere, a black sheep had been shivering in the cold, waiting hopefully for twenty-five years to be invited in.

When Jason had gone out to the kitchen to pour them both another glass, Jen had grabbed her phone and texted:

Jessie had a baby girl a couple of weeks ago by the way. Violet. Your half niece! I forgot to tell you but I thought you should know. Jen

As soon as she had sent it, she'd known that she shouldn't have. She had turned her phone off and hidden

163

it under a cushion. In the morning, when she'd switched it on again, having completely forgotten her misdemeanour, there was a terse message from Cass:

Obviously I won't be sending a card.

Jen had deleted both texts – her own and Cass's – and tried to forget it had ever happened.

Now she surreptitiously turned her mobile over, in case it lit up to tell her there was a message or, God forbid, a text that Jason might catch sight of.

'Let's do something.' She stood up, purposefully.

'Too miserable out,' Jason said.

'Well, then, let's watch something. We can't sit here doing nothing all day.'

'*Casablanca*? *Now, Voyager*? *Angels with Dirty Faces*?' Jason rattled off their rainy-afternoon favourites, each of which they had seen at least twenty times before.

'You choose. I'm going to make some tea.' She slipped her phone into the pocket of her oversize cardigan. In the kitchen, once she knew Jason was occupied with hunting through the DVD shelves, she dug it out. Two missed calls. Cass must have phoned straight back. No messages.

She thought about sending a text, saying 'What do you want?' but she worried it might sound confrontational and, anyway, she couldn't risk getting into a text exchange – not with Jason around. The only thing to do was to switch her mobile off. There was no way Cass had her home number. She never gave it to anyone these days, and they had always been ex-directory, ever since some of Jason's students had got hold of it and started calling at two or three in the morning, drunk and thinking they were being hilarious. Actually, Jen had thought she was pretty hilarious herself when she'd taken the phone out of his hand one night and told them to go fuck themselves.

She would have to worry about Cass later.

Two hours on, dabbing at her eyes with a tissue, although her mind had only been half on the thwarted romance of Bette Davis and Paul Henreid, she sneaked up to the bathroom, switched on her mobile again and it immediately began to buzz with missed calls and then messages.

She listened to the first one. Cass's voice, familiar even after such a short acquaintance, sounded strained. The connection was bad and Jen had to struggle to pick up all the words. She played it again.

'Hi, Jen. I am so, so sorry to be calling you but I don't know what else to do. My mum's had a car accident. She's in hospital. She's in a bit of a bad way and I need to let Dad know, but he's not answering his phone because he's obviously with Amelia. I hate to involve you, but could you just call him? He'll answer, if it's you. Just tell him she's in King's.'

She left the name of the ward and then said something that sounded like she was there now.

Jen sat on the edge of the bath and tried to think what to do. There was no point even listening to the other messages. She knew exactly what they would be. Cass had sounded desperate. Her mother was hurt, and she needed her father. Fuck. But Jen really didn't want to be the one to break it to Charles. Telling him this news would let him know that she knew the whole story, that she and Cass had been in contact, that his cover was blown. And she couldn't risk sending him a text, in case Amelia happened to read it. What kind of a person would she be if she ignored Cass's plea, though? And what if Cass got so desperate that she stopped being careful, stopped worrying about whether Amelia might see something she shouldn't.

She had no choice. She sent Cass a message that simply said:

I'll call Amelia on the landline at 5 and keep her occupied so u can get Charles on his mobile then. OK?

A few seconds later, she got a reply:

OK. Thanks.

Half an hour later, she phoned the Twickenham house. Thankfully, Amelia answered so she didn't even have to try to make polite conversation with Charles before he handed her over. Her mother-in-law chatted happily about their Christmas shopping plans. Jen assumed that Charles was in the other room, being told the bad news. She had no way of knowing.

23

Poppy had insisted that Jen meet her for lunch, and because Jen didn't know how to refuse without alerting her sister-in-law to the fact that something was wrong, she had accepted. And, besides, she missed her. She had heard nothing more from Cass since her mother's accident, and she had convinced herself that it had been a one-off, an emergency, a never-to-be-repeated panic response. Now she had to work at getting her life back to normal. Her genius plan on this occasion was to let Poppy do the talking and to provide supportive and interested asides, while offering up nothing about what was going on in her own world.

The advertising agency where Poppy worked three days a week as an account manager (having persuaded them she could do her full-time job just as well part time when she had become pregnant with Maisie, she now lived in fear of proving herself wrong) had recently introduced an open-plan environment. The staff were meant to hot-desk, but every one of them had immediately chosen their favourite spot and stuck to it, piling it high with files and trinkets that screamed, 'This desk is mine, keep away!' The proximity of your workmates was, Poppy had told Jen at the time, supposed to encourage creativity and the sharing of ideas but, in actual fact, all it encouraged was resentment and irritation. Did X really have to talk so loudly on the phone? Was it essential for Y to smack her lips after every sip of coffee? Did Z's wife deliberately give him tinned-salmon sandwiches every day so that the whole office smelled like cat food? Apparently so. Consequently, she liked to get out at lunchtime whenever she could find the excuse.

It was, it had suddenly struck Jen on the walk over, Rory's birthday. Every year around this time, the date would pop into her head uninvited. It was something to do with the trees changing colour, the leaves falling off, the days getting shorter. Maybe it was just the particular smell of autumn? Bonfires and fireworks and damp dogs. Sometimes it didn't hit her until a week later, but she never escaped the memory completely. He would be eighty. Assuming he was still alive. The thought made her feel panicky. Look at Cass's mother. Anything could happen. Would Rory have left instructions anywhere, a list of people to contact, if anything happened to him? She doubted it.

Poppy and Jen had a favourite bench in Soho Square where they would find each other whenever they arranged to meet up. Today, someone else was already sitting there, and Jen smiled as she saw her sister-in-law, recognizable from a mile away with her bright red coat and her pink-streaked brown hair, give them a dirty look as she passed.

Poppy had another date lined up, she told Jen, when they had settled themselves on an empty seat.

'This one's called Benji –'

'Benji? I hate that name. It sounds so wet. Like a character on kids' TV,' Jen interrupted before she could stop herself.

Poppy sighed. 'I am not going to dismiss him because he has a wet name. If we end up getting married and living happily ever after, you can ask if you can call him something else. OK?'

'Fair enough.'

'He's forty-four, divorced, works in IT. One kid that he has at the weekends.'

'Are they all divorced with kids?'

'Pretty much.'

'God, how depressing.'

'Well, unless I start trying to date twenty-year-olds, I just have to accept that most of them are going to have baggage,' Poppy said irritably. 'And, besides, *I'm* a single parent. What's the difference?'

'Same rules?'

'Exactly the same.'

'OK, well, let's hope this one is brave enough to show up.'

They both took a bite out of their sandwiches. Jen prayed that Poppy would have some other news, something else to talk about. She dredged around in the depths of her brain for something anodyne to bring up, some neutral ground that wouldn't involve family, and emerged with nothing.

'I'm worried about Dad,' Poppy suddenly said, and Jen felt her head whip round like the girl in *The Exorcist* before she could stop herself.

'Why? Has something happened?'

'Have you seen him in the last few days?'

Jen shook her head.

Poppy wasn't waiting for an answer. 'No, you haven't, have you? He just seems a bit preoccupied.'

Phew. It was all just a hunch of Poppy's, then. Charles hadn't started talking in tongues or smiting his chest and saying he needed to unburden himself of a terrible secret.

'Maybe he's worried about something at the business and he doesn't want Amelia to worry with him?'

'No. I think he'd tell the rest of us either way. I was at home the other day and his phone rang and he looked like he was going to have a heart attack.'

'I think you're imagining that,' Jen said. She didn't know what else she could say. There was no doubt in her mind that whatever was happening with Charles had to do with Cass's mum. Maybe the prognosis was bad.

'He went out of the room before he answered it. I mean, what's a seventy-three-year-old man doing with a mobile, anyway?'

Jen could have offered up a lot of reasons, actually. Instead, she shrugged non-committally. 'I guess he thinks he needs it.'

'And then, when he came back in, I asked him who it was and he said Uncle Jamie, but he looked awful, really bad.'

'Well, your Uncle Jamie is quite boring.'

Rather than crinkling with a smile, Poppy's eyes looked like they were filling up with tears, a very un-Poppy-like phenomenon. 'I think he's ill, and he doesn't want anyone to know.'

Oh God. 'No. I can't believe that. Look at him. He's never looked better.'

'Not all illnesses make you look bad, Jen.'

'I can't believe he'd keep something like that from Amelia. Or you and Jason, for that matter.'

Poppy sniffed dramatically. 'What if there's something really wrong, and they've told him there's no hope, so he thinks why burden us all with that?'

Jen tried to fake a laugh. 'Have you been spending too much time with Jessie?'

She was rewarded with a watery smile. 'You think I'm overreacting?'

'Massively.'

'Maybe. But when you see him next, will you just ask him if he's OK? See if you think there's something not right?'

Jen hated that she couldn't put Poppy's mind at rest. Reassure her that her father was in great shape. Physically, at least. She could no longer vouch for his mind. 'Of course.'

'I can't bear that thought – that they're getting older and, inevitably, something will happen to one of them, one of these days.'

Jen rubbed Poppy's upper arm. 'I know. But not for a long time yet, hopefully.'

'I'm being stupid, right?'

'It wouldn't be the first time,' Jen said, laughing.

On the way back to the hotel, she stopped by Ryman's and bought a birthday card. A generic-looking watercolour of a bunch of flowers. Blank inside.

Back on reception, she agonized about what to write. In the end she decided that 'Happy Birthday from your daughter Jen' would suffice. She had added the 'your daughter' bit at the last minute, just in case. It would do. It would let him know she was thinking about him. Despite the fact that she had thrown all his letters away, she could remember the address. If he still lived there. If he still lived anywhere.

She dug a stamp out of her wallet and shoved the card into the retro 1950s postbox that was mounted on the wall by reception. One of the doormen usually emptied it every afternoon and walked round to the post office with whatever was inside. If she changed her mind, she could always get it back from them later.

When her mobile rang, late in the day, and there was Cass's number again, she told herself not to answer. But she couldn't help herself. Before she really knew what she was doing, she had pressed the 'accept' button and moved out to the back room, signalling to Neil that she would only be a moment.

'Hello?'

'Jen? It's Cass. Richards.'

'I know. Hi.' She waited to hear what Cass had to say. She assumed there must be a reason for the call, some other message Cass needed to get to Charles for some reason.

'I just called to say thanks, really. For helping me get hold of Dad the other day.'

There it was again, that 'Dad' word that sounded so alien in reference to Charles.

'I know it must have been awkward for you. He said Amelia was standing right there when I phoned, talking on the landline in the living room. And Poppy was there too, did you know that? He had to pretend I was some relation of his. Well . . .' she laughed, 'I am, I suppose, but you know what I mean.'

'Right.'

For some reason, this made Jen feel even more uncomfortable, the idea of Charles confiding in Cass about getting one over on Amelia and Poppy. It wasn't playing fair. She decided to steer the conversation back to safer ground.

'How is your mum?'

Cass filled her in with the latest details – the prognosis was looking better than they'd feared at first. Her mother was making progress, on a slow but steady road to recovery. Jen listened, chipping in occasionally when it seemed appropriate.

'Cass,' she said, when Cass had finished her update. 'Why did you call me?'

'I just thought you'd like to know how things were,' Cass said. 'I don't know, really, I just felt like I should.'

'I'm glad your mum's going to be OK, but I can't stay. I'm at work.'

She felt uncomfortable having this conversation. Passing the time with the sister Jason still didn't know he had.

'OK. Well, it was good talking to you,' Cass said.

'You too. Take care.' Jen ended the call, shut her phone off, stuffed it into the bottom of her bag, tried to pretend it wasn't there.

She hadn't clapped eyes on Charles since Cass would have told him the news, for which she was grateful, because while she assumed Cass had said nothing about her involvement (surely, if she had, he would have called her in a panic, begging her to keep his secret?) she actually had no way of knowing for certain.

Last weekend had been an Elaine weekend. Jen and Jason had sat in her mother's spotless living room for three hours, eating a roast off their laps, sipping tea and listening to tales of her High Wycombe neighbours. Actually, because Jen had been so relieved not to have to see Charles and Amelia, she had felt particularly well disposed towards her mum and in no hurry to get away. There was something quite soothing in the minutiae of Elaine's stories about people Jen didn't know doing things she didn't much care about.

Her mother was starting to look a bit frail, Jen had thought. Probably not to anyone else, but she had noticed how Elaine put her hand on the back of an armchair to steady herself as she went out to the kitchen to produce more biscuits. And the way she let out a little sigh as she sat down again. She was older than Amelia – she'd been thirty-seven when she had Jen, which was ancient for a first-time mother back then, and probably went some way to explaining why Jen wasn't followed by a stream of brothers and sisters.

It had taken Elaine ten years to get pregnant, she had told Jen once, and that was one of the things that had made Jen so special. She hadn't wanted to be special, she'd wanted company, and so she hadn't reacted as generously to her mother's remark as she might have. Later, she had found out that Elaine had actually been pregnant many times but that Jen had been the only one strong enough to survive to full term. She remembered feeling desperately sorry for her mum then. Elaine had told her this when Jen had first got married. Not in a scaremongering way, more because she thought Jen ought to know that it might take a while when – there had never been an 'if' – she decided to start having children herself. In the event, she had found both getting and staying pregnant easy. In fact, she had loved it, both times. She'd been lucky.

She had felt a lump appear in her throat. All her mum had ever wanted was a family, and she had ended up with Jen and no one else, just as Jen had ended up with only her. It couldn't have been any easier for Elaine than it had been for her. And then Jen had lucked out. She had found herself a whole other tribe and joined them. But she was still all Elaine had – well, her and Jason and the girls. And none of them paid her mother enough attention.

Usually, she would have been surreptitiously checking the clock, her mum's list, anything that would give her an excuse to leave.

'I fancy another cup of tea,' she'd said at about five to four, the time she ordinarily started trying to edge her way out of the front door. She'd looked at Jason hopefully.

He'd nodded. 'Why not?'

The expression on her mother's face had been worth it. Jen might as well have announced that she was staying for a week. Or moving back for good into her little bedroom that was now a dumping ground for things Elaine liked to put aside for the jumble but then had no way of ever delivering. Jen resolved to bring the car over and clear it all out for her, one of these days.

Elaine had started to ease her way out of her chair. 'Lovely,' she'd said, beaming.

'I'll make it.' Jen had jumped up. She let her mum wait

on her far too much. She always had. She thought about the way she had always hated Jessie treating Amelia as her slave.

'Well, then, I'll come and keep you company,' Elaine had said, still beaming.

By the time they'd left, about an hour later, Jen had felt a righteous glow of having done the right thing. It was that easy.

Walking along Charlotte Street on Tuesday morning, she put her head down as she passed Masterson Property, just in case it was one of those days when Charles had decided to check up on his empire. Safely past, she let out the breath she hadn't even realized she had been holding on to.

She was behind the desk, congratulating herself silently on having crossed the bridge without the troll catching her, and trying to concentrate on allocating suites for the following weekend (when two equally big stars – one an actor, one a musician – were checking in at the same time, and both their entourages had demanded they be given the best room), when a familiar voice startled her.

'Jen . . .'

She looked up, and there he was, standing right in front of her.

'Charles. What are you doing here?'

He smiled. It seemed like a genuine smile, a friendly, hopeful smile. Certainly not the smile of someone who was hoping to silence her by chopping her up into very small pieces and distributing her across the gardens of some of the most prestigious properties in Central London. 'I was walking past, so I thought I'd drop in on the off-chance you had time for a coffee. We missed you on Sunday.'

'Oh. I'm on an early, so I've already had my break.'

This was a lie. She had actually come in late. She shot a look at Neil, willing him not to contradict her, but he was absorbed in something and didn't even seem to have heard. She was thankful he was there, though, so there was no chance of her and Charles having to have any kind of heart to heart.

Charles pulled a mock sad face. 'Oh well, I guess I'll just have to wait for the weekend to catch up with my favourite daughter-in-law.'

'I'll be there,' Jen said, forcing a smile.

'It wouldn't be the same if you weren't,' Charles said, with what seemed to be a twinkle in his eyes. It was impressive, the way he could pull it off. Still be Charles without really being Charles at all. Without ever having been, come to that.

He looked tired around the edges, though. She could see why Poppy was concerned about him. There were dark rings under his eyes.

'Have a good week,' he said, waving goodbye as he went.

'My wife says your father-in-law's a fox. She keeps telling me I should ask for his autograph,' Neil said, once Charles was out of sight.

'He wouldn't mind,' she said, knowing Charles would love it. He was nowhere near famous enough for an incessant flood of autograph hunters to have made signing anything a chore, and he still got an obvious thrill from being recognized.

She knew she shouldn't, but she went out the back and got her phone out of her bag –

I hope your mum is still recovering OK.

– she texted, and then she pressed delete, quickly, before she could change her mind.

24

The corridors of King's were starting to feel like home, Cass had spent so much time there. Luckily, Masterson's was being completely cool about her having as much time off as she needed. She was keeping her hand in, anyway, huddling outside by the front doors with the smokers, phoning her clients, checking up on how things were. She had had to clarify with her dad first that he wasn't going to say anything to anyone at work about a close friend having had an accident, because that would have been a bit of a giveaway. Of course he wasn't. He had never publicly acknowledged Barbara in more than twenty-five years, so why would he start now?

He was cut up about it, though, she could tell. She had wondered in the past whether he had only stayed on friendly terms with her mum to stop her from blabbing his secret. Keep your enemies close, and all that. But, if any good had come out of what had happened, it was that she now knew that he cared. He turned up at the hospital whenever he could, even if he could only stay for a few minutes each time.

The first time she had met him outside, and he had been clutching a bunch of flowers that she had had to break to him he would have to leave in the car or chuck away before he could go in. He had pulled her to him and, despite everything that was going on, she had relaxed completely in his embrace for a few seconds. She couldn't remember the last time he had hugged her like that. Their relationship since she had become an adult – well, since he and her mum had split up – had become so spiky and testy that if he'd ever even tried to embrace her she probably would have pushed him away most of the time.

'She's doing OK,' she had said when they'd broken off.

'Thank God. I got here as soon as I could.'

'Sorry I had to ring you. I didn't know what else to do.'

'Don't be silly, sweetheart. It was the right thing, of course it was. Apart from anything else, you shouldn't have to be going through this on your own.'

He'd reminded her so much of the dad he'd been when she was growing up then. Strong and kind. Able to make her feel safe and protected. The thought that she might lose her mum – even though that had dissipated as soon as she'd got to the hospital and seen the consultant, who had assured her that Barbara's injuries, while bad, weren't life threatening – had terrified her. Her two aunts – her mother's sisters – had made it clear to Barbara long ago that they disapproved of her relationship with a man who was not only a husband already but a father too. They had refused to visit while she lived in the house he paid for. Barbara, in turn, had announced she wouldn't go to see them until they would accept her partner. The stalemate had meant that their contact had gradually dwindled, their closeness fractured. It had never recovered. Even when Barbara and Charles had separated, she had steadfastly refused to get back in touch. They had shown their true colours. Consequently, Cass had never even met them.

Beyond the aunts and their children – whose names she

only knew through other, more distant relations with whom Barbara still exchanged Christmas cards – there was only her dad.

He'd followed her through the labyrinthine sour-smelling corridors to the side ward where her mum was already recovering from the first of what would turn out to be several operations. And then he'd sat there and held her hand while they'd waited for Barbara to wake up.

It didn't feel like the kind of thing you ought to admit to, but it had brought them closer.

Some of the nursing staff had been a bit twittery and overexcited when they'd recognized him. Not that they were unprofessional enough to let it show; you could just see it in their eyes. Charles had retained sufficient presence of mind to introduce himself as Cass's godfather, an old and dear family friend, and they had taken him on face value, because why wouldn't they? That had hurt a bit. She understood why he had had to, of course, but she couldn't help wishing it hadn't come so naturally.

Still, she had told herself, he was there. That was really all that mattered.

Now her mum was most definitely on the road to recovery. She would have to stay in hospital for a while yet. There were still more operations to come, with pins and rods and God knows what else. But she was not in danger. The accident had made Cass think, though. Anything could happen. You could lose your family in a moment. A flash. One day they were there, and then nothing. Gone.

She had called Jen on instinct. She'd felt she had a right to know what was happening, that she might be curious or worried. Or maybe just eager to hear that the drama was over, that Charles's attention could refocus on his real family. She'd got the impression Jen had been keen to get off the phone, though. She had probably thought she'd never hear from her again. Swept her back under the carpet where she belonged.

Neil was checking the rooms list. Jen watched his finger move slowly down the printout, stopping on every line, hovering for a moment and then beginning its agonizingly arduous journey southwards again. It was like this every time. A job that should have been a cursory glance at a computer screen to check the status of guests coming and going became a full-blown production in his hands. She watched, fascinated. She could never work out whether he was doing it to waste time – which really wasn't Neil's style – or just because he liked to be thorough. Either way, she had to fight the urge to rip the piece of paper from his hands and throw it in the bin.

'Hold 401 and 403 for the Clancys,' she said, referring to a family of parents and two children who wanted rooms next to each other, if possible.

'I'm just checking it.'

'I've gone through the list. It's fine.'

The finger was still poised, hovering. 'I want to have a back-up plan.'

'Neil, the hotel's half empty tonight. There's not going to be a run on double rooms before they get here.'

'You never know,' Neil said. Jen knew that, one day, Neil's over-attention to detail would probably see him save the day in some kind of emergency. He would be hailed a hero and complimented for his meticulous work ethic. Meanwhile, the rest of the reception staff would have developed twitches.

The phone rang and she left him to it, thankful for the diversion.

'Fitzrovia Hotel.'

'Ah,' a voice she recognized said. 'Is that Ms Jennifer Masterson or Ms Judy Sampson?'

Jen felt her mood lift a little. She glanced in one of the mirrored tiles behind reception and gave herself a quick once-over, patting down a rogue spiral of hair without even realizing she was doing it.

'It's Jen . . . nifer.'

The hotel insisted on full names on all the staff name badges, so Jen had had to accept that any of the guests who took the trouble to learn her name would use the hated long version.

'Morning, Mr Hoskins, how are you today?'

'I'm well. And it's Sean. I hate Mr Hoskins. That was the name of my PE teacher and, well, you know . . . there have been years of therapy, that's all I'm saying.'

Jen laughed. 'Well, in that case, it's Jen. I hate Jennifer. No reason. I just do.'

'Good, I'm glad we got that sorted. How are you? How's the faithless father-in-law?'

Jen shot a glance at Neil. There was no way he could hear Sean's end of the conversation.

'Oh, that,' she said, as lightly as she could. 'That's got even weirder, actually.'

'You're kidding? What? Prostitutes? Animals? Oh, wait, I know . . . ladyboys?'

'None of the above.'

'Don't tell me . . . vegetables? Or kitchen utensils?'

'Not so far as I know. Now, what can I do for you?'

She knew she really shouldn't have this conversation now. Not while Neil was right beside her.

'I want to book in for a few days. Hold on, I've got the dates . . .'

When she got off the phone, Neil was still painstakingly studying the rooms list.

'I'm putting Sean Hoskins in room 328 from next Sunday,' she said, just to wind Neil up.

The only reason she answered the phone when it rang this time was because she was distracted. She was pottering happily around the kitchen, fixing dinner. She was looking forward to seeing Sean again, she had realized on the way home. It was actually quite cathartic to be able to make light of her situation with someone, even if he didn't know the half of it. Just to exchange an uncomplicated bit of chat with no hidden subtext or mines to avoid.

Jason had taken a glass of wine upstairs with him to have a bath. Jen could hear the radio on up there. Soon he would start singing along to Absolute 80s. She found the same station. Sang along herself, even though she had a voice that she had always thought sounded like an ailing walrus.

She picked up her mobile and answered without even checking to see who was there.

'Hello.'

'Hi, Jen.'

She recognized the voice immediately. Took the phone away from her ear to check the name. Cass.

Cass sounded relaxed. 'How are you?'

Jen turned the radio down, lowered her voice, even though she could still hear music coming from the bathroom.

'Um . . . I'm fine. How are you? Is your mum still OK?'

'Is this a good time? Can you talk?'

For some reason, this question made Jen nervous. 'Not really. Well, for a minute . . . Jason's upstairs.'

'She's still progressing. One step at a time and all that shit. Literally, in her case, actually.'

'Right . . . thank goodness . . .' She didn't know what else she was expected to say, so she just waited.

'It's taken its toll on Dad, though, don't you think? He's aged.'

She didn't have time for this. 'I think Jason's going to be down in a minute –'

'Of course. Sorry. He's why I'm phoning, actually. Him and Poppy and Jessie.'

Jen put her hand on the table to steady herself. Somehow, she knew she wasn't going to like what came next.

'Mum being so ill has made me realize how on my own I am. If anything happens to her . . . well, you know what that feels like. And what if it was Dad who got sick? I wouldn't even know. He could be dying, and no one would tell me.'

'I'd contact you. Of course I would,' Jen said weakly.

Cass ignored her. 'And so I've made a decision. I need to get to know my family. I have three half-siblings. I think I want to . . . I've got a right to meet them.'

Jen felt her face go hot. She sat down. 'No, Cass . . . I don't think that's a good idea.'

'Why? Because it might upset Amelia? That's why I'm talking to you. She wouldn't even have to find out. You could tell the three of them about me, and we'll take it from there.'

'No way. If you want to be a part of Charles's family, then talk to Charles. I don't think anyone's going to thank me for getting involved.'

'You know he'll never say yes. He'll just be terrified his world is going to come crumbling down. And, besides, you involved yourself, remember? I'm not the one who made contact. I'm not the one who texted after we met.'

Jen breathed in deeply to try to calm herself. It didn't really work. 'I just wanted to know what Charles was up to.'

'Which was also nothing to do with you. Either you're a part of their family or you're not, Jen. Either you're involved or you're not, already. You can't have it both ways.'

'And what about your dad? How's he going to feel, if you break up his family?'

'Like I said, I won't. Not if we handle it properly. Not if you explain to Jason –'

'You don't think he'd go straight to Charles and demand to know the truth?'

'He won't need to know it's come from me. You could tell him you'd found out some other way . . .'

Jen could hear Jason stomping around upstairs. He'd be down in a few minutes, smelling of limes and basil.

'You know where they are. If you want to meet them, I can't stop you.'

'But you can pave the way. Please, Jen, think about it. Would it be better for Jason for me just to jump out from behind a tree, shouting, "Surprise, I'm your little sister!" or for you to break the idea to him gently?'

'I can't talk about this now.'

'OK. I'm not trying to make trouble. I just need a family. Same as you.'

Jason was thundering down the stairs, whistling to himself.

'I have to go. I'll call you.'

'Thank y—' Cass started to say, but Jen cut her off.

By the time Jason breezed into the kitchen, Jen was chopping tomatoes to make a pasta sauce. She tried not to let him notice that her hands were shaking.

'I think I should go and see Mum again on Sunday,' Jen said later, when she and Jason were settled on the sofa, glasses of wine in hand.

'We went last week,' he said, more bemused than anything.

Jen rarely, if ever, suggested spending any more time with her mum than she had to. A combination of her feeling as if she really ought to make more of an effort, and the fact that Riverdale no longer felt like home, had shifted her perspective, though.

'I know,' she said, on the defensive already. 'But we went to Charles and Amelia's five weekends in a row before that.'

'I thought you wanted to. You usually do.'

'It's not about what I prefer. I just feel like Mum's getting older suddenly and I should do my duty, that's all.'

'Let's go the following weekend, then. I've told them we'll be there now. Jessie and Martin might be coming.'

'You should have checked with me first. I've told my mum we'll go already.'

This was yet another lie – she was getting adept at this, a skill she had never wanted to acquire. Something to put on her CV, maybe, she thought, if she ever decided on her dream job – 'Special skills: fibbing and bullshitting' – but suddenly it annoyed her that Jason had just agreed for them both to spend Sunday at his parents' without consulting her. Obviously, this hadn't bothered her in the slightest for the past twenty years, but she had decided to take offence now.

'Right . . .' Jason said slowly.

For some reason, this irritated Jen beyond belief. Her light mood of an hour ago completely evaporated.

'What? Right, what?'

'Nothing. I'm just surprised.'

'I just decided it wasn't fair, that's all. We spend five weekends out of six with your parents.'

'Because that's what you've always wanted . . .'

His weary patience was starting to drive her crazy. She knew the way it would go. Jason would acquiesce to her demands, but with a kind of quiet resentment that he would deny if questioned. They would be a little bit touchy with each other for a day or so, but then everything would be back to normal – Jen and Jason, so grown up and committed that they almost never fought. She used to think this was a good thing, for some reason. A sign of their compatibility. They had been parents for twenty of their twenty-two years together. They had put the girls first, had a policy never to argue in front of them. It had worked so well that she was starting to wonder if, perhaps, they had forgotten how to fight at all.

'Forget about it. I'll go on my own.'

'What'll I tell Mum and Dad?'

'That I've gone to see my own mother. What's the big deal?'

'Couldn't you go to Elaine's on Saturday? And then we can still do mine on Sunday.'

'I'm not going to spend both of my two precious days off doing family stuff. There's no way. I'm going to my mother's on Sunday, and you can either come with me or not. It's up to you.'

Jason sighed. 'OK. I'll ring Dad.'

The relief was immense, but even as she was celebrating her victory, she was feeling irritated that he had given in so easily. She found herself thinking, Stand up for yourself. If you think I'm in the wrong, then fight back. What's the worst that can happen?

They spent the evening watching TV in silence. Jen wanted to break it, wanted to tell Jason what was going on in her life – the reasons why she couldn't face going to Twickenham this weekend, or any other – but she couldn't, and she didn't know what else to say.

At one point, she snapped at him when he changed channels without warning.

'Fuck's sake, I was watching that.'

'Sorry. You only had to say.'

'I just did, didn't I?'

She sat there fuming for a moment, and then realized

that the last thing she should be doing was taking out her anger and frustration about Cass on Jason.

'Sorry,' she said. 'For biting your head off. Watch what you want.'

'It's fine,' he said, turning back to the original channel and picking up the paper. 'There's nothing on, anyway.'

She kept waking up in a cold sweat. For a foggy moment she would wonder what was wrong, and then Cass's voice would come crashing into her sharpening consciousness: 'I've got a right to meet them.' Jen would look over at Jason, always sleeping peacefully, face down like a toddler, and wonder what she had started.

If she tried to think about it dispassionately, from the point of view of someone not connected to the family, she could easily understand Cass's thinking. As Cass had pointed out herself, she was only a few years older than Simone. If Jen put herself in Cass's position, which wasn't that much of a stretch, it wasn't hard to see how scary the idea of being all alone in the world might be. She had avoided that path by grafting herself on to the Mastersons. Why shouldn't Cass who, after all, had a much more legitimate claim – to some of them, at least – than Jen, want to do the same?

But then she would always come back to the reality. What Cass thought might improve her life – the jury was totally out on this, by the way; Jen had no reason to believe that Jason, Poppy or Jessie would want to welcome her into the family, in fact, quite the opposite – would potentially ruin five others. Six, if she included herself, because she would undoubtedly get caught up in the fallout. Not

Cass's fault, admittedly. Jen knew that all the blame lay squarely with Charles. And with Cass's mum, obviously. But that didn't make it OK. One wrong move wouldn't cancel out the other.

26

Emily was home from college for the first time since she had left at the end of September. Jen had been so excited to see her, so pleased and relieved to have another presence in the house, that she had driven across London to meet her from the train, and had embarrassed her daughter by jumping up and down and waving when she spotted her walking along the platform. Actually, the girl she had waved at had looked something like one of her daughters, but not quite. Emily had cut her long red hair to shoulder length, added a heavy fringe that almost covered her eyes, and dyed the whole thing black with a few electric-blue streaks.

'Wow,' Jen said, as she held her at arm's length.

'I think that's parent speak for, "What the hell have you done to yourself?"'

'You look great,' Jen said, not really convinced. 'Maybe I should do mine too.'

'Don't be stupid, Mum,' Emily said. 'You'd look ridiculous.'

'You've got skinny,' Jen said as she hugged her daughter tightly, trying to keep the judgement out of her voice. 'There's nothing of you.'

'Mum –' Emily protested.

Jen interrupted. 'I'm not telling you off. I'm just warning you I'm going to be forcing food on you all weekend, that's all.'

'Great. I'd be disappointed if you didn't.'

'I've had mothering withdrawal symptoms. You're going to have to take the full brunt of my unfulfilled maternal instincts.'

Emily laughed. 'Christ. I'm calling Simone and telling her to get down here quick.'

Jen leaned over, buried her face in her daughter's hair. 'I am so glad you're here.'

With Emily there, the house seemed like a home again. Jen and Jason back to doing what they did best: being devoted parents, a happy couple, a family. It felt as if the whole building breathed a sigh and relaxed. The atmosphere lightened up, as if someone had added a touch of helium into the mix.

Although Jen was grateful, she tried not to analyse too much. Tried not to acknowledge that something couldn't be right if she and Jason could only be themselves when one of their daughters was present. Tried to enjoy the weekend and not dwell on life beyond it.

Emily prattled on, oblivious to any underlying tensions, while Jen prepared pasta and pesto, and chocolate mousse, and laid them all out for her daughter to devour. She and Jason watched fondly, as gripped as a pair of feeders by the sight of their offspring enjoying her food.

'So Josie and I have decided we're going to share a flat next year,' Emily said.

Jen resisted the temptation to say, 'Which one is Josie again?' She found it hard to keep up with Emily's fluid social life.

'And we're trying to decide which of the other girls to

ask if they want to come in with us. We need five, really, to get somewhere we can afford.'

'Do you really need to start looking yet? You've only been there five minutes,' Jen said, spooning more cheese on to Emily's meal.

Emily pushed her hand away. 'God, Mum, that's enough. Yes, totally. Everyone's obsessed already, and all the good places get reserved by Easter. If you miss the ones that go through the uni accommodation office, you have to just look randomly, and everyone says you get ripped off that way.'

'What if you and Josie fall out before you move in? I mean, it's months away.'

'As if,' Emily said, conveniently forgetting that her back catalogue of friendships read like a history of the Roman Empire complete with fallings out and betrayals and secret pacts. Luckily, without the beheadings so far – although she was still young.

'How's the course?' Jason asked.

To his delight Emily had chosen to study drama, and he loved to compare his own teaching methods with those of her tutors.

'Awesome. We're doing lots of physical stuff at the moment. I think they're trying to knock everyone into shape before we start stage fighting after Christmas. I'm knackered, to be honest.'

Once she had finished eating, and was looking like she had already gained a few pounds, Emily announced that she was going out. Her childhood best friend, Catriona, had opted not to go to college and still lived with her parents round the corner. It was her birthday and the reason Emily had made the effort to clear her overstuffed Leeds social life and travel home (only calling to announce her intention a few hours before she had arrived). Jen had practically knelt down and prayed her thank yous on the spot. It hadn't occurred to Emily that her parents might have plans of their own. Which, of course, they didn't.

Although Jen was tempted to ground her now – like she used to do when Emily was thirteen – so loath was she to break up the party, she kissed her daughter on the forehead and told her to make sure she handed over her dirty washing before she left.

'Do you want me to pick you up later?' Jason asked, clearly keen to resume the chauffeur role he had complained about for years.

'No. Thank you. I don't know what time I'll want to leave.'

'Well, call me if you change your mind. And promise you'll get a taxi if it's late. No walking. I'll pay you back.'

Emily rolled her eyes. 'Thanks, Dad.'

'She's got skinny,' he said to Jen, once the front door had closed.

Jen laughed. 'That's what I said. I think students are contractually obliged to live on a couple of bowls of cereal and a few vodka shots a day, though.'

'She looks more like Jessie every minute, don't you think?'

'So long as she only inherits her looks, and not too much of the other stuff.'

He snorted. 'God help us.'

Without asking, he opened a bottle of white wine and

handed her a glass. Jen felt as if she had gone back in time, back to before the cracks started to appear. Even without Emily actually being there, the house felt different. Just knowing their daughter would be back later had completely changed the dynamic between her and Jason for the better. They finished the wine, chatted about Emily and how happy she seemed and how great it was that she loved her course, called Simone and passed the phone back and forth between them, tripping over each other's sentences, and stayed up later than they had in a long time, both secretly hoping Emily would come home early and fill the room with her presence.

Eventually, they gave in to tiredness and went up to bed. Jen felt closer to Jason than she had in weeks. They would get through this, somehow. She didn't quite know how, if she was being honest. The whole situation had got so complicated, the secrets too big, the deceptions already too hard to explain. But she wasn't going to worry about that now. Now she felt loving and happy and optimistic. She turned to Jason as he switched off his bedside light, put her hand on the side of his face, willed him to kiss her. It felt alien, a habit they had somehow got out of without even realizing it. She thought, briefly, about when the last time had been. Couldn't remember.

'Night, love,' Jason said, and he pecked her on the cheek. 'Don't stay awake all night listening for Em to get home.'

He turned on to his side, facing away from her.

Jen lay back on the pillow, staring at the dark shadows on the ceiling. 'Night.'

*

Of course, she stayed awake, waiting to hear the front door open and shut, and Emily's delicate fairy steps as she tiptoed up the creaking stairs. She felt completely and utterly alone, the hopeful mood of the evening long gone. She missed Amelia dreadfully, she realized. Her whole adult life, if she had had a problem, she would turn to her mother-in-law for advice and comfort. Gossip and news, and anything of a sensitive nature that an elderly relative might not fully appreciate, she shared with Poppy first. But everything else – and at those times when she needed a sympathetic shoulder to cry on and not Poppy's wisecracks – she looked to Amelia. Before her own mother, that went without saying. Elaine could be judgemental in a way that Amelia never would.

And there was no one in the world she wanted to confide in now more than the one person she knew she never could.

She felt a tear roll down her cheek. Sniffed and tried to stem the tide. She had never felt so helpless before, so completely at a loss about what to do. She thought briefly about Cass and then pushed her out of her mind. She had to worry about her own family, she couldn't start fretting about Cass too. She looked over at Jason, could just about make him out in the dark. He was breathing deeply, making occasional tiny snoring noises like a purring cat. She couldn't believe she was letting this thing – this secret – start to drive a wedge between them. OK, so maybe there had already been a crack in their relationship, a hairline fracture, but she had never thought it was irreparable. They had lost their way a little after Emily went to college, had struggled a bit for things to say and to feel as if anything was worth the effort, but she had been sure it was a temporary thing. They had just needed to find a new way to be, a different version of themselves that would see them through the next twenty years. But then this had happened, and now she couldn't even act like everything was normal, like it was all going to be OK. Because it wasn't. She didn't see how it could be.

At about twenty-five past three, she heard the click of the door and, a minute or so later, Emily on the stairs on her way up to her bedroom. Jen waited for a moment, rubbed at her eyes to remove any telltale signs of crying, and then couldn't resist getting out of bed and creeping across the landing, coughing softly as she neared the door so as not to startle Emily too much.

Not that that worked.

'Jesus! Mum, you scared the shit out of me.'

Emily was sitting in front of a mirror, wiping her make-up off with a flannel. She had mascara streaked down her cheeks.

Jen laughed. 'You look like Alice Cooper.'

'Are you OK? Why are you up?'

'I couldn't sleep. Did you have a nice time?'

'Fab. We went to Pacha with some of Catriona's friends from work.'

'Well, in that case you're home early. Do you want anything? Chamomile tea? Water?'

'I have water. Go to bed, Mum.'

'Hot chocolate?'

Emily smiled. 'We have hot chocolate?'

'I bought it specially. I think I'll have some, anyway. Help me sleep.'

'Well, in that case . . .'

Jen leaned down and hugged her, and was gratified to feel Emily hugging her back. 'Get into bed, I'll bring it up.'

'Love you.'

'You mean you love the fact that I'm going to make you hot chocolate.'

'Well, that too.'

'I'll take it.'

When she came back, Emily was tucked up in bed, duvet up round her chin, looking eight rather than eighteen.

'Stay here and keep me company while I drink it,' Emily said.

Jen settled herself down on Simone's bed, across the room, the way she used to after Simone first went to college and Emily, even at sixteen, had found it hard to get to sleep without the comforting presence of her elder sister there.

The next thing she knew, it was twenty past six in the morning and she was snuggled under Simone's duvet. Across the room, Emily was asleep on her back, pyjama-clad limbs splayed out from under the covers. Jen thought about getting up and going downstairs, or creeping back into her own bed for a couple of hours, but in the end she just turned over and went back to sleep.

'Are we going to Granny and Grandpa's for lunch tomorrow?' Emily asked over what amounted to lunch for Jen and Jason but breakfast for her, next day. They had decided to have another stab at Christmas shopping in the afternoon – only, this time, in the calmer environs of Kingston.

Jen was aware of Jason looking at her. It had occurred

to her that it actually might be a good idea to go and see Charles and Amelia after all. Having Emily there would take the tension out of the visit and would buy Jen a Sunday away from them next weekend without, hopefully, having to have too much of a negotiation about it.

'Well, I was going to go to Grandma's . . .'

She saw Emily trying to mask a disappointed face. It wasn't that she didn't love Elaine. It was just that she had bought into the whole myth of the Mastersons just as much as Jen herself had.

'. . . but then I thought maybe I could leave that till next weekend. Although she'll be sorry not to see you.'

'Fab. I'll make it up to Grandma at Christmas.'

Jen looked at Jason for confirmation, and he rewarded her with a big smile.

'We can go to Mum's next weekend, though, can't we?' she asked.

Get him to agree while he was feeling well disposed towards her.

'Of course.'

'Goodness,' Amelia said, when she opened the front door. 'You've done something to your hair.'

'Do you like it, Granny?' Emily said as she put her arms round her grandmother and planted a kiss on her cheek.

Jen hung back, not wanting to face Charles alone.

'Well, yes. It's . . . different.'

'You hate it,' Emily said, laughing. 'That's OK, you can say so.'

'Well, not hate, exactly,' Amelia said, with a smile. 'It'll just take a bit of getting used to, that's all.'

'Well, don't get too used to it. I'll probably change it again in a couple of weeks.'

'I used to bleach my hair white, sometimes, when I was young. Peroxide. Terrible stuff.'

'Did you really, Amelia?' Jen couldn't imagine it, somehow.

'Well, it was the sixties. I had a beehive, too, for a while.'

'Cool. Do you have any photos?' Emily linked Amelia's arm and walked towards the living room with her.

'Somewhere. In the attic, I think.'

'Can we see them, Granny?' Emily asked. 'Please.'

Amelia chuckled, flattered that her granddaughter was interested. 'I'll see if I can dig them out. After lunch.'

Charles appeared at the door of his study. 'Good God,' he said, in mock horror. 'Morticia Addams.'

He looked a little strained, Jen noticed. There were dark shadows under his eyes. Emily threw herself into his proffered hug, and Jen felt a sharp stab of regret that she could never enjoy those comforting bear-like embraces again, like she used to.

'I'm trying to persuade Granny to do hers like it. What do you think, Grandpa? You'd love it, wouldn't you?'

'Are you kidding? I've been asking her to be an Elmo for years. It's my fantasy.'

'Emo, Grandpa. Elmo's a muppet.'

'Well, that too.'

Jen breathed in the so familiar scent of the Masterson home. Lilies. Baking. Furniture polish. Cigars. Despite everything, it still smelled like comfort.

'Jen,' Amelia said, throwing her arms around her and planting a soft kiss on her cheek. 'I've been getting worried.

I've phoned you a few times. Have you been working extra shifts?'

Jen looked over at Jason, who was chatting happily to Charles and Emily and, hopefully, out of earshot.

'Just in the run-up to Christmas,' she said, hoping she wouldn't get struck down. She hated lying to Amelia, but it was better than having her think she had just been ignoring her calls. Which she had.

'I knew you must be busy,' Amelia said.

She accepted what Jen had told her at face value. Of course she did. That was the thing about Amelia: she was naturally trusting. If Jen told her she was flat out at the hotel, she would accept that as the truth. Just as, Jen knew, she would have done if Charles had said he had to entertain a client in the evening, or visit the Bath branch for the night. It would never even have occurred to her that someone she loved so much would lie.

'You work too hard,' Amelia said, taking Jen by the hand and leading her towards the kitchen. 'Come and let me spoil you rotten. Jessie and Martin and the baby are here. They arrived last night.'

'Great.'

'Jen, darling!' Charles exclaimed as they passed him in the hall, deep in jokey conversation with his son and granddaughter. 'Don't think you're getting past me without a hug.'

Jen reluctantly allowed herself to be embraced, half-heartedly patting Charles on the back as she did so.

Then he held her at arm's length, beaming a smile at her. 'You're sitting next to me at dinner.'

This was another one of his in-jokes. They all, for some

reason, always sat in the same places at the table when they came for lunch. It had become a long-running gag and, from there, part of their tradition. It meant that Jen knew she would have to sit at Charles's right-hand side, like it or not.

She plastered on her game-face smile, and waited for the afternoon to be over.

Thank God for Emily. She was so full of her new life, so oblivious to anything else that might be happening, that she filled every available space with her stories. It didn't even faze her that her grandparents didn't quite follow some of what she was saying.

'Tinie Tempah?' Charles interrupted at one point. 'Is that one of your friends?'

'No! He played in town, we all went, a whole gang of us.'

'Ah!' Charles said, joking but still not entirely sure what about. 'He's like Tiny Tim.'

'Tiny Tim's in *A Christmas Carol*, Grandpa.'

'No. "Tiptoe Through the Tulips". You remember. Or maybe you don't. I suppose you're too young.'

'For God's sake, Dad,' Jessie said, handing Violet over to Martin.

'Even I'm too young for Tiny Tim.' Jason laughed.

Jen, who ordinarily would have loved these half-deliberate misunderstandings that were guaranteed to rile Emily to the point of hysteria, tried to smile along.

'Is he very small?' Charles said, a twinkle in his eye.

'No . . . what?'

'And he has a bad temper? Or maybe he hardly has a

temper at all, that's what the tiny bit means. He's a normal-height man with a very small temper.'

Emily rolled her eyes. 'You're so funny, Grandpa.'

'I am, aren't I? I can't help myself.'

Just a normal Sunday lunch. Jen took a sneaky look at her watch. Only a couple more hours.

Although the afternoon being over also meant dropping Emily off at King's Cross on the way home. Her bag, stuffed full of clean washing and tins of tomatoes and bags of pasta, was waiting in the boot of the car.

Jen was worried that, when the time came, she might just grab on to her daughter's ankle and refuse to let her go.

27

It was a beautiful day in Brighton. Freezing, but clear and sunny. The sea looked glassy. Smooth, and almost still. There were no boats anywhere to be seen. Or people, for that matter. The undercliff was deserted. Cass dug her hands deep into her pockets and crunched across the gravel towards the water. It was probably too cold, she thought. She was clearly the only person stupid enough – or adventurous enough – to think that a run along the front was a good idea in the sub-zero temperature.

She had been shivering non-stop since she'd left home, despite the layers she had piled on top of one another. She was going to have to break into a run just to get warm. Pulling up the hood of her sweat top, she struck out towards the marina.

She liked to run down here whenever she could. Twice, three times a week, maybe. She wasn't a natural runner. It hurt every time. She had a drawer full of ankle supports and knee stabilizers and blister plasters, and she almost always had to walk part of the way, but nothing else gave her the same feeling of satisfaction. It was all about the moment she got back home, and the smug glow that stayed with her for the rest of the day.

It cleared her mind. That was the main reason she did it. Of course, there was the fitness factor, but she could have achieved that just as well in the gym at the end of her road. Running was all about blasting the cobwebs from inside her head. Making sure she was able to think clearly. It made her better at her job, she was sure of it.

Since Jen Masterson had invited herself into her life, Cass had been coming down here even more frequently. Sometimes just to walk, if she couldn't face a run. She had thought she was reconciled to her place on the outside of her father's family. She had had enough years to come to terms with it, after all. She couldn't believe how much her meeting Jen had unsettled her. It was as if Jen had opened the door to the sacred Masterson family home just enough so that Cass could peek through, and now she couldn't get the image out of her head.

One scene, in particular, had taken root and kept popping into her consciousness whenever she wasn't being vigilant. She knew it was something she had created as much from vignettes in old 1940s films and department-store grottos as from anything that had any basis in reality, but she couldn't shake it. She had never seen her father on Christmas Day. Both she and her mother had always known that that would be out of the question. Over the years, Cass had created the perfect mental video of his family Christmas, in the big Arts and Crafts house in Twickenham that she had once sneaked up to London and looked at the outside of, but had never entered.

She had tweaked the details every year to take into account the ages of his children. Sometimes she would make one of them fat, just to amuse herself. Or surly. She liked to imagine Charles surrounded by stroppy recalcitrant offspring, silently wishing he was spending the day in

Iver Heath with his calmer, more compliant, eager-to-please youngest daughter. She hoped that he, at least, missed her.

It was funny, she hadn't thought about that for years – not since her mum and dad split up, anyway. After that, she had just worked on maintaining a relationship with her father. She had been terrified she would lose him. The rest of his family became an irrelevance. But after her conversation with Jen every bauble, every fairy light she saw set her off. And now that she had the latest images of most of the family firmly lodged in her head, it was easy to reconstruct the whole scenario. She had even caught a glimpse of Amelia on a picture Jen had scrolled through rather quickly. She had looked nice, actually. Sweet-faced and maternal. Just add in a few random grandchildren, and the whole thing was complete. A warm, happy, nuclear-family Christmas.

Cass had seen how shocked Jen had been by her revelations about Charles. Something was rotten in the state of Denmark. The foundations on which Jen had constructed her adult life were subsiding into the mud and her perfect existence threatening to go down with them. It had been clear from the look on her face just how much she thought she had to lose.

And then, when she'd called her the other day, she could sense the panic in Jen's voice. She could understand why. But she had no intention of blowing the whole thing wide open and destroying her dad's marriage to Amelia. She had never had a vindictive streak, despite all the many fantasies she'd indulged in where Amelia – and occasionally Jason, Poppy and Jessie – contracted terrible disfiguring diseases or conveniently fell under a very big bus. She just wanted to make contact with her half-siblings, that was all. Let them know she existed. She hadn't really worked out what would happen then. Cass had never been a great one for forward planning.

One day, they might be all she had, that was the point. Surely they would understand that, would know that she wasn't there to be a home-wrecker. They might not welcome her with open arms – in fact, she wasn't stupid, she knew they wouldn't. Quite the opposite, probably, but a door would have been opened. It might take years for one or all of them to come round, so she had to start laying the foundations now.

And if Charles decided he had to take it out on her and her mum, well, that was a risk she was prepared to take. And actually, seeing him at Barbara's bedside, seeing how concerned he was, how close they still were, she didn't believe for a minute that he would cut off contact. OK, so he might be angry for a while, but he'd come round. She had to look at the bigger picture, the long game.

The marina still seemed to be an impossible distance away. Usually, she liked to give herself a goal, set a target and force herself to achieve it. Today she decided to let herself off. She turned round and began a slow jog back towards town.

Back at work on Monday, Jen breathed a sigh of relief. The good atmosphere between her and Jason had lasted the whole evening after Emily's tearful departure, as they picked through the bones of the weekend, happy to be on common ground. She had a two-week respite before she would have to face Charles and Amelia again. Amelia had told her not to even think about their planned Christmas shopping trip while she was so busy at work, and Jen had hugged her tightly, hating how easy it was to pull the wool over her mother-in-law's eyes.

On Sunday evening, lying in bed with Jason, feeling warm and safe and loved, she had thought, perhaps, that they might have sex, but Jason had simply put his arm round her, pulling her close, kissing the top of her head. She could have initiated it herself, of course. Back in the old days, she wouldn't have thought twice about it. But things were different now; this wall had grown up between them, and she couldn't remember how things had been before, couldn't locate a sledgehammer to knock it down. She felt awkward, embarrassed, afraid of rejection. She had contented herself with snuggling into his chest, happy to feel some kind, any kind, of connection between them.

'What the hell?'

Poppy's voice jolted Jen out of her relative complacency. She didn't sound happy.

'What's wrong?' Jen put down the sandwich she was eating for lunch, and waited.

She racked her brain for ways in which she might have pissed Poppy off. She hadn't even spoken to her in nearly a week, because she had been avoiding her calls. Ah, yes, she hadn't spoken to her in nearly a week, because she had been avoiding her calls. That would be it.

'I've been calling and calling. Where have you been?'

'Sorry, I've been busy, and then Em came home . . . I'm here now, aren't I?'

'You're supposed to be my best friend. But I went on a date with a strange man – who I met over the internet, as you know – a week ago, and you haven't even asked me how it went. He could have been a psychopath. I could have been lying dead in a ditch for days, for all you cared.'

Jen always forgot that, deep down, Poppy shared some of Jessie's tendency for melodrama when pushed. She usually kept it well hidden, too self-aware to let it show. Jen wasn't in the mood to indulge her.

'I knew you weren't dead in a ditch, because I got your messages. I just haven't had a second to call. I'm really sorry. How was it?'

'It was fine. I think.'

'This was Benji?'

'It was. I'm seeing him again.'

'You liked him, then?'

'I don't know. I have literally no opinion of him. He seemed nice enough, I just can't really remember anything about him. He could walk in here now and I don't think I'd even recognize him. That's how much of an impression he made.'

'Well, that sounds like a great start for a relationship.'

Poppy wasn't intending to budge too far from her bad mood. 'Like I said, he seemed nice enough.'

'Hasn't he got a daughter?'

'Yes. Samantha, or Tamara, or Amanda. Something like that.'

'There you are. That's something. Almost.'

'Anyway. I'm seeing him for lunch today. Star Cafe, one fifteen.'

'Shit. If I wasn't on early lunch, I could have come and checked him out through the window.'

'No, well, you're clearly too busy,' Poppy said petulantly.

Jen resisted the urge to tell her sister-in-law that she had real problems weighing on her own mind. Things that carried much more weight than whether she liked a new man she had just met, or if she was getting enough attention. And that a big part of the stress of those problems was trying to protect Poppy from ever finding out about them. She knew that Poppy was feeling slighted. She could sympathize, but she just couldn't do much about it at the moment. And she couldn't risk explaining herself too fully either.

'I'm sorry I haven't been around much lately, OK? I get that you're pissed off with me.'

'Is something wrong?' Poppy said sharply.

'No.'

'Then what is it? And don't tell me work.'

'Nothing.'

'So you've just not been calling me back because you couldn't be bothered? And Mum said she's hardly spoken to you too.'

Jen bristled. It wasn't fair that she was being asked to explain herself, that she was the one being made to feel like the bad guy.

'Poppy, I've been busy, OK? I know my job's not as high powered as yours, but sometimes I do have to work long hours . . .' Even as she said it, she knew it was the wrong thing to say, but she was out of inspiration.

'Wow. Have I done something to piss you off?'

'No. Look, I really don't have time for this. Everything's

fine, I'm just working extra hours, and I only have five minutes left on my break, and I still haven't eaten my lunch.'

'God forbid you make Neil or Judy wait five extra minutes –'

'I have to go, Poppy. I'll talk to you soon.'

'Are you in this evening? I'm coming over.'

'No. I'm not.'

'When, then?'

'Look, I'll see you soon, OK? I'll call you. Bye.'

She pressed the end button without giving Poppy the chance to say any more. Now all she needed was for either Poppy or Amelia to sympathize with Jason because Jen had been doing so much overtime. He'd give away in a second that he had no idea what they were talking about, and then where would she be? She was going to have to offer to do some extra shifts, just to cover her tracks. She wrapped up the remains of her sandwich and threw it in the bin. She had no appetite for it now.

The last thing she wanted – she would ever have wanted – was to fall out with Poppy. Ordinarily, she would have loved to relive Poppy's date with her. They would have cried tears of laughter as Poppy gave her a blow-by-blow account, and Jen teased her mercilessly about every aspect. They would have shared every last detail, however humiliating or personal. That was how they were; they told each other everything.

Not any more.

Jen could feel herself on the verge of tears. She splashed water on her face in the staff bathroom, and then had to patch up her make-up because she had made her mascara run. She looked at herself in the mirror over the sink. She looked gaunt. She knew she had been losing weight – stress always did that to her – but she hadn't realized quite how much. She looked wired, too, as if she could do with a good night's sleep and a week in rehab. She made herself as presentable as she could, and then walked out to reception.

David looked at his watch as she approached the desk. She was . . . what? Two minutes late.

'I'm covering for Neil, because he had to meet someone for lunch.'

'Sorry,' she said quietly. There was no point getting into an argument about it.

'It's fine. I'm just telling you he had to leave on time. He couldn't wait for you to get back . . .'

David had a passive-aggressive management style that sometimes drove Jen mad. She would much rather he just said, 'You're late, don't do it again,' and left it at that. But that wasn't his modus operandi.

'. . . and with Judy off sick, I obviously couldn't leave the desk completely unmanned.'

God forbid. Someone might have wanted to complain about having no whisky in their minibar and had to wait thirty seconds for her to get back from lunch before they could do so.

She took a deep breath. 'I know. I'm sorry. I was on an important call and couldn't cut it short.'

'It's just that we can't have the guests having to wait –'

'Jesus, David, I know,' she snapped.

In Hotel Top Trumps the general manager outscored the reception manager on all counts. She wanted to tell him to fuck right off, but she knew she couldn't.

She caught her breath again. 'I'm sorry. It won't happen again.'

Thankfully, that seemed to appease him, and he walked off in the direction of the restaurant. Jen watched him go, knowing she could have handled that better. She put her hand over her eyes and willed herself to get through the day.

'Are you OK?'

Jen jumped. She hadn't noticed there was anyone in the reception area. Sean Hoskins was standing at the desk. She smiled her professional smile. Or at least, she tried to. It wasn't coming out quite right.

'I'm sorry. I didn't see you there.'

'I was hiding. It looked like you were being told off.'

'No. It was nothing. I'm sorry. Are you checking in?' She was far too well trained to admit to any problems amongst the staff.

'Yesterday. Really, though, do you want me to wait for him outside, when he's on his way home, and do him over? I'm only offering because he's clearly way smaller than me, and he looks a bit asthmatic.'

Jen actually laughed, it was such a ridiculous thing to say. 'To be honest, if I thought it would help I'd do it myself.'

'Ah, so he *was* ticking you off, then. Double booking? Angry guest? Cockroaches in the restaurant?'

'No! Of course not. Nothing to do with the hotel. Personal stuff that I shouldn't let affect me at work. It's unprofessional.'

'Father-in-law?'

Jen's phone, which she had forgotten to switch to silent

and which was lying on the desk beside her, began to ring again. No doubt Poppy following up with some more reproachful words. She glanced down, unable to ignore it completely. It wasn't Poppy. It was Cass.

'For fuck's sake,' she said, before she could censor herself. She picked up the phone and turned it off. 'Sorry.'

'Don't be. Are you OK? Do you need to deal with that call?'

'No,' she said firmly. 'It wasn't anyone important.'

'You wouldn't be human if you didn't let your real life affect your work life. To be honest, that's why I set up on my own – so I could be as grumpy as I liked, if I was having a bad day. You should try it. It's very cathartic, actually, being rude to people who are rude to you first.'

'It's a nice idea, but I'd be sacked in five minutes.'

'I'll tell you what, you can start with me. I'll be unforgivably dismissive to you next time I'm passing, and you can tell me where to go. Trust me, it'll feel good.'

David was crossing back over the reception, a sheaf of papers in his hand. He smiled a smile of recognition.

'Mr Hoskins. Glad to have you back. Is everything OK?'

'Excellent. I was just telling Ms Masterson here that she is one of the most helpful and polite receptionists I've ever had the pleasure to deal with.'

'Well, I'm glad to hear it.'

Jen waited until David had gone through to the back room, and then snorted. 'That sounded so fake.'

'Pleasure. Right, I can't stay here all day trying to save your career. I'm going to be late.'

He waved a hand at her as he went. Jen laughed at his

retreating back. It was so sweet of him to try to cheer her up. He made it seem as if it mattered to him, as if making her feel better was important. It had worked too. She felt herself relax for a moment.

And then she remembered Poppy and Cass, and she felt the suffocating weight settle back down on her shoulders, crushing her.

28

They hadn't had a real fight for years. Not a proper, all-out, I-wish-I-was-married-to-someone-else kind of fight. And Jen hadn't seen it coming either – it was just suddenly there, and they were in the middle of it, trapped in the heart of the fire with no emergency exits in sight.

It was Jen's fault, she knew it was. She should have just kept her mouth shut – carried on grinning and bearing it – or, at least, thought about what she said before she said it. There must have been a way of getting across what was on her mind without making it sound like a direct attack on his parents. But she had just blurted it out, as soon as they were tucked up in bed. Five more minutes and they would have been asleep, and this conversation would never have happened.

Deep down, a part of her knew she just felt like having a row, letting off steam like other couples. Shouting and screaming – although she was a little afraid of what she might say, if pushed – until she had got all the tension and anxiety and frustration that had been building up out of her system. It was all too much. She had always been proud of the fact that they rarely fought, had thought it showed understanding, respect – maturity, even. These days, she wondered if it just meant that they had never cared enough, that they had been content to let their relationship drift and run aground in the safe shallows.

She had started to get herself into a spin on the way home, having put in an extra three hours to cover for Judy's absence, and so that Jason would nod and say, yes, wasn't it awful, when Amelia or Poppy mentioned to him how overworked she was. She was exhausted. Physically, mentally, emotionally. Her last communication from Cass had lodged itself right at the forefront of her mind, pushing all rational and logical thoughts to the side, leaving her unable to think straight, unable to even stick her head back down in the sand – where she felt, if not safe, at least hidden. Out of the path of the bullets.

And then it had hit her with a deafening thud, as she sat on the bus, that their long weekend away for Charles and Amelia's anniversary was just round the corner. She had blocked it out somehow, focused on how she was going to get through Christmas and pretended that this enormous ditch wasn't lurking in the way, waiting to trap her before Christmas even arrived.

It couldn't happen. It. Could. Not. Happen. No way could she spend three nights away with her in-laws now. No way.

Once home, she claimed exhaustion and another impending migraine and ran herself a bath. Jason was all sympathy and made her a brie sandwich that she ate in silence, sitting on the bed in her pyjamas, having protested that she needed an early night.

As soon as the words had come out of her mouth, she regretted saying them. She had hoped she might get through the night unscathed if she could only feign sleep, but Jason had insisted on accompanying her to bed and was now sitting up beside her, light on, book open.

'I think we should cancel the holiday.'

Jason looked confused, no idea what had hit him. 'What? Why?'

'Because I can't face it.'

'Where's this come from?'

'I don't know. I just . . . I don't want to go.'

'You're knackered. Get some sleep. You'll feel differently in the morning.'

'Don't talk to me like I'm one of the girls, Jason. Jesus!'

'Well, you're making no sense.'

'How much more explicit do you need me to be? I think we should cancel the cottage. I just don't think it's such a good idea after all.'

'It's all booked . . .'

'It's . . . I can't. I just can't.'

She had no way of explaining to him what her real problem was. She should never have started this.

'Did Mum say something to upset you?'

Jason knew that Jen and Amelia often talked on the phone, had no idea that Jen had been screening her calls lately and letting them go to voicemail if her mother-in-law rang. That was something else she was going to have to address one of these days.

'No. I just think it might be a nightmare, that's all. I can't face three nights – actually, four days – of us all cooped up together.'

'It was all your idea. You can't just change your mind.'

'It was a stupid plan. I don't know what I was thinking.'

'God, Jen, it's three nights with my parents. We've been

away with them before. You love spending time with them.'

'You don't understand.'

'Too right, I don't. And I am not about to turn round and tell them we've decided we don't want to go on the holiday we've booked with them, after all. The holiday that was all your idea.'

'I don't think they'd care.'

'What are you saying? That my mum and dad would rather not spend a few days with us? Wow, Jen, that's extreme.'

'Of course not. Just with me. I don't know. Maybe I just shouldn't come.'

'They love you. OK, what is going on?'

'Nothing. I'm just tired, and we see so much of them already.'

'It'll do you good. You haven't been yourself lately. God knows what's up with you –'

'I told you,' she said, more harshly than she'd intended. 'I'm knackered. I don't want to use up my holiday running around after your mum and dad.'

'Since when did they expect us to run around after them? They're usually the ones insisting on doing everything.'

'You know what I mean. It's OK for you, you get weeks off over the Christmas break.'

'Is that what this is about? That I get more holiday than you do? And, of course, I never have any coursework to mark, or tutorials to plan. And do you have any idea how hard it was for me to organize time off during term time? Finding people to cover my classes –'

'Jason, I'm not having a go at you. I'm just saying that I

don't get to have time off very often, and when I do it's precious. I feel like I just need a few days to flop about and do nothing.'

'Well, you should have thought about that before you told Mum and Dad we were taking them away. It's too late now. Anyway, you're off for Christmas, aren't you? That's, what? A couple of weeks later –'

'Which we'll spend with your parents,' she interrupted. 'I just want some time for just us. I don't know . . .'

'You're being ridiculous.'

'I can't, OK? I can't face it, I can't go.'

'There's something you're not telling me.'

'No.'

'There is, there must be. Something's happened.'

Fuck it. Maybe she should just get it out there. Maybe he should know exactly what his father was capable of. She closed her eyes, took a deep breath.

She couldn't do it. Couldn't detonate the bomb under all their lives.

'I could say I was ill, or something. You go, take them out, spoil them, everybody's happy.'

'What, another convenient migraine?'

Shit. 'That's harsh.'

'Well, they do seem to happen at the most opportune times.'

'What if I really was ill? I couldn't go then, so what's the difference?'

'The difference is that it would be true. I'm not going to lie to get you out of a few days in the country. It's ridiculous.'

'Why do you care so much if I come or not? Surely it's better if I'm not there, if I feel like this?'

'Because we're doing this for them. This is supposed to be their anniversary present. From both of us. What the hell is up with you?'

'I don't know. I can't explain.'

'It's like you've been body-snatched. You're moody, you're secretive. You don't want to spend time with my family. I spoke to Poppy the other day, and she said she'd barely heard from you.'

'I've been busy,' Jen said, rather desperately. She wished she'd never started this conversation.

'With what?'

'Just stuff. I don't know. Work.'

'Work? If this is what three hours' overtime does to you, then God help us if you ever have to cover an extra day. And it's not like we even have the girls at home now.'

'You have no idea how stressful my job can be. Just because it's not academic . . .'

And so, the argument lurched from Jason's failure to appreciate that Jen had spent years doing something unfulfilling because it fitted in with the family's needs, to her lack of supportiveness about his ambitions to be Head of Department, on to his lack of willingness to take her job seriously, and her tendency to think she knew better than everyone else did about how they should live their lives.

She accused Jason of never having counted her mother as being as important as his own, which made him snort and tell her it was a bit late for her to be putting herself in the running for daughter of the year.

'What the fuck does that mean?' she shouted.

'What do you think? I've lost count of the excuses

you've made in the past not to have to spend any time with Elaine.'

'That's not true, and you know it,' she countered, knowing that he was right.

'You make up the rules to suit yourself. You always do.'

Eventually, they arrived right back where they had started.

'I'm not going, and that's final. I don't care what you tell them.' Jen slammed her water glass down on the bedside table, spilling the contents. It dripped down on to the carpet. She ignored it. Of course, she actually cared very much about hurting Amelia, would have hated for her mother-in-law to think she didn't want to spend time with her.

'You're being totally unreasonable, and you know it. We'll talk about this tomorrow when you've calmed down a bit.'

'Don't shout,' Jen heard herself saying, although she was fully aware that she was the one who had raised her voice first. She didn't even know why she had said it, since they were alone in the house. The neighbours, maybe. The walls of their terrace were thin.

Jason glared at her, and she waited for him to say, 'Don't you dare tell me not to shout, when you're shouting yourself.' But instead, he just flung down the book that he was still holding, having failed to read a single page, on to the floor, turned out his bedside light, and said, 'I'm going to sleep, but I'll tell you now, there is no way I am going to cancel this holiday, or that you are going to cry off with a fake illness. Grow up, Jen. Sometimes we have to do things we don't like.'

Jen thought about getting up and flouncing out. Going to sleep in either Simone or Emily's single bed. Instead, she did nothing, just rolled on her side, facing away from him.

This was so unfair.

For the first time ever, she was thankful to be on an early the next morning, up and out long before Jason surfaced. Usually, he would wake up just enough to mutter, 'Have a good day,' at her as she crept around getting dressed, but if he heard her this morning he didn't give himself away. She made his lunch, as she always did (although she suspected he threw it away and ate cafeteria junk most days, but she still liked to provide him with a healthy option), left it in the fridge, and then went out into the dark, damp morning, on time for once.

Jen knew that, later in the day, one of them would send the other a conciliatory text and that, on this occasion, it should be her, but at the moment she still felt too hard done by, too wounded by some of the things he had said. Too upset that she hadn't got her own way, if she was being honest. It had shocked her when he'd fought back. She had expected resistance – after all, what she was saying had been so completely out of left field, totally without precedent. She had known he might dig his heels in, take what she was saying as an assault on his family, refuse to budge. But she hadn't expected them to shout at each other, hadn't thought it would end up turning so personal.

It was funny – well, not funny exactly, more interesting, and maybe a little bit sad – the way he had just assumed her problem was with Amelia, and there had been no way for her to disabuse him. She had come dangerously close to blurting out the fact that it was Charles she didn't want to be around. She had stopped herself, even in the middle of a fight, to protect him. To protect them all. And without being able to tell Jason exactly what her problem was, she was always going to sound like a spoiled child.

As always, when they had had one of their rare arguments, Jen veered between feeling contrite and indignant in the aftermath. She should never have suggested they cancel the holiday. These were his parents they were talking about. But, honestly, it was ridiculous. Jason should never have assumed they would spend every Sunday having lunch with them. He should have told her how it was going to be, made it part of his wedding vows. ('Will you take me and my mother and father to love and to cherish, will you spend all your free time being taken in by his hokey charm and complete and utter bullshit?') What she really meant, of course – although she was deciding to ignore the fact now – was that he should have ignored her when she had insisted they spend the majority of their weekends with the Mastersons instead of with her own mother. The fact was, he should have just manned up at some point over the past twenty-odd years.

Jen mulled this over in her head, going through another angry phase, and wrestling with her computer, trying to put through a payment that had been rejected twice already because the connection kept going down.

'Jesus Christ!' she said, far too loudly, and slammed a pile of papers from one end of the reception desk to the other. Luckily, the reception was deserted. She took a deep breath and tried again.

The internal phone rang. The display lit up: 'Room 328 Mr Sean Hoskins'. Jen grabbed it eagerly, happy for the distraction.

'Morning. You're up early.'

'Oh good, you're on. I'm coming down.'

'What –' Jen started to say, but he'd hung up.

A couple of minutes later, the lift pinged and Sean appeared, smiling broadly.

She mirrored his smile. Actually felt ten times better for seeing a friendly face. The thought flitted across her mind that she was glad she was on duty alone, that no one else was around.

'Do you need any help with anything?'

'No. To be completely honest, I'm bored out of my mind and I came down in the hope that you'd take pity on me and chat to me for five minutes.'

Jen had no idea if what Sean was saying was true, or if it was another one of his jokes, but she felt flattered, nonetheless. 'With pleasure.'

Sean leaned his elbows on the desk. 'OK, what shall we talk about?'

She laughed. 'Hold on, this was your idea.'

'I don't care. Anything's better than morning TV.' He picked up a newspaper that was lying behind the desk. 'I'll open this at a random page, and we can discuss whatever's on there.'

He opened it with a flourish, closed his eyes and pointed blindly at the page.

Jen looked. 'Wow. Libya.'

Sean closed the paper again. 'OK, well, maybe not that. Let's start from the front.'

In the end, they chatted for about twenty minutes, about everything from the monarchy to Taylor Swift's love life via the euro crisis. Jen forgot all about her fight with Jason. Or, at least, it was pushed from the front of her mind to the back.

After a while, another guest arrived and started tapping his nails impatiently on the reception desk.

'I won't be a moment,' she said to Sean, hoping he might hang around a little longer.

'I should go,' he said. 'I hope your day gets better.'

'See you later,' Jen said, realizing that she actually already felt in a cheerier mood. 'Have fun.'

She made a restaurant reservation for the impatient man and then, still feeling better disposed towards the world than she had earlier, sent Jason a cheerful text. Not an apology, just a friendly message:

You ok? I feel a bit knackered and rubbish! Xxx'

She hoped it would give off the signal that she wanted to be friends again. This was how they always operated after a fight. Eventually, one of them would give in and make a jokey or, at least, a light-hearted overture. The other one would capitulate immediately, and the disagreement would be forgotten and probably never mentioned again. They never had a debrief. There would be no discussion of who had been in the right or in the wrong, or who owed who an apology. Not even an attempt to work out how they could avoid going over the same ground in the future.

She wondered, though, if they had just been brushing

all their grievances under a carpet for all those years, rather than hoovering them away for good. Whether, one day, one of them would lift the corner up and they would all come seeping out and suffocate them.

29

By home time, she had still not received a response from Jason, which could have meant one of two things – that he had been teaching solidly and hadn't received her message, or that he wasn't ready to make up and so had decided not to respond. She knew which she thought was the case. If Jason had been feeling bad, wanting everything to be OK between them, he would have been checking his phone regularly all day.

She knew that, whatever happened, the holiday was still going to go ahead and she was going to be there. She tried to summon up any relaxation techniques she might have picked up in random yoga classes she had attended here and there. What was all that stuff about being in the moment, not dwelling on the past or the future? She wished she had listened more carefully, instead of always using the time to run through what she needed to buy for that night's dinner. She had never been very Zen.

Sean was coming back into the foyer, laden down with a box full of bits and pieces, and with an old advertising sign under one arm, as she was getting ready to leave. She saw him refuse an offer of help from Graham Roper the Doorman Groper with a smile.

'Had enough?' he said as he passed.

'Something like that. Or it could just be the end of my shift.'

'They actually let you leave? I thought you all lived here in a big dormitory in the basement.'

'See you tomorrow.'

'Unless,' Sean said, looking at her hopefully, 'you fancy a quick drink or something? I mean, I know you've had a long day . . .'

Jen reached straight for her default answer in situations like this. It had happened many times before – businessmen, away from home without their wives, propositioning the nearest halfway attractive woman in the hope of a bit of illicit excitement. She had never accepted one of their invitations yet. Actually, she had always assumed Sean didn't have a wife. Hoped he didn't, maybe, she realized now.

She felt herself colour a little. 'We're not allowed to drink in the bar. It looks bad.'

'We could go to the pub on the corner, then. If you say no, I'm just going to have to sit there on my own like a sad old alky. You'd be doing a good deed.'

She thought about the frosty house that would almost certainly be waiting for her. The easy conversation she had had with Sean in the morning. Would it be such a crime to have a quick drink, a bit of light-hearted chat with a friend, and still be home in time to make dinner?

'Well, if you put it that way. Just one, though. I don't want my husband to think I've abandoned him.'

She waited for Sean to leave his packages behind

reception, and they walked to the nearest cosy pub on Rathbone Street. Jen was sure Jason must have lunch or a quick drink here and there with female colleagues. In fact, she knew he did, and it had never bothered her. She had never been one of those women who view every other female for miles as a threat. She didn't think he would mind her chatting to Sean Hoskins over a vodka and slimline tonic. If she had been in a better mood she would have sent him a jokey text – 'Gone for a drink with a cute male guest. Be back in time for dinner, or maybe tomorrow morning!' or something like that – but as he still hadn't replied to her earlier missive she decided he didn't deserve it. Let him wonder where she was, for once.

Sean got them both drinks, and they settled at a table by the front window.

'So,' Jen said, once she had taken a sip. 'Good day shopping?'

'You make it sound like I'm a Kardashian.'

She laughed. 'OK, then. Good day sourcing stock?'

'Yes, thank you. I did have a good day acquiring vintage items to sell in my emporium. It was a house clearance today, actually, so I came away with a lot of bargains.'

'How do you know what you're looking for? Did you train in . . . something?'

Sean nodded. 'I got a degree in biochemistry from Brunel, that helped.'

'You know what I mean, have you done courses – "Old junk for beginners" – that kind of thing?'

'That's amazing! That's the exact module I took. That

and "Make money out of shit your granny's throwing away". In actual fact, it was just always a passion of mine, and I somehow turned it into a living. It's the kind of thing you have to learn on the job.'

'I'll swap you. I have a load of old tat in my house I could sell.'

'And I am perfectly capable of arranging for someone to have eggs and bacon brought to their room between eight and eight fifteen in the morning. Toast on the side. Orange juice. See, I'm a natural.'

'I think you'll find that's the room-service department, but nice try.'

Sean made a mock surprised face. 'What? They won't even trust you with that?'

Jen shook her head. 'Too specialized.'

Sean laughed.

He had an appealing laugh, Jen thought. It sort of came out of nowhere, like he couldn't help himself. It made you feel it was genuine and not out of duty or politeness. It was a laugh that made the listener feel flattered.

He asked about Jason and she told him about his job and then worried that she bored him a bit about the girls and their achievements, although he seemed interested. She didn't mention that they were in the wake of a major argument. That would have been too disloyal. Sean, it turned out, had never married.

'Are you a sociopath?' Jen asked lightly. 'Or maybe you fancy yourself as a playboy? Do you have a load of eighteen-year-old girlfriends dotted all over the country?'

'God, no, I'm far too lazy. I mean, I've had girlfriends, of course. I've just generally had them one at a time and

233

age appropriate. I always assumed I'd get married one day – it's just never happened.'

'You can tell me, did they all say no?'

Sean laughed his taken-by-surprise laugh again. 'You've got me. I'm a tragic loser. Would you like another?' He indicated her glass.

'No, I'd better not.' She looked at her watch. An hour and a quarter had gone by without her even noticing. 'Shit, is that the time? I should run.'

'Do you always do this when it's your round?'

'Always. I'm actually just going to go straight to another pub, where I'm going to con someone else into buying me a drink.'

'I haven't even asked you about the father-in-law yet. Any more drama?'

She frowned. 'Way more. It's complicated. I can't . . . I shouldn't talk about it, really. It doesn't seem fair on Jason. He still doesn't know.'

'Of course, sorry. I was just being nosy, and it's absolutely none of my business. I don't think it's good for you, though. Bottling it up and trying to deal with it on your own.'

Jen put an arm into her coat. 'I'm fine,' she said, smiling. 'To be honest, it's been lovely not having to think about it for a bit. Thank you.'

He walked out with her. She didn't know why, but she headed straight down to Tottenham Court Road rather than walk back up Charlotte Street with him, and past the hotel.

'Oh, I'm back in two weeks,' he said as they parted company, having established that Jen wouldn't be around when he checked out the next day. 'Big vintage fair in Regent's Park, and I have a hundred and fifty square foot to fill.'

'Great,' she said, glad she would be seeing him again so soon, and then she worried it had sounded too eager. 'And thanks again for the drink.'

While she was walking to Goodge Street station, she thought about Sean. She'd always liked him, he was so easy to talk to and he always said something that made her smile. The distraction meant she had managed to get through most of the day without dwelling too much on her fight with Jason, or the whole mess that was her life with her extended family. In fact, for the past hour or so, she had forgotten about her problems completely.

She arrived home in a much more forgiving mood than she had been in when she had left in the morning. Life was too short for arguing. Jen could be the big person and make the first conciliatory move.

Jason was preparing dinner in the kitchen when she got there. Look! Everything must be OK! I'm preparing a meal for you!

She greeted him with a smile, putting in all the effort she could to let him know she was apologizing, without actually saying it.

He offered a hesitant one back. 'I only just got your text.'

Jen didn't believe him, but she knew it was said as an explanation – an apology, even – for his lack of a reply. 'That's OK.'

'Did you have to do more overtime?' he said, without a hint of a subtext, as far as she could tell.

'A couple of us went to the pub, actually. It was only a quick one.'

For some reason, she didn't offer up the identity of the person she had been with. It didn't seem important, and she wouldn't want him to worry about why she had picked the day after they had had a fight to go for a drink with a man he had never heard of, however innocent it might have been. She would tell him later. If he asked.

'Good for you.'

They would tiptoe around each other a bit awkwardly for the rest of the evening but, by tomorrow morning, Jen knew from experience, everything would be back to normal. They wouldn't resolve anything, they would just paper over it and hope the paper didn't stretch so much that it ripped.

'Oh, I spoke to the woman who owns the cottage,' Jason said, with a grimace.

They were sitting in the living room, struggling for something to say, waiting for the lamb and baked potatoes to be ready.

'I asked her about getting a harder mattress for Mum and Dad, but she pretty much told me to get lost.'

'Well, I don't blame her, really,' Jen said. 'What's she supposed to do? Buy a new one for every guest who comes to stay?'

'She did say she might be able to find a board to put under it.'

This was, Jen knew, Jason's way of saying that the holiday was still on, there was nothing more to say, move on, next.

She decided to let it go. 'Well, that might be OK,' she said, and turned back to her book.

Subject closed.

30

'There's a letter for you here, somewhere.'

David rifled through the drawer of the reception desk. He made it sound as if a letter arriving for a member of staff was an event, which, in fairness, it probably was.

Jen's heart started to beat faster. She knew instantly who it would be from. Only one person had ever sent her a letter here before. Not many people, surely, even wrote letters these days. Certainly no one under seventy-five.

'It came yesterday. I put it in here for safe keeping.'

She resisted the urge to push him out of the way and look for it herself. It was painful watching him scrabble around. She knew all the letter would contain would be a cursory summary of the four or five years since the last one, and probably a thinly disguised request for money, but she felt hungry suddenly for details – any details, however trivial and impersonal – about her father's life. It felt blissfully uncomplicated, somehow, the idea of family that had no connection to the Mastersons. Even dysfunctional and often disappointing family.

It was funny, finding out the truth about Charles seemed to have made her feelings soften towards her own father a little. No one was perfect. There were only degrees of imperfection. At least, with her own dad, she knew what she was up against, she knew exactly who he was.

Finally, David spotted something and produced it with a flourish. 'Ta da!'

She grabbed it from his hand, put it in the inside pocket of her jacket. She would have to read it on her break.

It was brief, that was the main thing that Jen thought when she unfolded the paper. There was always that moment of anticipation. A sharp excitement, like Christmas morning. Maybe this was the time he would explain himself – or, at the very least, try to engage her in a real and meaningful way. She knew it was ridiculous. Knew there was no reason to think it would ever happen. Rory had never been verbose.

He thanked her for the birthday card. 'Eighty! Can you believe it?' Then there were the usual anodyne pleasantries – 'How are you? How are the children?' that kind of thing. He obviously wasn't entirely confident with their names, even after all these years. He had separated from Maxine, his live-in girlfriend of the last ten years or so, the letter said. 'Water under the bridge.' She had cleaned him out, leaving him with just the flat – which was in his name, anyhow, so she'd had no choice – and very little else. So there it was, the plea for funds. She would almost have preferred it if he'd just come out and said it: 'Dear Jen, send me fifty quid, yours, Dad.' At least then there would have been no grey areas, no room for hopeful, pitiful interpretation.

She wished, as she always did, that her feelings about him were straightforward. She stuffed the letter back in its envelope and put it in her bag, intending to tear it up as she had all the others. Not that there had been many. An intermittent trickle. She had never answered any of them.

'I'll write back to him. Tell him what he can do with his begging letter.'

Jason had only met Rory once – when he had turned up, out of the blue, at the little flat in Kingston where they were living when Simone was born – and, having heard Jen's tales of his prowess as a father, had been less than impressed.

Rory had started writing to her a couple of years ago. She had never found out how he had got the address. In the confusion and excitement and ultimate disappointment that followed the arrival of that first letter, she had never thought to ask.

It had been written on blue paper. The kind you buy in a pad and tear off sheet by sheet. Jen had recognized the handwriting immediately. Had felt faint, sick, elated all at once. It was years since she had heard from him – thirteen, probably. His visits had stopped suddenly, a few months after he had left home, and he had disappeared out of her life so completely that it had been almost as if he had never existed. A fictional character from a book she had once loved.

Jason had been at work and she had flirted with the idea of saving opening the letter until he got home, so that they could share the moment together. She had been unable to wait, though, her fingers tearing at the envelope even as she had mulled this over.

She had known as soon as she pulled out the flimsy sheet of paper that it was going to be an anticlimax. It was only a few lines long. Thirteen years of history encapsulated in a few short sentences. Sorry he hadn't been in touch. He had heard she'd got married. He was struggling a bit himself.

She had stopped herself from tearing it up just long enough to show Jason, when he came home that afternoon. That was the only time she had cried, watching her husband read the pitifully inadequate offering she had been waiting her whole adult life to receive.

'You don't need him,' he had said as he'd hugged her. 'You have me. You have all of us.'

The other two occasions when Jen had seen him, Rory had simply materialized in front of her at the hotel, and claimed to have been passing. They had spent five minutes catching up, and then he had disappeared out of her life again for another few years. Once, he'd pressed her for money, but not the other time, so she had occasionally allowed herself to believe he had some vestige of family feeling in there, somewhere – even though her rational self knew it was improbable. More likely, she was a box he felt he had to tick from time to time. She tried not to care. A leopard can't change his spots, she had told herself, more than once.

'What's the point?' she said now. 'He's not going to change.'

'After everything he's done to Elaine ... to both of you. I don't know how he's got the nerve.'

'He's just no good at being a father. It happens.'

'It was his choice.'

'Maybe. Or maybe he just can't help the man he is. Nobody can. And some people aren't strong enough to fight it.'

'You've never had a good word to say about him.'

'And I still don't. I'm just saying, perhaps I shouldn't always judge him so harshly. Perhaps he's not that much worse than most people, he's just not so good at covering it up.'

'Well, God help the world, if that's the case.'

'Who am I to pass moral judgement on him?'

'His daughter. Who he walked out on, when she was eight years old. If you can't hold him to account, then I don't know who can.'

'I turned out all right, didn't I?'

'Despite him. That's to Elaine's credit.'

'Exactly. Things might have been much worse if he'd stayed. If he'd pretended he and Mum were happy for my sake, but it had all been a lie.'

Jason exhaled loudly. 'It makes me angry, that's all, that you had to go through all that. And, whatever else, there's no excuse for him cutting you out of his life except when he needs something.'

'I just . . . I'm tired of feeling like I hate him. He's a miserable, lonely old man. What's the point?'

'The point is that he was one of the two people you should have been able to trust more than anyone else in the world. And he let you down. Big time. I find it hard to get past that.'

'I just don't think life is that black and white. A lot of parents fuck up.'

'Well, you're a nicer person than I am.'

Jen knew this conversation could only be unproductive. And dangerous.

'I'm going to open a bottle of wine.'

She stomped out before he could say anything else.

Water under the bridge.

As she lay awake that night, listening to Jason's breathing, the phrase from Rory's letter popped into her head again. She saw her dad handing her a twenty-pence piece, dressed up in his best suit, on his way out for the night. She was about five.

'Look after the pennies,' he'd said, with a twinkle in his eye.

And then, in the kitchen, her helping her mum make dinner.

'Many hands make light work,' her dad had said as he came in to help himself to a beer from the fridge.

She blinked back a tear. So she had inherited something from him, after all. It was a useless attribute, faintly embarrassing, definitely not one to boast about, but it was his. Proof that he'd once been a daily presence in her life

Cass heard the phone at the other end ring again. Over and over. Eventually, it clicked through to answerphone and she hung up. She had left enough messages. It wasn't as if Jen didn't know why she was ringing. She was clearly ignoring her calls.

The first few times, Cass had assumed Jen was at work – or with her family. Of course, she wasn't going to answer. Cass had understood. She had left messages – hopeful and friendly, at first, getting increasingly curt and recriminatory as time went on. And then she gave up and started ringing off when she got no reply, knowing that Jen would see her number listed as a missed call. Knowing her point would be made.

It wasn't fair.

Jen had set herself up as the portal to the Mastersons. The gatekeeper. And now she was freezing Cass out. She had put the shutters up, and she thought that that would be enough. That if she pretended Cass wasn't there, she might just go away. A bit like when children think that, if they close their eyes, you won't be able to see them. Out of sight, out of mind.

Really, Cass thought, she had had enough of being pushed aside. She had spent her whole life on the sidelines, steadfastly hoping that by being good and dutiful and discreet she might one day be allowed to be in the spotlight. It was never going to happen, she knew that now. Not if she just sat back and waited.

Truthfully, she had had enough of being ignored. She had told Kara this, when they'd had one of their long phone conversations last night. One of the things she loved about Kara was her disregard for the consequences. She adored drama. Cass knew that anyone else – if there had been anyone else she could have confessed her feelings to – would have told her to think twice, to tread carefully, to think about the lives she might ruin (her own most of all). Kara, on the other hand, had reacted exactly as Cass had known she would.

'Fuck it. It's not like you haven't given her every opportunity to do things properly.'

'I know.'

'She should consider herself lucky you're even waiting for her to tell you when the time is right. You could have just steamed into the family home and announced yourself. I don't know why you didn't, really.'

'Yeah, cos that would really endear me to them . . . It's much better if she breaks it to them, lets them get used to the idea.'

'Well, I don't think I could have been so patient. What if she never does? What are you going to do then?'

'Move on to Plan B. I just need to decide what Plan B is.'

Kara had laughed. 'If you need help formulating it, you know where I am.'

31

'Jenny!'

Elaine's smile gave away that she was delighted to find her daughter standing on the doorstep when she opened the door. Jen turning up midweek wasn't a regular occurrence. In fact, she couldn't remember ever having done it before. She had decided on a whim. Phoned her mother and suggested it before she could talk herself out of it. She had just wanted to do something nice for once, something extra-curricular.

Elaine's house was at the end of a terrace on a small neat estate. It was the house Jen had grown up in, one of an optimistic 1970s collection of identical three-up two-downs, with weeping willows in the front gardens, in a quiet cul de sac where the local kids could ride their bikes safely. At least, that had been the idea when it had been built. None of the weeping willows had lived through the bike-riding children becoming rampaging adolescents with too much time on their hands, and nothing to do with it.

It had been designed with young families in mind. A kind of starter home, Jen imagined. Elaine had never left, had never had the wherewithal, once Rory and his sporadic income had gone. She had watched as a never-ending cycle of happy couples with tiny children had moved in for a few years, and then moved on to bigger houses or divorce. She didn't know many of her neighbours now. It had started to become too hard, trying to forge new friendships as the invisible doors revolved, and so she had stuck to the few people who had stayed put as long as she had. There weren't many of them left.

Elaine stood back to let her into the small hall. She was smartly dressed: A-line skirt, baby-blue blouse, outdoor shoes with clicky low heels. Jen noticed that her hair was neat and her make-up just so.

'Have you been out?'

'Oh, just the Co-op. I wanted to get a cake in.'

Jen bit her tongue. 'Great.'

The idea of Elaine, dressed and made up with nowhere to go but the Co-op, struck a chord of guilt.

'I'll put the kettle on.'

'So,' Jen said purposefully, 'I've brought a ton of bin bags. We can load up everything from the spare room and I'll take whatever's any good to Oxfam and the rest to the tip.'

'Are you sure? I could easily do it myself.'

Jen put an arm around her mother. 'And how would you take it anywhere? You don't have a car.'

'Well, it's really kind of you, Jenny. It'll be a great help.'

Jen experienced a righteous glow. The kind you get when you help a blind person across the road or give anything silver-coloured to a beggar. There was no such thing as altruism – it was all about how it made *you* feel, not them.

'And I'll go through the attic while I'm here. Might as well.'

She said this without really thinking. God only knew what was up there, and how long it would take to sort. Jen didn't think anyone had climbed the rickety metal ladder in living memory. She had certainly never set foot up there, her childhood fear of spiders having given its dark corners a horror-film atmosphere she had been keen to avoid. Since she had become a mother herself, she'd forced herself to overcome that particular neurosis, unwilling to pass it on. She would still rather never encounter anything with more than six legs but, if she did, at least she no longer cried and screamed and ran out of the room.

'I can't have you doing that, it's a terrible mess up there. Just helping me with the spare room is enough. I'm really terribly grateful.'

'Don't be silly. At least I can have a quick scout around and see if there's anything obvious that can go –'

'No, Jenny,' Elaine said sharply.

Jen almost did a double take.

'I . . . I just mean, we won't have time to chat if you're up in the attic . . . Why don't you leave it for another time?'

'That's crazy. I've got the car here and the whole afternoon –'

'I can do it myself,' Elaine said, sounding slightly desperate now.

'You can't get up that ladder.'

'Well, I'll ask Dominic, from up the road, one of these days. His son would offer, I'm sure.'

Jen had no idea why her mother was being so adamant.

Assumed that, unaccustomed as Elaine was to being offered any help from her daughter, she didn't know how to accept it. She was probably afraid of putting her out too much. Scared that if today turned into a production number, then Jen wouldn't offer to visit her again any time soon.

'Tell you what. I'll do half an hour up there, that's all. You can time me. And then we can have tea and cake and do the spare room together.'

Elaine, she noticed, was looking anxious. Her patent happiness at seeing her daughter seemed to have waned.

Twenty-three minutes later, Jen understood why.

'I was protecting you.'

Elaine looked at the fireplace, the carpet, anywhere but Jen.

'From what? From my own father?' Jen rifled through the battered cardboard box she had dumped on the table. 'There are . . . what? Seven years' worth in here?'

Elaine eased herself down on to the sofa. She looked like she might have fallen over if she hadn't.

Jen picked up one of the still-wrapped gifts. 'To Jenny, love Dad' written on the label. She tore it open. Bouncy deely-boppers wobbled about on a purple head-band.

She reached for another in gaudy Christmas paper, ripped into it. A *Now That's What I Call Music* CD: 'Kayleigh', 'West End Girls' and 'Alive And Kicking'. Some of her favourite songs when she was thirteen.

'How could you?'

'I thought I was doing the right thing.'

'You let me think he just didn't care about me. That he'd forgotten me the minute he walked out of the door. And he sent me presents till I was . . . what . . . fifteen?'

Elaine was studying her hands. 'I'm sorry, Jenny.'

'No wonder you didn't want me to go up there. What else might I find? Letters? Did he write me letters?'

'Sometimes.'

Jen stood up, made to go towards the ladder again.

'I burned them all.'

'You . . .?'

'Jenny, love, you have to understand. I had to make a decision. He was so unreliable.'

'Did he ever try to see me?' Jen could hear how cold her voice sounded, couldn't do anything about it.

Elaine's voice was getting smaller and smaller. 'I couldn't have him take you out when he'd been drinking, could I?'

'It's not as if he ever hurt me, or took me down the pub and then came home without me.'

'Of course not.'

'Then I don't understand.'

'All those times he was supposed to pick you up, and then he didn't come –'

'What? So because he was a bit flaky, you thought it would be better if I never had any contact with him again?'

'I thought it would be better for you. I thought if he kept letting you down, it would break your heart.'

'And losing touch with him altogether wouldn't?

'I'm sorry, Jenny –'

'Jen!' Jen raised her voice. 'It's Jen, for God's sake. How hard is that to remember?'

'I'm sorry. You're making me nervous.'

'I need to understand why, that's all.'

'I just wanted you to be happy.'

'And it never occurred to you to let me decide what that would take? For Christ's sake, Mum.'

Elaine made as if to stand up. 'I'll make us some tea.'

'No. I have to go. I need to get back home.'

She grabbed up the box and left before her mother had a chance to protest.

When she got to the house, she left the presents in the boot of the car and told Jason she had worked a few extra hours. She knew if she filled him in on what had really happened, he would talk her out of what she had decided to do next.

'Judy's still sick,' she said, wrinkling up her face.

She hoped he couldn't see she'd been crying again.

Another Sunday, another painful afternoon sitting in Charles and Amelia's front room. Jen had thought about trying to get out of it, knew she wouldn't be able to pull off another migraine, couldn't face the argument with Jason that would inevitably follow.

So she sat at the table, monosyllabic, as closed in and uncommunicative as a teenage girl. Picked at her food. Spoke only when spoken to. Sulked.

'Are you unwell, sweetheart?' Amelia said, laying a gentle hand on her arm. 'You do look a bit peaky.'

Jen looked up, became aware that her mother-in-law was looking at her, concerned.

She forced a smile. 'No, just a bit knackered. Hard week at work.'

'Still doing extra hours?'

Jen nodded weakly.

'So have you heard Martin got a new car?' Charles looked at Jason as he said this so, thankfully, Jen didn't feel she was expected to answer.

'Another one? Do you think maybe he'd give me one of the old ones? Charitable donation.'

She let them chatter on, barely tuning in to what they were saying, nodding and smiling here and there when she thought she should.

That morning neither she nor Jason had leapt out of bed in order to make the other tea so they could have their usual Sunday morning catch-up. They had both just lain there, feigning sleep, until it had felt like a decent hour to get up.

By the time they left to go home, Jen felt as if she had barely strung two words together all afternoon. She longed to confide in someone about what had happened at her mother's house but she had forgotten how to talk to her mother-in-law.

She hated knowing that Amelia was concerned about her but, at the moment, it didn't feel like there was anything she could do about it. She was just grateful it was all over for another week. That was all she could do now – take her life one step at a time, and try to fight fires along the way. It was exhausting, but there didn't seem to be another way. She had no idea how long she could go on like this, but trying to think of a solution was like trying to unravel the mysteries of the universe. She didn't even know where to start.

32

It wasn't the most salubrious of areas.

Jen held on to her bag as she walked from the bus stop, trying to look as confident, as casual, as she could. Trying not to give off a vibe that said, 'I'm a stranger here, I don't really know where I'm going and I clearly must have something in this bag worth stealing, otherwise why would I be holding on to it so tightly?' In truth, there was nothing in there she couldn't replace – except for the photos. She knew she should have had them copied before she came.

She had decided not to mention where she was going to anyone – not Jason, not Poppy, not Amelia. She didn't think any of them would understand. She filed the idea away in her 'Secrets' file. At this rate, she was going to need an entire cabinet devoted to them.

She had caught the train down to Croydon, and then the bus to the other side of the town. She'd asked the driver to tell her when they got there, and he'd pulled a face and said, 'Look out for all the boarded-up shop fronts,' a phrase that was only marginally better than, 'Get out at the chalk outline of the dead body,' and which hadn't exactly made her feel at ease.

She knew from the map that her dad's flat was close by. She had never been there before, obviously. She wasn't quite sure why she was there now. It was stupid, really. A whim. If it wasn't for the fact that she just wanted to get inside – somewhere, anywhere – and shut the door before she got mugged or worse, she would have turned round and gone straight back to the bus stop.

She was taking a chance that he would be home. She hadn't called ahead to check. She couldn't have, even if she'd wanted to, because she didn't have a number – and, anyway, once she'd made the decision to come, she'd had to move quickly before she changed her mind. She hadn't really thought through what she would do if he wasn't there. Leave a note, maybe. 'Jen was here.'

She wasn't expecting to gain a father, just maybe a bit of closure. Perhaps they could have some kind of a functional relationship for the last however many years he had left on earth. Jen could visit and take him out to the shops or the pub, and he could act like he gave a shit who she was.

She found the house on the edge of the estate. She made a note that, if she got lost on the way back to the bus stop, she should turn left at the salivating pit bull, tied to a child's climbing frame with a bit of string that it could have chewed through in about a millisecond, if it had the brains to realize it. Number 25 had the guttering coming away on the upper floor, but an attempt had been made to plant some flowers in the tiny front garden. Unfortunately, someone had then decided to store their shopping trolley on top of them. Jen rang the bell for the ground-floor flat, and waited. After what seemed like an age, she heard noises in the hall, and then a voice.

'Who is it?'

'It's Jen.'

'Jen who?'

Great. Now she was taking part in a live-action knock, knock joke.

'Your daughter, Jen. Jennifer. Jenny. Jesus, Rory, how many Jens do you know? Let me in.'

She listened as he pulled back a bolt, then a chain and, finally, a deadlock. She felt sick. She barely knew this man, hadn't even clapped eyes on him in more than four years.

He peered round the door, an old man with a slightly too flat nose and thin sparse white hair, who vaguely resembled her father. Jen didn't know what reaction she had expected – maybe, in her most hopeful imaginings on the way here, delight that his daughter had finally sought him out, or even a gruff, 'What do you want?' What she got was the indifferent politeness of an acquaintance, and not a very close one at that.

'Oh, it's you. You'd better come in,' he said, pleasantly enough.

Jen followed him down the corridor to the tiny kitchen at the back.

'Cup of tea?' he said, as if it had been four days, not four years, since they had seen each other last.

'Lovely.'

There was something about him that was so familiar, that took her right back to when she was seven or eight, and he was an everyday fixture in her life. She couldn't put her finger on what it was. It certainly wasn't the way he looked. Back then, Jen knew more from photographs than memories: he had been tall and dark and in good shape. He was always sporty, she could remember that much, and he would try to encourage her to play football in the park with him. She had wondered in the past whether having another child, a son, might have made him want to spend more time with his family, might have made him stay.

'So, to what do I owe this pleasure?' Rory said as he fussed around with mugs and tea bags.

'I don't know ... I ... I got your letter, and I just thought, well, it's been years ...'

'Come to see how the old fella looks, now he's an octogenarian?'

'You look well, actually.'

'So you're still at that hotel? I wasn't sure you would be.'

Jen nodded. 'We live in Wimbledon.'

'What ... you and ... um ...?'

'Jason. My husband's called Jason. We have two daughters, Simone and Emily. Both at college.'

Rory bristled. 'I know that. Well, not the college bit. Clever girls, then, are they?'

'They are.'

They sat in silence for a moment, while Rory poured water into the mugs and then squeezed the tea bags before plonking them on the counter. His flat could do with a good clean, she noticed. The kitchen counters had a sticky-looking film over them. There were cobwebs around the corners of the window. The whole place smelled slightly of stale air and unemptied bins. Clearly he was missing having someone to look after him.

'So you and Maxine have split up?'

Rory handed her a mug of tea – or, at least, that's what she assumed it was. It looked like a cup of dishwater with some milk thrown in.

'She moved out a while ago. No big deal.'

'How have you been?'

'Oh, you know, getting old.'

'Are you doing OK, though? Healthy?'

'Not too bad, considering. I manage. Jean from next door comes in now and then and gets some shopping for me.'

Jen stopped herself from asking whether Jean from next door was his new girlfriend. It wasn't out of the question. 'Right.'

Rory waved a pack of Hobnobs in her direction. 'Biscuit?'

She took one.

'How are your girls?'

'Simone and Emily. They're both at university, like I said. I have photos. Look.'

She produced them from her bag, with a flourish, and showed him the girls all the way back to when they were babies. Last time she had seen him, when he'd walked into the hotel four years ago, she had only had a few recent snaps of her two girls on her phone, and nothing of when they were growing up – plus she hadn't wanted to deal with him then, had wanted to get him out of there as soon as she possibly could – so now she took him through the whole story. Then she dug out her iPhone and showed him the most up-to-date pictures she'd taken of them both, and of Jason. She flicked through any with Elaine in quickly, before he really noticed.

He examined them all carefully. 'Lovely girls,' he chuckled, once she'd got to the end.

'Emily reminds me of you. She has this thing she does where she flicks her hair out of her eyes . . .'

Rory pointed up at his balding head. 'Not any more.'

'No, but you used to. I remember.'

'You do?' He smiled, as if that made him happy.

Jen felt as if she was about to burst into tears. He was so like himself, so like the man she remembered, but also immeasurably different. She didn't know what she was doing here. It was too late, truthfully, to start thinking of this man as her father. You couldn't make it real, just because you wanted it so much.

'So I just wanted to make sure you were all right, really. It's been a long time.'

'Well, last time I came to see you at your hotel, I got the impression you'd rather I hadn't.'

Jen could remember it clearly. She'd been busy at the time, but she could easily have taken ten minutes to speak to him properly. Instead, she had felt angry that he could just waltz back into her life after years of silence, and expect her to be pleased to see him. And she hadn't tried to hide her irritation.

'I'm sorry, a lot's happened since then.'

'We're all getting older.'

Jen inhaled deeply. 'Mum ... I found the things you sent me. In Mum's attic. I never knew.'

Rory gave a gruff half-laugh. 'That'd explain why I never got thank-you notes, eh?'

'I feel awful, Dad. I had no idea.'

'Well, it was all a long time ago.'

If he felt relieved that she now knew the truth – emotional that he had been vindicated, after all these years – he wasn't showing it. Maybe he had got too used to the idea of them being strangers.

'I thought you'd just forgotten about me.'

'I kept it up for a few years, but once you got to being

a teenager I gave up. I shouldn't have, I know that now. I just assumed that, now you were older, you would have got in touch with me if you'd wanted to, and so you must have decided you didn't want to. It was only years later that it dawned on me you might never even have known I was trying to stay in contact.'

'I still don't understand, though. Why didn't you just turn up? Insist on seeing me? Take me to McDonald's, anything? Just because Mum said you couldn't –'

'It's not worth raking it all up again, love. What happened's happened.'

'But I'd like to hear your side of it. I've always thought . . . well, that you weren't bothered, to be honest. Can you just tell me what went on? I feel as if . . . I need to know everything, that's all. Just to understand . . .'

It was her own fault, she thought later. She had pushed him for an answer.

33

In one way, it all made sense. Jen had always had a memory, deeply buried somewhere, of her father getting teary-eyed one Saturday, saying goodbye. She had always dismissed it, assumed that she had invented it to make herself feel better.

In another, it was the most unimaginable thing she could ever have heard. She simply couldn't take it in. It was like hearing the rules of the universe – the quarks and the strings, and the idea that all the matter in the world came from something the size of a pinhead. You could follow the words. You could even accept that what you were being told might prove to be the case. But that didn't mean you understood it. It didn't mean you could process that thought and fully comprehend it.

'I don't believe you,' she said, when Rory told her.

'Then don't,' he said, flatly. 'It's better if you don't.'

'Mum would never . . . I mean, hiding presents, maybe, but . . .'

'I never blamed her. I drove her to it. I was staying out all night. I was drinking. We were unhappy.'

'And then you left.'

'Yes. I tried to keep on being there for you but then, one day, I'd had a couple of beers before I got there – I wasn't drunk, but I suppose she could smell it on my breath – and that was it. She told me she was taking me to court.'

'I don't remember any of this.'

'Why would you? We tried to protect you from it. Anyway, things were different then. Everything was loaded to the mother's side, and they agreed with her. Stopped my visitation, and that was it.'

'That was it? You didn't try to . . . I don't know, overturn the ruling?'

'Of course I did. I cleaned up my act. Gave up drinking. Tried to have the decision reversed, but Elaine wouldn't have it. Threatened she'd call the police if I ever came round again.'

Jen had tried to imagine her mother so fired up with anger and revenge that she would choose to deny her her father, rather than give him anything.

'I don't want you to blame your mother, Jenny. It would never have happened if I hadn't been so . . . I know that, for a fact. I ruined our marriage, not her. Who could blame her for wanting to punish me in the worst way she knew how?'

'Why have you never told me any of this before?'

'What would have been the point? I'm glad you're close to your mother. I wouldn't want to get in the way of that.'

Jen had exhaled loudly. 'So what am I meant to do with this information now?'

'Nothing. You asked me. I told you. There's nothing to be gained by it going further than this room.'

'Shit. I wish I didn't know.'

'Sometimes,' Rory said, 'ignorance is bliss. If you ask me, the truth is overrated.'

'I'm sorry, Dad.'

'For what?'

'I just am. I never knew . . .'

'Me too,' he said, and that was the closest she had ever come to hearing him express real regret for the way things had turned out.

As she left, about twenty minutes later, keen to be back to familiar ground, and having run out of things to say, she gave him a quick hug, something she had never done before. Well, since she'd been an adult, at least.

'How are you doing for money?' she asked as she put her jacket on.

'Well, my pension . . . you know . . .'

She handed him a ten-pound note out of her purse.

'I'll try to come again.'

'That would be nice,' he said, and he sounded like he might mean it.

Jen wasn't sure if she really would, though. She had enough complications in her life.

34

She had travelled home from her father's in a trance. She could hardly take in what she had heard. Could barely understand what was happening to all the safe certainties she had always relied on. The idea of her mum taking Rory to court – to prevent him from ever seeing her – was almost incomprehensible. Her mother had always known that Jen had been devastated by her father's apparent lack of interest in her.

She hadn't intended to tell Jason what she'd learned, because that would involve telling him where she'd been, and she wasn't sure he'd understand why she couldn't have communicated her plans to him in advance. Then she would end up saying something like 'Because if I'd told you, you'd have told me not to go' and they would have found themselves in another fight. But by the time he got home from work, she was so wound up, so desperate to confide in *somebody*, that she could hardly wait until he'd taken off his jacket. If he hadn't arrived then, she might well have gone next door, introduced herself to the neighbours she had never even spoken to, had studiously avoided for years, and told them the whole sorry story.

She couldn't decide if she felt better or worse for knowing. It was too late to forge the bond with Rory that she'd been longing for all her life. There was a comfort in discovering that he had always thought about her, but she couldn't shake off the overwhelming feelings of regret and resentment that that knowledge had been kept from her when she had needed it the most. The awful, nagging feeling that it was too late – there was no rewriting history, however much you might long to.

Eventually, frustration brought tears to her eyes. She rarely cried. She hated herself when she did. And now, these days, it seemed like she couldn't stop. Her life felt out of control. She had no idea which way was up any more; so many of the stable pillars holding her upright had been knocked down.

Even if she had decided to make a promise to herself to keep her visit a secret, Jason would probably have got it out of her somehow, because the first thing he said when he walked into the kitchen was . . .

'God, are you OK? You look awful.'

Jen tried to make a joke of it. 'Thanks. You don't look so hot yourself.'

'What's up?'

And then it all came out.

'Jesus,' he said, when she'd finished the whole story.

'Part of me wishes I didn't know, really, but it's made me realize it wasn't all one-sided. It wasn't that my father was a villain and my mother was a pitiable victim. They both have things to answer for.'

'Elaine must have had her reasons.'

'I'm sure she thought she did. But she lied to me. She made me believe he didn't care, when he did, all along.'

'Are you kidding me?' Jason snapped. 'You really think he cared?'

'He said he really tried – cleaned up his act, tried to show he was reliable.'

'You only have his word for that part.'

'Why would he lie?'

'I don't know. Because he's old and he's realized he needs to get some sympathy quick, so someone'll look after him in his dotage. Because he's hoping you'll take pity on him and give him some beer money. You didn't, did you?'

'No,' she lied. 'Of course not. He didn't ask. I don't understand why you won't give him the benefit of the doubt.'

'If someone had told me I couldn't see Simone and Emily when they were little, I wouldn't have relied on the Royal Mail to ensure I had a good relationship with my kids.'

He rooted around in the box that Jen had finally brought inside, after steaming out to the car to get it. Exhibit A for the defence. He picked up one of the gifts with a flourish. 'I wouldn't have thought a pair of . . . sparkly balls on springs . . . would make up for the fact that I never saw my daughter. I'd have been outside the house every day, making sure I saw her whether I was allowed, or not.'

'Well, lucky for us that you're so perfect,' Jen spat back.

'You're going to forgive him now, after thirty-odd years of hating him? What, he's going to start turning up for Christmas dinner and taking the girls on outings?'

'Don't be stupid. He's an old man. What would it hurt, if I visited him sometimes?'

'Fine. Just don't bring him here. I don't want anything to do with him.'

'Jason, he's *my* father. Surely, if I want to renew my relationship with him, then you should be happy to go along with that?'

'I have listened to you talk about how he let you down, how unhappy he made you, for twenty-two years now, I can't just –'

'Exactly. Because that's what I believed, but it turns out I was wrong. Surely I owe it to him to at least get to know what he's really like?'

'You're really telling me he couldn't find a way to be a father to you, somehow? That Elaine just said "keep away" and he said "OK, then", and that's *all right*?'

'No . . . what was he meant to do?'

'You have to earn the right to be called a father, Jen.'

'Like Charles?' she said, sailing dangerously close to the wind.

'Yes, like Dad. You have to be there and involve yourself and be a role model –'

'You don't think Charles has ever fucked up?'

'I'm sure he has. But the difference is that he always put family first. He took his role as a father seriously.'

'He certainly did.'

'There's no point talking to you, if you're just going to be sarcastic. Honestly, I have no fucking idea what is up with you these days,' Jason said and then turned and left the room.

She heard him storming up the stairs.

Jen sat at the kitchen table. She couldn't be bothered to start on dinner. They could call out for a takeaway, who cared? She didn't know why they couldn't seem to have a conversation these days without it turning into, if not quite a fight, then an argument. An exercise in points-scoring. They had gone from being people who probably fought too seldom to be healthy, to people who fought at the drop of a hat. They seemed to have lost the middle ground completely. The safe place where they could meet and be each other's unconditional supporters club.

She had had no intention of bringing Charles into the conversation, of course. She certainly wasn't ever in any danger of giving away what she knew, but she hated the way Jason still looked on him as some kind of hero. She had wanted to topple his halo, snap it in half and stamp it into the ground. She had just wanted Jason to acknowledge that his father wasn't the greatest in the world, and hers the worst.

The one person she knew would understand was Cass. She almost picked up the phone to call her, thought about it for a split second, and then came to her senses. She hadn't had any communication with her since Cass had declared her desire to get to know her siblings. There had been countless calls since they had last spoken, and Jen had simply ignored them. There had been no more messages after the first couple of days, but Cass's number was sitting there, resentfully, in her phone's history. A constant reminder of the threat.

Meanwhile, down on the south coast, Cass was sleeping soundly. She had decided what she was going to do next.

35

Work on Monday felt like a respite. Time at the hotel was uncomplicated. It could be boring, tedious, repetitive, soul-destroying, but it was definitely uncomplicated.

She tried to tell herself that she was glad to be back, because her job gave her a certain satisfaction, and not just because Sean Hoskins was due to have checked back in yesterday.

She had remembered this while she was sitting on the bus, gawping mindlessly out of the window, trying to wake up slowly. She had smiled at the recollection. Having someone to share a few friendly chats with would make the week pass more quickly – although, in turn, that would make next weekend come round sooner, and she wasn't sure that was a good thing. She had no desire now to spend time with either her in-laws or her own mother. She hadn't spoke to Elaine since her trip to see her. She couldn't face it. Couldn't think of what she might say that wouldn't feel like an accusation. Couldn't imagine how she would ever trust her mother again.

And then, next week . . . well, she couldn't even think about next week at the moment, or she'd slit her wrists.

Early mornings at the hotel were always quiet, even in the height of the summer holidays. Jen liked the luxury of having the time to check through future bookings, to make sure any special requests were catered for. Once

Neil had arrived, and they had exchanged a polite couple of words about their weekends, she was glad when he drifted off into one of his silences.

The lift pinged to announce it had reached its destination, and Sean stepped out, pushing a hand through his swept-back hair, and waving a greeting as he saw them.

'Morning. How's things?'

Jen and Neil both smiled their hellos.

'Do you need help with anything?' Neil asked, already waving to attract the attention of one of the doormen, who might be needed to flag down a cab.

'No. Thank you. All my stock has already been delivered to the venue. I just have to go down and move it around a bit before we open. And the walk'll do me good.'

'Where is it again?' Jen felt like she didn't want him to rush off, she wanted to keep him there for a bit, re-establish the easy way they'd had of teasing each other the last time he was down.

'Regent's Park. Have you not seen them building the marquees for it? The London Antique and Vintage Fair?'

'It's in a tent?' Jen raised her eyebrows in mock shock.

Sean laughed.

'No,' Neil said. 'A marquee.'

'If either of you want to come down, I can give you passes. I wouldn't want you paying the admission fee, it's extortionate.'

'It sounds just like being at Glastonbury again – only with people trying to sell you vases, instead of Ecstasy.'

'Exactly,' he said. 'Or, in my case, a bit of costume jewellery from the fifties.'

'Sadly,' Jen said, 'I don't think my budget runs to antiques.'

'Well, you'd both be very welcome, if you have an hour to kill.'

'There's a taxi here, if you'd like it,' Dan the doorman called over.

Sean started to move towards the door.

'Do you need any restaurants booking or anything?' Jen asked as he walked away.

She felt like she wanted an excuse for him to have to talk to her later. She didn't know why. Just a diversion, really, she told herself. A reason to think about anything other than home. She could feel that she was trying too hard, acting a little too desperate for him to think she was fun and sparkly and witty. She told herself to get a grip.

Sean laughed. 'Yes, if I want to humiliate myself this evening I'll let you know.'

'Ha ha.'

Once, years ago, she had accidentally booked the wrong restaurant, and Sean had turned up at Tamarind instead of Benares to meet some associates for a Michelin-standard curry, only to find there was no table available. He would have been within his rights to be furious, embarrassed in front of his acquaintances, but he had chosen to take it graciously. He had never let her forget it, though.

In the afternoon, she hung around after her shift had finished, pretending she had work to do. She had hoped Sean might pop back during the day, or that he might come home early, and they could have another little flirty chat before she finished her shift. It wasn't that she was interested in Sean – or that she thought he was interested in her – she told herself. It was just that the thought of home and spending a long evening tiptoeing around safe subjects with Jason was exhausting.

She felt completely on her own. Cut off from all her support systems. Her head hurt with the responsibility of being the keeper of all the secrets. It was like a sick joke; find the person least comfortable with keeping things to herself, and tell her *everything*.

In the end, she gave up and started on the long journey home.

She was being ridiculous.

She was walking along the road from the bus stop, past the shops, concentrating on avoiding the puddles, when she became aware of a woman sitting on the wall of their next-door neighbour but one's house. Something was familiar – a manicured hand pushing back long brown hair, a black pea coat.

'What the hell are you doing here?' she demanded as she drew close to Cass.

'Waiting for you.' Cass smiled, as if nothing was amiss, as if it was perfectly normal for her to have travelled up from Brighton to sit on a wall yards from Jen and Jason's house in the drizzle.

'You never answer my calls any more, so this seemed like the best way to get to talk to you.'

'Are you psychotic? What if Jason sees you? He could get back from work any minute.'

'He'll have no idea who I am. As you well know. And anyway, he's home already. I checked.'

Jen felt her heart stop. 'You checked?'

Cass laughed. A laugh that made Jen want to slap her.

'Don't worry, I didn't ring the doorbell. I mean, I saw him through the window. From the other side of the road.'

'What do you want, Cass?'

'I told you, to talk to you.'

'I mean, what do you want here? Now? You're not expecting me to take you home and introduce you? When he still doesn't know you even exist? I don't think that's the way to give your relationship the best chance.'

'Stop being so melodramatic. I just wanted to say hello. See where my brother lives.' She peered along the road. 'I thought your house would be bigger, somehow.'

'Well, much as I'd value your professional opinion, it'll have to wait for another day.'

'This isn't fair, you know, Jen.'

Jen sighed. 'It's not that I don't feel for you. I understand. I do. But you have to let me tell him in my own time. At the moment, honestly, I can't imagine when that might be. It's Charles and Amelia's anniversary coming up –'

'And after that, there'll be something else. I'm trying to do it the right way but I don't know how long I can wait, in all honesty.'

Jen knew what Cass was saying, knew what message she was hoping to get across by being here, outside their home: I could just turn up any time out of the blue and knock on your door and introduce myself. If you don't tell him, then I will.

She could feel her heart beating in her ears. Her palms sweating. Panic.

'I have to go in.'

'It's not going to go away. I'm their sister, and that's it. Nothing can change that.'

'Please, Cass. *Please* . . .'

Cass stood up. 'It's OK, I'm leaving. I'm not threatening you. I just . . . you never return my calls, so how else am I supposed to find out what's going on?'

Jen watched as she moved away along the road. Waited until she saw her flag down a taxi. She had no idea what to do.

Jason was watching the news in the living room when she let herself in.

'That you?' he called out as she shut the front door.

'I'm late, I'm going to get on with cooking.'

She went straight through to the kitchen, dropped her bag on to a chair, took off her coat and sat down at the little table. She was finding it hard to breathe. There was no doubt in her mind that Cass's visit had been a statement of intent. She knew the truth was going to have to come out at some point, but she couldn't face it. Didn't feel strong enough to deal with the questions and the accusations and the hurt.

Did Cass really think that Jason, Poppy and Jessie wouldn't go straight to their father to get the truth verified? That it wouldn't become inevitable that their relationships with him would never be the same again? That Amelia wouldn't have to find out, eventually? That the whole family wouldn't crash and burn around her?

Cass was naive, that was the thing. She was young, she hadn't properly thought through the consequences. And she might just be headstrong enough to detonate the bomb herself, if she thought Jen wasn't taking her seriously enough.

Jen tried to imagine the conversation with Jason, the collateral damage that would follow. She couldn't do it. Not yet. Not now.

'Are you OK?' Jason was standing in the doorway, looking concerned.

Jen jumped to her feet, forced a smile on to her face. 'Long day.'

'Want me to cook?'

'No. Thanks.'

'Jessie called. I said you'd phone her back.'

'Oh. Right. Maybe a bit later. I want to get started.'

Another one to add to the 'Avoid' list. Jessie didn't have Poppy's witchy senses – she had nowhere near enough empathy with other people to ever really worry about what they were thinking – but her favourite topic of conversation, after herself, was the rest of the family and Jen was in no mood to indulge her.

Jason was hovering in the doorway. 'You sure you're all right?'

She forced herself to sound positive. 'Yes.'

'OK,' he said, and moved back towards the living room.

Jen breathed a sigh of relief. She didn't feel able to stand up to his scrutiny, she was still shaking from her encounter with Cass.

They ate with the TV on, not talking. Jen couldn't think of anything to say that didn't verge on dangerous territory.

'I think I'm going to have an early night,' she said, as

soon as the clock hit an hour Jason wouldn't question. 'I'm knackered.'

'OK. I'll come up in a bit. Night, love.'

'Night,' Jen said sadly, scared to go over and give him a kiss in case she tripped and fell into the ever-widening gulf that had sprung open between them.

It had occurred to her that she might be tying herself up in knots to save her relationship, when there seemed to be less and less of a relationship to preserve every day. That she might be fighting a losing battle. Flogging a dead horse. What did that say about their marriage, that it could start to crumble so easily?

She tried to remember what they had had in common, when they first met – before the kids, before she had even met his family. They had shared a sense of humour, a few interests. They had wanted the same things. Was that it?

She still had faith, deep down, that they could get through this somehow, though. That they could emerge, if not unscathed, then intact. That, somehow, she could keep her family together. She had to. Because if the Mastersons fell apart, then what would she have, what would be left? Who would she be?

36

'Asleep on the job?'

Jen jumped, tried to look as if she was working. Sean was standing looking at her, a wry smile on his face. She tried to return it, but she was having trouble behaving like a normal, functioning human being. She had spent the night awake but pretending to be asleep. Terrified her world was going to come to an end and there was nothing she could do to stop it. She felt wired from lack of sleep and sheer panic. She tried not to let it show on her face. Tried to seem professional.

'I was concentrating.'

'Yeah, right.'

'OK, I was napping. It's been a long day.'

She hadn't expected to see him today, had thought that as she was on a late shift he would have gone out before she arrived, and probably wouldn't be back until after she left. She attempted to match his tone, to fall back into jokey friend mode. Tried to look as if everything was normal.

'What are you doing, skiving off?'

He laughed. 'I'm completely ready for the big opening tomorrow, so I thought I'd call it a day. What time do you get off?'

Was he asking her out again?

'In about half an hour. But I have to rush home. I've

got . . . something on.' Why had she said that? Now she had made it look like she really did think he'd propositioned her when, in actual fact, all he'd said was, 'What time do you get off?'

'Sounds like fun. Well, I'll probably see you tomorrow.'

'Good luck with the opening.'

'Oh,' he said, reaching into his jacket pocket. 'Here are your passes. Just in case anyone wants to come down.'

He disappeared into the lift before she could say thank you. She hoped she hadn't offended him. The truth was that a drink would have been nice. Sean was good company. Easy to talk to. Attractive. Definitely attractive. Which was exactly why saying no had been the right thing to do.

Just as she was going to get her coat, her phone buzzed. Jason. She took it out to the back room.

She was still reeling from the evening before. From the narrow escape and the additional layers of complication that were now stacked on top of the web of lies she had built. Cass wasn't to be trusted. Unless she had conveniently fallen under a train on the way home, Jen was going to have to come up with a plan, a way to manage the situation. That had clearly been the message Cass had been trying to send her.

'Hi. You OK?' Jen asked.

'Yes. You?'

'Knackered, but . . . fine, yes.'

'Listen, I just wanted to warn you Mum and Dad are popping over in a bit. They want to talk about the holiday, make the final arrangements. They're not expecting to be fed.'

Oh God. She couldn't face it. She just couldn't.

'Oh. Shit, Jase, I'm sorry. I was just about to ring you. Neil's gone home sick and they asked if I'd stay. Just till nine. I thought we could do with the overtime.'

She could always go and sit in Caffè Nero with a book for a few hours.

'That's convenient,' Jason said.

Jen knew she was rumbled. She couldn't admit to it, though, she had to stick to her guns.

'I'm not making it up, Jason. Jesus. There must be something going round –'

'It's just that you didn't mention it till I said my parents were coming over, that's all.'

'Fine,' Jen said huffily. 'I'll say I can't do it, then.'

'No, no, you go ahead,' he said.

She knew he was angry with her. 'Well, you'd clearly rather I didn't.'

'You know what, Jen? You do whatever you want. I'll see you later.' He put the phone down without even saying goodbye.

Jen rubbed her fingers into her temples. Even though she knew there was no way for Jason to understand what was going through her head at the moment, even though she was keeping a huge secret from him, even though she was, indeed, making up the fact that she had been asked to do overtime, his attitude still annoyed her. How dare he think she was lying?

She picked up the phone before she had a chance to talk herself out of it, checked that Neil was occupied with a guest, dialled the number without even thinking through what she was going to say.

He answered after the second ring.

She spoke before she had a chance to think. 'Oh, hi. It turns out I don't need to rush home after all, so . . . if you fancy a drink . . .'

'Sorry, who is this?'

Oh God. Jen felt herself blush. How many people had he invited for a drink in the past ten minutes? 'It's Jennifer. Jen. From reception.'

'I know! I was kidding,' Sean said.

Jen could hear a smile in his voice. She, on the other hand, felt like an idiot.

'Same place, or do you know anywhere better?' he asked.

'No,' she said. 'Same place is fine. I could meet you in there in about five minutes, if that's OK.'

She wondered what she had got herself into. Shit, what was the worst that could happen? She'd spend an hour or so in the company of a charming, entertaining and supremely uncomplicated man with no obvious baggage – or at least, if he did have, it couldn't impact on her – she'd have one vodka and tonic, and then she could still hide out in Caffè Nero nursing a coffee for the rest of the evening. It would be an hour's respite from indulging her worrying, if nothing else.

She told Neil she was leaving, put her coat on over her uniform and headed for the pub.

37

For some reason, she suddenly felt hopelessly self-conscious. All the easy chatter she'd indulged in the last time they went for a drink seemed to have deserted her. She scoured the hidden recesses of her brain for an anecdote – anything that she could talk about and make herself seem even vaguely interesting – but they were empty. What if that's it? she thought briefly. What if I've used up every entertaining thing I will ever have to say, and all I'm left with is the weather and *Britain's Got Talent*? Luckily, Sean was on good form, happy to fill in the gaps while they stood at the bar sipping their drinks, waiting for a table to come free – Jen had insisted on buying, this time – and eager to talk about the Vintage Fair.

'It's like a small village,' he said when they eventually sat down.

'Do the antiques people look down on the vintage people?'

'I think they do! There's antiques on one side and us vintage people on the other. It's like apartheid.'

Jen laughed and felt herself relax a little.

Sean swigged back the last of his beer. 'How's things with you?'

'Fine,' she said defensively.

'OK. That's good.'

Jen sighed. 'All right, well . . . not fine, actually.'

'Let me get us another drink and then you can either tell me, or not. Up to you.'

She knew she should say, 'No, thank you, I should leave and get home to my husband,' but sitting in the pub chatting definitely beat trying to while away the next two hours in a coffee shop. Or going back to the house to face Charles and Amelia, for that matter. She did manage to ask him for a Diet Coke, though. She didn't think Jason would appreciate her coming in from work slurring.

'So,' Sean said, putting her drink down in front of her. 'I'm all ears, if you want to offload on someone. But don't feel you have to. I wouldn't want you to think I was being nosy.'

'I . . . I don't even know where to start, really.'

She suddenly felt like it would be such a relief to unburden herself. To share the whole sorry story with somebody who knew none of the players, who had no preconceived ideas of how badly any of them had behaved, no expectations to be shattered. She didn't even need him to comment, she certainly wasn't expecting him to give her any advice. It would just be cathartic to get the entire weight of it off her chest.

'At the beginning?'

'I haven't . . . no one else knows any of this . . .'

Sean looked at her. 'I'm not about to turn something you tell me in confidence into a bit of gossip. That's not my style.'

Jen inhaled deeply. 'OK, well . . . I know people always say "it's a long story", but this really is.'

'That's all right. I haven't got anything else to do.'

So she told him about Cass being Charles's daughter, not his mistress, and the way her relationship with Jason had started to fracture since she'd found out the truth about her father-in-law. She told him about her dad. About Poppy and Jessie and Amelia, and the perfect family she had surrounded herself with. About Cass and the implied threat that she could blow the whole thing apart, if she wanted to. How she felt as if she was walking on quicksand, sinking deeper with every step.

She stopped every now and again to check he hadn't fallen asleep – or if he was in the throes of terminal boredom – but he always encouraged her to go on. Of course, he had no idea that her father-in-law was the great Charles Masterson, social commentator and proponent-of-bringing-moral-values-back-into-society extraordinaire, and she made sure not to mention his name. She might wish a lot of things on Charles, these days, but even she didn't want to be responsible for letting that particular cat out of its bag.

When she got to the end, to Cass turning up on her doorstep out of the blue, Sean sat back and exhaled a long breath.

'She sounds a bit unhinged, if you want my opinion.'

'Honestly, I don't think I can take any more. I have no idea what to do, it's all such a mess.'

'Can I ask you something? What were you hoping to achieve? I mean . . . listen, I have no idea what I'm talking about, really, but she's not going to go away, this Cass. She's always going to be his daughter.'

'I know. I mean, I don't know. I suppose I was hoping

she'd decide she didn't need to get to know them, after all . . . that I could persuade her –'

'And then the family could just carry on as normal? Is that even possible, do you think?'

'Not now, probably . . .' She paused. 'I honestly don't know if Jason and I will survive it.'

'If it's a choice of Cass telling him, or you breaking it to him gently, then I know what I'd recommend. He's not going to blame you. You've been put in an impossible situation.'

'I know. It's just the idea that once I do, that'll be it, there will be no taking it back. Even if he can forgive me for keeping it a secret all this time, he'll go straight to his father and accuse him. He'll tell Poppy and Jessie, how could he not? Amelia will . . . Oh God, I can't even think what it'll do to Amelia. The minute I utter those words, I'll have destroyed the family. My family.'

'It's your father-in-law who's doing that. You'll just be the messenger.'

'Yes, and we know what happens to them.'

'What's the alternative? A slow lingering demise, because you can't act normally around them? Maybe sudden death is better?'

'I keep hoping there's some other solution, that's all. And I keep thinking that every day I don't tell him is another day I don't have to deal with the fallout.'

'Do you really think there could be?'

'Not really. Not any more. It's just . . . we have this stupid weekend away booked. Once we've got through that . . . Amelia's been looking forward to it for months. And then it's Christmas. My girls will be home for the holidays.'

'There's never going to be a perfect time.'

'I know that. It's . . . not yet, OK. Not now.'

'I don't even know where to start. You poor thing. It must have been a nightmare.'

It was the fact that someone was being sympathetic. That for the first time, someone – anyone – had acknowledged how difficult her position must be, how impossible the situation she was in. She couldn't help it. She felt her eyes well up again, blinked furiously to try to stop the tears coming. She felt so stupid. The last thing she needed was to start crying in the pub, but she didn't know how to make it stop.

Sean looked at her, horrified. 'Oh God. I'm sorry. I didn't mean –'

'It's not your fault,' Jen sniffed. 'This is ridiculous. You must think I'm the one who's unhinged.'

'Are you kidding? If what's been happening to you had happened to me, I'd be a basket case.'

'I think I probably am.' She dug around in her bag and found a tissue, dabbed at her eyes, attempted to stem the tide.

'Actually, you do a pretty good impression of being a well-rounded, balanced person. Well, most of the time, anyway.'

'I feel exhausted, just trying to remember what secret I'm keeping from who. It's like I can't have a normal relationship with any of my family any more. I'm just avoiding everyone.'

'I don't think it's healthy, if you really want my opinion. It's too much for one person to have to deal with.'

'I feel a lot better, just for having said it all out loud.'

Sean smiled. 'This is you feeling better? Jesus, I'd hate to be around if things get bad.'

Jen laughed, which must have looked fairly demented, she imagined, given that she still had tears and no doubt mascara and God knows what else running down her face.

'The thing is, I keep telling myself everything'll be OK, somehow. That if I ignore it all, it might just go away and things will go back to how they used to be. But I know I'm kidding myself, really.'

'Maybe you should just bite the bullet and tell Jason. I know you were trying to protect him but if, in doing so, you're pushing him away too, then that can't be a good thing, can it?'

'I don't think he'd take kindly to me having met his sister.'

'He'd get over it. And maybe it wouldn't be such a bad thing for him to see what his father's really like.'

'It's not just that, though. I've realized lately that it's more fundamental. We've lost something. Or maybe it was never there in the first place. I don't know who we are as a couple any more. We've only ever really been together as parents. I don't know if, without that, we have anything to hold us together. I've got no idea what we have in common outside family. I used to be so pleased with myself about how close Jason and I were. I thought we had it pretty perfect. Now I realize we were just deluded.'

'You've been together a long time . . .'

'What if I just made myself love him because I fell in love with his family?'

'Come on . . . really?'

Jen nodded. 'I don't know . . . I've started wondering that lately.'

'You can't be carrying all these secrets around with you. You'll make yourself ill.'

He put a hand on her arm as he said this. She knew she should move it away, but she couldn't make herself. She looked up at him and saw that he was looking directly at her. She felt her stomach flip.

'I don't know what to do,' she said, only partly meaning in relation to her problems.

'I can't help you there,' he said, pulling his hand back.

She could feel a burning sensation on her arm where it had been. She wondered briefly what it would be like to lose herself for a few hours with this man. Just once to have something that was uncomplicated and spontaneous. To be made to feel like she was wanted again, that she counted. But that wasn't her. She had always had very strict rules for herself, and she wasn't about to break them.

'Maybe you need to put yourself first,' he was saying. 'Stop worrying about how everyone else feels.'

She had no idea what possessed her. Even years ago, when she'd been single, she had rarely been the one to make the first move. And now here she was, a mother of two, happily married – at least, until recently – and monogamous for more than twenty years, leaning over to kiss a man she barely knew in the middle of a pub.

She didn't even think about the other people around them. Whether any of her co-workers from the hotel might have stopped in for an after-work pint. She didn't think about Jason or the girls. And, for a brief minute, she forgot all about Charles and Amelia, Cass, her dad, her sisters-in-law, her mum. Everything.

Sean hesitated for a moment, but then she felt him relax and respond.

She was vaguely aware of a voice saying, 'Get a room,' but she blocked it out. Personally, she hated to see overly physical public displays of affection, but now was not the time to worry about upsetting the locals. She could feel Sean's hand on the side of her face, holding her there, as if he was afraid she might disappear if he didn't.

It was so long since she had kissed anyone other than Jason. Lifetimes ago, she knew that. Before marriage, before children. In fact, she couldn't even remember when she had last kissed Jason like this. When they had leaned into one another as if their lives depended on it, rather than pecked politely at each other's cheeks like a pair of friendly parrots. She had forgotten how powerful a kiss could be. She'd forgotten she could feel like this.

After what seemed like an eternity, they moved apart.

Sean was looking at her intently, bluey-grey eyes fixed on hers. 'I wasn't expecting that,' he said, and the way he said it, the hoarse catch in his voice that hadn't been there before, made Jen feel light-headed.

'I still have a couple of hours. We could go back to your room . . .' There. She'd said it. It had sounded like it was coming from someone else, it was so unlike anything she would ever say, had ever said. Now it was out there. She couldn't take it back.

'Are you sure that's what you want?' he said, but she was already up and putting on her jacket.

Outside, she could hardly look at him. She felt as if she was in a trance. She knew what she was about to do was wrong, but she was powerless to stop it. Sean reached out for her hand, and then, before she knew what was happening, they were standing in a doorway and he was kissing her again, this time with even more urgency. Somehow, she managed to ignore the fact that they were in the street, that she had a husband at home, that she wasn't the kind of person who would ever do something like this.

After what seemed like hours, they surfaced for air. Sean cradled her face in his hand.

'God, you're gorgeous,' he said, and she felt her legs buckle.

She smiled up at him. 'Let's go,' she said before she could change her mind. 'We might have to walk through reception separately, though.'

In the couple of minutes she'd had to think, she had already worked out that she could tell whoever was on duty that she had forgotten something earlier, and then go through to the back room and up the service stairs to meet Sean on the third floor. She would probably need oxygen to revive her once she got there, and she wasn't sure how erotic Sean would find an asthmatic wheeze. She hadn't worked out how she would leave later, either, what excuse she would give for having been lost in the hotel for however long she was there. That she'd fainted, maybe. Passed clean out in the back room and lain under a table undetected for an hour or so. She couldn't think about it too much or she'd bottle out.

She went first, figuring that this would give her a fighting chance of catching her breath before Sean showed up. She felt fuelled up with adrenaline. She knew what she was doing was crazy – and wrong – but she couldn't seem to stop herself.

Neil was on the desk along with Karen, one of the juniors. They smiled when they saw Jen come in. She'd banked on there being at least one guest needing attention, but reception was deserted. She tried to steady her breath. Just a normal evening. I've left something behind. I've come back to get it. Big deal.

'I think I left my wallet here,' she said, rolling her eyes as if to say silly old me and my forgetful ways. 'I think it must be out the back, somewhere, probably fell out of my bag.'

'I'll help you look,' Karen said.

Ordinarily, Jen would have thought how nice, how thoughtful. 'No!' she said, far too vehemently. 'It's OK.'

As if by magic, a couple with two children, and enough bags to start a Louis Vuitton store of their own, fell out of a taxi and it was all hands on deck to get them unloaded and checked in before the younger of the two kids, a toddler, got sued for noise disturbance. Jen felt sorry for any dogs within a two-mile radius.

She slipped out the back and was on her way up the stairs, leaving them to it. When she reached the third floor, she found room 328 and waited outside, praying no one would be delivering room service next door before Sean arrived. She wished she'd said yes to another vodka and tonic. She needed the Dutch courage.

Thank God it was only a couple of minutes before the

lift pinged, and there he was. Jen took him in as she watched him walk down the corridor towards her. He was tall, dark and almost, nearly, handsome. OK, so he wasn't necessarily conventionally good-looking, but it was all about his confidence and humour and that knowing smile he had. She liked his smile, she had decided. He always looked like he had a secret, and a fairly dirty one at that. He pushed his hair back off his face in a way that reminded her of herself when she was nervous. Thankfully, though, he wasn't sporting the same ginger curls.

'Hi,' she said, apprehensively.

Sean rubbed his hand along her upper arm in a reassuring gesture as he unlocked the door. 'OK?' he said, and she nodded.

She was struck by the fact that it felt strange being inside one of the rooms. Ordinarily, there was no reason for her to be – and, in fact, she couldn't remember the last time she had been. Sean's room was a junior suite, which basically meant a bedroom with a tiny sofa area. Jen was relieved to see that it was tidy. She wasn't sure she could take coming face to face with his dirty underwear draped across a chair.

'Do you want a drink?' he said, opening the minibar. Even though she did, she managed to say no. She had to keep a clear head.

There was an awkward pause when neither she nor Sean seemed to know what to do. It was as if they had left the pub with no doubts about what they wanted but now that they were in private, self-consciousness had crept back in. She could see the bed looming up out of the corner of her eye. She tried not to look at it.

Sean walked over and leaned down to kiss her again, and suddenly it all made sense. She felt his hand move inside her uniform jacket, across her collarbone. He started to unbutton her blouse and she shuddered, half from pleasure, half from fear. This was it.

He pulled away and looked at her. 'Are you sure you're all right?'

She nodded. 'Just nervous.'

He kissed her again, and she tried to lose herself in it like she had in the pub. It worked too. After the first couple of seconds, she just gave in. It was going to happen. She wanted it to happen.

When they broke apart again, Sean was silent for a second. And then he took a step away from her.

'Shit. Jen, we can't do this.'

She thought she'd misheard for a moment. Tried to work out what else he might have said.

'It's not that I don't want to. God, no. But you're married. You have a family. I . . . it's just not right. I can't take advantage just because you're having a hard time at home. It's not me.'

Jen stepped back, felt like all the blood was draining from her head. The room was spinning.

'It's not me either. I mean, I don't go around propositioning men. I've never . . . But I thought this was different. I thought . . .' She felt so stupid. She had basically thrown herself at him, and now he was rejecting her. She fumbled with the buttons on her shirt, trying to do them up again.

'If you were single . . . but you're not. It wouldn't be fair.'

She felt as if she was in a film. The stupid lonely

middle-aged woman making a fool of herself by practically jumping a man she hardly knew. The audience would be shouting, 'Don't do it!', laughing at her, feeling sorry for her. Why had she ever been deluded enough to think this man would want her?

'But,' she said, a note of desperation creeping into her voice, 'why did you kiss me, then?'

She waited for him to say, 'Actually, it was you who kissed me first,' which, technically, would be correct.

She didn't know if she could bear the humiliation.

'Because I think you're lovely,' Sean said. 'But I should never have asked you for a drink.'

'I feel so stupid,' Jen said. 'I'm so embarrassed.'

'When you wake up tomorrow, you'll be relieved. You'll know we did the right thing.'

Suddenly, all she wanted was to get out of there. If she could avoid seeing Sean for the next couple of days, he could join the ever growing list of people she had vowed to try to steer clear of. (She was going to have to move to a desert island, at this rate. That or spend her life savings on some kind of facial reconfiguration.) She had no idea how she could pull that off, so long as she worked at the hotel, but it was the only way. She would pretend this had never happened.

'I have to go.'

Sean reached out a hand to take her arm. 'Jen. Don't be silly. Let's go back to the pub. We can have another drink, at least.'

She pulled away. 'No. Really. I should just leave.'

She walked out before he could say anything else. She didn't know where she was going, she just wanted to put as much distance between herself and Sean as she could. How could she have been so stupid? She had misread the signals completely. She had lost her mind, betrayed Jason, made a fool of herself.

She remembered all the other people in the pub, the voice saying, 'Get a room.' Anyone could have seen them, two saddos in their forties, necking away like randy teenagers. Overheard her suggesting they go to his hotel. Was anyone in there laughing now at the deluded married woman who had made an idiot of herself, practically begging a man who wasn't interested to have sex with her?

She fought back tears. She had no idea who she was any more. The Jen she had always been, the one she thought was a pretty good person, would never have even thought about kissing a man who wasn't her husband. Let alone done it. Let alone been the one to initiate it. She couldn't even think about what had happened afterwards, what she'd said to him. She could feel her face flushing at the memory.

She practically ran down the stairs and back out through the door to reception.

'Did you find it?' Karen asked pleasantly.

Jen had to think for a moment to remember what she was talking about. 'Oh. Yes.'

'God, you were ages back there,' Neil said. 'I nearly sent out a search party.'

Jen didn't trust herself to say anything else, so she just waved her hand. She ignored Graham Roper the Doorman Groper's shout of goodnight and headed down the street.

She didn't slow down until she had reached the heart of Soho, thronged with people leaving work, meeting friends for a drink or a meal. She looked at her watch. It was still only twenty past seven. If she went home now, there was a chance Charles and Amelia might still be there. She couldn't safely assume they would have left until about nine. She had forty minutes to kill before she could start on her journey back to Wimbledon.

She wandered around until she found a Costa Coffee, bought herself a latte and sat staring out of the window.

'I'm sorry I snapped at you,' Jason said as soon as she walked through the door.

She couldn't even look at him. She thought that, if he could see her face, he'd read what had happened written all over it.

'How was work? You must be shattered. Did you eat? I ordered pizza when Mum and Dad left and I got a huge one, in case you hadn't had time. It's in the fridge.'

'I'm fine. Not hungry.'

'Drink?'

'Actually, I think I'll just go to bed. I'm on an early tomorrow.'

He didn't object. Didn't beg her to stay up and tell him about her day. She was grateful. She wouldn't have known what to say. They kissed cheeks as she passed him on the way to the stairs. She tried not to think how different a kiss it was to the one she had experienced a couple of hours ago.

'How were Charles and Amelia?' she said, suddenly remembering that she should show some interest.

'Good. They missed seeing you.'

'Sorry. Night.'

'I'll try not to wake you when I come up,' he said to her retreating back.

'Thanks.'

She felt the weight of their polite exchange nearly suffocate her. She wanted to run back down the stairs and tell him everything that had happened from the beginning right up to tonight, so that he could tell her not to worry and that everything was going to be OK. But she knew if she did, he wouldn't, so instead she just kept walking.

She tried to keep her head down when she saw Sean crossing reception next morning. She was on her own – as the person doing the early shift always was before seven thirty – but she had been counting on him not being up and about so early. There was no reason for him to be. The Vintage Fair didn't even open until ten.

She thought about picking up the phone, pretending she was on a call to a customer, but it would be just her luck for it to suddenly ring while she was talking. She busied herself with some papers, hoped he might keep moving if she kept her head down.

He had been right when he'd said she would be relieved nothing more had happened when she got up in the morning. She had gone to bed feeling angry and humiliated, and woken up feeling ashamed and regretful. What had she been thinking? It was made ten times worse, of course, by the fact that it hadn't been she who had turned down Sean's advances, it had been the other way round. If she had got her way, she would have slept with him, cheated on Jason – who, as far as she was aware, had never so much as looked at another woman, who was one of the only people she knew who was straight up and honest and exactly the person he claimed to be – destroyed her marriage, probably. She had nothing to resent Sean for, really, she should be grateful, but all she felt was shame and embarrassment. She didn't want to have to speak to him.

Sean, on the other hand, had different ideas. Jen could sense him hovering near the desk. In the end, she had no choice but to look up.

'Have you got a minute?'

It must have been obvious she was a trapped audience. She couldn't go anywhere, even if she wanted to.

She looked over to check that Dan the doorman was comfortably out of earshot. 'I don't really want to talk about it, to be honest. I made a fool of myself, that's it.'

'I thought I should make sure you knew that it wasn't that I didn't want to. I think you're absolutely . . . well, you know. Under any other circumstances . . . I just thought it would add to your problems, that's all, and I would hate to do that.'

'It was the first time . . . I don't usually go around throwing myself at strange men.'

'I know that. And, for the record, it didn't feel to me like you were throwing yourself at me. It felt like I was encouraging you. I was the one who kept suggesting we go for a drink. I knew you were married. I should never have done that.'

She looked right at him for the first time. 'So why did you? If you have such a strong moral code –'

'Because I really liked you. Like you. And I wanted to spend time with you, get to know you better. I knew I was potentially putting myself – us – in a difficult situation, but I couldn't stop myself.'

'I should still never have done what I did.'

'Tell you what, let's toss a coin for it. Heads it was all my fault, tails it was yours.'

Jen smiled, despite her miserable mood. 'You were right . . . when you said I'd be relieved in the morning that we hadn't . . . you know.'

'Whereas I have been kicking myself. It's not every day a woman I've had a huge crush on for years kisses me. Or lets me kiss her,' he added hastily.

She tried to ignore the fact that he'd said he had fancied her for years. 'Thank you,' she said, 'for trying to make me feel better.'

'At your service,' he said, waving his hand with a mock flourish. 'Now I should go on my sad, single, lonely way and get ready for the day ahead.'

'Bye,' she said, as casually as she could. 'Have a good one.'

'I guess I'll see you tomorrow.'

'Yup,' she said, looking down.

She knew she wouldn't, in fact, see him because she was off the following day, and then he would be gone. She decided not to say anything, though. If she did, she was scared they would have to mark the moment, say an awkward goodbye, and she wasn't sure whether she could cope with that. When she found out he was coming down again, she would have to book holiday, take time off sick, something. It didn't bear thinking about.

She spent the day trying to push all thoughts of him to the back of her mind. She had enough to worry about in her real life without dwelling on what might have happened. There but for the grace of God, she heard her father say. People in glass houses.

38

It was here. No amount of wishing it would never happen – that the cottage would burn down, or one of them would contract a deadly contagious disease, or war would break out, anything – could change the fact that the day she had been dreading, more than any other, had finally come.

They were travelling up separately, thank God, because neither Charles nor Jason could bear to be the one to leave their car at home. The plan was to meet in the pub in the village of Great Milton late morning, and then head over to the house, which was a five-minute drive away, to meet the owner and collect the keys, at twelve thirty. As they turned off the motorway and travelled down ever smaller roads, Jen's heart began to sink. She simply had no idea how she was going to get through this.

Since, well, since *that* evening, not only could she hardly bear to face Jason, but she could hardly bear to face herself in the mirror either. She would be overtaken with waves of shame and embarrassment, or fear of being found out. If this was how she felt after one near miss, she couldn't even begin to imagine how Charles had got through the last twenty-five years. She almost felt sorry for him.

Every time she thought about Sean, she ran through a whole spectrum of emotions in record time. She felt ridiculous, regretful, ashamed and, occasionally, slightly turned on – although she tried to suppress that one as much as she could. Mostly, she just felt bad. She tried to imagine how she would take it if she found out that Jason had been with a woman, snogging in a crowded pub and then pushed up against a doorway in the street, caught up in a moment he couldn't resist. It made her sick to think about it. In the end, she had to stop herself from going over and over it. It had happened. There was nothing she could do to change things. Move on.

On the plus side, her indiscretion had temporarily helped to drive thoughts of Cass to the back of her mind. There was only so much she could torture herself with at once. Her head simply didn't have space to house all the things she was anxious about at the same time. She had never been great at multitasking.

There were, she had noted last time she'd counted, eleven missed calls or texts from Cass logged on her phone since the afternoon she had come to the house. Jen had taken to leaving her mobile turned off, switching it on every now and again in case of emergencies, trying to ignore the rising floodwaters. If she allowed herself to dwell on it, she would begin to panic, heart racing, palms sweating, head swimming.

As she was packing up the last few bits and pieces, she heard Jason's phone ring, knew by the way he answered it that it was Poppy. She stayed in the kitchen, listening to his jokey exchange with his sister. She breathed a sigh of relief when it sounded like he was ending the call, but then suddenly there he was, in front of her, phone held in his outstretched hand.

'She wants a quick word with you.'

Jen pulled a face that she hoped said, 'I haven't got time.'

Jason thrust the mobile at her anyway, and went back out of the room.

'Hey,' she said, before Poppy could strike first and ask how she was. 'How's things?'

'Great. I wanted to tell you to have a good time. I've asked Jason to get a box of champagne truffles from me and put them in their room.'

'Lovely. I might eat them on the way, though.'

'And I'm sorry I snapped at you the other day.'

'It's fine . . . it was me . . .'

Thankfully, Poppy's mind was on other things, and Jen's words were enough for her to assume that everything was back to normal. 'Oh, and I really like him.'

Jen was momentarily confused. 'Like who?'

'Ben.'

'Who's Ben?'

'Benji. The guy I met through . . . you know. You'll be glad to know he says I can call him Ben.'

'Benji who was so bland you couldn't even remember what he looked like after the first date you had with him?'

Poppy sighed. 'It wasn't that he was bland. It was . . . I don't know . . .'

'Forgettable? Uninteresting?'

'No. Why are you being so mean?'

'I'm not. I'm just telling you what you said.' She reminded herself that she would be on trial, after their last conversation. She had to try harder.

'I was only joking. Tell me what he's like. How many times have you seen him?'

'Four. We just had lunch again yesterday. And he's nice. Funny and sweet and good company. And he's attractive too, just not in a way that hits you in the face, that's all.'

'Did you speak to his mother or his ex yet?'

'No. Only because we haven't been out for a proper evening date yet. And it feels a bit silly, now I've got to know him. Plus, he did say it would be OK, which must mean he has nothing to hide, right?'

'Oh no, I am totally not getting involved in that one. You do whatever you think is right.'

'We're meant to be having dinner at the weekend. He couldn't do a dinner at the weekend if he had a family, could he?'

An image of Charles shot into Jen's mind. She had remembered, the other day, that before he semi-retired Charles often used to entertain potential wealthy buyers at the weekends. Or so he said. He used to say he had to woo them to convince them that they should let Masterson Property find them their new home. Funny, how she'd forgotten that. Don't say anything, she told herself – the way you sometimes have to remind yourself not to laugh when someone tells you a piece of really bad news.

'Of course not.'

'I don't know. Maybe I'm being naive.'

'I suppose you have to trust people sometimes.'

'Mmm . . . Maisie, don't . . . oh, you did.'

Jen laughed. 'What's she done?'

'Fed a bit of toast to the cat. I swear my vet thinks there's something wrong with me, because she keeps telling me to put him on a diet but then every time I go back, he weighs a bit more. It's because Maisie keeps shoving food at him whenever she thinks I'm not looking.'

'I'll leave you to it,' Jen said, seeing her excuse to cut the call short before Poppy started asking questions.

'It's OK. I can talk to you and keep an eye on her at the same time.'

'Oh no, I'm not being responsible for Jerome keeling over from obesity. I'll talk to you soon.'

She could hear Poppy laughing as she hung up.

The village was small and pretty, with just one shop along with the pub, which was lovely, old and beamed with shedloads of both character and characters who, Jen assumed, were the locals. Under normal circumstances, it would have been idyllic. They had promised themselves dinner at Le Manoir aux Quat'Saisons, just up the road, one night as a treat. Somewhere Jen had always wanted to go, but she couldn't even bring herself to look forward to that now.

Charles and Amelia were already seated at a table in the corner of the pub lounge, when they arrived. Jen busied herself with chairs, unwilling to look either of them in the eye. When she did finally have to admit defeat and sit down, she noticed that Charles looked older, strained and tired. Did that mean Cass's mother – God, she really must find out her name – had suddenly taken a turn for the worse? She had been doing fine, the last Jen had heard.

'It only took us an hour door to door,' Amelia was saying. 'Of course, Charles drove far too fast, as usual.'

'Fifty would be far too fast for your mother,' Charles said jovially.

'Gosh, Jen, have you lost more weight since we saw you last?' Amelia said, and not as if that would be a good thing.

Actually, Jen thought, she might well have lost a few more pounds, not that she was about to admit it. 'No, I don't think so. It's probably this coat.'

'You look tired. It must be all the extra work.'

Jen leaned over and gave her a hug. 'Not this weekend.'

'You must have a rest. Don't think you have to be running around after me and Charles all the time.'

'Good heavens, no,' Charles piped up.

Jen forced herself to smile at him. She was here now. She had to get through this weekend with the minimum of permanent damage.

'If anything, we should be running around after you – after all, you're paying.'

'Shall we have an early lunch? I'm famished,' Jen said, in an attempt to show willing. She didn't even wait for them to answer. 'Let me get some menus.'

The cottage was every bit as chocolate-boxy as it had looked in the pictures. It was set off the main road, down a little lane that led to fields at the end. Pale rough stone, with characterful leaded windows and a small porch. Jen knew from the photos she'd seen online that there was a big, cosy farmhouse kitchen, an overstuffed living room, and three decent-sized bedrooms upstairs. When they'd booked, she had optimistically hoped she might persuade one or other of the girls to come along. Then she had just thought it would be fun to spend some time with them. Now she would probably have used them as a human shield. Of course, they both had lives of their own, and better things to do than spend three nights watching their mother tiptoe neurotically on eggshells around the rest of their family.

The woman who handed them the keys – imagine the poster girl for the WI in the 1970s, only not so sexy – did a double take when she spotted Charles. Jen saw Amelia smile happily with a pride that she immediately then tried to suppress. Amelia had never been one to show off.

'Mr Masterson,' the woman said, her voice dripping with obsequious admiration, 'I had no idea.'

Charles held out a hand to honour her with a firm shake. The Pope offering a blessing. 'Pleased to meet you. What a delightful place.'

'I have to say,' the woman gushed, 'I so admire your world view.'

'Thank you. It's always nice to feel one's work is appreciated,' Charles said graciously.

Jen looked at the house, the lane, anywhere but at her father-in-law.

Inside, it was a bit overdone country-cutesy for Jen's taste. There wasn't an inch that hadn't been covered in a chintzy floral fabric. She felt as if she was inside a bouquet. The whole place screamed Middle England as loudly as a red-jacketed huntsman with a pack of baying beagles at his heels. She could actually feel Britain's moral backbone forcing her to stand tall and be counted. They went their separate ways to unpack.

Jen and Jason had earmarked the second biggest of the double bedrooms, making sure that Amelia and Charles had the largest and prettiest. Their own view was of a herd of cows, contentedly mooching around, most of them the wrong side of fat. The sight made Jen feel uneasy.

'I hope they're dairy and not for eating,' she said as she looked down on them. 'I'd hate to think they were all pottering about happily, not knowing their days were numbered.'

'They're girls, by the look of it,' Jason said, peering out of the window. 'I think that means they're dairy.'

'Since when could you tell the sex of cows just by looking at them?'

'Call me an expert, if you like, but I don't think male cows get pregnant. Or have udders.'

'They're pregnant!' She slapped his arm playfully.

'Or maybe just fat. Can cows get pregnant in November? I have no idea. They're definitely females, though.'

Jen's mood dropped as quickly as it had risen. 'Oh God, if they have boys, do you think they'll take them away and sell them for eating?'

'Christ, your glass really is half empty at the moment. What's wrong with you?'

'Nothing. Just thinking aloud.'

'You're not going to be in a funny mood all weekend, are you?'

'No. God. Of course not.'

She didn't want to revisit the topic of her unwillingness to spend this time with his family – especially not with Charles and Amelia next door. She could hear them moving around, the low murmur of his voice and her slightly higher tone.

'Good.'

Jason, Jen felt, had never quite forgiven her for saying she didn't want to be here and, ever since, she had felt as if he was trying to bite his tongue. Like he had more to say to her on the subject, but he knew it would be better in the long run to keep it to himself.

She hated it when he was like this. Resentful and closed off. All her instincts were telling her to ask him what was wrong, provoke him into saying whatever it was he wanted to say, but she forced herself to ignore them. Just get through the next few days. Everything else could wait.

She shoved clothes into drawers, mentally counting down the hours until it would all be over. It didn't sound so bad when you said seventy hours. Seventy hours could go by in no time. Four thousand two hundred minutes. Two hundred and fifty-two thousand seconds. What was that song from *Rent* again? They'd been to see it once, a few years ago, and she had sung the lyrics in her head for days.

'I hope Dad hasn't picked up on your reluctance to be here.'

'Jason, for God's sake.'

'Didn't you notice how quiet he was at lunch? And I feel as if he's been like that for a while now. Not himself.'

'I've said sorry. I'm here, aren't I? Stop trying to make me feel bad.'

'Keep your voice down, they'll hear you,' he said.

She wished they could clear the air properly for once. Get everything out in the open, and then see where they were after that. But that was out of the question, obviously. They never did, and this certainly wasn't the time or the place to push the issue. Jason was never going to understand how she felt. She was never going to be able to tell him a fraction of the things that were taking up space in her head. She just had to learn to be better at deception, to be more convincing when she said that everything was fine, she was happy to be there, happy to be spending time with his mum and dad. Once these next few days were out of the way, she could go into overdrive building bridges. Shore up their foundations, before she had to tell him the news that might rock them again. From then on, she was only going to look ahead to the future, never back. No use crying over spilled milk, the cliché-offering voice in her head – Rory's voice, these days – said.

'Whatever is wrong with Charles, it has nothing to do with me,' she said now, trying to keep a light tone in her voice. 'I'm happy to be here. We're going to have fun. All right?'

'Sorry,' he said. 'I didn't mean to have a go at you. Come here . . .'

He put his arms around her, and she let him pull her into a hug. She pushed an image of Sean out of her head. Felt herself blush with shame or embarrassment, or both.

'I'm an idiot,' he said. 'Of course it's all going to be OK.'

She nuzzled her head into his chest, willing it all to go away and for them to be back where they were a couple of months ago, living in blissful ignorance.

When they had first booked the cottage, Jen had entered into the spirit of things by researching days out on the internet, planning what they could do that Amelia and Charles would find entertaining. She had enjoyed it, storing up surprises like Christmas presents. There was to be a visit to Woodstock and Blenheim Palace, a day spent sightseeing around Oxford itself, and she had mapped out a couple of local and not too arduous walks, in the hope that the weather would be fine.

The first afternoon was cold but pleasant – the sharp, watery November sun low in the sky, doing its best – and so, once they had unpacked, she suggested a stroll through the countryside, ending up at another nearby village that had a shop selling tea and cakes, and from where they could easily get a bus back. She chivvied everyone into their coats and out of the house. Keeping on the move seemed to be the key to getting through the holiday in one piece. The Devil makes work for idle hands. Don't stand still long enough to get into an argument. Stay occupied, and then there would be no question of anyone saying anything they shouldn't. Don't think about Sean. Don't think about Rory and Elaine. Don't think about Cass. Don't think.

She set off at such a pace that, after a short while, Jason called out to her to ask her to slow down or they weren't going to be able to keep up. She did as he asked, but she still walked ahead, trying to enjoy the countryside. Jason was lagging behind with Charles and Amelia. Let him try to get to the bottom of what was preoccupying his father. She'd be interested to hear what Charles had to say.

Every other person they passed greeted Charles like the long-lost Messiah. These were his people. No doubt, if he dropped dead on one of their beautiful footpaths, they would erect a statue to him. His chest puffed up a little more each time, like an amorous pigeon.

Amelia was talking about one of their neighbours. Someone Jason clearly knew or had heard her talk about before. Something about him putting in for planning permission to create a roof terrace that would overlook their garden. Jen could hear Charles chip in every now and then, usually when Amelia asked him a question. She kept her head down, kept walking, tried to appreciate her surroundings. Just get today out of the way. One day at a time.

39

'Happy anniversary.'

Charles held his glass of champagne aloft (only the best – Jen and Jason might be paying, but Charles had ordered – and Jen had tried not to gasp when she'd seen the price on the wine list).

'Happy anniversary,' she echoed, a smile plastered on to her face. She was trying.

'Thank you, darling,' Amelia said, misty-eyed.

'Well, it certainly is an achievement. Not many couples can say they've been together – and happy – for forty-five years.'

'Well, forty-seven really, since we dated for two years before we married.' Amelia looked at Charles fondly as she said this.

He smiled and touched his glass to hers. Jen looked away.

They were having dinner at Le Manoir, the beautiful Raymond Blanc restaurant that was part of an opulent country-house hotel that had been way outside Jen and Jason's budget. This meal would probably set them back a couple of weeks' wages each. Not that she begrudged it. Or, at least, not that she had begrudged it when they'd booked it. She had been excited about being able to repay Charles and Amelia, in however small a way. They had saved her, taking her into their family, rescuing her from her own sterile life. Of course, now that excitement had been replaced with dread, resentment, anxiety. All of which she felt she could have come by much cheaper, if she'd wanted to.

They sat in one of the small, pretty armchair-stuffed reception rooms, having a pre-dinner drink and looking out over the gardens.

They had managed to get through more than twenty-four hours – twenty-nine and a half, in fact – without major incident. Last night, after their walk, Jen had offered to cook for them all in the cottage, and because Amelia was tired out she had reluctantly agreed. Eschewing all offers of help, Jen had rustled up what she thought was her best dish, a chicken tagine, made with Moroccan spices and couscous. She had taken her time, relishing being on her own, trying to delay the moment when they would all have to sit down to eat together.

Carrying the steaming dish towards the table, with three expectant faces smiling at her, she had remembered what Miss Janine, her ballet teacher when she was at primary school, used to say, over and over again: 'Smile, girls. It doesn't matter if it hurts. If you put a smile on your face, no one will know.' God, she'd hated ballet. And Miss Janine, for that matter.

And then, later, once they had gone up to bed, something momentous had happened. Put out the bunting! Alert the media! Hallelujah! Jason and Jen had had sex. She didn't really know how it had happened. He had initiated it – spurred on, she thought, by the fact that they had got through one day unscathed and she had so clearly been on her best behaviour. In truth, she was knackered, and willing sleep to help the hours to go by, but she knew that if she knocked him back it would be months before another perfect moment presented itself and he would feel he could try again.

It was nice. No, she thought, that wasn't fair, it was more than nice. Not exactly *Last Tango in Paris*, but then, if it had been, she wouldn't have enjoyed it so much. She'd have been worrying about all that cholesterol in the butter. It was what she needed. It was comforting. It made her feel emotional in a sort of 'Thank God, I thought it was never going to happen again' kind of way. At one point, they got a bit giggly about the fact that Charles and Amelia were just the other side of the wall, and they had to make sure they kept the noise down. That was the best part, in all honesty. Her and Jason sharing a joke like they used to, laughing like they didn't have a care in the world.

Afterwards, they had fallen asleep wrapped up in each other and a tangle of sheets. When she had woken up, he'd still had his arm across her and, even though it was weighing heavily on her chest and she'd felt like she might have a coronary, she had left it there.

In the morning, she had waited to go downstairs for breakfast until Jason was out of the shower, dressed and ready to accompany her. In the kitchen Amelia was sporting a gold bracelet that Charles had given her as an anniversary gift. Ostentatious? No, Jen thought ungenerously. All she needed was the matching necklace and she could join the Beastie Boys.

'It's beautiful,' she'd said. Because it was. Guilt made for fabulous presents.

Charles glowed with husbandly pride. Look at me. Look what a perfect spouse I am. Look how much I must love my wife, because I've spent a small fortune on her!

'Show Jen your present,' Amelia had demanded, and Charles had been obliged to produce a little box from his pocket – an Asprey box, no less – which he'd handed to her proudly. Inside, nestled on its silk cushion, was a beautiful gold money clip.

'Gorgeous,' Jen had said, holding it out to return it.

'Look on the back,' Amelia had insisted.

Jen had reluctantly taken the money clip out of its nest and turned it over. 'Here's to forty-five more' it declared on the reverse side, with the date.

She'd felt suddenly sick. 'What a lovely sentiment,' she'd said, looking Charles straight in the eye for the first time in weeks. She couldn't help herself.

He hadn't even flinched.

Later, they had driven to Woodstock in their two cars, mooched around in the village shops for a while, had lunch in a cafe and then explored Blenheim Palace and its luscious gardens in the afternoon. By the time they'd got to Le Manoir, Jen had felt like she could almost see the end in sight. Not counting the meal and sleeping time, they pretty much only had to get through the same amount of time as they had already survived. A day and a half. If she slept in late, went to bed early, it should go by in a flash, they would have done their duty for the foreseeable future, she could go home, bury her head in the sand and wait for it all to go away.

Fat chance.

She never should have accepted that third glass of wine.

It wasn't that three glasses made her feel out of control, it was just that once she had polished off the third, it then became inevitable that she would say yes to a fourth and, maybe, if it was on offer, even a fifth. And then all bets were off.

They were actually having a pleasant evening. That was what had allowed her to let her guard down. The food was exceptional, just as Jen had imagined it would be. They had walked around the grounds oohing and aahing at the organic vegetable plot, even though it was too late in the year for much to be going on. They had tried to spot the fat carp in the pond, but it was too dark to really be sure, and then they'd felt their way over the bridge to sit in the little pagoda.

Soon her pretend jollity started to feel no different from actual jollity. If you act like something is a certain way for long enough, then eventually it might as well be. The lines blur. Fiction becomes reality. Charles was telling an anecdote, it was funny, they were all laughing. Everything was going to be fine.

They picked their way along the dark road, back to the cottage, hugging the hedges every time a car came towards them. At one point, Jason reached out and took Jen's hand and she felt a wave of something approaching happiness. It made it awkward a couple of times, when they had to go into single file, but she didn't let go. She didn't want to spoil the moment. Another image of Sean popped into her head, and she pushed it away. That woman wasn't her. In fact, Jen didn't know who she was, or where she had come from. She gripped Jason's hand more tightly.

Once they got in, they should all have just gone their separate ways to bed, congratulated themselves on a great night and slept it off, but someone – Jason, actually – decided it was a good idea to open another bottle. Jen could remember briefly thinking, 'This isn't the most sensible thing we could be doing. I should say no.' But the next thing she knew, she was accepting a glass – her fourth of the evening – and joining in yet another toast, with enthusiasm.

They moved into the living room, turned the real-flame gas fire to high, and settled into the deep armchairs. She had never been a great drunk. She didn't like the feeling of not being completely focused. Plus, she had discovered when she was a student that she had a tipping point. A point at which long-dead and buried slights came back to life, and deeply suppressed resentments had a tendency to bubble up to the surface.

Four glasses of wine and she could usually manage to shove it all back down again, bury her true feelings where no one would see them. Five and, well, anything could happen. Consequently, she would always endeavour to move to soft drinks when she hit the happily tipsy three-drink high, content to watch other people around her make idiots of themselves and knowing she would be the one feeling fine in the morning.

Later on, she would try to blame it on the wine – as if, without that extra glass, she would have been able to hold her tongue for ever. Underneath it all, even she knew that wasn't the case.

Jason filled their glasses up again. Amelia, clearly not used to having so much to drink, started getting into that loop that drunk people sometimes get into of saying the same thing over and over again.

'Forty-five years,' she said, for maybe the fifth time that evening. 'Forty-five years. Can you believe it?'

Jen had always loved how her mother-in-law was when she was a couple of drinks down. She became endearingly ditzy. 'Away with the fairies,' Charles would say (affection-ately, Jen had always thought). 'Ooh, there she goes. Yes, she's gone,' he would laugh indulgently.

And Amelia would inevitably look at him with big doe eyes and say, 'Who, dear? Who's gone where?'

It was yet another long-standing family joke. The kind of gentle, loving banter born of a long-standing shared history that Jen had always craved. Now when he said it, though, it just seemed patronizing – as if he was laughing at his wife, not with her.

'She's off,' Charles said.

Jason laughed. Jen smarted on Amelia's behalf.

'I'm not off anywhere, dear,' Amelia said in a sing-song voice. 'I'm staying right here, with my lovely family, until you all go to bed.'

'You do that, Mum,' Jason said warmly.

'I hope we'll still be here for *your* forty-fifth.'

'If we are, they'll be feeding us with spoons,' Charles said, laughing at his own joke.

'I won't care. Just park me in a corner and I'll be fine. I just want to be there.'

'They have to get there first. Jen might see sense and run off with the milkman.' Ha ha. Aren't I hilarious?

'We don't even have a milkman,' Jason said. 'She'd have to find one first.'

Usually, Jen would have joined in, holding her own and giving as good as she got. Tonight, she said nothing.

'As if Jen would ever do anything like that,' Amelia said, mistaking – as she always did, when she'd had a couple of drinks – teasing for accusation.

'He's joking, Amelia.' Jen put her hand on her mother-in-law's, and squeezed it.

'Of course he is. I knew that. But really, though, I hope you two will always be as happy as we have been. I'm sure you will be.'

Jen said nothing.

'I've been so lucky,' Amelia said.

'Charles is the lucky one,' Jen said, trying to make her voice sound light and casual. Just joining in the banter.

'Well, then, we're both lucky. Not many couples can say they've been as happy as we have, for as long as we have.'

'No,' Jen said, looking pointedly at Charles, 'they can't.'

Did she imagine it? Did he have the good grace to look uncomfortable, just for a split second?

Jason was smiling, oblivious. Happy that he thought everyone was having a good time. For some reason, this irritated Jen enormously. How could he not see what a gruesome old fake his father was?

She sipped her drink. Sip. Sip.

Charles held his glass aloft. Proposed another toast.

319

'Here's to my beloved family. I love you all more than it's possible to imagine.'

'Hear, hear,' Jason said, leaning over and clinking his father's glass.

'How lovely, darling,' Amelia said, eyes glistening.

Jen smarted.

'What do you say, Charles?' Jen could hear an edge in her voice, but she couldn't remember how to turn it off. Actually, scrub that, she didn't want to. 'Do you think it's unusual these days for two people to have the kind of relationship you've had?'

Charles assumed his moral-crusade TV-persona stance. He sat up a little straighter, cleared his throat. 'Sadly, yes. I don't believe –'

Jen had no time to listen to any more of his bullshit. She had spent her whole adult life being taken in by it. She interrupted, before he could finish whatever it was he was going to say.

'What? A devoted, monogamous . . . honest relationship?' She stared at him defiantly.

Jason, she noticed, was starting to look a little concerned. He had stopped smiling and was looking between her and his father, as if he was watching a tennis match. He must have picked up that her tone was off. This wasn't happily tipsy Jen, this was angry, bordering on drunk, Jen.

'Everything OK?' he said, with a slightly desperate note in his voice.

At this point, someone should have suggested they call it a night and go to bed. Jen would have woken up in the morning horrified by her near miss (again, this was in danger of becoming a habit) and determined to stay resolutely sober around her in-laws for ever more. Sadly, the voice of reason hadn't shown up this evening – or, if he had, he'd brought a bottle – and so they still sat there, knocking back their wine, trying to hang on to the remnants of what had been a nice evening.

'Isn't this a lovely area?' Amelia said, to no one in particular. 'I'm so glad we came.'

Jen squeezed her hand again. Tried to remind herself that she mustn't give anything away in front of her.

'I mean exactly that, actually, Jen. People of my generation took their vows more seriously, I think. Look at the divorce rates. You can't argue with the fact that couples, these days, are far less likely to stay together than they used to.'

'Maybe it's just become harder to keep secrets.'

'What is up with you?' Jason hissed. 'Have I done something?'

'No. Of course not. I'm just interested in Charles's views on this, that's all.'

'You're behaving very weirdly.'

She ignored him. Turned her gaze back to Charles. Waited.

'Yes, I'm sure there is an element of that,' he said, calmly. 'Anyway, the important thing is that Amelia and I have been very lucky, and happy, and we're blessed to have had the life we've had.'

He knocked back the last of his wine. Point made. Now let's move on and talk about something else.

Jen breathed in. Breathed out. Fuck it, she wasn't going to let him get away with that one. She felt as though she was watching a film. She could see herself on the verge of blowing it all. Couldn't find a way to stop herself, even though she knew she should. It all felt as if it was happening to someone else.

And then she hit the detonate button.

The next day, she could hardly bear to think about it. It was one of those moments – if he hadn't said what he'd said, if they had said goodnight as soon as they got back to the cottage, if they had been talking about anything else – that changes the world. Watching it back in her mind, everything slowed down at this point, she could see the words edging out of her mouth. There would have been time to take them back, laugh it off, pretend everything was fine. Except that, of course, it was too late.

She'd laughed, she had actually laughed. He thought it was that easy. Throw out a few platitudes and wait for his adoring family to lap them up. Trusting, hanging on his every word, as they always had done. It was pitiful.

'So your relationship has always been honest?'

Jason put a hand on her arm. She shook him off. She noticed Charles had gone a shade paler.

'We really should go to bed.' Jason stood up.

But, too late. The train hadn't only left the station, it had already been derailed. There were casualties sprawled out beside the tracks. Jen stayed firmly rooted to the spot.

'Jen, you've clearly had a bit too much to drink. We all have, probably. Jason's right. We should go to bed.' Charles stood up too, as if to set an example of how it should be done.

Jen noticed that Amelia had finally picked up on the

tension and was looking wide-eyed, a study in shock and innocent bewilderment – Bambi just after his mother had been killed – aware that something was happening, but not sure what. For her adored mother-in-law's sake, she should just shut up, leave it while she still could. Except that she couldn't. There was something too satisfying in seeing Charles start to squirm.

'Why don't you answer my question?'

'OK,' Jason said. 'Now we really are going to bed. You're right, she's just had too much to drink, Dad. She'll apologize in the morning.'

Jen fumed. 'Don't speak on my behalf.'

'I have no idea what's going on here,' Jason said.

Jen turned on him. 'No, of course you don't. Because you have no idea what kind of a man your father really is. And don't you dare tell him I'll apologize. Because I won't. He's the one who should be saying sorry. Begging forgiveness, more like.'

The silence was tangible. There might as well have been tumbleweed blowing through the living room. Cowboys putting their drinks on the bar and turning round slowly, guns drawn. Jen knew, in that moment, that she had already gone too far, but she also felt a sense of triumph. Take that.

Charles gently prised Amelia's glass from her fingers, put it on the coffee table. 'We've *all* had too much to drink. Let's just go to bed.'

'What the hell's the matter with you?' Jason said angrily, still focused on Jen.

'Why are you all arguing?' Amelia said quietly. 'What's happened?'

Charles, Jen noticed, was looking cornered. He knows, she thought. He knows that I know. It felt thrilling. Shocking. Almost a relief.

'You should call it a night,' he said. 'You've hurt Amelia's feelings. I'm sure you'll regret some of the things you've said in the morning, so it's best if we just all go now and sleep on it, before somebody says something they can't take back.'

How dare he? The man who had been deceiving his wife for over twenty-five years was telling her she had gone too far. Not only that, but his speech was clearly a plea – a warning, even – to her not to blow his secret.

'*I've* hurt Amelia's feelings? No, really, did you just say that?'

Jason was still hovering by the door in the hope that he somehow might be able to spirit Jen away. 'She's just upset because she heard from her own father again for the first time in years . . .'

'No, Jason.'

'Just because you're angry at your own parents, don't take it out on Dad.'

Too late. The fuse was lit. Take cover.

'OK, that's it. I'm not going to let Charles manipulate you all into thinking he's the perfect husband and father any more . . .'

'Jennifer,' Charles said, in a low voice.

She didn't even look at him. Fuck him. She had a poison dart and she was damn well going to throw it.

'. . . so maybe, as he seems to suddenly prize honesty so much, you should ask him to tell you about Cass and Iver Heath and . . . the fucking dog . . . and where he used to go when you thought he was staying away for work . . .'

She sat back. It was out there. She could never take it back. Try as she might to protest that she was just saying anything she could think up to wound Charles – that it had no basis, no foundation in truth – she knew that she had pulled back the curtains just enough so that his family could see through to the other side. She could attempt to drag them shut again, but she knew it was too late.

And, in that instant, she knew she had made a terrible mistake. A mistake that would change everything.

40

Jason had moved out.

There had been no shouting, no fighting once they had got home. It was just that everything had shifted. He had started looking at her as if she was a person he barely knew, a hostile stranger. They hadn't been able to find a way to communicate that would get them through this. The paths they had always navigated so easily had become choked with weeds, debris piling up, blocking the way.

They had driven back from Oxford in deafening silence, after returning the keys to the cottage's owner and fabricating a family medical emergency that meant they had to leave a day early.

'I'll still have to charge you the full rate,' the woman had said, not even pausing to offer her sympathy first. So much for her being Charles Masterson's biggest fan.

'Fine. Whatever. I really don't care,' Jason had said and then got back into the car, slamming the door so hard the windows in a nearby house had shaken.

Jen had tried to talk to him a couple of times, tried to apologize, to explain her side of the story, but he wouldn't have it, cutting her off and turning the radio up full blast.

'I don't want to hear it,' he'd said, putting his foot down.

She had felt wretched. Tears falling silently down her cheeks as she watched the fields and then the houses rush by. They were home in a record-breaking fifty-five minutes.

She had hardly seen him since. Not after the first few days. There had been one afternoon when he'd turned up unexpectedly, and her heart had lurched when she'd seen him standing on the doorstep – he had rung the bell, even though he still had his keys. But he'd made it clear that he'd only come to deal with the practicalities of what they should do with the house. ('You can stay in it, I don't care. I want the girls to have somewhere to call home still.') Jen had cried and pleaded and, eventually, begged, but Jason had been immovable. In his mind they had said all they needed to say.

There was no going back.

The immediate aftermath, the moments after impact, had been apocalyptic. Once the words had come out of her mouth, her concern had been for Amelia and Jason. It was as if in that split second she had sobered up, seen, for the first time that evening, what really mattered. Jason had looked at her, confused, brain working overtime to try to fathom what she was saying.

'What are you talking about? Who's Cass?'

She had felt herself deflate. There was no victory here. 'No . . . Jason . . . I've said enough. Forget it.'

'What do you mean, forget it? You made some kind of insinuation about Dad, you can't just pretend you didn't. Dad?' He had turned to look at his father.

Jen had followed his accusing look. Charles's mask had slipped, a mixture of fear and anger clouding his face. Amelia was just sitting motionless in her chair, white-faced, unreadable.

'Don't listen to her,' Charles had spat. 'She doesn't know what she's saying.'

Jen had bristled, wanting to defend herself, but also knowing that the best thing that could happen at that moment would be for Jason and Amelia to think she had been bluffing, throwing something out there that had no facts to back it up.

Jason was having none of it, though. 'What? She made up a random woman and implied that you were having an affair, or something? That is what you were implying, isn't it, Jen?'

Jen had looked at the floor, waited for it to swallow her up, but it hadn't obliged.

'Mum. Do you know what this is about?'

Jen hadn't been able to fathom Amelia's reaction. Maybe she had just gone into shock, refusing to compute what she was being told.

'I think Jen's just had a few too many glasses of wine,' she had said calmly. 'I think you're both right, and we should all go to bed.'

Charles had jumped on that, as if it was the most meaningful thing ever said. 'Yes, come on. Things will all seem different in the morning.'

'No!' Jason had raised his voice. 'There's something going on here.' He'd suddenly sat back down, as if it had just sunk in that something really serious had happened.

'And you said Dad wasn't really staying away for work when he said he was. What was all that about? Care to elaborate, either of you?'

He'd looked back and forth between the two of them. Jen was determined not to be the one to hammer the final nail into the coffin. Charles was looking like a man facing a firing squad. Jen had stayed silent. Charles had run a hand over his eyes.

Jason had swung round to Amelia. 'Mum, why aren't you saying anything? Don't you want to know what's going on?'

Jen had been wondering that too. Why was Amelia being so passive? If that was me, I would be beating my husband around the head, screaming at him to admit to whatever it was he had to admit to, she thought. Although shouting had never been Amelia's style.

'I'm so sorry,' Charles had suddenly said. He had crumpled, like a Chinese lantern just before the flames consumed it. 'I'm so sorry, both of you. I don't think you're ever going to be able to forgive me.'

He'd told them then, leaving out only the part about still being in contact with Cass's mother. Jason had listened in silence. At one point, he had reached out his hand and taken Amelia's. She'd let him, no more animated than she'd been before. When Charles ran out of steam and stood waiting for a reaction, braced for anything that might come his way, Jason had stood up, looked straight at his father and said, 'You disgust me.'

Jen had stood to follow him as he walked out, but he'd turned back and hissed at her. 'I don't even know what to say to you. You knew all this, and you didn't tell me?'

'I didn't know what to do . . .' She'd known that the best thing would be to leave him. He needed time to take in what he'd just learned, but she'd wanted him to reassure her that everything between them was OK, that they would get through this together.

'At least do me the courtesy of sleeping down here,' he'd said as he moved towards the door. Then he'd stopped, remembering his mother. 'Mum, are you going to be OK? I can drive you back to London, if you don't want to stay here.'

'I'll be fine, sweetheart,' Amelia had said quietly. 'And you've had far too much to drink to drive.' She looked suddenly much older than her years, fragile and vulnerable.

Jen had felt her heart was going to break as she looked at her mother-in-law sitting there, pale and in shock. What had she done?

'Jason . . .' Charles had said pleadingly, but Jason had gone. 'Amelia, love, we need to talk. Privately.'

He'd turned to glare at Jen.

'I hope you're happy.'

'I —' she had started to say, but he'd stormed out, slamming the door behind him.

She had been left with Amelia, and no idea what to say to her.

'I'm so sorry,' she'd muttered as she got up to go – she didn't know where, she just knew she couldn't stay in this room any longer. 'I didn't mean for it to come out this way. You know I never would have wanted to cause you any pain.'

Amelia had sat there, staring ahead of her. 'I knew. I've always known.'

Jen had thought she'd misheard. 'You . . .?'

'Yes.'

Amelia had stood up and walked over to the door. For a split second, Jen had thought – hoped – that her mother-in-law was going to embrace her. But Amelia had walked straight past her and opened the door.

'Amelia?' she had said, but her mother-in-law kept on walking.

Jen had spent the night shivering and crying on the sofa. She had barely slept until the early hours, when the wine and exhaustion caught up with her. She'd woken to hear the sound of a car pulling away and had rushed to the window, relieved to find it was only her in-laws. She had no idea what had passed between them in the night, but she was still reeling from Amelia's revelation that Cass's existence wasn't news to her.

She had crept up the stairs and crawled into bed beside Jason, savouring the warm closeness of his body before he awoke and, she knew, she would have a lot of explaining to do. She tried to convince herself that he would get over it. Maybe not as far as his father was concerned, but she had to be hopeful that she could make him realize the position she had been put in, the agony she had gone through over whether or not to tell him, the reasons for her silence.

She had snaked her arm around him and he'd grunted softly in acknowledgement. She'd allowed herself to believe that everything was going to be all right. Then Jason's body had stiffened.

'Shit.' He'd moved out of her embrace and sat up. 'Shit.'

Jen had waited, unsure what she should say or do.

'Tell me everything you know. I don't want any more lies or cover-ups.'

So she had, leaving nothing out, including the frantic calls from Cass when her mother was in the hospital, and the fact that Charles was still very much a part of their lives.

'What should I have done?'

'Told me. Told me as soon as you found out. God, you must have thought I was fucking stupid.'

'No. I didn't want any of you to get hurt. But then Cass just kept pushing and . . . I don't know . . .'

'So my whole fucking life has been a fraud,' Jason had said. 'I can't take this in. I can't . . . oh God, poor Mum.'

'I think they've gone back to London,' Jen had said gently. 'I heard the car.'

'This is going to devastate her. That bastard.'

She had been relieved that, at least, it seemed Jason could see Charles was the only real villain there.

She'd decided not to mention Amelia's comment the night before. She had stuck her nose in enough. Instead, she'd reached out and stroked his shoulder.

He'd flinched, as if he had just remembered she was there. 'How could you have kept it from me? The fact that my father is a cheating bastard and that I have another sister. That, in fact, I've had another sister for more than half my life and never known it.'

'I'm sorry –' she had started to say again, but he was on a roll.

'You know what, it's not the idea that you didn't tell me that's so bad. It's the way you finally let it out. The vindictiveness, the pleasure you had at throwing that information into my dad's face. And in front of Mum.'

She knew he was right on that point. She had no defence. 'I should never have –'

'What was it? Were you so jealous of my family? Your own is so fucked up that you couldn't bear for mine to be happy?'

'No, Jason! God . . . no. It's not my fault that I stumbled across the truth. It's not my fault that your family turned out not to be so happy, after all.'

'Does Poppy know?'

'Of course not. I couldn't tell any of you. How could I?'

'Jesus Christ, this'll kill Jess. You know what a daddy's girl she is.'

'That's why I couldn't say anything.'

'Until now. Until you just announced it in front of Mum. If this is hurtful for me, then I can't imagine how she must be feeling. To find out that you have no idea who you're married to. That everything you thought was important is a fiction.'

'I think you need to talk to her.'

He wasn't listening. 'I've never seen that side of you. It was so . . . ugly. So spiteful. You've broken up my family, Jen.'

'No, that's not fair. I'm really sorry for the way I handled it, but it's Charles who has broken up your family.

Don't shoot the messenger.' She heard Sean's voice as she said this. Shook her head, as if that would dislodge the image.

'How can you be so flippant? This is . . . Jesus. I have to get back up to London, I have to worry about my mother first. Everything else can wait. Pack the stuff up.'

'Let's not leave it like this. Please, Jason. You have to understand I didn't mean to be hurtful. I just . . . he pushed all my buttons, everything had got too much. I had so much pressure on me. And I'd had too much to drink . . .'

He was already on his feet, getting dressed. 'Be ready to go in twenty minutes.'

He hadn't moved out right away. They had tried to work their way through it, for a couple of days, her tiptoeing around him as if he was more likely to forgive her if he didn't notice she was there – but the resentful silences were suffocating. And he simply couldn't get over the fact that, if it hadn't been for Jen, none of this would have happened. He wouldn't have fallen out so badly with his father that they were no longer on speaking terms (this she didn't believe; she knew their relationship was damaged for ever by what he had discovered, but the way he had discovered it was irrelevant – or, rather, it would become so eventually, she hoped). She'd tried to make him understand that, even though she had handled it with as much subtlety as a bull who went straight from his spree in a china shop to a glass factory making priceless chandeliers, what she had done in reality was to expose the truth. She hadn't created it. She hadn't sent Charles out with instructions to father children by other women.

Jason was having none of it, though. Whenever she tried to talk to him about it, he simply shut her down.

She'd waited for the implosion to come in Charles and Amelia's marriage. She'd just assumed that Amelia would kick him out. She couldn't imagine her being able to come to terms with his years of deception, whatever she had said. Who could? Obviously, she no longer had a direct line to her in-laws, but, whenever she asked Jason, he said that his father was still living there. Not that he would go to the house unless he had the reassurance that Charles was out. He wanted nothing to do with him, he said. He had seemed as bemused by his mother's lack of action as Jen was.

Sometimes – often – she'd found herself thinking about Amelia, her perfect life in pieces, sitting in that too-big house. The look on her face when she said, 'I've always known.' What did that mean? That she'd sanctioned Charles's double life? Could she really have understood that Charles and Cass's mother were, to all intents and purposes, a couple? For sixteen years of her marriage? Don't ask, don't tell?

Jen had thought about calling her, more than once, just to check she was coping, but she knew she was the last person Amelia would want to talk to. And who could blame her?

'This isn't for ever, is it?' Jen had said, once she'd taken in what Jason was telling her. That he had found a flat of his own and was moving out.

'Honestly, I don't know. How could we ever be a family

again? I'm not punishing you, Jen, I just don't see how that could happen.'

Despite everything, it had shocked her how easily he could dismiss their relationship.

She'd felt as if she had gone on to autopilot, going through the motions, treading water until she could get her life back on track. She'd felt as if all she could do was wait and see what happened.

41

Jen had never really thought about how small her life was. How contained. How she truly had put all her eggs in one basket before she'd thrown it on the floor and stamped on it. Without her family her days were empty. The house resounded with silence. The weekends dragged on endlessly.

The Mastersons popped into her head at all hours of the day or night. Everything she did connected to one or other of them in some way. A walk through Soho Square would conjure up a snapshot of Poppy sitting on their bench waiting to meet her for lunch and a catch-up, an announcement about a new theatre production would have her calculating which dates she could tell Jessie she would be free to go, a flash of Lang Lang on the TV had her reaching for the phone to let Amelia know to turn over to Sky Arts. There was nothing that didn't evoke them. It felt as if she was possessed.

She could get through the weekdays easily enough. She was busy at work and professional enough not to let the guests see that anything was wrong. Only once – when regular Mr Sommers asked her if she'd been ill since he saw her last, because she looked so thin – did she cry at work. Not so much cry, it was actually as if someone had opened up a fire hydrant. The tears seemed to be coming out horizontally and with such force that they were propelled violently across the reception desk. Mr Sommers, being a sweet man, had ignored his obvious desire to run away or to put up an umbrella, and had come round to her side, led her out to the back room and let her sob all over him. He'd had the sense not to ask her what was wrong, because he would have been there all day. As it was, she'd had to offer to pay for him to have his shirt laundered.

And then she'd had to force herself to think about other things on the bus and the Tube to and from the hotel, after she'd burst into tears one morning on the Northern Line and a man who had been sitting next to her got up and moved, muttering about her under his breath as he went. Funnily enough, no one on London Underground had put their arm round her and offered to let her deposit tears, mascara and snot all over their clothes.

This had always been her mum's technique, when Jen was little. The forcing yourself to think about other things, that was.

'Think about our holiday we had in Poole,' she would say, when Jen couldn't sleep. Or, 'Remember how much fun you had when we went to Whipsnade? Think about that day from beginning to end. Everything, right from the moment we made the sandwiches to take with us, to when we got home and went to bed.'

It nearly always worked, and the young Jen had become very adept at focusing her memory to block out the bad stuff and keep her mind firmly rooted in a happy past event. Now, though, she had to try to find memories that didn't contain Jason, because they would definitely set her off. And recalling a family holiday to Dorset when you were seven didn't really cut it when you were forty-three.

She thought about calling her mum, telling her the whole story, saying she was sorry for the way she'd spoken to her last time she'd seen her, and asking her to come and help her get through this. So Elaine had made mistakes. Jen now knew only too well how easy that was. Knew that nothing was black or white, right or wrong. But she didn't know where to start. How to break the silence.

She waited for Poppy to contact her. She had no doubt that Jason would have told his sisters everything. Even Jessie, who probably would have had to ramp up her hysteria to eleven so that people would realize she was actually serious, this time. She wondered if he would describe in detail the way she had thrown her discovery in Charles's face, unaware of or not caring about the fallout she was causing. It wasn't really his style to stir things up, but she could imagine that he might want them to know the worst about her, to make sure she was paraded in her true colours. And who could blame him?

It didn't matter that Charles was the chief villain of the piece. What mattered was that she, Jen, had been the one to open the closet and let all the skeletons out. And once they were out and dancing about in plain sight, no one could ignore them any more.

If there was one lesson she had learned, though, it was no more secrets. If she had come home, that first day, and told Jason that she had seen his dad behaving oddly with a strange woman, things might have been tricky for a while, but they would have got through it together. So he would still have ended up estranged from his father. But, at least, their marriage might have remained intact. She had made the wrong choice, she knew that now – keeping her discovery to herself – but she tried to comfort herself with the knowledge that she had, at least, made it for the right reasons.

A couple of weeks after the world fell apart, she received a text from Cass.

WTF is going on? Dad says they all know. Are u ok?

She ignored it. Nothing good could come from going down that route again.

A while later, she received a note from Jessie. Over-blown and accusatory: 'I don't know how you could have done this to us, after everything my family has done for you.' She couldn't finish it. Put it in a drawer until she felt strong enough to continue.

She had still heard nothing from Poppy, had picked up the phone on more than one occasion and begun to punch in her oh-so-familiar number and then lost her nerve at the last minute. On the fourth or fifth occasion, Poppy picked up. Jen was so surprised she almost dropped the phone. Poppy, as ever, started speaking as soon as she answered.

'I don't want to talk to you.'

'Please, Pop –'

'Stop calling me.'

And, just like that, the line went dead.

*

What to tell Simone and Emily had been the one thing she and Jason had agreed on. The truth about everything, with one small omission – the way Jen had behaved on fight night. Both girls were heading home for the big anniversary party, fired up and excited by the thought of a Masterson get-together. Unaware it had been unceremoniously cancelled.

'I don't know if I can do it,' Jen had said tearfully, when Jason had suggested he come over and they break the news together – to try to at least show their daughters they were still capable of having a functioning relationship.

'It's not about you, it's about them. You have to try.'

Jen had driven to Euston to collect them, Simone and Emily having coordinated their movements so they would both end up arriving on the same train.

Simone had been full of her plans to travel to America in the summer holidays. Her college had organized some kind of exchange programme, and she was going to work in a legal centre in Boston for a month or so. Jen had been thrilled for her when she had been accepted, but now she was struggling to act enthusiastic about anything except sitting in a darkened room and sobbing.

She had bitten her lip to try to stop herself from crying in front of the girls. She hated it that her daughters' happiness was about to be trashed.

'Mum, is something wrong?' Simone had asked. 'You look . . . I don't know . . . you don't look well.'

'What?' Emily had demanded, having failed to pick up on the atmosphere herself. 'What's wrong?'

Jen had reached a hand out and squeezed her knee. 'I'm

OK. A bit stressed. But I'm not ill, if that's what you're worried about.'

'What about Dad?'

'Dad's fine. Neither of us is ill.'

'Promise?'

'Promise.'

By the time they had got home, Jason was lurking in the hall, looking like a man who didn't know how to relax in his own home. Like a guest who hasn't yet been offered tea and made to feel comfortable. As soon as they had all hugged their hellos, he'd asked them to come and sit at the kitchen table. He wanted to get it over with, Jen could see. Get it over with and get out of there.

'There *is* something wrong,' Simone had said, looking at her mother accusingly.

'What's going on?' Emily had been amusing herself, piling her hair on top of her head into two buns and securing them with pencils. She looked like a little girl.

'Everything's OK, girls,' Jason had said, looking at the table and allowing his body language to give away that it definitely wasn't. 'It's just . . . Mum and I have decided to live apart for a while.'

He'd paused to let what he was saying sink in. Emily's eyes were brimming over with tears in a second. Simone sat stony-faced.

'Why?' Emily had wailed. 'What do you mean, live apart?'

Jen had put a hand over hers. 'Dad has got a new place and I'm going to stay here.'

'Have you met someone else?' Simone had said, looking him straight in the eye.

'No! As if —'

'Neither of us has,' Jen had added hastily. 'That's not what this is about.'

'Then what is it about? What's going on?'

In their discussion of what best to tell their daughters, she and Jason had decided to cite irreconcilable differences. Tell them that they had grown apart. It seemed like the easiest, kindest way to go.

'We just feel like we need some time on our own, that's all.'

She had looked at Jason for some support, and he had picked up on it. Their communications system hadn't yet completely broken down, then.

'We're still talking, look. We don't hate each other. Far from it.'

That did it. Jen had stifled a sob. Simone squeezed her hand.

'It's nobody's fault,' Jen had managed to say. 'No one is to blame.'

'This is . . . awful,' Emily had said. 'I mean, how could you do this to me?'

'Oh, shut the fuck up, Em,' Simone had said. 'This isn't about you.'

Emily had ignored her. 'And what about Granny and Grandpa? They must be devastated.'

Jen had taken a deep breath. 'That's another thing . . .'

When she'd finished, Emily had looked disgusted. 'Grandpa has another daughter? Gross.'

'Poor Granny,' Simone had said quietly.

'Yes,' Jason had said. 'Poor Granny. I need the two of you to keep an eye on her when you're home.'

Neither Jen nor Jason had mentioned that she and Amelia had had no contact since that night, or that Jason had no intention of ever being in the same room as his father again. They had thrown enough disturbing information their girls' way for one day. The rest could wait.

'I don't have to tell you how important it is that no one outside the family gets to hear about Granny and Grandpa's problems,' Jason had said, still protecting his father despite everything.

Simone and Emily had nodded earnestly in a way that had made Jen want to cry all over again.

When Jason said he had to leave, Emily had clung on to him like she used to do when she was tiny and he would leave for work. Jen nearly joined her, gripping on to him like one of those tiny koalas she used to put on her pencil when she was at school.

That night, both Simone and Emily had stayed in with her and they'd all cooked together, like they used to do before the girls left home, and then they'd squashed up on the sofa, alternately comforting and needing to be comforted.

She knew Jason was angry, knew that it was too much, all at once, for them to be able to try to carry on as if everything was normal. But it still both shocked and hurt her how definite he was, how quickly he had decided that there was no possible future for them.

42

She buried herself in work. She wrote her own name down for every extra shift that came up. It helped that she was usually so tired when she eventually got home that she could go straight to bed without having to work out how to get through an evening. A couple of times she went for a drink with Judy, but their hearts weren't really in it. They were work friends. They really only had work in common. Jen had told her colleagues that she and Jason had separated but none of the other details, so she couldn't even unburden herself over a few drinks. And Jen knew that Judy would really rather be heading home after a long stint at work than keeping her company, however much she would protest otherwise.

Christmas came and went. The girls came home prepared to tough out Christmas Day with their mother, and she went overboard with her efforts to show them that everything was as normal as it could be – thereby guaranteeing that, of course, it wasn't. She had sent Elaine a card and the cashmere-mix jumper along with Simone and Emily, who were dispatched to visit their 'other' grandmother on Christmas Eve. Jen was relieved to hear that her mother had made plans to share lunch the following day with one of her long-standing neighbours who was also on her own. She had still had no contact with Elaine since their argument.

She waited, sure there would be word from Jason's family. All of the Masterson women were meticulous about the etiquette of Christmas, keeping lists of cards received and sent. She had teased them all about it for years, being much more scattergun in her own approach. She had even once bought Amelia a beautiful teal leather notebook on which she had had the words 'Christmas Cards' embossed in a gold colour. She prepared herself to be happy with even the most generic card, the blandest of holiday greetings. A corporate message. No matter how many times she checked the post, nothing arrived.

Jason stayed away too. She called him a couple of times on the pretext of needing to talk about something practical. He was polite but all business. She tried to ask him about the rest of the family, but he was evasive, anxious not to engage. She had been cut off as effectively as if a surgeon had spent a day excising any last part of her from their lives. Twenty-two years of history dropped into the surgical waste bin. It seemed that, as far as the Mastersons were concerned, you were in or you were out. There was no in between. And she was most definitely out.

She gleaned what she could from her daughters, treading carefully to try to avoid making them feel they were being used as spies. Charles was still living at the family home. Jason, Poppy and Jessie were, as yet, refusing to have anything to do with him.

She was careful to avoid walking past Masterson Property if she could help it. And Soho Square, where Poppy worked. She knew it was inevitable that she would spot one or other of them, Poppy or Charles, near their offices one of these days; she was just hoping she would see them before they saw her, so she could prepare herself. She had no idea how Charles would react, if they met. Did he feel any sadness for her, was he prepared to shoulder the guilt himself? She doubted it.

Twice she had seen his angry figure approaching the front doors of the hotel and she'd hidden in the back room, asking her confused colleagues to claim she was absent. Neil told her that he'd come in once, when she genuinely wasn't there, demanding to see her. She told them she couldn't face any of her husband's family, so devastated was she by Jason's decision to leave, and they seemed to accept it. She felt like a sitting target, perched out in public view on the reception desk like an unsuspecting grouse innocently going about its daily business on August the 12th.

It occurred to her that she could leave. Go anywhere. Do anything. She no longer had any ties. But she knew that, apart from the girls and their sporadic trips home, these people – Neil, Judy, David – and this job were all she had. That didn't bear thinking about, really.

So she did nothing. Went to work, went home. Phoned her daughters. Tried to remember to eat or to wash or to comb her hair. Tried to pretend she was fine.

Failed.

A few weeks after the holidays, Jen was pottering around the house trying to find displacement activities to keep her from brooding on what had happened in her life – crying over old family photos, sorting out the attic and weeping over a pile of her and Jason's never-used wedding presents, that kind of thing – when the doorbell rang. She wasn't expecting anybody, so she steeled herself for either the 'No, thank you, I have enough dishcloths and, even if I didn't, ten pounds for two is just insanity' or the 'Leave me the name of your charity and I'll look it up online, but I am not going to hand you, a stranger, my credit card details on the doorstep' conversation that she generally found herself having at least once a week, and went downstairs.

She opened the door with her best 'Don't mess with me' face on, to be greeted by her mother, suitcase in hand, nervous smile on her face. Jen felt a moment of unprecedented elation, and then her heart sank when she remembered how things had been left between them.

'Oh, thank goodness you're in,' Elaine said, walking past her into the hall. 'I let my taxi go and, as soon as I did, I suddenly thought, What if she's at work, or something? I suppose I should have rung first, but I thought you might put me off.'

Elaine always rambled on when she was nervous.

'What . . .?' Jen said. 'Is everything OK?'

'I've come to stay for a few days,' Elaine said. 'If that's all right.'

For a minute, Jen wondered whether in her self-obsessed miserable state she had invited her mother up and then immediately forgotten about it. And then she remembered that she hadn't even told her what had happened. She had decided she didn't want to hear Elaine's concern and sympathy. She didn't need it.

'What are you doing here, Mum?' she demanded.

Elaine had never come to see her unannounced. She hated London. And anyway, they didn't really have the sort of relationship where they would just swing by for cake and gossip.

'You need your family around you,' Elaine said.

And Jen thought, Yes, I do. Jason and the girls. Poppy, Amelia, Jessie. 'Really,' she said. 'I'm OK.'

And then – just to prove her point – she burst into tears.

'So, Simone told me you were looking awful.'

Elaine had steered her daughter into a chair and was now hunting through the kitchen cupboards, for Jen knew not what.

'Wow. That's nice to hear.'

'You know what I mean. Now, do you have any whisky?'

'Mum, it's not even midday. And you don't even drink.'

'Who cares? Needs must. You can just have a glug in your coffee.'

'Thank you but, one, I don't have any whisky and, two, if I did, I wouldn't drink it in the morning.'

'It's good for stress,' Elaine said, still flinging cupboards open, as if Jen might have a secret supply that she hadn't wanted to own up to.

'So is punching people, apparently. I might take that up. Soon.'

'OK, well, we'll just have the coffee. And you need to eat something. You're too thin.'

She was right on that one. Jen had lost more weight. Preparing meals when there was only one of you just felt like a waste of time. Jen realized sulkily, too, as her mum was looking her over with a critical eye, that she was still in her pyjamas – even though she had been up for hours – and she couldn't recall having washed them in living memory. She was pretty sure the remains of yesterday's make-up was on her face somewhere, too, just not necessarily in the same arrangement it had been when she'd first put it on.

Elaine plonked a coffee down in front of her and she drank it down in one, and held her mug out for a refill. She needed caffeine if she was going to be able to deal with her mother.

'You're a mess,' Elaine said.

Jen grunted to show she'd heard her.

'Did you have breakfast?'

'Wasn't hungry,' Jen mumbled, and then she obediently ate the huge bowl of Fruit 'n' Fibre that her mother put in front of her.

'Right, bath. I'll go and run it for you. You could wash your hair, too, it's practically in dreadlocks. And bring those disgusting PJs down when you get out, and any other washing you have.'

Forty-five or so minutes later, scrubbed and shiny in clean sweatpants and her favourite old T-shirt – at least Elaine hadn't made her dress up, that would have been a bridge too far – and sitting at the kitchen table while her mum blow-dried her hair like she used to when Jen was a pre-teenager, she did feel, if not better, then more like a member of the human race and less like a cave dweller.

'Right, food shopping,' Elaine announced, once Jen's hair was dry.

Jen had never seen her mother like this, taking charge, galvanized into action, a woman with a purpose. The thought of being needed seemed to have given her a new lease of life.

The idea of trailing around Morrisons seemed way too exhausting, though.

'I don't really need anything.'

'I've looked in all your cupboards, and you can't live on instant noodles and tins of mushroom soup. You need some vegetables. And protein.'

It suddenly became clear why Simone and Emily hated it so much when Jen lectured them about their eating habits.

'How long are you staying?' she asked, trying not to make it sound like an accusation. She didn't have the strength for a fight. In fact, she had no intention of ever arguing with anyone about anything again. Ever.

'Till Tuesday morning,' Elaine said, with a big 'Isn't that fantastic?' smile on her face.

Jen tried to mirror it back at her, but it came out more like a snarl. 'Great.'

Later, when she managed to get away from her kidnapper for a couple of minutes, Jen hid in the loo and called Simone.

'Did you know she was coming?' she hissed in a loud whisper.

'Sorry, Mum. I didn't like the idea of you being on your own.'

'I can't spend all this time with her. I'll strangle her.'

'I thought I was doing a good thing,' Simone said quietly.

Jen hadn't wanted her to feel bad. Simone and Emily had no idea about the ill feeling Jen was currently harbouring towards Elaine. She would never have wanted to poison her girls against either set of grandparents and, consequently, was having to bite her tongue every time she spoke to them. Which was often. Both daughters currently phoned her pretty much daily, checking up like a pair of worried aunts.

'It's just a bit too soon for all the post-mortems and life lessons, that's all. Thank you, though, sweetie, for worrying about me. But you don't have to. I'm going to be OK.'

'I checked with Auntie Poppy, and she thought it was a good idea too,' Simone said.

Jen's stomach lurched. She still hadn't had a conversation with Poppy, missed her like she had been bereaved. She desperately wanted to ask what Poppy had said. Did she hate her? Did she think Jen was responsible for the family breaking down? Was she still in touch with her father, or had she cut him off? She knew Poppy must be suffering almost as much as she was. But she also knew she mustn't start using her daughters for espionage. Knew she had to encourage them to have a healthy relationship with the family they belonged to by blood, just as she didn't.

The fact that Poppy had agreed Simone should ask Elaine to check up on her meant that she was concerned for Jen's welfare. That was a good thing, surely. But Poppy also knew how Jen felt about her mother. Knew the tricky, uncomfortable relationship they had always had so maybe this was her idea of a punishment.

'It was really thoughtful of you,' Jen said, softly now. 'I'm sure it'll be fine. Thank you.'

Over the first home-cooked healthy meal Jen had eaten in a while, Elaine gamely talked about anything other than Jason: her neighbour's out-of-control dog, the number of shops in her local high street that were in danger of closing down, the weather. Jen could visualize the list, and she almost warmed to her mother as she thought of her poring over it, racking her brain for conversation subjects, interesting or not. Her own failed marriage sat there in a corner – fat and grey, eating buns and hosing itself down noisily with its trunk – and they both chose to ignore it.

She thought she might actually be starting to feel a bit better just by virtue of being clean and presentable and having gone out of the house for any reason other than work (a trip around Morrisons – my, she was positively back on the social scene).

'Let's go to Richmond tomorrow, if it's nice,' Elaine said as they were clearing up.

Jen had barely said a word all evening, just let her mother witter on, more talkative than she had ever known her to be, barely listening.

'I've heard it's lovely down by the river.'

'You don't have to do this, Mum,' she said. 'I'm not a convalescent.'

'Who said you were? We can't sit around here all day. I just thought it might be nice to do something fun.'

It all felt like too much effort. 'Let's see how we feel in the morning.'

'Now I'm going to make you some hot chocolate, and you're going to bed.'

'It's half past eight.'

'I don't care. You can read for a while, if you want.'

Jen couldn't help it. She laughed. 'Since when were you the kind of mum who made hot chocolate?'

Elaine looked hurt for a moment. 'I used to, actually, when you were little. I'm worried about you, Jenny. I want to do something to help.'

'To make yourself feel better, you mean?'

'Yes, maybe. If that's how you want to look at it, then fine. But let me look after you.'

'Fine,' Jen said, huffily, unable to get up the energy to argue.

By nine o'clock, Jen was in bed with a warm drink. Elaine actually tucked her in.

'It's like I'm in a straitjacket. I can't breathe.'

'Things'll get better.' Elaine leaned down and pecked the top of her head.

Jen lay there, trussed up like a mummy. Stared at the ceiling.

She'd dropped off almost as soon as Elaine had left the room, and hadn't woken again until about thirteen hours later. Her congealed once-hot chocolate still sat on the bedside table. She took her time and came downstairs, having showered and dressed, so that Elaine would have nothing to lecture her about.

The agenda for the day in Richmond was clearly 'Take

Jenny's mind off it!' because Elaine went into overdrive, talking about the river and the ducks and the little shops, and should they have lunch in a pub or Zizzi. Jen had never heard her mother talk so much. She nodded along, feigning interest, occasionally interjecting something anodyne enough that her mother might think she was following what she was talking about. She appreciated what Elaine was doing, she really did. She just wasn't sure she wanted her mind taken off it.

By the time they got home, Jen had been beaten into submission. Rendered as obedient and pliable as a hostage with Stockholm Syndrome.

Bath. Home-cooked meal. Clean pyjamas. They watched *Antiques Roadshow* on TV, and it was quite therapeutic – until Jen remembered how Poppy used to like to rewind and freeze at the point some posh old biddy was told her priceless vase was actually worth about fifty quid. She would try to find the exact frame where the news hit her and her face gave away how devastated she was, before she plastered a smile on and said it was fine, she would never want to sell her heirloom, anyway.

Thinking about that made Jen cry. She tried to hide her tears from her mum, who seemed to be engrossed, but before she knew it Elaine was next to her on the sofa, clamping Jen to her side and telling her to 'let it all out'. She may well have regretted saying that, because Jen did. She couldn't stop herself. To her credit, Elaine just sat there with her arm around her daughter, patting her like she needed burping. She didn't ask any questions, didn't make Jen talk, for which Jen would have been grateful if she'd been capable of rational thinking.

By the time Jen had cried herself out, she felt much better, if somewhat foolish. Elaine's response, once Jen had steadied her breathing and blown her nose noisily on a tissue her mum had produced from somewhere, was to make them both a cup of tea.

'*Downton Abbey*?' she said, once she was back from the kitchen with a full tray – pot, milk jug, plate of biscuits, everything. (Jen hadn't even known she had a milk jug. Couldn't imagine what would ever have possessed her to buy one.) She nodded and her mother settled in beside her, and they watched in silence. Jen found her presence strangely comforting.

'What are you going to do while I'm at work tomorrow?' she asked, when they said goodnight. 'I'm on an early, so I won't even see you in the morning.'

'I'm sure I can find plenty to amuse myself,' Elaine said, and kissed Jen on the forehead. 'Sleep well.'

She knew something was up the minute she put her key in the door when she got home from work the following afternoon, because Elaine was practically standing to attention in the hall.

'OK, what's going on?' Jen demanded as she headed into the living room and saw that the piles of detritus she had accumulated in the past few weeks had been replaced by open spaces and shiny woodwork.

'Oh, you've tidied up. Thanks. You didn't have to.'

'I had lots of time,' Elaine said. 'Not that I mean you shouldn't have left me on my own all day,' she added hastily, scared of being seen to criticize.

'It's OK, Mum. I'm going to get changed,' Jen said.

She looked in on the kitchen as she passed through the hall. It sparkled like something out of a Flash commercial, light bouncing off the faux marble worktops and hitting her square in the eyes. Upstairs, her bedroom (which, this morning, although Jason had long since vacated it, still bore his imprint like a crime scene, exactly half of the wardrobe empty while her clothes spilled out on to the floor, two drawers of the tall boy barren while the other two overflowed, half of the dressing table bearing the chalk-outline dust imprints of his deodorant and aftershave) looked like a ten-man makeover team had spent a week smartening it up. Her clothes seemed to be arranged by type. Trousers, skirts, dresses, tops all segregated. Apparel apartheid. Toiletries were lined up in order of height. Shoes stood side by side in neat pairs. So that's how Elaine had spent her day. Either that, or the mice had decided they finally needed to start earning their keep.

Jen felt tears well up, yet again, and forced them back down. While she wasn't sure that erasing every trace of Jason from her life was what she wanted, she couldn't fault her mother's kindness. She changed out of her uniform – putting it on a hanger, for once, instead of draping it over a chair – practised a smile in the mirror and headed back downstairs, determined to seem grateful.

43

'Let's talk, Mum,' Jen said. 'I mean a proper talk. Not skirting around the issue, not shouting at each other. Or me shouting at you, I suppose I should say.'

Elaine looked trapped in the headlights, a rabbit scared out of its skin. 'I don't want to get into a fight, Jenny.'

'Neither do I. And could you call me Jen? Just once in your life?'

She took a deep breath, realizing that this wasn't a great start for a rational discussion.

'Thank you for everything you've done today. I really appreciate it.'

'I don't know how else to help you.'

Jen poured herself a glass of wine. 'Want one?'

'A tiny one, maybe.'

'Really?' She couldn't remember ever having seen her mother have a drink.

'Really small. Dutch courage,' Elaine said, with a nervous laugh. She sat down at the kitchen table, fiddled nervously with the cuff of her blouse.

'I understand why you hated Dad. I really do. I can't imagine what it must have been like, being married to someone who treated you like that.'

'If I thought we could have kept it together for your sake . . .'

'I get it, I truly do. I wouldn't have wanted Simone and Em to grow up watching their father come in after being out all night, God knows where. Of course you were right to kick him out. It's the rest of it. After . . .'

Elaine sighed. Took a minuscule sip of her wine. 'I don't know what to tell you. I thought I was doing the right thing. It seems I wasn't. I can't change it, however much I want to.'

'I just . . . I don't understand how you could think it would be better for me to believe my dad had forgotten all about me. It makes no sense.'

'I know now, I accept that I was partly motivated by anger. After everything he'd done to me, I didn't want him to be able to pop up twice a year with a present and have you thinking he was father of the year.'

'I don't think that was likely.'

'We all make mistakes. It's just that some are bigger than others, that's all.'

Jen couldn't argue with that. She had lost count of how many she had made herself in the past few months.

'Sometimes it's hard to know what the right thing to do is. And I didn't have anyone to ask for advice. It was a terribly lonely existence, to be honest.'

Jen felt suddenly overwhelmed. 'For me too.'

'I realize that now. I think . . . I thought you were so young, the best thing I could do was to protect you. Maybe I should have talked to you more.'

'Mum . . .' Jen said, and then she stopped.

She hadn't told anyone the full story of everything that had happened to her over the past couple of months.

Nobody had the whole picture, from her seeing Charles and Cass in the street to the night she blew Jason's family apart, via her indiscretion with Sean. She felt so weighed down by the need to get it all off her chest, to confess. To paint as bad a picture of her behaviour as she could, and then see what the fallout was.

'Can I tell you something?'

'Of course you can,' Elaine said, but she looked worried, as if she wasn't going to like what she heard.

Jen started at the beginning, told the entire tale, leaving nothing out. She saw Elaine's eyes grow wide when she got to the part about going back to Sean's hotel room with him.

'You poor love,' was all her mother said, when she'd finished.

'It's all my fault, though. Everything.'

'You know as well as I do that's not true.'

'It feels like it is.'

'Charles Masterson made his choices. They had nothing to do with you. And you won't get anywhere by spending your time wishing you'd behaved differently, because there's nothing you can do about it. I should know. You just have to move on.'

Jen gave a half-laugh. 'Well, that's easier said than done.'

Elaine put her bony hand over her daughter's, patted it. 'I didn't say it was easy. Just that it's the right thing to do.'

'I'm glad you're here,' Jen said. She meant it.

By the time Elaine left, on the Tuesday morning – Jen had arranged to go into work late, after having taken her to Marylebone and made sure she got on the right train – Jen

360

felt as if she'd turned a corner. Jason was gone, but she had to try to get on with her life.

'Bye, Jenny . . . Jen . . . sorry,' Elaine said as she kissed her daughter goodbye.

She said 'Jen' like it was an alien word, like she had picked it up phonetically and had no idea what it meant. But at least she said it.

'I will get used to it, it might just take a while.'

Jen gave her a hug. Almost asked her to stay. 'I'll come down soon. I promise.'

Her relationships gradually started to drift back to the way they had been before. People stopped asking her how she was feeling every five minutes and started having normal conversations again – about what their kids were up to, or the weather, or the price of petrol. It was a relief, if she was honest.

She started visiting Rory regularly, taking him cakes and cans of lager – even though she knew he shouldn't really have either. He seemed pleased to see her. Even, she suspected the second time, had tidied up in anticipation of her visit. The cobwebs were still there, but they looked as if they had been shifted about a bit. She thought he must have flapped a duster in their direction, at least. She didn't even try to fill him in on what had happened to her life. He had only just learned to remember Jason's name – it would be too confusing to ask him to forget it again.

They kept their conversation to the present. Jen had realized it was pointless expecting Rory to account for the past. It was what it was, and there was nothing she could do to change it. And after a while, she stopped wanting to punish him, stopped looking for explanations and apologies. She started to enjoy hearing about the mundanities of his day. His on-off relationship with Jean, his feuds with the Meals on Wheels volunteers, his one-man campaign against the noise of his upstairs neighbour. If she didn't so much feel she had gained a father, then she had at least gained an old man who she was starting to care about. It was almost like having another child to worry about. A crabby, wrinkly child with hair growing out of his nostrils, brown teeth and a tendency to pick fights with everyone around him. But she liked having someone else to care about.

She wondered what had happened to Cass, whether she had managed to maintain a relationship with her father, given what had happened. She actually hoped that she had, hoped that some good might have come out of this mess. In the end, she didn't have to wait long to find out.

44

It was the headline that screamed out at her. 'I am TV star's love child', it declared. 'See pages 6 and 7'. Next to it was a picture of Charles – not one she recognized, but recent. Looking dapper, looking pleased with himself, unaware that his house of cards was about to come tumbling down.

And beside that was a photo of Cass. Glamorous, dressed up, made up to the nines and posing for the camera.

Jen could hardly get the money out of her purse to pay for the paper, her hands were shaking so much. Once she had it, she didn't even move away from the newsstand. She just opened the pages up, right there and then. She needed to see the worst.

On page six was another picture of Cass, looking hurt and hard done by, but also, it seemed to Jen, a little coquettish as well. The piece went on to describe how poor old Cass Richards had been forced to live in the shadows for the past twenty-five years while her bigamist, in all but name, father presented himself as some kind of pillar of the community and forged a career as an outspoken upholder of all things right and illiberal.

There was a snap of Cass's mother too – Barbara, Jen finally discovered her name was. She could see that Barbara bore a strong resemblance to Cass, an older but more

363

glamorous version. She looked younger than Jen had imagined – fifty-five, the article declared – still a vibrant, attractive woman. The button nose and slight overbite were there, along with a mane of glossy ash-blonde hair and amber-coloured, possibly lifted, eyes. She must, Jen thought, have been stunning when Charles had first met her. She wasn't far off now.

She hoped desperately that Amelia hadn't seen the article, although she knew the chances were that some kind soul would draw her attention to it. Schadenfreude had a way of bringing out the worst in people. She couldn't even begin to imagine the agonies her mother-in-law would go through once she knew her life was being held up for scrutiny and ridicule. Charles, she knew, would be mortified. His whole grim past had raced up to knock him down. It was unlikely *Newsnight* would be picking up the phone to have him air his views on the Big Society now.

Another small picture showed Charles and Amelia on the beach with a mini Jason, Poppy and Jessie. Jen felt sick. She had no idea how the paper had got hold of that particular photo. Cass must have had it squirrelled away somewhere from years ago. Used it as a voodoo doll, most likely.

She took out her phone to call Jason. She wanted to make sure she broke it to him gently, before it hit him in the face. Wanted an excuse to speak to him, as much as anything.

'I've seen it,' he said, when she told him why she was calling.

The way he said it made her feel like it was all her fault all over again.

'Poor Amelia.'

'Jen, I'm busy, actually. I'll talk to you another time, OK?'

He had put the phone down before she could say anything else. She knew he still wanted to punish her.

It was unbelievable how many people come out of the woodwork as tabloid readers when something like this happened. They were positively queuing up to tell Jen about it. Some (Neil, Judy) had her best interests at heart, she knew, wanting to cushion the blow, as she had tried to do for Jason. For others (Margaret from housekeeping, a neighbour Jen had argued with once when their car alarm kept going off, Graham the doorman), it was their best ever day and they would have walked barefoot over the Himalayas to be the one to break the news and see the expression on Jen's face when she heard it for the first time.

The papers made a meal of it for a few days. Jen kept her head down, didn't answer her front door in case they had sent a reporter to ask for her side of the story. The whole thing felt like it was happening to someone else's family. Which, in a way, it was. Jason's. Jen was thankful, at least, that the girls were enough of a step removed for no one to think of contacting them to ask for their opinion.

'Maybe,' Elaine said, when Jen spoke to her on the phone, as she did most days now, 'a part of Charles is relieved it's all out in the open.'

Jen knew better. Charles had stayed with Amelia all these years for a reason. He would never have wanted his son and (acknowledged) daughters to know exactly what kind of a person he really was; he prized his status, his social standing and his burgeoning TV career too much. And, for all she knew, he had really loved his wife. He'd just had a funny way of showing it.

She picked up the phone to call Cass, without even stopping to think.

'Hey,' the familiar voice said. 'I guess you've seen the paper.'

'What the fuck were you thinking?' Jen said. 'Have you got any idea how hurtful this is? What it'll do to Amelia?'

'I wasn't the one who spilled the beans in the first place,' Cass said defiantly. 'I wasn't the one who pulled the rug out from under Amelia's life.'

'But . . .' Jen could hardly speak. 'In the papers? For the whole world to see? That's so . . . vindictive . . .'

'That's not why I did it. Nothing was going to change, don't you see? They were sticking together in that stupid house like nothing had happened.'

'Grow up, Cass,' Jen said. 'Stop acting like it's all about you.'

'I suppose you know what it's like now, being on the outside? Once they lock those doors, there's no getting in. Trust me, I tried.'

Jen did something she had never done before. She put the phone down without saying goodbye.

She couldn't help thinking about what was happening in Twickenham. Who was there? Did Amelia have all her children around her to soften the blow? Had she finally thrown Charles out, now that all their dirty laundry had been aired so publicly? Were they talking about Jen, or was her name never mentioned? Written out of their collective history.

She felt an ache in her stomach when she pictured them all sitting around the table, the places where she and Charles used to sit probably both empty now. She would try to push the thoughts to the back of her mind. Even though Amelia and Charles were still the girls' grandparents, they were no longer her family. She had to forget about them.

She waited for the media attention to die down. She resolved to go out more, stop brooding, stop looking at the internet, and take back control of her life.

If only she knew how.

45

Cass wasn't sure she liked seeing her picture in the paper. It was definitely a flattering shot, and she was sad enough to care that that was the case, but it was just that she looked a little desperate, a bit like a wannabe. Like one of those kiss-and-tell girls, or a fame-starved *Big Brother* contestant. It was odd seeing her name too. Cassandra Richards printed there for all of the paper's however many millions of readers to see.

The interview hadn't been part of her plan. After she had turned up at Jen and Jason's house (God, that had been scary – her heart had been pounding out of her chest when she sat on the wall, anticipating Jen's reaction when she arrived home), she had waited, breath held, heart fluttering, for news.

She had been in no doubt that Jen was going to have to tell at least Jason, even if not the others, about her existence after that. She had shown that she could expose Charles's secret any time she liked. Not, to be honest, that she had had any intention of doing so. She held no ill will towards Jen. She liked her, hoped that one day they would all feel like family. She was never really going to blow it all apart herself. She just wanted to give Jen a nudge. Let her handle it how she wanted to, but hint that she ought to do it sooner rather than later.

Then, the next thing she knew, her dad was telling her

mum that the whole family knew. That his other three children weren't speaking to him. She knew that her mother had waited, just as she had, for his marriage to fall apart, for his secret to be made public. For him to beg to come back and be a family with the two of them again.

Nothing. Nothing had happened.

He had stayed at home in Twickenham with his doormat of a wife. She had thought perhaps Jason, or one of the others, might get in touch with her. Curiosity, if nothing else, would surely drive them to seek her out. She could hardly stand the suspense. Waited, thinking every day that today was going to be the day.

Nothing.

She had thought about getting back into contact with Jen, but she had the feeling her approach wouldn't be welcomed. Her dad seemed unhappy and angry and she knew that, whatever had happened, however his story had come out, it had not been a happy experience. And then she had heard via Charles that Jason and Jen's marriage had broken down, and she knew she should keep well away. She'd felt bad, she honestly had. Jen hadn't deserved for it to rebound on her.

Only once did she and her father talk about what had gone on. He had phoned her, not even waiting to exchange pleasantries before getting straight to what was on his mind. 'Did you get in touch with her? With Jen?'

She had known he would be angry, would think that she had acted as a catalyst somehow, so she had avoided giving a straight answer.

'She contacted me,' she had said. 'She came down to Brighton to confront me.'

He had left it at that, seemingly not up to the fight, and she had been grateful.

Now, of course, things were different. Since the article had come out in the paper, he had avoided her completely. All of her colleagues now knew about their relationship – that had been an embarrassing Monday morning – so he couldn't really fire her, but she knew that their closeness was over. At some point, she was going to have to think about looking for another job, or maybe she should just use this opportunity to set up on her own as she had always wanted to? He would never forgive her for this.

She didn't really know why she had done it, why she had picked up the phone and called the number the paper gave out for people wanting to pass on bits of gossip. It was the anticlimax. The deathly calm after the storm. She had been so sure that everything was going to change, that she would be able to begin the undoubtedly long and slow process of getting to know her siblings, that when she was confronted with a blank wall, a sea of nothing, she had felt cheated.

As soon as she had done it, had said the words to the person on the other end, who had gone from sounding bored to practically salivating when she had spat out why she was calling – Cass would have sworn she could hear the drool hitting the receiver – she had had second thoughts. But, by then, it was too late. She had alerted the tabloid media to the fact that Charles Masterson was a fraud – and a fraud with a love child, at that. She hated that phrase. 'Love child'. As if the only children born of love were those whose parents were sneaking around while their partners' backs were turned. She didn't have to go through with telling the story herself, but it would be out there now, regardless.

She had thought, probably foolishly, that at least by agreeing to do the interview she could make sure the piece wasn't too unsympathetic to Charles. She could do some damage limitation. Make sure they made a note that he had always been a kind and loving father, all things considered.

When she had read the finished article, there didn't seem to be much mention of that. Charles came across as a hypocritical Lothario, while she was made out to be, it seemed to her, pathetic, needy and bitter. The scorned daughter looking for revenge.

Her mum, who she had not warned until the day before, had been furious. Splashed across the Sunday press as a stealer of another woman's husband. To be fair, Cass thought, trying to make herself feel better, that was exactly what Barbara was. Not that she had ever told the neighbours that, of course.

She had quite enjoyed talking to the journalist, at first. It had felt cathartic to get the whole story off her chest, to have her point of view heard, for once. They had met in a little cafe in Hove, after the pictures had been taken in a small hotel room that the paper had arranged. Someone to do her hair and make-up. A stylist who persuaded her into a dress that was considerably shorter than one she would ordinarily wear. They all kept telling her how great she was going to look. And she, like an idiot, had fallen for it.

The reporter – a woman in, probably, her mid-fifties, with a neat black crop and her glasses dangling from a chain round her neck – had been super friendly at first, praising Cass's bravery in coming forward, telling her that her father would thank her in the end, because living a lie must be like living a kind of hell. As the interview had gone on, it had become obvious that this was going to be some kind of a hatchet job, though. The woman – Angie, that was her name – had kept asking Cass for sleazy details about her parents' relationship, how often Charles had stayed over, did he ever buy her mum under-wear, that kind of thing. Cass had tried not to answer, but Angie would always sidle up to the same subject again, putting words into her mouth, choosing to read silence as acquiescence.

By the time it was over, she had felt lower than she had ever felt before. There was nothing she could do now but wait for the story to come out, the shit to hit the fan, the grenade to go off.

She had bought a bottle of wine and taken it home. She hadn't even invited Kara over to share it with her.

46

Jen was mooching around Selfridges Food Hall after work one afternoon. Judy had invited her over for dinner with her family on Saturday evening – an event Jen was dreading because, fond as she was of Judy, they had never really socialized away from the hotel, and she wasn't sure what they would find to talk about. She was caught between aisles, hunting for something to take as a gift that didn't cost too much, but that looked like a treat and not an offering from a food bank.

She was trying to decide between a box of salted caramels or champagne truffles when she turned round to check whether anything else took her fancy and bumped right into her. Poppy. Her former best friend and sister-in-law. Or, at least, Jen assumed she was soon to be her former sister-in-law. She and Jason hadn't discussed divorce, but it was starting to feel somehow inevitable.

In fact, they hadn't really discussed anything. She hadn't even spoken to him since the day the story broke in the papers. He had left her polite, procedural messages a couple of times, about the house or the girls, but nothing more. She had tried calling him back at odd moments, hoping to catch him unaware, so that he would answer, but he never did. More than anything she missed having someone to chat about the mundane stories from her day with, and who would chat about theirs with her. Even the silences she had come to dread seemed comforting, in retrospect, because at least they had been shared.

'Sorry,' she said, on autopilot, before she looked up and registered who it was.

Poppy gasped. Let out a little 'hi' before she thought better of it.

Jen stood nailed to the spot. Her instinct was to throw her arms around Poppy and hug the life out of her, but she knew it wouldn't be welcomed.

'Hey . . .'

She noticed that Poppy could barely look at her. She looked like a startled antelope, caught in the moment before she made a bolt for freedom.

'Jen,' she said quietly.

'It's so good to see you. I . . . are you OK? Can I talk to you, just for a minute?' Jen had no idea what she was going to say, she just knew she had to say something.

'I don't think I really have anything to say to you. Sorry.' Poppy turned to walk away, nearly knocking over a display of tins of loose-leaf tea with her shoulder bag as she did so.

Jen nearly smiled. Poppy always carried unfeasibly large bags. Jen had never had any idea what was in them, apart from accumulated random mess that Poppy never got around to sorting through.

She put a hand out and grasped Poppy's coat-clad arm, as if to stop her running away. 'Just come and have a coffee. Ten minutes, that's all. There are things we need to talk about.'

She marched her through to the main shop before Poppy could object again, down the escalator to one of the little cake and coffee areas. She steered her to a table in the corner and barked an order for two white coffees at a waitress without even asking Poppy what she wanted.

'None of this was ever meant to happen.'

'This?' Poppy said, a look of cynicism on her face.

'Me and Jason, Amelia and Charles. I didn't set out to ruin everyone's lives.'

'I'm sure you didn't.'

'It wasn't my fault that your dad was living a double life. I didn't ask to know about it.'

'I don't understand why you would have said it like that. In front of Jason. In front of Mum. As if you hated us. After everything –'

'God, no, Poppy. I adored . . . adore you all, you know that. That was just it. I couldn't bear seeing what Charles was doing to your mum. To all of you. I kept it to myself for months. It was awful knowing, having to face you and Jason. Not being able to confide in you . . .'

The coffees arrived. Poppy stirred hers violently, spoon clanking against the china, liquid sloshing up to the rim of the cup and threatening to spill over. 'And the way you chose to tell Jason was to blurt it out on our parents' anniversary?'

'No one could regret that more than me.'

'Yes, I suppose that's true,' Poppy said.

Jen thought she could sense her soften slightly. 'I miss you. All of you.'

'Maybe you should have thought of that.'

'I didn't think at all, that's just it. Everything had piled up on top of me, and I could hardly breathe. I felt like I was suffocating under the weight of it all. I'm so sorry.'

'Jen . . .' Poppy said.

Jen sat with bated breath, waiting for what would come next.

'. . . I accept your apology. Thank you.' Poppy stood up, fished in her bag for her purse. 'But now, if you'll excuse me, I've got to go.'

'No, Poppy . . .'

Her cold acceptance was harder to bear than the anger Jen had expected. It was so emotionless. As if she didn't care about her relationship with Jen, or lack of it, she was simply being polite to a not much liked acquaintance.

'Wait . . .'

Poppy put a five-pound note on the table and walked away before Jen could say any more.

From Simone that evening she heard that Jason, Poppy and Jessie had started to see their father again. Hesitantly, at first. There had been recriminations, tears, resentment. But the newspaper article that Jen had thought might blow them apart irrevocably had, in fact, had the opposite effect. The Mastersons were closing ranks. Battening down the hatches. Pulling up the drawbridge. And she was firmly on the other side of the moat. It shocked her to the core that they were all prepared to take part in the deception – because that was what it was, she knew that now – that they were a happy, harmonious, devoted family.

She called Jason, to ask him about what had happened to make him forgive his father and move on, but he told her in no uncertain terms that it was none of her business.

A few days later, Emily told her that they were planning another family get-together. A party to make up for the fact that the big anniversary celebration had been cancelled.

'I'm coming down for it,' she said excitedly, as blissed out and unquestioning in the face of this good news as a tambourine-wielding chanter dancing down Oxford Street.

'I'll stay at yours, though, obviously. If that's OK.'

'They're . . . what? Everything's forgotten? Back to normal?'

'Pretty much, thank goodness,' Emily had said. 'Grandpa's really sorry for what he did. He says he made some stupid mistakes, but he's realized now what's really important to him, and he's trying hard. It's sweet, really.'

'Right . . . well . . .' Jen had said, knowing it was pointless to even try to deprogramme her. The cult had sucked her right back in. 'It'll be lovely to see you.'

That Monday morning, Jen had half considered phoning in sick, partly because she genuinely wasn't feeling great – something in the takeaway curry she had had the night before had left her feeling a little worse for wear – but mostly because she knew today was the first time she would see Sean again since, well . . . since . . . and she honestly wasn't sure if she could face it.

Judy had been full of it on Saturday night – which had been pleasant, actually. Not great fun, not something Jen felt she wanted to repeat every weekend, but a nice enough way to get through a lonely evening. Obviously, Judy knew nothing about the million ways Jen had humiliated herself the last time she and Sean had met.

'He definitely likes you,' she had gushed. 'Maybe now that you're single . . .'

'I'm not single. Officially, I'm still married.'

'You know what I mean. It'd do you good to get out there.'

Truthfully, Jen had considered it. They had Sean's details on file, obviously. She had actually had a sneaky check to see if his mobile number was there. Written it down on a piece of paper. A couple of times she'd even come close to calling, but she wasn't sure what she would have said. 'Hi, remember how I debased myself by practically jumping you last time we met? Fancy a repeat performance, only this time I'm not wearing a wedding ring?'

Actually, that was a lie. She was still wearing her wedding ring. It would have felt wrong to take it off and, besides, it was practically welded to her hand, these days. Held on by bits of finger flab bulging out above and below. She would have needed a hacksaw to remove it. She had no idea if Jason still sported his. It didn't feel like something she could ask the girls and not seem altogether pitiful.

She had even taken particular care with how she looked before she left home. Her hair was flattened to within an inch of its life. She had actually put her make-up on in the bathroom – rather than on the bus, as she usually did – so she thought her eyeliner might be straight, for once. Sometimes she arrived at work looking as if she was hoping to audition for Kiss. It wasn't that she was hoping Sean would ask her out again. More that she didn't want to feel he was looking at her and thinking, Yikes, I had a lucky escape.

Because things had calmed down, because her life was back on an even keel – even if it wasn't a particularly enjoyable one – she had stopped looking so gaunt. She was actually eating meals, rather than occasionally remembering to stuff in a bag of crisps before she passed out. She still couldn't really be bothered to cook for herself. But Morrisons had a nice line in microwave meals for idiots, and she could just about summon up the energy to take them out of the cardboard and stab them with a fork, most nights. She knew not being super skinny suited her better. That she had one of those faces that needed a bit of flesh on it, otherwise she could start to look like something Alexander McQueen might have decorated a handbag with.

She was so caught up in thinking about what the day might hold that she didn't concentrate on where she was going and, before she knew it, she had forgotten to take her detour and she was walking right past Masterson Property. She told herself not to look inside, but the more she did so, the more her eyes were determined to disobey her. Charles wasn't there. Of course, he wasn't. Or at least she didn't see him, but her heart started to beat out of her chest, thinking about how close she'd come. By the time she reached the hotel, she was practically having palpitations.

It didn't help that she couldn't decide whether she wanted to be there or not when Sean checked in. Consequently, she jumped every time anyone approached the desk, and then experienced alternate waves of relief and disappointment when it wasn't him. By lunchtime, she was a nervous wreck.

In the end, he showed up while she was dealing with an

irate businessman who had left his shoes outside his room to be cleaned, and they had never been seen again. Jen was trying not to look at his feet, because he had the hotel's fluffy towelling slippers on with his power suit, and, even though she was genuinely apologetic that such a thing might have happened, she was also a bit scared she might laugh.

She noticed Sean out of the corner of her eye. Felt herself turn an attractive shade of raspberry. Which, together with the hair and her green uniform shirt, probably made her look like a faulty set of traffic lights. Or a 1970s ice lolly.

She promised the businessman a full forensic investigation and directed him to the nearest shoe shop. Sean was taking his time, chatting with Judy, being his usual charming self. Once Jen was free, he looked over her way. Obviously, they were in public, so she knew he wasn't going to say anything that might embarrass her.

'Did I hear you telling that man you lost his shoes?'

'They were stolen from outside his room.'

'And you've sent him to Aldo in the hotel's slippers?'

'It was either that, or lend him my heels. And I'm only a size five.'

Sean smiled. 'Do you see why I keep coming back here? There's never a dull moment.'

'We do our best.'

'See you later.' He smiled, and moved off towards the lift.

Judy was beaming at Jen, as if Jen had just told her she'd won Receptionist of the Year.

'See,' she said, as soon as the lift doors closed. 'I told you he has a crush on you. It's patently obvious.'

Jen rolled her eyes. 'Stop trying to make something out of nothing, just because you're bored.'

She felt secretly pleased, though. Whether he still liked her in that way or not, he was clearly making the effort to stay friends. The residual humiliation she still harboured deep down ebbed away a little.

47

A little while later, Judy answered the phone and passed it over to Jen, a knowing smirk on her face.

'Mr Hoskins for you,' she said smugly.

'Hello,' Jen said, turning away from her slightly.

'I just want to ask you one question,' Sean said at the other end. 'Did you sort all your problems out and everything's fine and you're happy and I should leave well alone, or did they get worse and you're an outcast living in a hovel with no friends, or neither of the above?'

'The second one,' Jen said.

'In which case, would you like to go out for a drink with me this evening?'

She thought about her empty house. Another evening in front of the TV with no Jason, Simone or Emily for company. Single women were supposed to go out with men, and she seemed to be a very single woman now. What was the worst that could happen? That she might almost enjoy herself for a couple of hours?

'OK.'

They arranged that he would collect her from reception at the end of her shift, like a regular date, now that she had no reason to be discreet. She knew that there was no chance of her launching herself at him as she had done before – or, indeed, at any man ever again; she had had enough rejection for one lifetime. She didn't even feel the butterflies that she had felt before, the sense of nervous anticipation. She still thought he was an attractive man but, truthfully, she really wasn't sure whether or not she actually fancied him, or if what had happened had happened because she would have been drawn to any man who had shown an interest in her when her real life got to be too much.

'So,' Sean said, when they had settled down with their drinks, 'I'm not expecting you to tell me what went on, but I can't say I'm not curious.'

'Oh no, you're not getting off that lightly,' Jen said. 'I'm going to bore you with all the details.'

She told him the whole story, right down to the fact that it was she who had blown the whole thing apart, and the mean-spirited way in which she had done so. She figured he might as well know the worst about her. She saw his eyebrows shoot upwards involuntarily when she explained exactly who her father-in-law was – the way people's always did – but if he had an opinion on Charles and his views, he kept it to himself.

'God, what a nightmare,' the master of understatement said, when Jen finally ran out of things to say. 'And you don't think maybe Jason just needs time?'

She shrugged. 'I don't blame him, if he hates me, after the way I treated his family. And then there was . . . not that he even knows about that.'

So far, they had avoided any mention of Sean's last visit. Jen knew that they should probably address it, but she would rather have had her eyelashes pulled out one by one than confront it head on.

Sean had other ideas. 'I hope you're not still beating yourself up about that,' he said.

She looked at the table. How interesting. Someone had carved 'Fuck Arsenal' into it. Wow. Had Samuel Pepys been sitting at this very spot?

'Because I'm not having that argument about who was most to blame again.'

'Don't . . .' she said.

He smiled, and she wondered whether there would now be an awkwardness between them that would cloud the evening.

Sean had other ideas, though. 'Do you fancy dinner?'

They ate at Pescatori. Chargrilled squid followed by monkfish in pancetta for Jen. She had walked past the restaurant hundreds of times but never been inside. It was far too fancy. She knew she wasn't going to let Sean pay for the whole thing, so her enjoyment was somewhat ruined by her trying to work out whether she had sufficient funds in her account to cover half the bill, or whether her card would be rejected. She and Jason still had their joint account but, other than the regular mortgage payments going out of it, and the direct debits for gas and electric, neither of them was touching it. Jen knew they would have to sort it out, one day, but it felt so final that she didn't want to be the one to bring it up.

She and Sean chatted easily. He was the kind of person who never projected any atmosphere. In a good way. He didn't leave you trying to guess what you'd said wrong, or whether you'd offended him. If there was a potential misunderstanding, he'd get to the bottom of it, usually with a joke. He was – or, at least, he seemed to be to Jen – blissfully uncomplicated. She could imagine he would be easy to live with. For the first time in weeks, she felt relaxed. Happy, even.

'Are your parents still alive?' she asked him at one point.

'Yes, but they live in Portugal. One brother, one sister. Both in London, both nice normal people. No family dramas for me.'

She decided she liked him even more.

Later, after Sean had insisted on paying for the meal in spite of her protests, they walked back in the direction of the hotel. Jen knew that neither of them was about to attempt to pin the other up against a wall or suggest they go to his room. They were doing it properly, this time. Taking it slowly. Actually waiting to see how they felt.

'If I was any kind of a man, I'd offer to take you home, but I have literally no idea where Wimbledon is, or how to get there.'

She laughed. 'I'll be fine. I'm used to it.'

'At least let me put you in a taxi.'

'No,' she said. 'It's not even late.'

'Then I'll walk you to the Tube.'

At Goodge Street they hugged for longer than they would have if all they thought they would ever be was friends.

'I'd like to see you again. For dinner, I mean, not just walking through reception,' he said. 'Tomorrow night? Not that I'm trying to rush things, but I'm only here till Thursday.'

'Tomorrow night would be lovely. I'm paying, by the way.'

He hesitated, clearly thinking that to refuse would be to insult her. 'OK. Thank you.'

'McDonald's all right?'

He laughed. 'Perfect.'

They hugged again and he kissed her briefly, his mouth against her mouth. She felt her knees buckle a little. OK, so who was she kidding? Maybe she did fancy him after all.

'Text me when you get home, so I know you're there safely.'

'What are you going to do about it if I'm not?' she asked, teasing him.

'Oh, I don't know. Call the police and ask them to scour the area between here and Wimbledon? I'm sure they have nothing better to do.'

'Night, Sean.' She headed into the station, a smile on her face.

It stayed there all the way home, even when the Tube changed its mind about going to Colliers Wood and stopped at Kennington instead, even when she just missed the bus at her connection and had to wait nearly twenty minutes for another one, even when it started to rain on the walk at the other end and she didn't have an umbrella. She liked him, he definitely liked her, and the embarrassment of the last time they had seen each other was a thing of the past.

Definitely progress.

'Is it wrong that I'm kind of seeing someone?' she said to Judy the next day.

She was taking her break out the back of the hotel, in between the bins and the air-conditioning units. Judy was waiting for her shift to start.

'No,' Judy said. 'Of course not. You're not the one who walked out.'

Jen and Sean had exchanged a bit of small talk over the desk when he had been on his way out for the day. Jen had warned him that, although she wasn't hiding the fact that they had had dinner the night before from any of her colleagues – well, maybe from Graham Roper the Doorman Groper, because the less he knew about what she did in her private time the better – it wouldn't do to be seen to be too flirty while she was at work.

Because she was on an early, and had been up since four thirty, she was already dead on her feet and had told Sean there was no way she could possibly make it past nine o'clock, so they had arranged to meet as soon as she got off her shift.

By six o'clock, they had had two drinks in the pub and were looking at menus in Zen Garden – Sean's suggestion. He had claimed a yearning for dim sum, but Jen knew he had chosen one of the cheapest – but still nice – restaurants in the area, because he knew she was going to stick to her declaration that it was her shout.

The evening felt more loaded than the night before. This was a proper date, there was no question, so self-consciousness had crept in, yet again, and was threatening to kill off the conversation. It didn't help that Jen had been struck by the thought, in the middle of the night, that if she and Sean continued like this, they were more than likely going to have sex, eventually. He was going to see her naked. The last time, when they'd had their near miss, she had been so carried away by the moment that she hadn't given it a second thought. Now, when half the excitement should be in the anticipation, she felt nothing but fear. She was a forty-three-year-old mother of two. She had not spent the last twenty years in the gym doing crunches just in case, one of these days, she might have to take her clothes off in front of a man who might not appreciate that her slightly pouchy stomach came with the job.

Ridiculous, she knew, but then her development, as far as relationships with men went, had been arrested at the age of twenty-one, when these kinds of things were paramount.

She pushed a white glutinous squidgy blob, which had started to remind her uncomfortably of her admittedly slim but untoned thighs, around her plate.

They sat in silence for a moment.

'How are the flour rolls?' Sean said, no doubt wondering where his sparkly companion had gone.

'Delicious.'

'My prawn dumplings are superb.'

'Great.'

Sean laughed. 'I know what this is. We've hit the awkward stage. It's suddenly dawned on us both that this might go further, and we've entirely lost the art of conversation.'

Jen immediately felt more at ease. This was a man who she could be totally upfront and honest with. Nothing seemed to faze him.

'Is it terminal?'

'Only if we allow it to be. In my experience, if we force ourselves to talk about anything, however banal, and then we go back to my room for ten minutes before you have to leave and we get to second base – no further, mind you – then the next time we see each other everything will be fine.'

'It sounds like you've been through this before.'

'Trust me, I'm an expert. That's why I'm still single.'

'No one except Jason has seen me naked in years,' she blurted out. She might as well put her cards on the table.

Sean held his hands up. 'Whoa. Who said anything about seeing you naked? That's at least base four.'

She laughed. 'How many are there?'

'I have no idea.'

'I just mean, I'm not thirty any more and . . . well . . . you know.'

'Who do you think I am? Ryan Reynolds? I'm interested in you, not your six-pack.'

'It's more like a Party Seven, these days, but I take your point.'

And that was it, awkwardness over.

They did go back to his room later, and just for ten minutes, like he'd said. Jen thought they'd got to second base. They lay on his bed and kissed and a few clothes got rearranged, anyway. She felt incredible. Sean could turn off jokey and go for passionate at the flick of a switch.

By the time she had to leave, she could hardly tear

herself away. She had no idea how those True Love Waits teenagers did it. No wonder they spent so much time praying and dry humping each other up against walls.

48

Even though she had to get up at the crack of dawn –
before it, actually, at this time of year – she could hardly
sleep for thinking about what had just happened. She had
travelled home in a daze. For the first time since Jason had
left, she felt as if she could see a future ahead.

Not that she thought she and Sean were going to settle
down and get a mortgage and a springer spaniel. She knew
it was highly unlikely that the first man she dated would
turn out to be the love of her life, or she his, but she knew
now that having a new relationship was possible. Meeting
someone else wasn't out of the question. And Sean was
funny, smart, attractive, kind, thoughtful and, maybe
above all, uncomplicated and unencumbered. There
would be no quiet resentments with him, no buried grievances. He was as upfront and straightforward as they
came. Not to mention that he undoubtedly still had the
ability to make her feel a little weak at the knees.

As she took her make-up off, she received a text from
him. It simply said:

Night, gorgeous. X

It made her feel special in a million different ways.

When her alarm went off, she didn't know where she was
for a moment. She had finally drifted off at about mid-

night and now, four and a half hours later, her body was refusing to believe that it was morning. She hauled herself out of bed and into the bathroom, automatically reaching for the shower taps. As she waited for the water to warm even one degree above freezing, she suddenly felt a wave of nausea. She pictured her gloopy flour rolls filled with something that almost resembled pork, and threw up violently into the toilet bowl.

Brilliant. Just what she needed. Food poisoning. Tonight was Sean's last night before he had to go back up to the Cotswolds – although he had already made arrangements to come straight back down after the weekend, once he could arrange for cover in the showroom. Neither of them, it seemed, could bear to wait for his next scheduled visit, which was five weeks away, to see if their burgeoning relationship had real potential – and they had arranged to go to the bar at The Langham for cocktails. They had talked about whether they should do something cultural – the cinema or, even, the theatre or a concert – but they had agreed that, as their time together was precious, they shouldn't waste it sitting side by side in silence. At least, not yet. If they ever settled down together, then they could do that every night.

She knew that, if she wasn't well enough to go to work, there was no way she could show up at the hotel for her date later on, even if she had got it all out of her system. She could, of course, meet Sean somewhere else, but that wasn't the point. You didn't take a day off sick and then go out in the evening. It just wasn't cricket.

She felt another wave coming. She gave in to it and then sat on the bathroom floor. This was so unfair. She silently cursed the Zen Garden. Pictured herself going in there to make a loud complaint: 'You ruined my blossoming love affair. I'm never eating here again.' She imagined they'd be devastated. The last of the big spenders, with her £27.65 bill, taking her custom and her £3.50 tip elsewhere.

After a moment, she realized she was feeling better. Not in that calm between the storms way that usually punctuates bouts of food-poisoning-related sickness, but completely fine. She remembered that she had felt nauseous a few days ago, too, when she'd got out of bed after the curry takeaway – although, that time, she hadn't actually thrown up. She thought about her thickening waistline, how she had lost her gaunt look and filled out in a matter of weeks. She thought about the way she had been floored by morning sickness for weeks when she was pregnant with Simone. She thought about the night she and Jason had had sex for the first time in months, the night before it all went wrong. She hadn't had her diaphragm with her, and why would she have? It would have been a bit like packing a surgical mask in case there was an outbreak of SARS. There had been no reason to think she would need it.

And then she thought, 'Oh shit. This can't be happening to me.'

There was no doubt in her mind, though. Even before she phoned David and told him she wasn't able to come in, went back to bed for a few hours in a state of shock, and then staggered out to the chemist's on the corner to buy the test that confirmed her fears, she knew.

She had to call Sean sooner rather than later, because Judy was bound to tell him she was sick, and she didn't want him to worry. She wasn't going to tell him the full story, though. Not yet. Not until she had decided what to do.

'Oh my God, I've poisoned you,' he said when he answered, so she knew Judy must have filled him in. 'Are you OK?'

'A bit wobbly,' she said – which was the truth, as it happened.

'Do you want me to come over? I can blow out my appointments, hire a Sherpa.'

More than anything, she wanted to say yes.

'No. That's so sweet of you, but I'm fine. And it's not a pretty sight, to be honest. Plus, I don't want you missing your appointments. That's what you're here for. I'll be fine by tomorrow.'

'And I'll be back in Moreton-in-Marsh. What time are you on in the morning?'

'Late. I start at nine.'

'I'm not checking out till about eleven, so I can give you longing looks across reception as I leave.'

'I'll look forward to it.'

'I'm going to go over to that restaurant and tell them to clean up their act.'

'No! Don't do that. I had a prawn sandwich for lunch, it could just as well have been that.' The last thing she wanted was for Sean to accuse Zen Garden of making her sick when, actually, it was her husband.

'And are we still on for next week? This isn't an elaborate way of you trying to avoid seeing me, is it?'

Jen forced herself to laugh. 'Of course not.'

'Because I can take it. I've been dumped many times before, I've got a hide like a rhino.'

'Nice image.'

'Call me later. I won't try you, in case you're sleeping.'

'I will.'

'Drink water.'

'I know. I'll talk to you later.'

'Bye, Jen.'

She sank back down on to the bed. She had no idea what she was going to do. So she did what she always did when something happened to her. She picked up the phone to call Poppy.

She heard it ring and ring. Imagined Poppy looking at the caller ID and deciding not to answer. When it clicked on to voicemail, she left a message.

'It's Jen. I know you don't want to speak to me, but something's happened. I need your advice. Please call me. I . . . I don't know who else to talk to . . .'

She put her mobile on the bed beside her and sat watching it for a while, willing it to ring. A watched pot never boils, the Rory in her head said. So she tried to distract herself. Told herself that maybe Poppy was at the cinema or on a date and would call later.

Nothing.

49

By Monday morning, she still had not heard from her sister-in-law, but she knew what she wanted. Emily had come down for the weekend and had submitted herself to being babied and pampered for the whole forty-eight hours. Despite everything else that was going on, Jen felt more herself – more comfortable, even – than she had been in ages. When Emily left, and the house was cold and too quiet again, she knew that she wanted this baby. Maybe, she thought, she was being selfish – as if she only wanted to have it to fill a hole in her life – but then it was her view that most people had children for selfish reasons, anyway, because what other reason was there? She certainly didn't think they were doing it for the kids' sake.

She knew, too, that her days with Sean were numbered, whatever happened. If he had any sense, he'd be back on the first train to the Cotswolds as soon as she told him the news. They had texted rather than phoned over the weekend, because, Jen had explained to him, she couldn't really chat with Emily home, and it was far too early to tell her daughter she was seeing someone. Of course, in her own head, she was thinking why tell her and go through all the drama that would precipitate, when it was probably all going to be over next week, anyway? Her plan was to tell Sean everything, face to face, on Tuesday evening. That was going to be a date to remember.

The other thing she knew was that she owed it to both the baby and to Jason to let him know sooner rather than later. She wanted him to have the opportunity to be a father to this child. And she had to admit that a part of her was even wondering whether this could be a way back. Whether Jason would see past everything else they'd been through and want to be a family again. Whether she would be welcomed back into the fold.

She allowed herself to daydream a little about them all sitting around the table again, the Mastersons. A high chair nestling in between her and Charles. Even Jessie was bound to come round when she met her new baby niece or nephew. She could almost smell the comforting aromas of the house in Twickenham, hear the laughter, taste Amelia's home cooking. She had no idea if it was even possible that they could recapture some of what they'd had, but she knew she had to give it a shot.

When Sean walked into reception the following afternoon, a flutter in Jen's chest and a quickening of her pulse let her know that she was pleased to see him. Either that, or she was about to have a coronary, struck down by the fear of the conversation she knew they had to have once they were alone.

He greeted her with a big smile. 'Oh my God, what's that?' he said dramatically, pointing out towards the street, once he had got his room key.

Jen and Judy both turned to look and, as they did, when he was confident Judy was facing the other way, Sean leaned over the desk and kissed Jen on the lips.

Judy laughed. 'I saw that.'

'Are you trying to get me fired?' Jen said, half thrilled, half horrified. Graham Roper the Doorman Groper was practically salivating in the doorway, hands in his pockets as if he was fumbling for change.

'Six o'clock?' Sean said. They had already arranged that they would revisit their cocktails at The Langham plan. Jen wasn't sure that she really wanted to tell him what she had to tell him in a crowded bar, but suggesting she could meet him in his room didn't seem to give off the right vibe either.

'Perfect.'

'Wear your uniform, it's kind of cute.'

'Perv,' she said, laughing.

After their first evening out, last week, she had brought a change of clothes with her on the second night they were meeting up. The first time he had seen her dressed in her civvies Sean had done a mock double take and said, 'Oh my God, you're female. I hadn't realized.'

Because it was a warm evening they decided to walk to The Langham – or, at least, Sean suggested it and Jen thought she should agree, even though she was desperate to get there and get it over with. He was so patently happy to see her that she felt as if she was leading her carefree tail-wagging retriever to the vet's to be put down. Walkies! Good boy! Sorry, Fido, this is where we say goodbye.

As they headed down Wigmore Street, she asked him questions about the area around where he lived, where he grew up, his school. It was like an episode of *This Is Your Life*. Anything to keep him from asking her about how she was.

Once there, they settled down in the bar and looked at the cocktail menu – although, of course, Jen had no intention of ordering one. She had tried to edge towards a table as far away from other people as possible, but it was obvious they wouldn't really get any privacy anywhere, the place was too crowded. She knew she had to say what she needed to say as quickly as possible, but then Sean reached for her hand and she couldn't stop herself from getting caught up in the moment.

'It's so good to see you,' he said, his blue-grey eyes fixed on hers.

She couldn't help holding his gaze. Damn, why couldn't she at least not have found out for a couple more days? It had been obvious to both of them, when they had last said goodnight in his hotel room, that the next time they met up would be it. Move straight to last base, do not pass Go. Now, obviously, there was no question that she was going to sleep with him, knowing she was pregnant with Jason's baby.

She gulped. 'You too.'

'My cousin Annie – you know, the one who married one of her teachers – she's looking after the showroom. She says I'm to tell you I can stay as long as I like. She's got it all under control.'

Oh God.

'Sean . . .' Jen said, in a tone that she hoped said, 'Listen to me, this is serious.'

It worked, because he sat bolt upright as if he was waiting to be told off. She had rehearsed over and over again, in her head, what she was going to say, but now it came to it, she felt tongue-tied.

'Is everything OK?' he said gently.

She knew she just had to spit it out.

'No. There's no easy way to say this –'

He interrupted her. 'OK.'

She breathed deeply. 'When I thought I had food poisoning the other day, I didn't. I'm pregnant.'

'God, I must be potent because we haven't even had sex . . .' Sean said, attempting a joke, although she could tell his heart wasn't really in it.

'Jason,' she said. 'I haven't . . . well, you know . . . with anyone else.'

'On a scale of what I was expecting you to say, that wasn't even on there.'

'I know. It came as a bit of a surprise to me too.'

'And . . . you're sure?'

She nodded. 'I'm so sorry.'

'For what? I can hardly be upset with you because you're having your husband's baby.' He sat back, looked anywhere but at her, fiddled with the collar of his jacket.

Jen felt a wave of feeling for him as she thought how he must have brought that jacket down specially, knowing they were going to have cocktails at a smart hotel. It was a little worn around the cuffs, she noticed. It had seen better days.

'It was a mistake, obviously. Right before we split up. Actually, the night before the big fight.'

'What does he think about it?'

'I haven't told him yet. I'm going to go and do it face to face.'

'Right.'

She told him then – because their thing was always to

be open with each other – how she knew the exact date the baby had been conceived, because of how her marriage to Jason had been in the weeks leading up to it. And that she had thought long and hard about whether to keep it, but she knew now that she wanted it more than anything.

'It might be my last chance and, even though I never would have wanted it to happen this way, I'm not giving the baby up.'

'I understand.'

'In all honesty, I don't expect you to. I'm not sure I do myself.'

Sean went quiet for a second. He could still hardly bring himself to look at her. 'Jen. Are you . . . do you think this might bring Jason round, make him want to reconcile?'

'I don't know. I mean, that's not why I want to have it.'

'I know that.'

'But I think if anything's ever going to make him change his mind, then this might, yes.'

'And is that what you want?' He looked up. Looked her straight in the eye.

She looked away. Was it what she wanted? 'I . . . I don't know. I think so. I think it would be the best thing for the baby . . . to have its family . . .'

There, she'd said it.

She noticed a waiter was hovering. Sean waved him away. Not now.

'I really like you,' she said, and it came out sounding like a massive cliché. 'And I'm truly sorry I messed you around. I didn't mean to.'

'I understand. Don't beat yourself up about it.'

'Do you want to go? I wouldn't blame you if you did.'

'Is that what you'd rather?'

'I don't know, to be honest. It's so good to see you, but I guess I should go home.'

'No. I promised you cocktails, so let's have cocktails. Virgin ones, obviously.'

'OK.'

He called the waiter over, and Jen ordered something that sounded like it would bring on a detox immediately, whether she wanted that or not. Sean ordered the same, and then changed his mind at the last minute and asked for something much stronger that involved several decisions about the type of olives and whether the ice was better cubed or crushed.

She wondered what they were going to talk about, now that she had hammered such a big nail into their coffin. Sean, being Sean, though, wanted to continue facing the issue head on.

'How do you think your daughters will react?'

She had been thinking about that all weekend. She was pretty sure that, beyond the initial reaction of 'Eew, Mum and Dad had sex', they would be excited. They were old enough, the age gap sufficient, that she didn't think either of them would feel threatened or usurped. And, even if they did, the idea of a reconciliation would bring them round soon enough.

'OK, would be my guess, eventually, although you can never tell. And anything that brings me and their dad closer together . . .'

'This whole thing must have been rough on them.'

'It has been.'

They sat there in silence for a few moments. Jen grasped around for something to say. Failed.

'And how about the rest of the Magnificent Mastersons?'

She smiled. He was trying so hard, and she was touched that he was clearly wanting to make it as easy for her as possible. She told him how Charles seemed to have been absolved, how they were a unit again. How she was hoping this baby might bring her closer to the whole family.

'And what if you get back together with him?' Sean asked. 'Will you go straight back into dutiful daughter-in-law mode with your father-in-law too? Everyone's forgiven, move on.'

'No. I don't think it could ever be like that again ...' She tailed off. It seemed so odd, so wrong, somehow, to be discussing how it might be, if she and Jason reconciled.

'You know my philosophy. Lay all your cards on the table – both of you – and then see how you feel. Everything up front.'

'Jason doesn't really do up front.'

'It's the only way. Always know what you've signed up for.'

'Maybe you should come with me. Act as my adviser,' she said, attempting a joke.

Mercifully, he laughed. 'You'll be fine.'

Thankfully, he didn't ask her what she would do if Jason didn't seize this opportunity to put her family back together. She wouldn't have known what to say. She hadn't thought that far ahead.

*

They had two drinks, and then Jen felt as if they should go home. She loved Sean's company, but she didn't want to prolong the agony. She didn't want it to seem as though she was giving him hope, by spending the whole evening with him. She was also a little afraid that, if she sat opposite him for too long, she might throw herself at him across the table, rip his clothes off there and then.

'I'll see you tomorrow, I suppose,' he said as they left. 'I guess I'll check out in the morning. Go back . . .'

Jen agreed to get a cab – she felt exhausted, both emotionally and physically – but not to Sean contributing to it.

'Thanks for being so understanding. And I really am sorry.'

'Will you stop saying that? I feel like a priest in a confessional. Would it make you feel better, if I told you to say three Hail Marys?'

She forced a laugh. She really was feeling wretched. Why did he have to be so reasonable, so nice about everything? 'I don't know the words.'

'OK, three choruses of "Don't Stop Believin'", then. It'll have the same effect.'

They hugged, and Jen felt him bury his face in her nicely straightened and smelling-of-coconut hair. She pulled away after a couple of seconds. Buttoned up her jacket. Got in the cab.

When she got to work the following morning, he had already checked out, leaving a note that said he thought it would be easier on them both not to have to say goodbye in front of her colleagues.

He wished her luck. Told her she deserved to be happy.

Asked her to let him know how things were going, because he would be wondering. There was no mention of him coming down again and, when Jen checked the future reservations, she couldn't find any reference to him. She had the feeling he would find another hotel next time.

She felt sad that it had ended like this, even though Sean had made it as painless as it could possibly be under the circumstances. She had treated him badly without ever wanting to, and he had behaved as, it seemed, Sean always behaved – rational, reasonable, wanting her to be happy. She felt as though she had lost a friend.

50

There was a split second when he first set eyes on her that gave away the fact that Jason was happy to see her. It was just a hint of surprise, the beginnings of a smile, but it was there. Luckily, Jen noticed it before he rearranged his face into something more unreadable – sterner, but with a hint of anxiety too. Otherwise, she probably would have backed out of what she had come to say, completely.

She was sitting on a low wall outside the house where Jason had his first-floor flat, in Kingston. She had managed to get the address from Emily, who would never have imagined that her father wouldn't have wanted her mother to know where he lived. She had guessed that he would be home about five, based on nothing but the fact that that was the time he used to arrive back when they lived in Wimbledon. Of course, he could have finished early, or have a rehearsal or a performance in the evening, or even a date – although she didn't really want to think about that. She knew she should have called ahead, but she hadn't wanted to give him the opportunity to avoid seeing her. Plus, she thought his unguarded reaction would tell her volumes.

She could sit here all evening, if she had to – the day had been pleasant and sunny, an early-spring warm spell, and she had brought a jacket in case it cooled down later – and the area where Jason had settled was nice enough.

She had started to wish she'd brought supplies, though. Pregnancy was making her feel permanently hungry.

She felt hopeful in a way that she hadn't in she didn't know how long. Everything was going to be OK. She was going to get her old life back. Maybe.

Thankfully, at about ten past five, she saw a figure that could only be Jason getting off a bus along the road. She breathed in and out steadily, to calm her nerves, forced her face into an expression that she hoped said 'It's OK, nobody's died' and stood up to greet him.

She hadn't seen him for weeks – nearly three months, in fact. Of course, he hadn't changed in that time – even though Jen felt she had, immeasurably. Or, maybe he had inside, who knew? Physically, though, he was the Jason she knew so well. Familiar. She even recognized the T-shirt he was wearing. In fact, she thought she might have bought it for him.

She had wondered how she might feel when she saw him. Whether her heart would start beating out of her chest, or she would burst into tears, but when it happened she felt blank. Removed, like she was watching herself go through the motions.

'What are you doing here?'

She remembered that she needed to get the good news out there quickly. 'Don't worry, everyone's fine. I just need to talk to you, that's all.'

'Why didn't you call first?' He didn't say this in an accusatory way, more confused.

'I don't know. I . . . can we just go inside?'

'Of course.'

She followed him in through the front door to an

unloved hallway. Upstairs, they entered a flat that was clean and neat, and full of bits and pieces Jen recognized. It was like a mini-me version of their house – or, at least, a negative version, furnished with all the missing pieces from the jigsaw. Put the two together and they would make one complete home. Even the smell was familiar. She watched as he filled the kettle, switched it on.

'It's a nice flat,' she said, searching around for something to say.

'Yes, it's worked out well.'

'How's work?'

Jason put down the box of tea bags he was holding. 'Jen, why are you here?'

Here we go.

'OK, well . . . I appreciate you might not want to know, or you might not even care, but I just found out I'm having a baby. That is, *we're* having a baby. Me and you.'

He couldn't have looked more surprised if she had told him she had been born a man. That she actually still had her old equipment in a jar somewhere.

'What? I mean . . . when?'

'The weekend away. Remember? I'm due in the middle of August.'

Jason sat on a chair opposite her, looking as if he might pass out if he didn't lower his centre of gravity quickly. She waited for him to say something else and, when he didn't, she carried on.

'Obviously, I would never have planned for this to happen. Not so long after Emily. But I couldn't be happier.'

'I can't believe it. Another baby.' He smiled at her, and she knew immediately that her news had wiped out months of bad feeling. She smiled back. 'I know. Crazy, isn't it?'

'All those sleepless nights. Are you ready for all that again? And then when she – obviously, I'm assuming it'll be a she – is a teenager, we'll be well into our fifties.'

Jen noticed how he'd said 'we'.

'Lots of women don't even have their first one till they're my age, these days. We started young.'

'We did.'

'Jason, I know things are different between us but I want . . . I'm hoping you'll be involved. I would hate for the baby not to know its father.' She looked at him for a reaction.

'Of course. I'd never . . . I'll do whatever I can.'

'I'd hate for it to grow up not knowing its whole family, actually.'

She couldn't help herself then, she asked him about Charles. 'I've seen him on the TV, now and then. He seems to be doing OK.'

Charles – having done a couple of mea culpa TV appearances (one of which Jen had caught by accident and then hadn't been able to turn over), which meant all was forgiven and that he could salvage something of his TV career, although he had had to shift his rigid viewpoint a little and was now presenting himself as some kind of lovable rogue – had, it seemed, embraced the forgiveness of his family with enthusiasm.

'I think he's really sorry for everything,' Jason said, parroting what Emily had said before. The party line. The Tao of the Mastersons. 'And, you know, it was all years ago . . .'

'And Cass?'

'God, no, none of us want anything to do with her. Not after what she did, going to the papers. Dad's cut off all contact.'

'They don't still work together?'

'She's leaving, apparently. And he's keeping out of her way till she does. He's trying really hard.'

He shut the conversation down by changing the subject without even acknowledging he was doing so, making it clear that this wasn't an area for discussion. As far as he was concerned, he had popped Cass's skeleton firmly back in his closet and she was staying there. Door locked. Key thrown away.

'So the baby'll be due in the summer . . .'

It was going as well as it could, they were chatting like two reasonable people who had a shared past, and who might well share some kind of a future, but Jen realized she could feel a weight settling on her. She couldn't understand why she wasn't floating on air at the prospect of Jason letting her back into his life so readily.

'I could move back to Wimbledon,' he was saying. 'If you thought that was a good idea, I mean. So I could be there –'

'Move in?' This suddenly felt like it was going a bit fast. So much felt unresolved.

'Not necessarily. Not at first. I'll rent somewhere. Just so we can be close to each other. And then we could maybe think about it later, after the baby's born. If you wanted to.'

Jen remembered Sean's advice. Get everything out in the open. Don't leave any explosives hidden that could blow you apart later on.

'Jason . . . even before it all happened . . . did you ever think that maybe we'd lost our way a bit?'

He looked at her as if he didn't know what she was talking about. 'What do you mean?'

'That once Emily left home we weren't the same? I don't know, that maybe we didn't know how to relate to each other without the kids around? Or your family.'

'I thought we were fine. I was happy.'

'It didn't bother you that we never slept together any more?'

'Well, you seem to be pregnant,' he said, trying to make a joke of it.

'You know what I mean.'

He sighed. 'I just don't see the point of rehashing all this now.'

'That's part of my point. We never talked about anything. We never sorted anything out.'

'If we're going to have this baby together – be a family again – then we have to move on. Just forget about everything that's happened. If I can, then so can you, surely?'

'It's not healthy, though. Nothing ever gets resolved. I'd rather we got everything out there, told each other exactly how we felt, got any lingering resentments or doubts off our chests, and then started again from there.'

'There's nothing to talk about. A new start is a new start. That's the whole point of it – you agree to forget everything that's gone before.'

'But then how will it be different?'

'Why would we want it to be different? When it was good, it was good.'

'When the kids were there?'

'So? Now there'll be another baby. You kept saying you hated not feeling like a family any more, once Em went to college.'

'I know. I did. I do. I don't know. And if I'm being honest, I don't understand how you could just give up on our marriage, just like that, without us trying to work through it. I know I handled things badly, but you couldn't even stay around and fight it out?'

'There wasn't any point.'

'But now I'm pregnant, you're happy to come back?'

'I never wanted us to split up. It's just there wasn't any other way.'

He was exasperating.

'And what happens eighteen years down the line, when this baby leaves home and we're on our own again? Can't you see what I'm getting at? We have to work out what went so wrong that we fell apart at the first hurdle, once it was just the two of us.'

'I hardly think it's going to be the same. Who knows what'll be happening in our lives that far in the future?'

'I don't know, Jason. I just feel like we should clear the air. Establish a few ground rules about how it would be.'

'Sure. There's plenty of time for all that,' he said, standing up to resume his tea-making. 'How's Elaine?'

Jen knew that, for now, the conversation was over. She would have to try to force the issue again, later on.

There was no denying it felt so familiar, so comfortable, filling Jason in on the way she and her mum had become closer than ever, telling him about work, asking about his students. Away from the topic of them and their relationship, they were pretty much able to slip back into a conversation as if they had been halfway through it the last time they saw each other.

By half past eight, she was exhausted. They had eaten a takeaway, sitting side by side on the sofa like they used to, and caught up with stories about the girls. When Jen was clearly dead on her feet – she remembered this from the last time she was pregnant, that feeling of wanting to hibernate, starting to feel tired and then, a split second later, having to go to bed or risk falling asleep where she stood – she called a taxi. They agreed that Jason would come to the house the following morning so they could talk some more.

There was an awkward moment when they said goodnight, and she hadn't known what to do. Who knew what the rules were regarding almost-ex-but-maybe-not-husbands? In the end, Jason had offered her a hug and she'd accepted it.

It had gone well, she thought. Much better than she had anticipated. Jason had seemed happy to put the past behind them – maybe too far behind, but that was another issue. Now there was a baby on the way, it seemed as if he could see a future for them. They could be a family again.

It was the right thing to do. Jason was a good man, a fantastic father. He was kind and considerate, could be funny, was always supportive. They could be right back where they were before. Two parents enjoying bringing up their child.

She ran her hand protectively over her stomach. She knew this was what she wanted; she just couldn't quite feel it yet.

*

Back home, before she even got her key in the lock, her mobile rang.

Poppy.

She hesitated before she answered. She was too exhausted for more confrontation. She was curious, though. It was the first time Poppy had returned one of her calls since, well . . . since. It was too hard to ignore.

'Hi . . .' she said gingerly.

'I'm going to be an auntie again!' Poppy squealed on the other end.

Jen stopped in her tracks, completely wrong-footed. 'Um . . .'

'Jason just called me,' Poppy said breathlessly. 'I can't believe . . . I mean, I know you still have things to work out . . .'

Jen put her bag down, flicked the kettle on. She wondered, briefly, if she'd entered a parallel universe, one where her whole adopted family hadn't rejected her without a second thought. Where her best friend hadn't refused to even speak to her.

This was what she wanted, but now she seemed to be on the verge of getting it, it felt unreal. Play acting.

She took a deep breath. 'I thought you didn't want to speak to me.'

Poppy laughed, as if that had all been a big joke and they both knew it.

'Well, that was then,' she said, as if that explained everything. 'Things have changed now, obviously.'

'Right . . .'

'There's a new little niece on the way. Or nephew.'

'And do you think Amelia –'

'Are you kidding?' Poppy said. 'A new grandchild? It's like a whole fresh start.'

Jen sat down, overwhelmed and exhausted by the emotions of the day. This could be it, everything she'd been hoping for. The Mastersons, it seemed, were offering to welcome her back with open arms. Slates wiped clean all round. She suddenly felt as if she was suffocating.

'Poppy, I'm knackered, actually, it's been a long day.'

'Of course. Call me tomorrow. I want to tell you all about Ben. I'm still seeing him, can you believe that?'

'Great,' Jen said weakly.

'We're even thinking –'

'Bye,' Jen cut her off. 'I'll talk to you tomorrow.'

She turned her phone off, wished she could pour herself a large glass of wine. Sat there not moving for the best part of an hour.

51

She slept only a little that night. Too many conflicting thoughts were fighting for space in her head. Could everything really go back to the way it was? Were the Mastersons prepared to welcome her back into the family, as if nothing had ever happened? On the one hand, it almost felt too good to be true. On the other, it made her uneasy. The Masterson tidal system gone mad. You were out, then you were in. Just like that. There were no half measures.

You were a member of their little army, or you were the enemy.

She drifted off briefly and dreamed that she was in the Twickenham house. It was lunchtime and everyone was there. Nothing really happened. It was more a dream about atmospheres than events. She woke up feeling as if she was in a cocoon. Safe, warm, loved. Accepted.

At about six thirty she gave up attempting to go back to sleep, went downstairs and made herself some breakfast which she promptly threw up again, and then lay in the bath staring at a damp patch on the wall until the water went cold.

She knew Elaine would be up and about already. All dressed up with nowhere to go. She had always been an early riser. Jen hadn't told her the news yet. Had been intending to go down over the weekend and deliver it in person. But she felt that she needed some non-partisan advice. That she needed, if she was being honest, her mum.

'You're up early. Are you on your way to work?' Elaine said when she answered the phone.

'No. I'm off today.' Jen tried to make her voice sound as upbeat and happy as she could. Tried not to blurt out her news without any preamble. 'How's things with you?'

'Good,' Elaine said. 'I'm going up to the shops in a bit. Not that I mean you've caught me at a bad time . . .'

Her mother was still a little anxious sometimes when they spoke. Still scared she might not have been completely forgiven. Jen felt waves of guilt every time she caught the nervous tone.

'Actually, Mum, I just rang because I've got some news. Good news.' She had thought long and hard before she picked up the phone about the best way to phrase it. 'Jason and me . . . we're having a baby. I'm pregnant.'

There was a pause, an intake of breath. 'I'm . . . that's amazing. Fantastic. I don't understand.'

'Me neither,' Jen said. She explained to her mother how it had happened. Told her how Jason had reacted to the news.

'I know it's none of my business, but does this mean you might be getting back together?' Elaine had always loved Jason.

'I think so. I don't know. Honestly, Mum, it's all a bit weird.'

She told her about Jason's plans for their future, about Poppy's phone call, about Charles's history having seemingly been swept under the carpet. 'It's almost as if none of it ever happened.'

'Well . . .' Elaine said, thinking it over, 'maybe they've worked through it, the five of them. They've decided what's really important for them. Stranger things have happened.'

'It just feels . . . I don't know. I mean, say I lost this baby –'

'Oh, Jen love, don't,' Elaine butted in.

'It's not going to happen. Just hypothetically. Would they still want me around?'

'You're over-thinking things.'

'Maybe. Jason's coming round later, so we can talk some more.' She sighed. 'It would make the girls so happy.'

'You think about yourself,' Elaine said. 'Make sure whatever you do, it's what you really want.'

'I will. Thanks, Mum.'

'And congratulations, by the way. A baby! I can hardly believe it.'

Jason arrived on the dot of ten. Big smile on his face, flowers in one hand. Jen checked herself for a telltale stomach flip. Felt nothing.

'The coffee machine's on.'

'I told Mum we'd pop over in a bit,' he said, thrusting the bouquet in her direction.

'What? Jason, no –'

'She's dying to see you.'

'Did you tell her?'

'Of course. If I hadn't, Poppy would have. Did Poppy call you, by the way? She said she was going to.'

'Um . . . yes . . . Listen, I wish you hadn't mentioned it to them yet. I feel like we need to get things straight between ourselves, before we start saying anything to anyone else.'

'We're going to be fine. And how could I not tell Mum? She's going to be a granny again, she's got a right to know.'

'No one else. Not yet. Not the girls.'

'Give me some credit.'

'I don't know . . . it's a lot to take on board.'

'Dad's not going to be there. He's off playing golf. I know you might not want to see him yet.'

'Just Amelia?'

'Just Mum.'

Jen thought about the house in Twickenham. It was more than three months since she'd set foot inside it, but she could still smell the distinctive aroma, could have led a guided tour, blindfold, of all the family memorabilia that cluttered every surface. The pull was magnetic.

'It can't hurt, I suppose. Since she knows, anyway. I'd like to see her. If you think that's what she wants.'

'She's desperate to see you.'

'OK. But we still need to talk. Properly.'

'Of course. There's plenty of time for that. I told her we'd be there about half ten, though.'

It started to rain as they drove towards Twickenham. Just drizzle, at first, and then big, heavy drops that hit the windscreen and seemed to bounce off still intact. The car didn't feel like the right place to have a heart to heart, so Jen let Jason fill her in on more of the family's news since she had seen them last. Charles, it seemed, had more or less given up doing any work for Masterson Property and was spending more time at home.

'Do you think Amelia had any idea?' Jen said, remembering her mother-in-law's comment on the night it all came out.

'Of course not,' he said, his face clouding over. 'How could they have been so happy, if she had?'

'How could they have been as happy as we all thought, if Charles was having a secret relationship?' Jen said.

She felt Jason bristle. 'Dad made a stupid mistake. He regretted it immediately, but it was already too late because the woman was pregnant, the damage was done. That doesn't mean he didn't love Mum, or their marriage wasn't genuine.'

Jen knew she should keep quiet, but she couldn't help herself. 'He didn't break it off, though, did he? He was with Cass's mum for sixteen years –'

Jason cut her off sharply. 'There's no point going over and over it,' he said.

Jen thought, We haven't really ever gone over it once properly, but she kept her mouth shut.

'Everything's back to normal, that's all that matters.'

Jen said nothing, stared out of the window at the dark grey sky.

52

She had expected a hint of coldness. Some resistance, at least. Had almost wanted it. A chance to clear the air. But the thing with Amelia was that she would never fight back. It had always been that way. However she might be feeling underneath, her default setting was to pretend that everything was fine with her world. Like mother, like son.

'Jen,' she said, smiling as she opened the door. 'It's so wonderful to see you.'

She pulled Jen into a hug, and Jen felt herself respond. It was irresistible.

'How have you been? Tell me everything you've been up to,' Amelia said cheerfully, as if Jen was a teenager returned from a gap year rather than the family outcast who had suddenly been offered her old job back.

'Oh . . . you know . . .'

She followed Jason and his mother into the kitchen. Nothing had changed; the Masterson museum was still intact.

'So,' Amelia said, filling the kettle with water. 'Did you hear that Poppy has a new boyfriend? Ben. She brought him to lunch last Sunday, and he seems like a lovely man.'

An image popped into Jen's head. Her running up to a strange man, begging him to save himself before it was too late.

('Back away from the front door!')

'Yes. I heard.'

'Clearly dotes on her so, of course, that means I'm pre-disposed to like him.'

('Run, run for the hills, before they suck you in.')

'I'm glad.'

Amelia put a mug of coffee down in front of her. 'Oh, wait, I have a new photo of Violet to show you.' She rifled through a pile of papers on the kitchen table and found what she was looking for. 'Look at that face! Isn't she a beauty?'

Jen looked at the picture. There was no denying that Violet was cute. She already had Poppy's eyes. Jessie's nose. 'Adorable.'

'Well, you'll see them next weekend, they're coming for Sunday lunch.'

Jen felt her heart sink. Almost heard it crash to the floor with a sickening thud. She looked over at Jason, who was smiling at her encouragingly.

'I promised my mum I'd go down there, actually.'

She waited for the world to end.

Amelia smiled. 'Well, maybe the weekend after.' She turned to Jason. 'I can't believe your father is playing golf in this weather. I told him it might rain.'

'I'll phone him,' Jason said. 'He might want me to go and pick him up.'

'Jason dropped him off at the club before he picked you up,' Amelia said. 'His car's in the garage.'

Jen couldn't even think about the idea that Charles might want to come home before she had left.

'I . . . um . . . I promised Judy from work I'd pop over

to hers this afternoon,' she lied, slightly desperately. 'I probably shouldn't stay too long.'

'Just let me sort this out,' Jason said cheerfully.

Jen looked at him pleadingly. Willed him not to leave the room. Alone with Amelia, she had no idea what to say.

'So,' Amelia sat down opposite her. 'How are things at the hotel? Are they still working you into the ground?'

Jen inhaled deeply. Smiled at her mother-in-law. She knew that Amelia was doing her best to make her feel welcome.

'Amelia, please. Shout at me. Tell me I ruined your life. Anything. Let's just talk about it.'

'I don't think that's necessary. We've all moved on.'

Jen was determined not to give up. 'There are things I still don't understand. When I . . . when it all came out, what did you mean when you said you'd always known?'

'It doesn't matter.'

'Please. I'm really trying to comprehend what happened.'

Amelia exhaled, looked towards the door to check Jason wasn't within earshot. Jen could hear him talking on the phone, presumably to his father.

'When Charles started seeing . . . that woman . . . I found out, I can't even remember how. She lived near us, went to the same church, if you can believe that. I thought it would just peter out.'

'You didn't confront him?'

'And drive him away? I had three children. And I loved him. Things were different then. And then, of course, I

423

saw that she was pregnant and I knew he'd be linked to her for ever, one way or another.'

'Weren't you afraid he'd leave?'

'Of course. But I knew he loved the children. And me, actually. I knew he'd never intended for her to replace us. And his television career started to take off. I thought, if I never made it an issue, there would be no reason for him to go. He needed to be seen as having a stable marriage. And I knew that if he thought I had been protected from the truth, he would want to keep it that way. Rather than have the whole thing blow up. Rather than see how hurt I was.'

'But . . . how could you live with that?'

'It was my choice. We were very happy, actually. I don't expect you, or anyone else, to understand.'

'So, all this time . . . you knew Jason, Poppy and Jessie had a sister?'

'Family isn't just about blood, Jen. It's about much more than that.'

Jen stirred her spoon round and round in her coffee. 'It turns out my father didn't abandon me. He tried to stay involved, sent me presents, tried to see me. My mother wouldn't let him.'

'I'm sorry. She must have had her reasons.'

Jen sighed. 'I wish things had turned out differently.'

'Well, sadly, things rarely turn out as we would want them to.'

'I'm sorry, Amelia. I genuinely mean that. I wish I could turn the clock back.'

'The others don't know what I just told you, by the way . . .' Amelia said.

Jen could hear Jason saying goodbye, heading up the corridor.

'. . . and I don't want them to. Everything's back to how it should be now. I don't want any more upsets.'

'He's going to wait it out.' Jason appeared in the doorway. 'The forecast says that it's meant to stop, apparently. He sent you his love, by the way.'

'Great,' Jen said weakly.

'Says he's looking forward to seeing you. Maybe we should tell Elaine we'll go the weekend after. You've probably seen a lot of her lately, right?'

Jen felt the walls closing in, the ceiling bearing down, the floor rising up. She needed to get out of there.

'I can't do this,' she said, once they were in the car and on the way back to Wimbledon.

Jason turned to look at her. 'This?'

'Us. I can't just slip back into our old life, as if nothing's changed.'

'You're kidding me, right? The whole family's willing to accept you back, and that's not what you want?'

'That's just it. It's not that you've realized you can't live without me, or you love me so much that you want to give us another try. It's like the whole family sat down and had a board meeting and passed a motion that I was to be reinstated.'

'Don't be so ridiculous. We're having a baby. Of course that changes everything. There's no point holding on to petty grudges – this is much more important.'

'And if I wasn't pregnant, do you think any of them would want to have anything to do with me?'

'You are, so there's no point even asking the question.'

'It's all a lie, this big happy family thing. Can't you see that? It's all based on quicksand.'

Jason did a double take. Jen had to stop herself from asking him to keep his eyes on the road. She reminded herself they needed to have this conversation. It didn't matter how hard it was.

'How can you say that?'

'Do you know that your mum knew all along? That it wasn't just your dad who was deceiving you all, she was too. For the right reasons, don't get me wrong. To protect you all. To protect herself, really. But that doesn't change the fact that none of it was real.'

'You don't know what you're talking about.'

'She asked me not to tell you. And I probably shouldn't have. But don't you see? That's half the problem. Everyone's pretending everything's fine. No one's facing anything head on.'

Jason, she noticed, was pulling over. She was glad – a moving car didn't seem like the most sensible place to have this conversation.

'How dare you criticize us. After everything that's happened.'

'And there,' Jen said, 'we have it, in a nutshell. You will always be "us". You'll never just be "you". I'm either married to you all, or none of you. I either buy into the whole myth, or I stay on the outside.'

'It always suited you before,' Jason practically spat. 'You could hardly wait to ditch you own family and join mine.'

'I'm getting out, Jason. I can get a bus home. I'd like you still to be a father to the baby. I'd like it to know its grandparents and aunts, but that's all. We can't get back together. I can't . . . I just can't do it . . .'

She opened the door before he could protest. As she walked up the road to the bus stop, hood up against the rain, she felt a weight lift off her shoulders.

53

Now that she had got things straight in her head – she wanted the baby, she didn't want Jason, didn't want the Mastersons except as her children's family, nothing more – Jen felt as if she could actually start to look to the future, start to see the positives rather than the negatives for once. She felt, if she was being honest, happy.

She found herself checking the future bookings every few days to see if Sean had pencilled himself in, but she knew the chances were slim. Although she had promised him she would let him know how she was, how things had worked out between her and Jason, she wasn't really sure he'd meant it when he said he wanted to know. She picked the phone up a hundred times to call him, and then chickened out. She couldn't stop thinking about him, though. Couldn't stop wondering if she'd made a terrible mistake.

In the end, she decided she had nothing to lose. She could spend her days wondering what might have happened, or she could find out once and for all.

She persuaded a reluctant Judy into phoning Sean's showroom and asking for an appointment with him. She had recently moved into a large detached house nearby, she told him, and was looking to find a few statement pieces. Money was no object.

'Look at how it backfired when you did this with the sister,' Judy said when she got off the phone, convinced her performance had been less than BAFTA-worthy.

Jen had finally told her the whole story behind the family break-up, filling in the gaps that had been left in the paper.

'This is different.'

'Why exactly?'

'Because Sean will be pleased to see me. Hopefully.'

It had crossed her mind several times that Sean might be thinking he'd had a lucky escape. Not to mention the fact that, even though he knew Jen was pregnant, the last time they had set eyes on each other she hadn't yet been wearing trousers with an elasticated waist.

She didn't even know what she was hoping for. She just knew she had to see him again, to understand how she felt about him. To see if there was anything there worth trying for. And to know if – after the way she had messed him around – Sean had any residual feelings left for her.

She travelled up on the train to Moreton-in-Marsh to make Judy's appointment. She had agonized over what to wear and had decided, in the end, not to even try to disguise her growing bump. He might as well get an instant visual reminder of the situation as soon as he saw her. She felt sick with nerves. At least, she thought she did. It might just have been a return to morning sickness.

Sean's vintage showroom was in a picture-perfect converted church with thick-stemmed wisteria growing around the door. Outside, ornate stone statues rubbed shoulders with bird baths and intricate wrought-iron gates that no longer led anywhere. Inside was like a treasure trove in the Tardis-like space. Jen picked her way through to the back, looking around for him, both anticipating and dreading the moment when he caught sight of her and realized what was going on.

'Ah, there you are.'

She jumped as she heard his voice. He sounded anything other than surprised to see her.

'Did you find it OK?'

'I . . . um . . . yes.' What was going on? 'You sound like you were expecting me.'

Sean smiled. Jen's heart raced, her stomach flipped, bells rang, choirs sang. She sat down on the nearest chair. An Eames classic, if she wasn't mistaken.

'You should never have told me about the way you arranged to meet your husband's sister. Plus, I've spoken to Judy countless times on the phone before, so I recognized her voice straight away. That and the name Lulu DeVille kind of gave it away.'

Damn Judy. 'I told her she should have come up with a more realistic name. I'm sorry. You must think I'm ridiculous.'

'I thought it was kind of funny, actually. And I'm intrigued. To what do I owe this pleasure?'

'You asked me to tell you what happened, so here I am.'

'Blimey. I meant send me a text, now and then.'

He was making light of it, but she could tell he wasn't as calm and cool as he was pretending to be. She couldn't work out if he was pleased to see her or not, though.

Without the element of surprise, there hadn't been an honest reaction she could gauge. She told him the whole story, everything that had happened since she'd seen him last, and he listened without interrupting. And then, Sean being Sean, he asked her questions about exactly how she felt, and they talked and talked about Jason and what might happen in the future.

'Nothing,' Jen said emphatically. 'I know that now . . .'

'God, that lot sound weird,' he said when she told him about Poppy and Amelia's about-turn. 'Sorry, I know they're your family and all that.'

And Jen, who had never said a word against the Master-sons as a whole, an entity, a corporation, to anyone before, said, 'I think they are a bit. And for the record, they *were* my family. Now they're just my children's family. Big difference.'

'For what it's worth – which is nothing, by the way – I think you've done the right thing.'

Later, once he'd closed up for the day, he insisted on cooking her dinner in his surprisingly-modern-on-the-inside but chocolate-boxy-on-the-outside cottage that was a few minutes' walk from the showroom. She knew she should head for the station and home, but she liked being around him too much – even when what he wanted to talk about was difficult.

Afterwards, despite her protests that she didn't want to intrude, he made up the bed in the spare room and she spent the night in there, lying awake for most of the time listening to the foxes out in the back garden and wondering what was going to happen. She knew what she wanted now. Seeing Sean again had confirmed for her that, more than anything, she wanted them to give it a go. She wanted a relationship that was based on more than compatibility, more than the fact that it was right on paper. One where they could be a couple first, and sod everyone else. But why he would want to be saddled with a pregnant woman, with baggage as heavy as her ever expanding belly, she had no idea.

She waited, hopeful that he might creep into her room, overcome with the desire to cement their relationship. Thought about creeping into his.

Neither of them did.

In the morning, he made her breakfast, dropped her off at the train station on his way to the showroom, saw her on to a train, hugged her goodbye and planted a kiss in her hair.

'Thanks for coming. Really,' he said. 'I mean, you could have bought something, but anyway . . . There is a recession on, after all, and everyone's meant to be supporting small businesses.'

Jen laughed. 'When I can afford two thousand pounds for a couple of old decanters in a wooden box, I'll let you know.'

'I think you'll find that's called a tantalus, and it's a very good investment. It stops the hired help drinking your best whiskey. It'd save you a fortune in booze.'

'I like my servants drunk. It adds to the air of decadence.'

'Ha! Remind me to come to yours for dinner.'

'Any time you like,' she said, suddenly serious.

'I'll call you,' he said. 'Or you call me. One of us will call the other.'

'Definitely.' She leaned over and kissed him on the cheek. 'One of us will definitely call the other.'

54

Jen still loved Christmas, only this year she had missed most of the build-up. Betty had been born on 9th August, a week and a half early, and her life had been in chaos ever since.

She had forgotten how much work a baby could be. Betty was gorgeous, that went without saying. Tiny – obviously – with a shock of dark curly hair. She had the Masterson big dark eyes, but also a look of Elaine around the nose and mouth – a fact which made Jen happy.

She and Jason had sold the house in Wimbledon, finally. They had had to let it go at a knockdown price in the end, but Jen had wanted it all tied up before the baby was born. No loose ends. Simone and Emily, fired up by the prospect of a little brother or sister (who was she kidding? No one ever even suggested it might be a boy) had come home on three successive weekends and helped her pack everything up, ready for the move.

The girls had taken everything that had happened in their stride. Jen thought that after the shock of Jason moving out, and Charles turning out to be the oldest swinger in town, they were prepared for anything. Although there had been a brief hairy moment, when Emily had thought Jen might be pregnant by a new boy-friend, and had turned into Mary Whitehouse in a split second, lecturing her about waiting and contraception.

Once Jen had managed to set the record straight, Emily had been all for it, assuming, as both girls did, that nothing would stop a reconciliation between their parents now.

The moment she had had to tell them they were mistaken had not been so easy.

She had wanted to put her family back together but, she realized now, it was never going to be possible to go back and rewrite history, however much you wanted to. Too much had happened. Too much had changed. But that didn't mean you couldn't change with it. Families came in all shapes and sizes. It was all about figuring out who you couldn't live without, and finding a way to make it work.

She and Jason could still be great parents, just not living in the same house. Plenty of other people did it.

Once Jason had realized she was serious, there were no histrionics; he hadn't tried to persuade her to change her mind. They had fallen into planning the practicalities – selling the house, using the money to buy two small places, close enough to each other but not too close, in an area that suited both their needs. She didn't know if he just didn't care enough, or if he thought she would come round eventually, but she was grateful, either way. She had never doubted that he would help support her and Betty. She just didn't want to be married to him any more. And once she went back to work she was sure he and his family would be there to help with childcare too.

She had seen them all occasionally since Betty's birth. At the christening, for a start. She had invited Judy and Neil (and Mrs Neil, who turned out to be called Sara and to be very nice and normal, and not a smart-arse at all) to beef up her side. They were polite enough with each other – friendly, but no more. Jessie was still struggling to acknowledge Jen's existence as anything more than a vague and not too well-liked acquaintance, but she was being a good auntie to Betty, which was all Jen really cared about. Charles, ever the polite gentleman, was always courteous and pleasant whenever she saw him. Funnily enough, neither he nor Amelia called her sweetheart any more.

They were still a clan. A unit, a clique, a gang. A cult. Ben had apparently been admitted to the ranks, and Jen was glad for Poppy. When she heard they were planning their wedding, she waited for the feelings of loss and bereavement that would arise from her being excluded from the process, but they didn't come. She wished the two of them well, that was all.

This year's Christmas Day couldn't be any more different from last year's. Last year, she had gone through the motions for Simone and Emily's sakes, sobbing into the gravy when she thought neither of her daughters was looking.

This year, they were in High Wycombe attempting to assemble a round table that threatened to take over the whole of Elaine's front room. Jen had had to bribe Simone and Emily to be there, to miss the traditional Masterson big day. They owed it to their grandmother on their mother's side, she had said. There had been too many years when they had all put their heads in the sand and decided to ignore the fact that she would have been spending Christmas Day alone. To be fair, now they were here, the girls were at least giving the impression of having a great time. They would spend Boxing Day with their other family, taking baby Betty with them.

Jen had taken all three of her girls to see Rory the day before. Simone and Emily had looked a bit bored, as they always did when they were asked to visit this slightly smelly old man who was, apparently, their grandfather. They were getting used to him. Betty was at her chubby best, smiling toothlessly at him as he smiled almost toothlessly back. He had bought Jen a bottle of Burberry perfume, from the market – clearly knock-off and undoubtedly not going to smell of anything except water after the first spray, but it was the thought that counted. He gave Simone and Emily vouchers for iTunes, which Jen had bought and paid for. He had got a bottle of wine in and some mince pies. He was spending Christmas Day, he told them with a wink, with Jean from next door.

She smiled as she looked at the faces around the table – her mother, her three daughters. This was her family. They were all she needed. Almost. She knew that at about four o'clock the doorbell would ring and Sean would be there, fresh from lunch with his brother and sister-in-law, probably laden down with sweet and thoughtful gifts for them all. It wasn't the first time he'd met them, but he would be on his best behaviour, she knew, still nervous about saying the wrong thing, still not quite at home enough around them to relax.

It hadn't happened quickly. Sean had been wary, understandably. Not only did he want to make sure that, this time, Jen really knew what she wanted, but he had the whole idea of having a child in his life – and one that wasn't his, at that – to contend with. In fact, they were still a work in progress, but so far it was definitely so good. And at least she always knew where she was, how he felt. They had no secrets from each other, that was one of their rules. To be honest, she found all the talking a little exhausting sometimes. She liked the idea of it in principle, but in practice it could get a bit wearing, airing their feelings and their grievances all the time. As faults went, it wasn't a bad one, though. And if Sean had been too perfect she would never have relaxed, she would have been looking around all the time, waiting for his fatal flaw to rise up and grab her.

One day, maybe, they would talk about the next step. About how to bridge their two worlds. There was no rush. Jen was in no hurry. He was there, and she thought – she was pretty sure – she loved him and he loved her. The rest could wait.

Acknowledgements

Firstly, a huge thank you to Beth Sampson who made a very generous donation to the charity DEBRA (www.debra.org.uk) in memory of her mother, Judy Sampson, in return for having me name one of my characters after her.

As ever, I'm indebted to everyone at Penguin (especially the fabulous Louise Moore) and at Curtis Brown (my agent, Jonny Geller, in particular). I'd name you all individually but I'd probably leave someone out accidentally, and imagine how awkward it would be whenever I came into the office then.

Thanks to Stephanie Moore and Charlotte Willow-Edwards for asking questions on my behalf, and to all those who answered them including The Mandarin Oriental, The Haymarket and The Four Seasons Hotels, Liv Smith Fallon, Kerry Hinbest and Joe Johnson.

the ugly sister

When it comes to genes life's a lottery . . .

As Abi would the first to know. She has spent her life in the shadow of her stunningly beautiful, glamorous older sister Cleo.

Headhunted as model when she was sixteen, Cleo has been all but lost to Abi for the last twenty years, with only a fleeting visit or brief email to connect them. So when Abi is invited to spend the summer in Cleo's large London home with her sister's perfect family, she can't bring herself to say no. Despite serious misgivings. Maybe Cleo is finally as keen as Abi to regain the closeness they shared in their youth?

But Abi is in for a shock. Soon she is left caring for her two young, bored and very spoilt nieces and handsome, unhappy brother-in-law – while Cleo plainly has other things on her mind. As Abi moves into her sister's life, a cuckoo in the nest, she wrestles with uncomfortable feelings.

Could having beauty, wealth and fame lead to more unhappiness than not having them? Who in the family really is the ugly sister?

'It's gripping stuff... it's no surprise that [Fallon's] characterisation is spot-on, or that her plots are intricate and involved. This is a great, intelligent read and I can't recommend it highly enough'
The Daily Mail

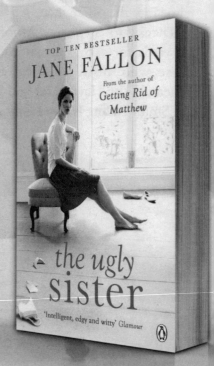

TOP TEN BESTSELLER

JANE FALLON

From the author of
Getting Rid of Matthew

the ugly sister

'Intelligent, edgy and witty' Glamour

*f*oursome

Rebecca, Daniel, Alex and Isabel have been best friends since university. Rebecca married Daniel, Alex married Isabel and, for twenty years, they have been inseparable. But all that is about to change...

When Alex walks out on Isabel, Rebecca thinks things can't get any worse. But then she finds out the reason why and she's left harbouring a secret she'd rather forget...

And there's more upheaval to come in Rebecca's life as her emaciated, neurotic, self-obsessed colleague, Lorna - her arch nemesis at work - suddenly becomes a regular feature in her social life.

Rebecca's once-happy foursome is now a distant memory and with hearts broken and friendships fractured, it seems that change is never a good thing. Or is it?

'Witty, well observed and free from chick-lit clichés, Foursome will have loved-up couples everywhere questioning just how close they really are.' *Heat*

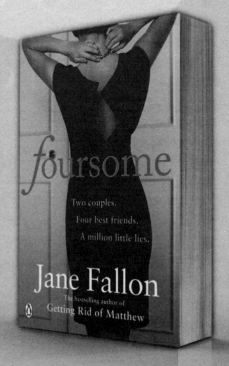

getting *rid of* matthew

When Matthew, Helen's lover of the past four years, finally decides to leave his wife Sophie (and their two daughters) and move into Helen's flat, she should be over the moon. The only trouble is, she doesn't want him any more. Now she has to figure out how to get rid of him . . .

PLAN A

- Stop shaving your armpits. And your bikini line.
- Buy incontinence pads and leave them lying around.
- Stop having sex with him.

PLAN B

- Accidentally on purpose bump into his wife Sophie.
- Give yourself a fake name and identity.
- Befriend Sophie and actually begin to really like her.
- Snog Matthew's son (who's the same age as you by the way. You're not a paedophile).
- Befriend Matthew's children. Unsuccessfully.
- Watch your whole plan go absolutely horribly wrong

Getting Rid of Matthew isn't as easy as it seems, but along the way Helen will forge an unlikely friendship, find real love and realize that nothing ever goes exactly to plan . . .

'Chick lit with an edge' *Guardian*